New Seasons Market

THE SHORES

BEYOND TIME

Book Three of the
CHRONICLE OF THE DARK STAR

KEVIN EMERSON

WALDEN POND PRESS
An Imprint of HarperCollinsPublishers

Walden Pond Press is an imprint of HarperCollins Publishers.
Walden Pond Press and the skipping stone logo are trademarks
and registered trademarks of Walden Media, LLC.

ISBN 978-0-06-230677-7

Typography by Carla Weise
19 20 21 22 23   PC/LSCH   10 9 8 7 6 5 4 3 2 1
❖
First Edition

FOR JORDAN

PRELUDE

EARTH YEAR: 2161
50 KM SOUTH OF THE MARS COLONIAL
TRAINING ACADEMY—MOAB STATION
UTAH EXTRACTION DISTRICT
NORTH AMERICAN FEDERATION

Far from where and when the universe as you know it is about to end, at the edge of a sheer cliff towering hundreds of feet above the crumbled desert floor, a green light began to blink. The light was on a glove, or something like a glove. Picture a thick pair of winter gloves, the kind with long gauntlets that stretch up your forearms, only now picture the fabric being a sleek, completely transparent material, so that you can see your hand and wrist inside, except for where wide white bands of padding cross the back of the glove in horizontal stripes. The green light was blinking on a small digital screen embedded just above the wrist, and it indicated that the gloves, along with a metallic backpack, a helmet with a golden visor, and a pair of heavy boots similar to what you might wear skiing—if there is even snow, in your when—were all in sync.

"Ready?" said a girl named Ariel, breathing deep. Her backpack emitted a steady particle hum. The interior surface of her golden visor shimmered with information about wind speed and distance. A message in the corner flashed: *Gravity Compensation 62%*.

Ariel was fifteen, the same age as the two students standing beside her at the cliff edge. Like her classmates, she was brilliant; they had all been specially selected to be here, and had traveled by mag-train nearly twenty hours from their population zone far to the north, across the parched, deserted interior of the North American Federation, to attend this four-week colonial cadet training program. But though Ariel would go on to work for the International Space Agency, where she would make many notable contributions to the study of long-transit nutrition, and though she would enrich her family's lives with her kindness and humor, and one time even thrill a crowd of thousands with a stirring piano performance during the *Starliner Einstein*'s launch party in the year 2204, she was not actually of any importance to the potentially cataclysmic events currently taking place at Dark Star. Had Ariel known this—and there was almost no way that she could have—it would have disappointed her greatly, as she was an ambitious young dreamer who, like most of us, couldn't quite shake the certainty that the world revolved around her, but alas, during those critical moments in the Centauri system, nearly fifty years in her future, Ariel would be asleep in a stasis pod on the *Einstein*, completely unaware.

The same was true for the two students beside her, and even for Ms. Yasmin, their instructor. Promising individuals with extraordinary lives ahead of them, all of whom would have been crushed to learn that, in terms of the fate of this universe, they really weren't that important.

But as you know, these things happen. Or in this case, don't happen.

However, there was a fourth student with them on the cliff that afternoon, standing not at the edge but about ten meters behind, who was quite important indeed. His green light was blinking too, but for him, the sight of it caused a different kind of anticipation than what the others were feeling.

"All right," said Ms. Yasmin, tapping her own controls. "Target that outcropping with your guidance system. Once you've been on Mars for a bit, you'll learn to size up these jumps on your own, but for the moment, best not to take any chances."

Ms. Yasmin was referring to a finger of smooth red

rock sticking up about twenty meters from the edge of the cliff. Another thirty meters beyond that stood a wide butte, like an island in the sky. Its sheer sides were colored a deep crimson, its top covered with crumbled tan boulders. The goal of today's lesson was to take a running start, leap from the cliff edge, and land safely on that spire's narrow flat top. Then jump again and reach the butte. They had all been learning how to use these MGS suits—short for Mars Gravity Simulation—and had been eager to take this afternoon elective hike with Ms. Yasmin. Getting used to Mars's low gravity was a key piece of training if you hoped to be accepted for the semester-long program at the International Mars Colony during your senior year of high school. Of course, the three students standing on the edge of the cliff dreamed of such a thing. The boy behind them, however, had a different dream in mind.

"Target locked," Ariel announced, first as usual.

"Got it," said the boy beside her, whose name was Theo.

"Yup," said Victor, next to him. He glanced over his shoulder at their fourth classmate. "Hey, Pete, you look like you're about to compromise your underwear integrity."

The fourth student just looked at the ground.

"Mr. Barrie," said Ms. Yasmin, "everything all right?"

Peter took this opportunity to flip up his visor and make a show of breathing deeply. "I'm just feeling a little ill."

One of his classmates snickered.

"The MGS suits can have that effect," said Ms. Yasmin.

Peter shook his head. "I don't think I'm up for it."

"Are you sure? You know the reward for reaching that butte is a BASE jump off the other side. It's quite a fun ride down to the canyon floor. And we won't be back up here for at least an hour."

"I brought my books." Peter motioned to his hip pocket and the outline of his virtual reader.

"Don't you need these credits?" said Ariel. It was weird, the way she seemed to care, although Peter thought she sounded more like she was offended. Why didn't he want this like she did?

And she was right: Peter probably did need the credits. Probably did want to spend part of next year on Mars. And yet he just shrugged.

"All right, well . . ." Ms. Yasmin tapped her controls. "I'll let the station know you're staying behind. I'm sorry," she added, looking at Peter sympathetically.

"It's fine."

Something made Ariel and Theo and Victor laugh to themselves.

Peter tensed, a wave of frustration rushing through him. That laughter—the kind that never seemed to include him, that he never wanted to be a part of anyway—that was part of the real reason he wanted to stay behind.

Ariel caught Ms. Yasmin eyeing them, and she backed up a couple steps. "Can I go?"

Ms. Yasmin finished configuring her settings. "Fire away."

Ariel gritted her teeth, her gaze full of purpose, and darted forward, boots clomping. With a burst of magnetic thrusters she leapt off the edge of the cliff, followed by Theo, Victor, and then Ms. Yasmin, all four of them arcing through the pale blue sky in a line of pinwheeling limbs.

Peter watched them land successfully on the narrow spire. He heard their laughter echoing off the rocks. Saw them slapping each other's backs and pretending to push each other off the sides, and for just a moment, he sincerely wished he could have just smiled and gone along with them. They leapt again, soaring high and far, and by the time they'd landed on the distant butte, their voices had been lost to the whipping desert wind. Soon after, they disappeared, BASE jumping into the canyon and essentially out of this story.

Peter sighed. That brief feeling of longing was

immediately replaced by a wave of relief. Now that his classmates were gone, he could turn his attention toward the trail they'd climbed to get here. It continued past this spot, drawing a zigzag of dust up the almond-colored slope of a broad rocky mountainside. In the distance, Peter could see where the trail disappeared briefly into a small relic forest and, beyond that, where it crested a bare rocky ridgeline that surely afforded an epic view.

He stripped off the MGS suit to just his sun-protectant base layers—they were made of a silver reflective material with a crisscrossing pattern of coolant wiring that was powered by a battery unit on the belt—and started up the trail. It was a January morning, but the temperature was already pushing one hundred. Though the sun had not yet begun to undergo the changes that would one day cause humanity to flee the solar system, it had become a danger to humans, due to the steady changes to Earth's climate and atmosphere over the previous two hundred years. You couldn't live near the equator anymore. Seattle was a popular beach destination in winter. Much of the United States had become uninhabitable desert land, suitable only for mining or, in this case, simulating some of the conditions on Mars. The prime habitable real estate these days was mostly near the Arctic, and so America and Canada had merged. More of a war, really; it had all happened before Peter was born.

His feet scuffed on the broken sandstone, kicking up clouds of dust. He was out of breath in moments; this ridge was over three thousand meters in elevation. He held a hand above his eyes and squinted against the harsh light, wishing he'd brought his goggles. At this altitude, the sun could cause retina damage if you weren't careful. Ariel had probably remembered hers. Where was Peter's mind sometimes?

Occupied, he knew. Not distracted, exactly, but busy. Like back there on the ledge. Instead of focusing on doing the jump test with the group, he'd been thinking about getting up to this high point, preferably alone, and seeing what there was to see. Why was he risking his chance at making it into the Mars program? Part of it was that reticence about his classmates; he found them hard to be around, with all their boasting and confidence and ambition, not to mention endless immaturity. Peter had ambition, too, but it wasn't about grades or achievement. He was one of the top students in his class, but he would never have bragged about it. He didn't consider the grades or the status they conveyed to be at all important. They were a game, a means to an end. What drove Peter was more like a yearning, a pure curiosity. A sense that he felt every day, like he was searching for something, some kind of understanding, of *awareness*, almost like there was a larger meaning to the world that nobody else knew about—definitely not his classmates—that he could nearly perceive, and yet not quite. The sensation made him feel big and small at the same time, like he was at once an infinitesimal speck, but then also the most important person in the universe.

Of course, we all feel this sense of importance from time to time. It can be helpful, for motivating us to make great discoveries about ourselves and the world around us, and yet it can also be harmful, when our actions end up hurting others. In his future, Peter would both make great discoveries and do great harm, but what was different about his version of this feeling, compared to that of his peers, or indeed nearly anyone on Earth, was that, in terms of the fate of this universe, he was shockingly close to the truth.

He climbed on, the terrain growing steeper, the switchbacks tighter, and soon entered the relic forest. The trail smoothed out and curved between short, rounded trees, the shadows a welcome respite from the heat. A sweet, herbal smell greeted him. The trees had gnarled trunks curved like question marks, with peeling bark and leaves that looked strangely reptilian. *Utah juniper*, Peter thought to himself. These trees had been all over this landscape a hundred years ago. Now they only huddled at the highest peaks, where the cooler temperatures provided just enough moisture for them to grow. Little islands of life. Peter heard a warbling birdcall. There had been nothing but vultures during their stay at the cadet program. A little farther up the trail and stubby round pine trees began to mix in: *piñon*. In a hollow, an orb of jewel-colored leaves: *manzanita*. Peter was probably the only member of his class who had actually read the ecology primer; who cared about the plants and bugs of a mostly abandoned wasteland. But to Peter, a plant was just as wondrous an organism as a human, if you looked at it closely enough. Maybe more so. You didn't hear these pine trees bragging about grades or internships or awards.

As he ascended, Peter felt himself opening up. Peaceful, complete. So much of the planet was damaged or ruined these days, *spoiled* by humanity's relentless growth and greed. Peter bristled when humans described themselves as something separate from nature, like they were above it somehow. Weren't they actually part of it? Of the design of this planet, this star system, this corner of the universe? Everybody forgot about that. Even when it came to Mars: Ariel and the rest of them just thought of it in terms of achievement, the next step in human conquest. But Mars was part of the design, too. It had once had oceans. Maybe there had once been Martian pines.

He ducked through the cool shadows, juniper

fingers scraping his arms. Soon he broke free onto the bare crest of the mountain. He scrambled up the last steep slope, a succession of slanted sandstone slabs, and reached the summit, where he was greeted with a 360-degree view of the vast empty desert.

Picture Earth, the way you know it, mostly: the sun, searing but still yellow in the sky, the south-western deserts of the North American continent a scribble of branching canyons striped in cinnamon and cream, though the sparkling rivers at their seams have long since dried up. The sky blue overhead, fading into a rim of chocolate haze: the ever-present pollution that cloaks the planet, yet in this desolate corner of the world it is still thin enough to see to the horizon. Here, the dust whorls from the great mining slags. There, the plumes of the omnipresent wildfires. The largest one, to the north, has been burning for two years, marching its way through what remained of the Rocky Mountain forests.

Peter spread his arms, closed his eyes, and breathed deeply. A mix of hot rock, sweet juniper, and sour wood smoke. Wind whipped around him, almost top-pling him. Made him smile. Being up here, so close to . . . what? God? Was that what it was, this thing he felt? Not exactly. But something. *The grand design,* he'd called it in his journal one time, by which most people might have thought he meant God, but Peter preferred to think of it as the universe at work. Around him, inside him. From a cell to a mountaintop to a distant planet . . .

It was so quiet. None of the silly jokes and dumb video streams. When Peter imagined being on Mars, *this*, right here, was what he yearned for: a world so silent that you might hear the whisper of true meaning. Except it would be impossible to actually find that there, stuck with your pod of teenagers the whole time. And while this solitary moment was nice, the strip of pollution and the dust and smoke reminded you that Earth had already been ruined. No, what Peter truly dreamed of when he closed his eyes was a world far beyond their inner solar system, somewhere untouched, somewhere new, that he alone could discover.

Peter removed his link from his belt and turned on the camera. He took a selfie with the great spread of country behind him but frowned when he viewed it. The image looked a bit too flat, too still to really capture how *alive* this moment felt. He switched the camera to its video setting, held it out again, and pressed record. The wind whipped around him, his black hair blowing this way and that. He turned in a circle, so you could see the whole panorama behind him. . . .

It could be said that what happened next was

coincidence, but that would rule out the power of curiosity. Simply put, Peter had an inspiration, and yet, is it that simple? Does that spark in our minds come merely from some interaction between our interests, emotions, and the world around us, or could it in fact be something more: perhaps our faintest perception of some energy that our earthbound senses can't quite perceive, or even an awareness of some higher dimension of reality?

Whatever the true cause, Peter imagined how much better this video he'd just taken would look if it was slowed down. He didn't even think that much about it. Just activated the slow-motion setting on the camera, began to record, and then spun around a few more times.

When he was finished, he caught his breath and watched what he'd recorded. It was too bright up here to properly see the screen, but it seemed to have worked.

Peter stowed his link, spent another moment with his eyes closed, and then started down the trail, through the shade of the relic forest, back down the switchbacks in the blistering sun. He returned to the ledge, got out his virtual reader, and read for some of his assignments. Soon after, as they'd promised, his classmates and his teacher returned. Peter didn't even mind.

It wasn't until later that night, in the dim light of

his bunk, that Peter had a chance to revisit his slow-motion video, and it was then, in the playback, that he saw the strange blurry shape that was flickering not far behind him on that mountaintop.

Someone had been standing there.

A figure, one that was clad in long black robes, with dark blue skin and more than two legs. It had been right there, looking upward, as if gazing directly at the sun.

Peter replayed the clip, then again, and each time, the figure was there, like a ghost. He checked the still photo he'd taken, which featured the same view. No figure. The video he'd taken at regular speed: no figure there either.

But in the slow motion, there it was.

Peter had one friend on the trip, a boy named Darius. He showed him the next morning, but Darius, his attention equally divided between Peter's link and a trio of girls walking by, just shrugged. "It's probably a VirtCom artifact," he said. "People say they see ghosts and stuff, but it's really just malfunctioning packets getting beamed to the wrong nodes. Maybe there was some magnetic rock up there catching a signal fragment. I heard about that happening somewhere else."

"Maybe." But Peter didn't think so.

A week later, as the cadet program drew to a close,

there was a second chance to practice with the MGS suits. Once again, Peter signed up. Once again, the suit made him "sick." Once again, he hiked to the deserted mountaintop.

He came to the wide vista and stood in what he thought was the exact same position he'd been in last time. He aimed his link at the spot where the figure had appeared. He had since downloaded an app that allowed for even slower motion capture, though it drained the battery quite fast. He was only able to shoot twenty seconds of video before his link died.

That evening, after recharging . . . there it was again. The figure was even clearer this time. It had large milky, pearlescent eyes. It seemed to have two noses, one above the other. And four legs, perhaps even many extra fingers. On one wrist, it wore a large silver watch. It was still gazing up into the sky, same as it had been last time.

What could it be? Over the following weeks after he returned home, Peter searched the VirtCom for any kind of character from a movie or stream that resembled this one. Any costume you could buy, any drawing that someone had done. He searched for mentions of VirtCom artifacts that only appeared in slow motion—by the way, how did that even make any sense? He searched for mentions of strange phenomena in the Utah Extraction District; there were many, alien and UFO sightings of all kinds, even claims of a whole town that had briefly vanished, in what used to be Arizona, but all those episodes had occurred over one hundred years ago, back before the area had been largely abandoned. Moreover, those accounts sounded far-fetched, at best. And yet . . .

Could this be some sort of alien being?

Whatever it was, Peter never shared his video with anyone after Darius. He wasn't the type to post much on his virtual profile anyway, but this felt strangely private, a secret all his own. Even more than that, over time, Peter began to believe that maybe, just maybe, the figure had been there specifically for *him*—like it was sending him a message, or it *was* the message, if only he could understand what it said.

The school year marched on, and afterward, life for Peter, as is often the case in one's teenage years, became busy. He didn't end up spending a semester on Mars, but he did finish school with a flurry of perfect grades, after which he went off to university to study advanced space travel mechanics and physics. He'd always been interested in the space program, but now it felt like a purpose, perhaps even a design . . . as if the stars were calling to him.

"Explain to me why we're going here again?"

"I just want to check something out." Peter led the way up the slope. Around them, deep red evening light bled over the sandstone.

"You know I was looking forward to sleeping on the subsonic, right?" said Mariah, trailing behind him. "Also, I packed for the beach, not for hiking."

"We're almost there."

They were on their way to vacation in Chile, where the oceans were still cool enough to swim in summer. All of their friends, who were also, as of today, fellow Academy graduates, had gone straight there on the subsonic transport, but Peter had insisted on flying in an old thruster that could barely clock six hundred kilometers per hour.

"This better be quick," said Mariah.

"It will be," said Peter, not really listening.

Crossing the UED, he'd begun to worry that he wouldn't remember the spot, but every contour was familiar to him, burned into his memory from hours of studying maps and rewatching his old videos.

He'd wanted to get back here for years. Finally, this evening, there'd been an excuse.

The juniper forest had been burned to black stalks at some point during the six years since his cadet days, but the view from the rocky mountaintop spine was still the same: magnificent folds and towers of earth in all directions, painted in burning hues as the sun settled into the polluted haze blanketing the horizon.

"Okay," said Mariah, arriving beside him, not breathing that hard—she'd always been more serious about keeping in shape. "This is pretty, but so are the beaches at Valparaiso, and there I could have a cervezarita."

"You know the reefs are fake, right?" said Peter, smiling at the familiar sensation of sand-bristled wind on his face, that smell of the hot rocks.

"Who cares? You can't find real ones anymore,

and snorkeling is fun. Also they're supposed to have the best fish clones. Even stingrays."

Peter was busy getting his link ready and positioning himself. When Mariah saw him aiming it in her direction, she put her hands on her hips and smiled.

"Can you move?" Peter said, watching the screen and waving his hand.

She slid over a step.

"No, I mean, like, behind me. Out of the shot."

Mariah arched her eyebrows. "How romantic." She shuffled down the rocky slope.

"Hey," said Peter. "Listen, you know how people always ask me what the secret was to graduating top of our class, or why, when I could have had any other position in the fleet, I put in for the outer planet survey training?"

"You're brilliant, ambitious, and . . . eccentric," said Mariah. "You don't *really* need me to tell you that again, do you?"

"There's something else," said Peter. He held his arms out. "This."

Miranda looked around. "What do you mean? This wasteland?"

"No. . . ." Peter started recording a video, using the latest ultra-slow-motion app. It might have been stupid to say what he'd just said, since there really was very little chance this would work again—

And yet didn't he know, somehow, that it would?

He recorded a clip and then played it back, his heart racing.

There it was.

The figure was still standing there, ghostlike. All these years later. Black robes, blue skin, too many legs. The only thing that had changed was its pose. Now it was looking down at its wrist, at that silver watch. The other hand was positioned over the watch, as if about to press it.

"It's really here," said Peter.

Miranda reluctantly peered over his shoulder. "What on earth is that?"

"Actually, I don't think it's from Earth at all. I saw this exact thing, this *being*, when I was here six years ago. In this exact same spot."

Mariah gazed up the slope, to where the video indicated the being should be. Then back at the screen. She crossed her arms. "You're telling me you brought me out into the middle of nowhere to see a VirtCom artifact? Of some weird cosplayer?"

"I don't think that's—"

"You know what, Peter? You're always playing your little mental games, and I'm usually fine with it, but this . . . whenever you're done making spooky videos, I'd like to go. You could have come and done this on your own time. And now *I'm* missing time that's really important to me."

"Mariah . . ."

She trudged down into the charred forest without looking back. Peter watched her for a moment. He should probably go after her.

Instead, he readied his link to make another video.

The sun had set, leaving a cooling world of magentas and lavenders, canyons settling beneath their shadow shrouds. Heat fled the world in gusts. Peter recorded, and then watched. The being still stood there, hand poised over its watch. The watch itself seemed to be giving off a faint blue light.

Peter looked back at the empty ridge. "I see you!" he shouted over the wind. It made him smile, in spite of his shivering.

Below, the thrusters of their ship grumbled to life. Mariah would kill him if he didn't get down there. He took one more look around this place, admiring its peace and emptiness. One more look at the spot where the figure was hidden by . . . time? Maybe. Now that he had finally graduated from the academy, perhaps he could find some serious scientists in the fleet to show these videos to. This could be his big discovery. Maybe he could even bring them here sometime. . . .

Of course, Peter couldn't possibly know that there would be no next time. At least, not here on Earth.

Because barely twelve short years later, as Peter was just returning from his second deployment in the Saturn moons, the world would be halted in its tracks by the stunning news that the sun had begun to change, that a supernova was mere decades away, that they had to evacuate Earth—first for Mars, and then for Aaru-5. All at once, everything changed.

Two years after that, when Peter heard from one of his commanding officers that the sun's changing state was confounding even the top scientists in the field, and that whatever had happened to it had apparently begun years before, he would think of that being, standing there on the mountaintop.

Had it known about the sun? Had it even had something to do with it?

Peter would wonder briefly whether he could have prevented the supernova by sharing his videos or leading a research team to the ridgeline, but on that night in 2167, such concerns had been far from his mind, and just as when he'd been younger, Peter decided to keep his discovery to himself. This time, however, it was because of something very strange that happened next, just before he returned to Mariah and his ship.

Peter had stowed his link and taken a last look around the vast landscape, enjoying the feel of the sandy breeze on his face. He'd just taken his first step down the trail—when he glanced at the ridgeline

again and had another idea, this one brazen, dangerous even. He scrambled up to where, on his video,
that figure appeared to be standing, and put his hand
into the exact spot.

Did he feel something there? Almost like his hand
began to tingle . . .

He took another step, moving completely into the
space where the being in the video seemed to be.

And then he surely did feel something. A sort of
buzzing. The energy of whatever was here with him—
or was it just the humming of his nerves? No, it had to
be more than that.

He began to stretch, to fade, but also to intensify.
As if his senses were miles away. Like the universe was
expanding around him, or like he was expanding into
it. He was no longer on the Utah ridgeline. Instead,
he found himself surrounded by a field of stars, so
many stars, but also so much blackness in between,
uncountable presence and unfathomable emptiness,
beginnings, endings, all without a true up or down,
all swirling. . . .

And then a shadow fell over him. Something
loomed, beckoning, drawing him in. He could see it
clearly now: a large, dark structure. It looked like a
doorway, with towering metal sides and a roiling black
center. The sight of it froze him from within. As he
drew closer, the sides of the doorway began to sparkle

with silver circuitry, as if it sensed him coming—

"Peter."

Something was beside him now, in the vast dark space. Something that shimmered with pale greenish-white light, something he couldn't quite see out the corner of his eye, unless he strained to turn as hard as he could, and even then still not quite—

A figure. But not that tall being with the robes and the many legs. This one was smaller, younger. It looked like a girl, except she seemed to be made of a million tiny mirrors reflecting starlight.

"I can show you," she said. Her voice was like glass, her words like an icy breeze that at first chilled him but then lit up inside him like energy.

"Show me what?"

"What you seek."

"The grand design?" Peter said instinctively.

"The higher viewpoints. I need your help, Peter."

He shivered. The doorway had grown larger and continued to draw him in. And now Peter spied something through it. On the other side was a great complex of circular black arms, bathed in iridescent green light. A machine, a space station . . . and yet he felt certain it was more than that: that it was also alive.

"Is this my future?" he asked.

"It can be," said the girl.

Whatever that structure was, it seemed so massive,

so beyond anything he'd ever known, that *anyone* had ever known. . . .

"Follow the space-time distortions," said the girl. "Trace the signal, written in gravitational waves. An event will happen soon in your timeline. No one else will know its source. That is where you must begin."

Peter's vision started to swim. He began to blur—no, it was more like he had many arms and many legs, branching in all directions, like he was at the center of many possibilities, perhaps, oh perhaps, all of possibility.

Older selves, younger, alternate histories and futures and beyond all of it,

Always looming,

That doorway, and the giant shadowy structure in the green light.

"Find me," she said again, "and all of this can be yours."

"I will," he answered.

The light grew, and so did the variations, branching and branching, all of it spinning faster as he sank into the great doorway. . . .

Peter came to and found himself lying on the rocky slope. Blinking at the field of stars, not all around him anymore, just the normal night sky overhead, Venus gleaming, the brushstrokes of the Milky Way.

Back on Earth. But from where?

His hip and shoulder ached. Throbbing from the back of his head. Peter found blood there. He propped himself up on his elbows. He was lying a few meters down from the spot on the ridgeline. He felt like he'd traveled a great distance, and yet there was the pink rim of the horizon, the sun having just set. There was the sound of the thrusters from his shuttle. Barely a moment had passed. . . .

He winced and saw the doorway behind his eyelids, the great structure beyond it, heard the glassy voice of that girl, like a dream.

Find me.

"Peter!" Mariah's voice echoed up the hillside.

He got to his feet, checked to be sure his link was in his pocket, and then, with a last look at the empty ridgeline, stumbled down the slope. Ducking through the burned forest, trudging down the trail, his mind far off.

"Finally," Mariah said as he entered the cockpit. "I swear I was about to—what happened to you?"

"Nothing," said Peter, his heart racing. "Just tripped. Total klutz. Ready to go?"

"Uh, yeah." She held out her link. It was playing a clip of their friends Rian and Jaime singing. "The subsonic had karaoke."

"Sounds fun." Peter strapped in and activated the liftoff sequence.

"They'll be in Valpo in under an hour."

"Nice." What were they talking about?

Mariah slouched in her seat. A minute later, she huffed and left the cockpit.

They flew across the twilit Utah desert. Across the midnight Gulf of Mexico. They spent a week in Valparaiso and afterward moved in together at the Helsinki officers' station. They broke up a year later, and the next time Peter saw her, they were in the virtual auditorium as Secretary General Wells made his fateful speech about the end of the solar system, Mariah fighting tears, while Peter tried not to smile. Six years after that, Mariah died on a rocket test mission, her craft burning up in the Martian atmosphere. Peter saw the streak of fire as he was prepping a flight team up at the orbital docks, where the superstructure of the prototype starliner *Artemis* was nearly complete. He only learned later that she'd been on board.

He had never told anyone about the strange being, or the girl made of light, the vision she had showed him. Instead, he'd worked his way up the ranks of the starliner program. Hard, relentless work, and some luck—or was it a grand design?—earned him command of the *Artemis*.

And four years later, while on board the great ship en route to map the rogue planet Kazu-4—a prime candidate to be the first waypoint designated Delphi—Peter revealed to his crew that they had a second, top secret objective: to analyze the source of mysterious space-time distortions and gravitational wave emissions, which, in the rush to evacuate Earth and plan the colonization of Aaru-5, had never been properly investigated.

Nor did he mention that these orders to investigate had not in fact come from ISA command. Sometimes Peter laughed to himself, when he thought of where those orders had really come from.

Throughout all the years between that Utah night and the moment when the *Artemis* encountered the great doorway in space—a discovery that would lock him and his crew on a course of events that would determine a good deal more than just the fate of this universe—scarcely a day went by when Captain Peter Barrie did not rewatch those old videos on his link and think of that great structure in the green light and the shimmering girl who had called to him from across the stars.

Indeed, every now and then, some fellow officer would notice him speaking quietly to himself as he stood on the bridge or studied the navigation charts.

"What is that little thing you're always muttering?"

Lieutenant Lyris had even asked him once, as they neared their mysterious destination.

"It's nothing," Captain Barrie replied. He smiled, and she smiled back, and though they'd become quite close, she didn't ask again. Later, when it was too late, she would wish she had.

On they sped through the dark of space, and as the great doorway, and his fate, drew ever closer, Captain Barrie kept repeating those same words to himself, like a vow:

"I am coming."

TIME LINE

2175: Humanity discovers that, contrary to all previous scientific understanding, the sun will soon explode in a supernova. The International Space Agency devises a plan to first evacuate Earth to colonies on Mars, and then leave the solar system altogether for the distant planet Aaru-5, a journey that will take 150 years.

2194: The *Starliner Artemis*, the prototype of the colonial fleet, is lost, eight years into its test voyage.

2209: Phase One of the ISA Colonization Protocol is completed. On Aaru-5, known by its inhabitants as Telos, the resulting firestorm destroys the surface of the planet, leaving only a handful of Telphon survivors.

2213: The last colonists depart Mars on the *Starliner Scorpius*.

2216: The sun goes supernova, obliterating humanity's home.

2223: The *Scorpius* arrives at Delphi, the first waypoint on the journey to Aaru, and is immediately attacked by a Telphon strike team. The *Scorpius* sustains massive damage and charts an emergency course to rendezvous with the rest of the fleet at Destina, in the Alpha Centauri star system.

2256: The Telphons intercept the starliners *Scorpius*, *Rhea*, and *Saga* in the Centauri system. After a fierce battle, the three starliners attempt to escape before Centauri A goes supernova. . . .

THE SHORES BEYOND TIME

1

Perhaps the greatest talent of the human species is the ability to convince itself of nearly anything. To tell yourself something is true and to believe it, sometimes even in spite of the facts. This is a skill both useful and dangerous: useful when it can provide hope, courage, and understanding; dangerous when it is used to deny the truth, to deceive, or to justify. Your history on Earth was a pageant of examples both grand and terrible. And yet there is no doubt that this human talent is essential when traveling across the vast depths of space.

To imagine you are walking on solid ground, when

really there are scant meters of material between you and a fathomless, frigid void. When that certainty of gravity is, in reality, just the product of your spacecraft spinning. To imagine that the light on your face is from your home star, and to forget, even if only for a moment, that your sun, the one that made you, is gone. To ignore how many forces just outside the window could knock out those lights, could stop that spinning, could tear a hole in your spacecraft and leave it just another cold, dead object, floating endlessly through space.

To believe you have a destination, one that will welcome you.

To imagine that, soon enough, you will feel like you are home again.

Faith, trust, belief in yourself—there would be no crossing the local arm of your galaxy without it.

And yet: no matter how strong your power of imagination is, in this universe, a reminder of the truth, of the odds you are really up against, can arrive at any moment.

"Red alert! All passengers report to your cabins and prep for emergency stasis lockdown. Repeat! Red alert! We are under attack. This is not a drill."

"Go!"

"Wait!"

Mina gripped Arlo's hand. She wanted to hug

him one last time, but he pushed her hard toward her walkway and leapt onto the staircase that led to his own, thirty flights up.

The elevators had shut down, solar lamps out, only red emergency lights flashing all around.

Mina backed away, her gaze still locked with Arlo's. How could this be happening? Just a moment ago they'd been standing there in line, smiling, arms around each other, waiting for the next drop shuttle to the surface of Delphi, when the first blasts had rumbled through the *Scorpius*. Wearing their neoprene bathing suits beneath their clothes for their scheduled turn in the thermal steam baths, so happy to be with each other again after that strange, formless decade in stasis. Everyone around them had been smiling, too, brimming with hope. One interval down, fourteen to go on the way to Aaru-5. Sure, there had been that trouble back at Saturn—most people had accepted that it was some kind of terrorist attack—but that was nearly a light-year ago, far behind them now—

"Mina, GO!" Arlo shouted again. "I'll be okay." And with a last look he turned and bounded up the stairs.

"All passengers report immediately—"

Mina fell in with the crowd around her scrambling to get to their compartments. *Oh my god. Oh my god.* They were going to die. The thought was like a knife slicing through her mind—but no. She had to focus. One thing at a time.

The floor shuddered again, more distant booms of explosions. Parents dragging wailing children, younger people slamming into elderly folks on their hover walkers.

Smash! One of the spherical cable transports tore free and crashed into the wall.

A *whump* of fire and smoke. Mina was thrown against the wall, her shoulder barking in pain. She shoved herself upright, kept going—

And then a searing, humming sound, a brilliant flash of light and a deafening explosion above her. Screams, alarms, the lightening in her limbs as the ship's rotation ground to a halt and artificial gravity failed, the roar of wind as air sucked out of core. Mina looked up and saw a giant circular hole with melted edges, debris funneling out of it into the dark void of space.

Arlo's deck was up there.

People around her stumbling. Her feet losing connection with the floor. She dragged herself along by the railing, slammed the controls to open her compartment door, and tumbled inside and spun and hit the close button.

No response.

Wind howled. Her guitar toppled over, sliding

across the floor and smashing against the door frame. She grabbed the manual handle, struggling to move it, her head already starting to feel light from the lack of oxygen—

The door slammed shut.

What about Arlo??

No time. Not now. As Mina shoved herself toward her pod, she performed that special talent: *He'll be fine,* she told herself. *If he made it to his compartment in time. Got into his pod. . . .*

And yet, even then, didn't she know?

Shutting the door had quieted the roar from the core somewhat, and now Mina heard the urgent announcement flooding her compartment:

"Core integrity failure. All passengers prepare for stasis pod ejection."

They were shooting her off into space! How would she survive? *It's okay, the pods have life support systems.* She knew this from the on-board orientation. You could be in space for months, years even. . . . *Or forever.*

Mina changed into her thermal wear, scrambled over the side of her pod, beside three others that were closed and dark—where was Liam? Where were her parents? Would they ever find out what had happened to her? She was going to die in space, she—

Come on!

She fumbled with the wires for the muscle stimulators, attaching them at her wrists and ankles. Another deep rumble and the red lights in the room died out, along with the warning voice. Only the mellow amber light from inside the pod remained. But beyond, tearing and crunching sounds, now a shriek as the door itself began to curl up from the floor, being ripped out into the depressurizing core.

GO!

Mina held the fluid line with trembling fingers, trying to press it into the port that had been surgically implanted in her forearm. Faster! The rumbling and tearing getting louder, like a wave. She finally secured the line, buckled herself in and slammed her fist against the power button.

Screaming wind. As she lay back, she saw the door frame peeling apart, the whoosh of everything sucking away—

The pod sealed shut. All those terrible sounds distant, just the hiss of the stasis gas and beneath that, the thundering of her heart.

"Pod evacuation system engaged. Launch in three, two, one . . ."

A whine and a crash, a blur and a shove and a flash of thrusters—

But everything around her was fading away, the stasis gas pulling her under. The last thing Mina saw, through foggy vision, was the side of the starliner core, alight in flashes of ejecting pods, and then the dark of space, stars everywhere, and bursts of light, explosions in the sudden silence, a brief glimpse of the shadow-blue world of Delphi.

Please find me, she thought. *Arlo . . . Liam . . . Mom and Dad . . . Please be okay. . . .*

*The core is tearing apart, but Mina doesn't make it to her
room, is instead sucked away, arms and legs pinwheeling,
through the gaping hole in the starliner core and out into
the darkness and cold, breath getting tight as she reaches in
vain for the ship, as she freezes—*

"Miss, please lie back," a voice said, as if from a
far distance.

Forms in a brightening fog. Movement. Faces . . .

"This is just a routine check of your vitals and your
pod. Assuming all is well, we'll be putting you right
back in stasis." The voice sounded closer now. Beyond
it was a babble of sounds: other voices, machinery,
someone wailing.

Mina blinked and saw the crisscrossing beams of a ceiling far above. The outlines of ships in the corners of her vision. A blurry silhouette beside her.

Frantic, terrified shouting somewhere nearby. The urgent beeping of a grav lifter.

"Where are we?" Mina asked, not even sure the words had left her lips.

"Four days out from Delphi," said an older woman's voice. Mina blinked and saw a medic leaning over the side of her pod. She was pressing a bio scanner to Mina's arm. "Your pod was salvaged from space after Core Three was destroyed. We're en route to Destina, the emergency rendezvous location near the fourth waypoint, at Centauri B. Hopefully, the rest of the fleet can interpret the few transmissions we were able to send before comms went down, and meet us there." She moved the scanner to Mina's forehead.

Mina pushed herself up onto her elbows and saw that she was in a hangar. The huge space was dimly lit, only a few of the light banks glowing, maybe to save power. There were hundreds of other pods interspersed among the smaller ships, making haphazard aisles. Most were closed, while teams of medical personnel hovered over open ones here and there. The moaning, wailing, and questions were coming from these open pods, the voices echoing.

Mina winced at a dull throbbing pain in her head.

"Headache, some nausea, muscle cramps," said the medic, "all normal symptoms of the rapid stasis procedure you went through when evacuating."

I was in space, she remembered, like it was a dream. But they'd found her. And yet, looking around the hangar, that couldn't have been the case for everyone else who ejected. There were far too few pods. "Who attacked us?"

"That is unknown at this time," said the medic. "It was a single ship, but with advanced capabilities and weaponry unlike anything we've ever seen."

"More like didn't even think was theoretically possible," said a younger man, a medical assistant, who was standing behind the medic, busily swiping a large tablet screen. "And those reports from the one ship of survivors who escaped the surface of Delphi? About the enemy soldiers' faces?"

"None of that is confirmed," scolded the medic.

"Are you saying they weren't terrorists?" said Mina.

"We don't think they were human at all," said the assistant.

The medic frowned at him.

"Where are they now?" Mina asked.

"We don't know."

"Are they attacking other ships in the fleet?" Mina thought of her grandparents, asleep on the *Starliner*

Osiris, not to mention countless other friends and acquaintances scattered throughout the fleet.

"We can't be sure. We have almost no information from the other starliners." The medic put away her scanner and started tapping at the control screen on Mina's pod. "If they'd wanted, they probably could have destroyed the whole ship, but they broke off the attack almost right after it began. Knocked out the refueling station, disabled our comms, and destroyed Core Three, and then just . . . vanished."

"But why? They—"

"You'll receive a full debriefing when we reach Destina," said the medic. "For the moment, we have thousands more pods to check and clear, and a thousand more injuries throughout the ship. The best thing you can do is let us get you back into stasis."

The medic held her link close to Mina's pod controls, her fingers moving from one to the other. She noticed Mina's gaze. "We're updating the software protocols for the upcoming journey. There we go." She shuffled through a shoulder bag, turned back to Mina, and held out a foil packet. "Eat this while your pod is rebooting. It's slow fuel with an extra vitamin and electrolyte concentrate. It's a thirty-three-year trip to Destina."

"Thirty-three . . ." Mina's heart started to race. "Is that even safe?"

The medic smiled darkly. "None of this is safe anymore." She stood.

There was a clunking sound beside them. Two zebra-striped bots had activated the magnetic levitation system on the stasis pod next to hers and were pushing it toward a large lifter with a stack of pods. Mina realized she would soon be just another body in that stack, and a shudder racked her body. Suddenly the walls of the pod were too narrow, the space too cramped.

"Here, take this too," said the medic. She held out a lozenge. "It's a relaxant."

Mina nodded and let the medic put it on her tongue.

"As soon as the reboot is complete, please re-engage stasis so we can get you safely stored. I know all this is overwhelming, but take my word for it, you're one of the lucky ones. If all goes well, we'll see you in a blink." The medic motioned to her assistant and they turned toward the next pod.

One of the lucky ones . . . Mina couldn't avoid the dark, painful cloud any longer. "Wait. I need to know . . . one of the passengers from Core Three. If he made it . . . Arlo Breton."

The medic frowned. "Family?"

"No, my boyfriend, but we'd been together over a year," she added, as if she needed to justify the terrible hammering of her heart.

The medic glanced at the assistant. "Check the manifest."

He ran his finger over his tablet, frowned, loaded another screen. . . . "I'm sorry."

Mina's breath hitched with fresh tears.

"If you want," said the medic, "there's been an impromptu memorial set up." She motioned toward the far end of the hangar. Through the gaps between ships and landing gear, Mina saw an area of wavering golden light, a few silhouettes in front of it. A wide spread of electric candles, video clips blinking from portable frames here and there.

"I can light a candle for him there," the medic added, "if you want."

"Thank you." She shuddered, her breath halting in her throat, and fought back the oncoming tears. "One more thing . . . my parents and brother, they were in a ship that was en route to Delphi, behind us, a Cosmic Cruiser. Is there any way to find out if they've caught up, or been in contact, or—"

The medic shook her head. "Like I said, comms were completely knocked out in the attack. We're flying blind. I know all this is difficult. We all lost people back there . . ." A shadow crossed over her face. The assistant looked at the floor, blinking at tears.

"I understand."

There was a beep from the pod controls and the medic stood. "Your settings are all ready. Stimulators are engaged, fluid line in. So, just eat your slow fuel and engage stasis. All right?"

Mina nodded, her throat tightening, a hole tearing open inside her, all her hope sucking out—*NO*. Arlo might be gone, but she wasn't giving up on her family yet.

As the medic walked away, Mina gulped down the pasty, bland slow fuel, but then instead of lying back down, she checked her link. She scrolled through her apps and opened a special one that Shawn's dad, Wesley, had designed for her as they were leaving Saturn, after they'd sent a link through space for Liam to pick up. A fresh flash of worry: Had Shawn and Wesley made it? Or were they lost too? She should have asked. . . .

The app opened. It used her link's light sensor to monitor the blinking of Mina's necklace: a silver chain that held a slim rectangular pendant with a rounded, green glass button at the end. Liam wore its twin around his neck. The necklaces were paired radio beacons, and Mina and Liam had been communicating with tap code, a laborious but effective method of using flashes of light to send messages, one letter at a time. The beacons were made of such retro technology that they did not save the messages they received, simply blinked in real time. This was part of what was supposed to make them cool, and why Mina had gotten the pair to share with Arlo. Just so they could blink at each other now and then, when they were on each other's minds—*oh, Arlo* . . . She'd given one to Liam just for the day on Mars, to test them out while she was on the *Scorpius* and he was stuck at the research station, never imagining that it would be her only link to her family across the galaxy.

When Mina had awakened at Delphi, before the attack, she'd found nine messages recorded by the app. The first ones had been from over six years earlier, as Liam was refueling. He'd said their parents were doing all right, and that their ship was steadily catching up to the *Scorpius* but also having trouble with their navigation systems—apparently they kept drifting ever so slightly off course for some reason— so they kept having to refuel. They were still going to make it to Delphi, but not until the fourth day after the *Scorpius* arrived.

His most recent message had been from about three months ago:

hi

If the *Scorpius* was four days out from Delphi, Liam and their parents should be arriving there at any moment. If the enemy ship—the *alien* enemy? Was that actually possible?—had really broken off its attack almost immediately, then her family might be safe. And yet what would they make of the wreckage? And would they even know where to go next?

"Miss . . ." Mina looked up to see the two bots approaching her pod. "Please engage stasis so that we may load you."

"One sec."

Mina pulled up the tap code key and began quickly tapping a message to Liam.

we've been attacked, she wrote, painstakingly, letter by letter.

heading for destina

It occurred to her that if the Cosmic Cruiser's long-range comms were also still down, as Liam had reported back at Saturn, they might not even know where Destina was.

near the fourth waypoint, second planet of centauri b hurry

"Miss, please." The bots had positioned themselves at either end of her pod. "We need to get this deck clear in case we have to scramble our military craft. It's for your safety."

"Okay." Mina kept watching the beacon. *Come on* . . . How long would it take her message to get back to Delphi? Was Liam even out of stasis yet? As she watched, she pulled off the necklace and hung it from a small hook that Wesley had attached to the inside lip of her pod. She'd forgotten to do this in the rush back at Delphi. Once the beacon was hung, she snapped the silver casing off its rectangular body, revealing its delicate circuit board. Then she slid her link off her wrist and secured it with a strap to the opposite side of the pod, so that the link and the necklace were across from each other.

"We have orders to enforce compliance if necessary—"

"Last thing," said Mina. She dug around the inner lining of her pod—there it was. She picked up a slim cable that attached to her link at one end. At the other end was a small sensor that affixed to the beacon's circuitry. This setup allowed Wesley's app to measure the relative strength and direction of Liam's signal, in order to determine how close he and the Cosmic Cruiser were to the *Scorpius*. He'd synced the app to Mina's stasis controls, so that whenever—*if ever*—Liam and her parents finally got within range, she would be awakened from stasis no matter what.

A light blinked in the app, indicating that it detected the beacon. "Okay, I'm ready." Mina lay back and, with a deep breath, engaged stasis. As the pod lid hissed closed, as she buckled herself in, she stared at the beacon. *Come on, just one flash before I go under. . . .*

But the beacon remained dark as the gas swirled

around her. Mina saw the two bots gazing down at her and shut her eyes. *Arlo,* she thought, a fresh well of sorrow opening within her.

Come on, Liam. . . .

The world receded again, into gray, into silence.

Light again. And that weird sensation of having sensation, of *being* again after a long cold nothing.

A foggy view of a cavernous ceiling. Closer, something was floating above her, oval shaped, and sliding out of her view.

Mina blinked, felt the sting of her dry eyes.

I'm in a hangar again. That's a skim drone up there.

Her lungs filled, then breathed out, the air adding condensation to the already moist flex-glass lid of her stasis pod. Twitch of her muscles, thump of her heart, a sore sensation in her chest, in her throat, a dull ache in her skull.

Thirty-three years . . . had it really been that long?

A light caught her attention. She twisted her sore neck to see something flashing on her link. Blurry . . . She blinked, moved her cold, twitching fingers to her eyes and rubbed. Looked again and saw a message: *Target Proximity.*

What did that mean? . . . But then she remembered the app, the beacon.

Liam! Mom and Dad!

The top of her pod hissed and yawned open. Mina lurched up, unbuckling, but immediately slumped against the side. Her vision spun, pain thudding in her head, a sour taste in the back of her mouth. . . . Were they really at Destina? She fumbled for her link and opened the home screen. Earth year 2256—April 18, as if Earth days even mattered out here.

A whoosh of thrusters overhead. That skim drone she'd noticed was across the hangar now, slipping into the airlock, the giant inner door beginning to slide closed behind it.

A familiar shape out of the corner of her eye: Mina craned her neck and spied her family's Cosmic Cruiser. They'd made it! But that skim drone . . .

"Liam?" she croaked.

The little craft hung there in the airlock, almost out of view. *Is that*— "Liam!" she shouted. "Wait!"

She tried to push up, get to her knees—

56

The entire hangar rumbled and a piece of tile smashed to the metal floor.

Finally, she registered the spinning red lights. The blaring of alerts. They were under attack again.

The airlock slid shut. Where could he be going? What was happening? Mina grabbed the beacon, not bothering to snap the casing back on, and stabbed at the button. As she did it, she dragged herself over the side of the pod and stood on wobbling legs.

come back

She stared at the beacon but Liam didn't reply. Another terrible rumble, everything rattling around her, making Mina stumble. She gritted her teeth and hurried toward the cruiser, tying her cold, damp hair back as she went. The airlock door on its side was open. She stumbled up the steps, into the familiar old hunk of junk.

"Hello? JEFF?" No answer. She ducked into the cockpit, but it was empty. The cruiser shook and she was thrown against the wall. Bracing herself, she moved to the back of the ship. Two empty stasis pods in one compartment. In the other—

Tears sprang from Mina's eyes as she raced between the two pods. "Mom! Dad!" There they were, their faces shaded by burns, but alive and peacefully asleep. Time seemed to loop on itself, as if she'd just seen them a few days ago—which in a way, she had.

Saying good-bye to them at their apartment door on Mars, Mina remembered how she'd hurried through their hugs and brushed off Mom's *love you* and how she'd been way more concerned with getting out of there with Arlo—

Arlo.

Mina fell against her mom's pod and sobbed, all of it hitting her now, finally. He was really gone. Forever. All the danger she'd faced back at Delphi, and the distance and loss and time that had passed, that still had to pass . . . And where the hell had Liam gone just now?

"Mina? Is that y-y-you?" said a staticky, robotic voice.

"JEFF!" She whirled and stumbled back to the main cabin. The floor shook again. Fresh spots in her vision. "Yeah! It's me! What's going on?"

"I am currently in command of the *Scorpius*," said JEFF, her family's personal bot, over the cruiser's local link, "though I have initiated a wake-up sequence and a command crew should be here sh-sh-shortly. We are under attack from the hostile Telphon force—"

"Who? Is that who attacked us back at Delphi?"

"Yes. The starliners *Saga* and *Rhea* have attached their magnet tethers and are beginning to tow us away, as the Centauri A supernova is imminent."

"Supernova? What do you mean? Another one?"

"Correct. We are about to deploy a counterattack

against the enemy ship that should—"

Mina's head hurt with the details. "JEFF! I just saw him leave. Where did he go?"

"He believes he can s-s-save Phoebe."

"Where is she?"

"Aboard the enemy craft."

"They captured her?" Mina glanced at the rear compartments. "Her parents too?"

JEFF didn't answer for a moment. "It is more complicated than that. I do not know that now is the time to explain fully."

"Okay . . . so Liam is flying after the ship that's attacking us, in a skim drone? And there's another supernova?"

"Acknowledged. Red Line for our safe departure is in twenty-five minutes."

"Does Liam know that?"

"He is aware of the danger, yes."

"But he's going to get killed! You have to send someone after him!"

"I am afraid that is not p-p-possible. All available processing power is being routed to rebooting the *Scorpius,* in order to get away from the supernova in time, and also to firing our countermeasures. We have devised a strategy to destroy the Telphon ship."

Mina could barely keep up. "But you just said Liam was headed for that ship!"

"Affirmative. I warned Liam against this as well. However he was still insistent on going after Phoebe."

"There has to be something you can do!"

"This is a difficult situation by any calculation," said JEFF, "but it is my duty to act in the best interests of the human fleet as a whole. I will be back in touch shortly."

Mina threw up her hands. "Are you kidding me?" They couldn't have gone through all this just to lose each other now! There had to be something—

"Mina."

The voice came from behind her. She turned, and before she could believe what her mind was telling her, she felt her heart shiver in the strangest way. "Liam?"

He was standing right there, not two meters from her. Her little brother, same as ever, in his black thermal wear and some kind of strange silver hoodie, and also what looked like a Haishang Dust Devils team shirt beneath that. He smiled, and Mina ran to him and threw her arms around him. "You're okay!"

And yet the second she hugged him she knew something wasn't right. The buzzing sensation, the way he felt cool to the touch, too cool . . . She pulled back, let go of him. "What's going on?"

Liam's mouth scrunched. "I know it's strange. I'm here, but I'm also not. I—I just came to let you know that I'm safe."

Mina eyed him. "Came from where? I just saw you leave. JEFF says you tried to rescue Phoebe—"

"I did . . . I mean, I am doing that, where you are. But . . . a lot has happened since then."

"What are you talking about?"

Liam made a strange face, wincing like his head hurt. And it almost seemed as if his body rippled, like she was looking at him on a holoscreen. Except she'd hugged him. He was here . . . or was he?

"Listen, I can't stay much longer. I just didn't want you to worry. Don't want Mom and Dad to, either. The supernova blast: you can use it to propel the starliners out of here. We timed it just right."

"What do you mean, *timed it just right*? We're trying to get away from it."

"I know. Tell JEFF that they can use the solar sails, if they haven't figured that out already. The blast will occur when they are at exactly the right distance to use its force and not be damaged by it."

"Liam, stop! I don't know what you're talking about! Who's *we*?"

"I, um—" His body contorted. His hand leapt to his head as if he was in pain, and somehow, a ripple of static seemed to rush through him. "Sorry, I don't have much time. But you have to be far enough away from the rifting event that will occur afterward, so that it doesn't destroy the ship's systems and leave you guys floating in space."

"I don't know what any of that means."

"I know. Just tell JEFF, okay? It will work. You'll make it safely away. That's all that matters right now."

"But what about you?"

"I'll be all right. Trust me." He winced again, balling his fists.

"You're not all right, Liam, I can tell." Mina's eyes welled up. "Why does it sound like I'm never going to see you again?"

Liam smiled. "You will. Someday, I hope. . . ."

"What are you saying?"

He grimaced. "I have to go. *You* have to go. Tell JEFF what I told you. And take care of Mom and Dad."

"Liam!" Mina shouted. "Don't leave!"

"I have to."

"Then tell me where you are! I'll come get you."

"You can't. There's no way . . . just get yourself to safety, okay?"

"No, I'm going to find you! You hear me?"

"Mina, don't. I, um, I love you. I'm going now. Bye."

And he was gone. Just like that. Mina stared at the space where her little brother had been. "Liam!" she shouted, but the cabin was silent, empty. Had that even just happened?

She wiped away tears, fought off a surge through her body to just collapse on the couch. All of this was too much. . . . "JEFF!" she shouted. "I need you *now*!"

"Yes, Mina," he replied over the local link.

"I just saw Liam. I think. I mean, it was him, but he wasn't here, not really. It was like he . . . appeared? And we spoke, and then he was just . . . gone."

"I s-s-see."

Mina cocked her head. "Why don't you sound surprised?"

"Well," said JEFF, "since Liam discovered the chronologist's watch technology on Mars, he has been able to accomplish various feats that defy what we would call the normal laws of space-time."

"You're going to need to explain what you're talking about."

"Yes, I would be happy to, but at the m-m-moment—"

The ship rumbled again.

"I know, I know: supernova, alien attack." Mina rubbed her face. "Okay, listen: Liam said that you can use the supernova blast to propel the ships to a safe distance from a rift or something."

"Acknowledged. Liam had previously mentioned to me something about the universe collapsing."

"Well, he didn't say that, but about the supernova: He said they'd timed it perfectly?"

"Who is *they*?"

"I don't know! But he said to use the solar sails and that would get us away safely. And he said you'd know what this meant."

"Just a moment, I am calculating . . . why y-y-yes, it does seem that with our expected velocity, and the timing of the supernova, deploying the solar sails will allow us to achieve a significant speed boost. It—that is fascinating."

"What is?"

"According to my calculations, when the supernova occurs, we will be at exactly the right distance to achieve the maximum possible thrust increase. Any closer, and we would have risked damage to the ship or the passengers. Any farther, and we would not have achieved quite as high a velocity. It is, mathematically speaking, perfect timing."

"What's your point?"

"Earlier, Liam stated that the timing of this Centauri A supernova was not an accident—that he believed the Drove were intentionally trying to kill us."

"The who?"

"The beings that Liam believes are responsible for causing our sun to go supernova. Liam has encountered a metal-suited man during his travels, who he believes is their leader."

"Hold on. These . . . the 'Drove'—they're different from the telephotos?"

"Telphons. Yes, they are two different species. But it seems that Liam's suspicion was wrong: this new data suggests that the blast is in fact timed to help us, not to harm us. Though that cannot be more than coincidental, unless . . ."

"Unless what?"

"Unless this is another example of your brother's anomalous behavior in space-time."

"Okay . . ." Mina shook her head. "So now what?"

"The crew has just arrived, so in a moment I will be able to r-r-relinquish command of the *Scorpius*. We are about to launch our countermeasure at the Telphon ship, which will hopefully destroy it; well, not hopefully when it comes to Liam—"

"It's okay," said Mina. "I don't think that's a danger for him." She felt a weird sensation as she said this. Not quite relief, because she *did* think he was in danger, she just wasn't sure yet from what.

"Acknowledged. I am handing off systems operations now. I will be back in touch shortly."

"JEFF, wait." But JEFF didn't respond.

Mina looked around the silent cabin and swore to herself. All of this was crazy! Telphons? The Drove? Time traveling? And where exactly was Liam? Was there any way she could find him? *He told me to go. . . .*

Arlo said that too. And he'd been right. And yet Mina wasn't sure she could stand losing Liam, too.

"Mina? Hey! Are you in there?"

Footsteps on the stairs, in the airlock.

Mina turned and suddenly someone was rushing at her.

"There you are!" Shawn threw his arms around her. "I'm so glad you're okay."

"Hey!" His short curly hair brushed against her chin. She gently pushed him away. "It's good to see you too. Is your dad—"

"Yeah, he's fine," said Shawn, out of breath. "They had me stored like six levels down. The alert woke me up. About Liam. Dad synced my link to yours, to go off if he was nearby." Shawn glanced around the cruiser. "Where is he?"

Mina explained as best she could, about Liam taking off after Phoebe, about the supernova, but she decided not to mention Liam's most recent appearance, or the strange things he'd said, adding simply, "I think they're okay, for the moment."

"That's good." Shawn looked at her, eyes wide with concern. "And you're okay, after stasis?"

"Close enough." But her mind drifted to Arlo again, and some tears escaped, which she quickly wiped away.

66

"Hey, it's, um, it's okay." Shawn patted her arm awkwardly. "My dad went to check the bridge, but he said if your parents were here, we should get them to the med bay. Are they . . ."

"Yeah, they're in back. Alive."

"Nice. Dad said they're going to need treatment as soon as possible. And also, the sooner they recover, the sooner we can find out what happened on Mars. Dad thinks the accident at the Phase Two research station might be connected to whoever keeps attacking us."

"The Telphons," said Mina.

"The who?"

"I don't know, they're some kind of alien army or something."

Shawn's eyes widened. "Aliens? Are you serious? Man, I *knew* this trip was going to be more dangerous than they said! What kind? Like, I mean, what do they look like—"

"I have no idea. JEFF might know, but he's busy." Another wave of feeling overtook her. She just wanted to sit down, to go back into stasis, to not feel this grief, not be in this moment at all—but no. *Come on!* Her parents were injured, her brother missing, the entire fleet in danger, and she could help. One thing at a time. "Let's just get my parents to the med bay."

They hurried to the rear compartment. Shawn

looked from her parents' pods to the empty ports where two other pods would have been. "Where are Phoebe's parents?" he asked.

"I think they're with these Telphons, too. Like they got captured or something."

"This all seems pretty weird."

"Tell me about it. Where's the closest med bay?"

"Dad said it's toward the bridge."

They activated the magnetic systems, and the pods levitated off the floor. Mina pushed her dad while Shawn pushed Mom, and they guided the pods out of the cruiser and across the hangar. Another rumble and a shriek of metal, the floor vibrating and making them stumble.

"That does not sound good," said Shawn, glancing warily at the walls and ceiling.

"Nope," said Mina, following his gaze.

In that exact moment, Mina's beacon blinked a single time beneath her thermal-wear shirt, but neither of them noticed.

They loaded into one of the elevators, rode up twelve levels to the main deck of the forward section, and pushed the pods down the wide hallway to the double doors of the med bay.

There was a large entry room where you normally would have checked in and waited for an appointment with a medic, but most of the lights were out, the chairs overturned. A large digital wall was heavily cracked, sparks shooting from the gaps.

Mina peered into the gloom. "Hello?"

A silhouette appeared in the red light down a corridor. "This way!" the woman called, waving to them.

They pushed the pods toward her, passing a set of sealed blast doors that normally would have led to another corridor, but when Mina pressed up onto her toes and glanced through the small, thick window, she saw only twisted wreckage and the black of space. The sight caused a fresh tremor of fear to ripple through her.

The woman motioned them into a compartment crowded with pods and patient beds in tight lines down both walls. There were a few more lights on in here, along with the blinking from pod readouts and bedside monitors. Four other medics and assistants were moving from one patient to the next, studying their readings and scans on holoscreens. Mina saw blackened burns, stained wound pads, pained faces. Most seemed to be unconscious, but here and there someone moaned in agony.

"I'm Dr. Inara," the woman said. Her blue lab coat was streaked and stained. Strands of her silver-and-black hair had sprung free from a hair clip, falling in front of her face. A welt there on her temple, as if she'd slammed into something. She moved her pad over the displays on Lana and Gerald's pods. "Are these Saunders and Chang? From the missing Delta Four Five cruiser?"

"Yeah," said Mina. "We need to wake them up right away."

"Hold on, I'm syncing their vitals. These pods haven't been updated in a while." Dr. Inara tapped her pad. "Wow, okay. It's a miracle these two are alive, all things considered." She read the scrolling data. "They've been in continual stasis for over forty-three years. Smoke inhalation, radiation exposure, the male has a fractured ulna . . ."

"Will they be okay?" Mina asked.

"They should be. I'm going to have to wake them at a slow acclimation cycle, in order to be sure their injuries remain stabilized and that their cognitive response isn't impaired."

"How long will that take?"

"About forty-five minutes."

Mina gritted her teeth. "Okay."

A technician brushed by her shoulder, moving around a nearby bed.

"Probably best if you find somewhere else to wait," said Dr. Inara. She gazed at Mina's parents again. "I'd love to know how they got here, when there's time."

"Yeah, so would I."

Dr. Inara eyed Mina quizzically but returned to her readouts.

Mina kept staring at her parents. Shawn pulled her arm. "Come on."

They retreated up the corridor and back out into the main hallway. Mina leaned against the wall. She felt a smooth humming there, the sensation of the ship's engines executing a burn. "I don't hear any more explosions. I wonder if the fighting is over?"

"Seems like it," said Shawn. "That was crazy back there on Delphi. My dad and I were standing in line at the climbing domes. If our stateroom hadn't been so close by . . ."

Mina winced, tears streaming out again.

"Arlo?" said Shawn. Mina nodded. "I'm sorry."

Mina wiped harshly at her eyes. "This is all too much."

"Good morning, Mina and Shawn!"

JEFF rolled down the corridor toward them, his panda face with its perpetual wide grin, his old wheels making their familiar crunching sound.

"Morning where?" said Mina.

"Good point," said JEFF.

"How are things going on the bridge?"

"Stable for the moment. We are en route away from the supernova. Our countermeasures against the Telphons were effective in warding them off, but we were not able to neutralize the threat entirely, as we had hoped."

"You mean they escaped?" said Shawn.

"Correct."

"What about Liam?" Mina asked. JEFF's eyes flickered for a moment and Mina felt a surge of adrenaline in her belly. "JEFF . . ."

"You said that you have seen Liam, and he told you he was okay."

"Yeah, but what do *you* know?"

More flickering. . . . "I have only limited information. Liam contacted me from the skim drone just fifteen minutes ago. He was on his way back toward us, with Phoebe, but the signal cut out. I believe the skim drone was shut down by the electromagnetic pulse we created when attacking the Telphons. Unlike the starliners, a skim drone has no EM shielding."

"Wait," said Shawn. "Are you saying he's stuck out in space?"

"I do not think so. Earlier, I placed a tracking beacon in Liam's shoulder, before the Telphons captured us. Up until a few m-m-minutes ago, that tracking beacon was giving off a signal. Then it gave a number of very strange error results and disappeared."

"Like the blast fried it?" said Shawn.

"No. The beacon was still functioning after the blast, likely protected by Liam's space-grade suit and the fact that it was implanted subc-c-cutaneously. Before the signal disappeared, it transmitted errors in its time code. I believe that Liam has traveled in time again, thus escaping from the marooned skim drone."

"Whoa, hold on," said Shawn. "Traveled *in time? Again?* He's done that before?"

"Affirmative. He and Phoebe were both gone for quite a few years on the journey here."

"Man," said Shawn.

"So . . . ," said Mina, "we're just going to fly out of here without knowing what happened to my brother?"

"You said that he visited you, and that he said they are okay."

"Yeah, but . . . that's not enough, JEFF! I need to know where he is!"

"I understand, but if my recent experiences with Liam are any indication, it is likely that our best course of a-a-action, given all the variables, is to wait for him to find us."

Mina sighed and clenched her jaw. "None of this makes any sense!"

"I know it is not ideal. For the m-m-moment, we are all safe. Now I must visit the maintenance portal down the hall and plug myself in for a much-needed s-s-system update. I would likewise suggest the two of you get some food. The forward galley has basic provisions."

"I am starving," said Shawn.

"Me too. JEFF, how much longer until the super-nova?"

"One hour, forty-six minutes, thirty-eight seconds, roughly. It is fascinating: the timing that Liam described will allow us to reach a speed nearly four percent faster than our normal maximum. I look forward to hearing how he arranged that." JEFF rolled down the corridor.

"I don't understand any of this," said Shawn. "Time travel . . ."

"Yeah, my brain hurts too. Let's get food."

The forward galley was nearly empty, only occasional crew members hurrying in and out, having just been awakened from stasis, on their way to their posts. The nutrition bots had laid out a sparse selection of quick-grab foods: nutri-bars, strips of OrangeVeg, and synthetic lime pudding.

"This is as bad as school lunch," said Shawn, grabbing one of each.

They sat alone in a sea of empty tables. Mina took a bite of nutri-bar and nearly gagged, but she eventually forced it down. Neither of them spoke, just tapped at their links, but with the VirtCom down there was nothing to do other than look at pictures or play games in offline mode.

Mina had a million questions rattling around in

her head, but for the moment, she scrolled through her photos. The dates on the most recent ones were decades old, yet to Mina, they'd been taken mere hours ago. First were the selfies with Arlo from right after they'd woken up at Delphi. Next were ones from all the way back on the ride from Mars to Saturn, when she and Arlo and their drummer, Kiana, had been practicing for the show they never got to play, a few moments when she'd managed to smile in between worries about her family. Before that, pictures of them messing around in the climbing domes back in their core while waiting for departure from Mars, before anything had gone wrong. Her and Arlo together on the space elevator, the rusty glow out the skinny window, a last photo of her empty bedroom that morning, when she'd been sad but more so excited to finally be getting on to a new adventure, never imagining what would happen next. . . .

Mina turned off her link and wiped her eyes. She finished her nutri-bar and stood. "I'm going to see if my parents are awake yet."

Shawn looked up from an old-school racing game he'd been playing. "Cool. My dad's going to meet me here in a couple minutes, but—" Shawn half stood. "I can come with you, if you need me, or . . ."

"No, I'm fine." She patted his shoulder. "Thanks for your help."

Shawn kind of blushed. "Anytime. Let me know how they're doing."

"Okay."

Mina returned to the med bay. As she started down the corridor, she paused at that sealed emergency door and gazed out through the tangled wreckage into space. Stars in all directions, the bright orange glow of Centauri A and the cool blue of Centauri B, both coin sized behind them. She felt a nervous rush: so little stood between her and nothing. Was that the last thing Arlo had thought? Before he froze? Did he see the stars in all directions, realize he was going to die? What would that have been like . . . ?

Mina shook it off and entered the compartment where her parents were. Dr. Inara wasn't around. Things had quieted down, most of the patients asleep, only a medic or two left checking monitors. The mellow blinking of lights and blipping of sensors here and there.

Amber lights glowed around the inner rims of both pods. Dad's was still closed, but Mom's was now open.

Mina put her hands on the edge of Mom's pod. She had an oxygen mask over her nose and mouth, a fluid line in her arm that attached to a bag hanging on a nearby rack. There was a bandage over the side of her head.

"Hey, Mom." Mina's eyes rimmed with tears again. She rubbed her mom's shoulder. "You're gonna be okay."

Mom's eyes fluttered. It was impossible to know if she saw Mina, but her lips moved, as if she was saying something, though it was too faint for Mina to hear.

"What's that?" Mina leaned closer.

Mom tried to speak again. Her brow furrowed and her fingers brushed weakly at the mask.

Mina checked over her shoulder, then slipped the mask down beneath Mom's chin.

"Mom. What is it?"

"No," Mom said. Her eyes were still closed, but she winced.

"You just need some time to recover," Mina assured her. "You've been in stasis a long time. Over forty years. I know that sounds crazy, but—"

"Ariana, don't do this."

"Mom, it's me, Mina." Was she referring to Phoebe's mother?

Mom's eyes popped open. "We have to go with you!" She gasped for breath, blinking rapidly, her arms moving like she was trying to prop herself up, but she was still too out of it. "Ariana, please! He's my son; I need to know—you can't—"

The words made Mina's heart race. "Mom! What are you talking about?"

Mom looked at Mina blankly for a moment, uncomprehending. Then she squinted. "Mina?"

"Yeah, it's me."

"Oh, honey . . ." Tears came to her eyes. Mina leaned into the pod and gently hugged her. "I'm so glad you're safe," sad Mom, and yet they'd barely hugged for a moment when she tried to look over Mina's shoulder. "Where's JEFF?" she said anxiously.

"He went to reboot, I think."

Mom gripped Mina's shoulders. "You have to stop them. Call security. Get to JEFF now. They're going after Liam but we can't trust them! They're the enemy!"

The words made Mina's brain feel slow, like heavy puzzle pieces were sliding together in her head. "Who? Do you mean Ariana?" Mom nodded. "Wait, she's here? On the ship? And she's the enemy? Is that what you're saying?"

"I just saw her," said Mom. "They're the ones who caused the accident on Mars."

"Mom, are you sure? I mean—"

"Mina, now!" Mom croaked. "They came back because they need JEFF. He's the only one with information on where Liam and Phoebe went, and we can't let them—" She tried to sit up again.

"Oh, is she awake?" Mina saw Dr. Inara crossing the compartment.

"Get to JEFF!" Mom hissed, her eyes pleading.

"Okay." Mina whirled and rushed past Dr. Inara. "Call security!" she said. "We have intruders on board. Paolo and Ariana Dawson!"

"I don't—"

"Tell colonial security to head for the bot service node on the forward deck!"

Mina raced back to the main corridor and sprinted in the direction of the elevators. The service node had to be one of these compartments—

She was just past the doorway when she skidded to a stop and darted back.

There was JEFF, lying on the floor. Or most of him was.

His smiling panda head was gone.

2

Ariana held JEFF's detached head in her lap.

Ariana, whose real name was Marnia-2, who had been born on the planet Telos, grown up there, raised a family there, before the humans had burned the surface of the entire planet in Phase One of their colonization plan. Who had lost her son in that firestorm, and whose daughter had, just moments ago, disappeared into the cold dark of space.

No, you haven't lost Phoebe yet, she told herself.

She stared into the android's bright eyes, its pink grin, and finished soldering the loose wires hanging from its severed neck. JEFF was the only one who had been with Phoebe and Liam since Saturn. The only one who might be able to help Marnia figure out where her daughter had gone.

"There," she said, putting the soldering pen on the floor. "Now, JEFF, can you hear me?"

"Hello!" said JEFF. "Please pardon my interruption in service. I am running diagnostics now to determine the cause of my brief system failure— Ah, that is the problem. I seem to be missing my body."

"Yes, sorry about that. It was the only way to fit you in these cramped quarters."

Marnia sat beside Calo-6, her husband and Phoebe's father, known to the humans as Paolo. Together they were squeezed inside the tiny cockpit of Liam's skim drone. The Telphons had salvaged it from space, where Liam had left it, and then they had used it to infiltrate the *Scorpius* in order to get their hands on JEFF.

"Now," said Marnia, "please tell me what has happened to you since we last saw each other."

"Acknowledged," said JEFF. He recounted how, in the aftermath of the underground lab explosion on Mars, Liam and Phoebe had discovered the observatory of an extraterrestrial being called a chronologist, and her dead body inside, and how Liam had used this chronologist's watch to see the future. How, after escaping Barro and Tarra on Delphi, Phoebe and Liam had used the watch together to travel to Phoebe's home world, but on their return, they had been pulled off course by a doorway in space-time. How they'd found themselves on the *Starliner Artemis*, in the past, just before it was sucked through that very doorway. How the chronologist, whom they'd earlier found dead, had rescued them and returned them to the Cosmic Cruiser just before they'd reached the Centauri system. How through all of this, Liam had been developing his ability to somehow manipulate time and space—so much so that, just before the Telphons caught them in the *Scorpius* hangar, JEFF had seen Liam from another point in time and helped him set up a plan to escape. How the last thing Liam had said was that he was going after Phoebe, and how the last readings of his whereabouts showed him perhaps moving in time again.

"She jumped out of our ship," said Marnia. "They were both in this craft. I talked to him, but then when we found it . . . they were both gone."

"I can only assume Phoebe is with him now," JEFF concluded, "wherever or whenever they have gone."

"You're saying they vanished from this craft . . . by time traveling," said Calo.

"That is, however improbable, the most likely solution."

"So where could they have gone?" Calo asked.

"That I do not know," said JEFF.

Marnia heard Liam's words in her mind: *We're going to find another way.*

"Could they have used that doorway again?" she asked. "Could they be trying to go after the Drove on their own?" She still had a hard time accepting that there was a race of beings out there with the power to blow up stars, but Phoebe had believed it, and here, right out her window, was a second star about to explode.

"I cannot be certain," said JEFF, "but Liam and Phoebe did learn that the Drove use doorways like the one they found to travel in and out of this universe. But the larger problem is—and again, this is according to Liam and Phoebe—that the very use of these doors appears to be endangering the universe as a whole. In his most recent message, Liam said, in effect, that this posed an even greater threat than the supernova itself."

"Wait, what most recent message?"

"Liam spoke with his sister just over an hour ago. He also said that he was okay."

"Did he say anything about Phoebe?"

"I do not believe so, but I would assume she is safe as well."

Marnia bit her lip. She gazed out the cockpit of the skim drone. The boiling Centauri A was fingertip-sized in the distance.

They'd risked everything by flying back to the *Scorpius* and sneaking on board, and they were barely better off than before. Luckily, their human identities had not yet been flagged, as the only people who knew or suspected Marnia and Calo's true identities were either dead, or, in the case of Lana and Gerald, still injured.

Calo had strongly disapproved of Marnia's decision to stop by their med bay. *Stupid*, she thought to herself now. For three years, she had fought any feelings of friendship for Liam's parents, knowing that they had been part of the very team of human scientists who had decided to exterminate her species, whether they did so knowingly or not. Even after Liam had saved Marnia and the rest of the remaining Telphons from the starliners' EMP counterattack, it was still hard to look at Lana and not feel that deep well of anger inside her, to envision her own young son, forever taken from her in the Phase One attack.

And yet she had still felt the need, for some reason, to inform Lana that they would find Liam and return him to her. Lana had been coming out of stasis at the time. She probably hadn't even heard her. Maybe that was just as well.

Marnia scratched at the false skin at her temple. Infiltrating the *Scorpius* had also meant reapplying her human disguise, and now every inch of her was itchy.

"How long until we can rendezvous with the ship?" she asked.

Calo checked the navigation screen. "A few more minutes." As he spoke, an orange light began to flash on the console. "Another short," he muttered.

"I thought you fixed them all."

Calo tapped the light and flipped through schematics on the navigation screen. "So did I. This thing was hit by an EM blast. For every circuit that was fried, there's another one that was almost fried and could go at any second."

"Are we going to make it?"

Calo highlighted the thruster circuits and bypassed the faulty panel. "Yes. We're almost beyond the starliners' long-range sensors. Tarra should be waiting for us there. Even if we had a total power failure now, we've achieved the speed necessary to make the rendezvous."

"Still, we can't afford to lose power. We still need air and heat."

"We'll make it."

"And then we'll try to find this doorway Phoebe and Liam were talking about." She turned to JEFF. "Did they say anything about where it's located?"

"Only that it is somewhere between here and Delphi," said JEFF.

"There's a lot of space between here and there," said Calo. "It could take us ages to find it. Can you be more specific?"

"I am afraid not." JEFF's eyes flickered. "My diagnostics indicate that you have disabled my transmitting functionality."

"Obviously," said Marnia.

"In that case, may I ask: Have you decided not to continue your attack on the human fleet?"

"The only thing we've decided is that we're not leaving our daughter behind," said Marnia. "There will be plenty of time to deal with your fleet once we have her back."

There was a crack as something hit the hull of the skim drone.

"Debris from the firefight," said Calo.

Marnia looked around and saw other pieces glinting here and there in their lights. Phoebe's voice echoed in her head. *You have to stop this!*

"The Drove," Calo said thoughtfully. "They cause

these supernovas . . . but why? Why would you want to blow up a star?"

"Because . . . you're trying to destroy the universe?" said Marnia. "Or destroy its inhabitants?"

"Yes, supernovas destroy," said Calo, "but they also create. Supernovas produce certain elements that are obtainable nowhere else in the universe. They also emit massive amounts of energy."

"What are you saying?"

"Well, the humans destroyed our planet, but their goal was to make something new. Something they could use. What if the point of blowing up these stars isn't to destroy? What if the Drove are trying to get something they need?"

"It makes sense," said Marnia. "But why does that matter?"

"Because if the Drove want something from the supernova, that means they will have to come back to get it."

Marnia felt a surge of hope for the first time in far too long. "And we could be waiting. And then follow them back to the doorway."

"Exactly."

She rubbed his shoulder. "It's a good plan."

Calo shrugged. "We still have no idea who these Drove are, or what we'll really be up against—"

A warning sensor began to flash on the console.

"What's that?" said Marnia.

Calo tapped the screen, twisted to see behind them. "Someone's coming."

"Tarra?"

"No, we're still a few minutes out from—"

"Hey! Bot-nappers!" a girl's voice called over the skim drone's link.

"Fly faster," said Marnia.

"This thing won't go any faster!"

"I know you can hear me! This is Mina, Liam's sister. My parents are with me but they're pretty severely injured. I figure you might know something about that."

Lights burst above them. Marnia squinted and saw the underside of a Cosmic Cruiser.

"You can't outrun us," said Mina.

An alert sounded in the skim drone. Lights flickered all across the console.

"They've slaved our controls," said Calo.

"Override it!" Marnia shouted.

Calo stabbed frantically at buttons. "There's nothing I can do. This drone is paired with that cruiser."

"Let us go!" Marnia shouted over the link. "We need to find our daughter. We—"

"We're not here to take you back," said Mina. "We

want the same thing. My brother's out there, too. We're coming with you."

Marnia froze. Calo shook his head. "Impossible! We're not going anywhere with you! Not after what your people did to our planet—"

"I'm sorry, but you don't have a choice," said Mina. Marnia could hear her voice shaking. "We can do whatever we want with you, now: take you back with us, or just slam you into one of these fragments from the battle. At the very least, that should be enough to break the cockpit and kill you two in the vacuum of space. Small justice, I'd say. Someone I loved very dearly died that way, along with thousands of others."

"Do it, then!" Calo fumed. "Our ship will just blast you out of the sky and you'll suffer the same fate!"

There was a pause and now another voice:

"Ariana, this is Lana." Her voice was so raw and weak. "We all have blood on our hands. I only understand a small part of what you've been through, but right now, it doesn't matter."

"It all matters," Calo grumbled.

"Quiet," said Marnia.

"We watched our children grow up together," said Lana. "No matter our differences, right now we want the same thing. That's why we flew out here. Our people are headed in the opposite direction. . . .

I'm not even sure we could catch them now if we tried. You have JEFF, and you have a ship powerful enough to search the galaxy for them. We're not going to kill you; forgive what my daughter said. I suppose you could kill us, if you want. I know we have a lot to reckon with, but right now, we're asking for your help."

Another link channel beeped to life in the skim drone. "This is Tarra. We see you're being intercepted. We'll have them targeted and neutralized in a moment."

"Wait," said Marnia, grabbing Calo's hand before he could reply. "This was what Phoebe wanted. If we'd listened to her the first time, she'd still be here."

"What she needs is to—"

"Calo!" Marnia hissed. "Listen to me: finding Phoebe is one thing, but Liam has some kind of power we don't understand. And when we find him, there's no way he's going to trust us. If he and Phoebe run off again . . ." She motioned to the Cosmic Cruiser. "He'll trust them."

Calo stared at her. "But they—"

"I know what they did, and what we've done since. But Lana's right: that has nothing to do with what we do, right here, right now."

"Our people will never go for it. Never mind the

strike team. When word gets back home . . ."

The word *home* stung, but Marnia knew what he meant: the Styrlax cargo ship parked near the smoking ruins of Telos, which housed the two hundred and twenty-three Telphon refugees—twenty-five now, as Tarra had reported that two babies had in fact been born since they'd left Telos for Mars—all that remained of their people in the universe, except for the fourteen members of this strike team. *Thirteen*, Marnia thought, *without Phoebe*. After attacking the *Scorpius*, the team had plucked enough stasis pods from space for all the Telphons back home—once their original users had been tossed into space, that is.

"They're asleep," Marnia said. "They won't know until it is over." Asleep and waiting until the human threat was eradicated before they would set off in search of a new home. Every one of those Telphons had lost as much as Marnia and Calo, or more; and he was right that they would abhor the idea of teaming up with the humans. Tarra, their commander, might not go for it either, though she had agreed to this search for Phoebe, at least briefly.

But neither Tarra nor the Telphons back home knew what Marnia and Calo now understood after talking to JEFF.

"Calo . . . ," said Marnia.

He sighed. Flexed his fingers. "I know." He keyed the skim drone's link. "Tarra, that's a negative. Do not engage. We are joining the human cruiser. Prepare to let all passengers aboard unharmed."

"But we—"

Marnia cut her off. "We'll explain when we arrive. We need each other . . . for now."

3

EARTH YEAR: 2211

HAISHANG COLONY, MARS

TIME TO DARK STAR FUNCTIONALITY: 16H:49M

"Liam."

"It's your move."

Mina is giving him that look, the one that's part glare and part pity.

"Sorry," Liam says. He studies the holographic game board between them and slides one of his pioneer groups from the mining planet of Betax to the swamp planet of Temina.

Mina pushes her long black bangs out of her eyes and frowns. "Why would you move there? The market for swamp exhaust is dead."

Liam isn't sure. Because he wanted to buy the exhaust cheap? Or because he was thinking about how Mina's stasis pod might be lost in space?

That's in the future, he reminds himself. *And besides, she's okay, remember? You found her pod, just before you left the Scorpius. . . .*

That's right.

Here, it is a sunny afternoon on Mars. Liam and Mina sit on the balcony. Mom and Dad are in the cool just inside the door: Dad reading a holoscreen, Mom applying moisturizing electrodes to her feet. *Did they wake up? Have their injuries healed? Forty-three years in stasis . . .*

Distantly, he feels that surge again, a nervous flare of adrenaline like there is a jet flame inside him that is permanently turned to "on." What if his parents didn't make it? What if they can't recover from such a long stasis? What if that's Liam's fault, for not getting them off Mars sooner, for missing the starliner, for—

And there it is again, behind his eyes: the great boiling fireball, about to explode. Centauri A, seething with lethal fury, ready to erase him and everyone he loves, and there's nowhere to run, the skim drone dead—

STOP, he pleads with himself. Here, they are okay. *See?* Here, everything is safe.

The feeling calms a little. Yes, here on Mars, he doesn't have to worry.

Overhead, the sun gleams through the geodesic triangles of the dome. Below their balcony, the avenue burbles with conversation and the whirring of the moving walkways. The dry smell of colony air with the slightest tinge of desert dust. . . . If Liam tilts his head, he can see through gaps between the apartment complexes and just catch a glimpse of the distant maroon shadow of Olympus Mons. A cool, mysterious place that he will soon get to know better than almost anyone.

His nerves fire again when he pictures the chronologist's observatory at the top. The darkness when they first climbed down inside. The way it toppled off its high perch, threatening to crush them as they sped away in the skim drone. The way everything has been unsteady ever since— *Stop! None of that has happened yet.*

"Hey."

"Liam, come on," Mina says.

"It's your turn," Liam replies.

"Ugh, I just went. While you were sitting there spacing out, I monopolized iridium mining in the entire inner system. So the sooner you move, the sooner I can finish demolishing you."

"Sorry." Liam shakes his head. Was he spacing out because he was thinking about the future? *You weren't back then. You are now. Remember, those are different.*

He looks over the game board and is almost surprised to feel a grin tugging at the corner of his mouth as he moves another one of his pioneer teams.

"Why are you smiling?" says Mina. "You're playing out your own funeral."

He wants to say that he likes it. This moment. That is what he is thinking now. He is tempted to tell her that he's been here quite often. That in their future, when she is on the *Scorpius* and he is crossing the void between Saturn and Delphi in the Cosmic Cruiser, he will use an alien watch to revisit this exact moment, many times. That it feels safe here. That he feels whole. He can sense those other versions of himself here, too, faint tinges of their energy.

But Mina would be very confused by this. Besides, this wouldn't be the memory he finds so comforting if he were to change it now. What makes it special is how it *was*, how his family was together, how at least for the duration of this game, he wasn't worried about the future at all.

He glances at his parents, sitting inside, looking

relaxed. Such a rare sight. *I could warn them.* About the explosion in the underground lab, about Phoebe and her parents and the coming attack. But would it change anything? The sun would still go nova. And even if his parents knew the dangers ahead of time, would things actually work out any better than they had? Or would that new future in fact end up being worse? As it was, they had so narrowly survived the events on Mars, at Saturn and Delphi . . .

Could I find out? Was there a way that he could look at these other possibilities? See what might have been? He has glimpsed such things before, and yet he feels the surge of nerves again, sees the boiling star—

Stop it! Just be here. Mina asked you a question! That's right, and this moment, just after Mina asks, is the one he wants to pay attention to most.

"Check our totals," the Liam on the balcony says, the smile tugging harder.

Mina glances at the columns of data along the side of the board and frowns. "Wait, how did you get more money than me? And how is swamp exhaust suddenly worth so much?"

Liam remembers now: his whole strategy was to let Mina invest in iridium mining, because he'd noticed that if you made too much money from the mining, you had to start paying a lot more for climate control.

And the most important ingredient for climate control systems was swamp exhaust. So while she had been moving to colonize the planets rich in ore, he'd been settling on what appeared to be the worthless backwater ones.

"You tricked me," she says with a huff, but smiles too. "I didn't realize you had such a good poker face."

He wants to tell her it's not a poker face. It's just the look he gets when he's thinking about so many things at once that it gets overwhelming. Except it was less of that back then, the first time. The *real* time. How had he done it? Had he actually bluffed, despite how that always made his stomach flutter? All the lessons on breathing, on keeping his spinny thoughts in line, when he was younger and used to have night terrors and his parents took him to that therapist, back when there still were therapists. And yet somehow during this game on the balcony, he had pulled it off, tricked his sister. Even impressed her.

He almost wants to cry now. This Saturday afternoon—would there ever be another like it . . . ?

"We should go," says a voice beside him.

"I know." *What's the hurry?* he wants to add, except he should remember; even in the past, time is still passing. "Just one sec." He watches his old self move his star bases into the ninth sector, reveling in the thrill of victory.

"I can't believe it," Mina says, staring at the board, at the spinning totals. "You're going to win. And I didn't even let you."

She looks angry but also smiles, and Liam feels his heart swell with pride. Then and now. Like a warm, safe sun.

He turns to the mainframe: "Okay. Let's go."

"Come on, wake up."

Not yet.

If only he could tell her that he's not asleep.

"Was the chronologist's watch your first interaction with the higher viewpoints?"

Liam and the mainframe walk down an avenue in the downtown of the colony. A mag-shuttle whirs by overhead. It's busy out here today; throngs of people flow through the rust-colored afternoon toward the grav-ball stadium. A match will be starting soon. Others shop, or just stroll. In the distance, Liam can see a crowd at Vista, atop the Earth Preserve. Are they looking at Earth? Has it burned up yet? Any day now.

A passerby glances at Liam's legs, perhaps wondering why he's wearing black thermal wear instead of the standard-issue, hand-me-down gravity clothing, or where he got such a cool, hard-to-find Haishang

Dust Devils jersey, the one Phoebe will give him on their last day.

No one seems to notice the mainframe. This doesn't surprise Liam, because even though she shines brilliantly, and appears to be made entirely of tiny, angled mirrors reflecting a vast field of stars, he can only really see her in the corner of his eye. In fact, she may only be visible to him. It seems, too, as if behind her there is something impossibly bright and massive, something *more* to her, but once again, Liam is unable to turn far enough to see it.

"Call me Iris," she says. "It's a bit more friendly than *mainframe*."

"You're reading my mind again."

The impression of her shrugs. "I am assimilating data."

"You make it sound like *I'm* the computer."

"Every living thing is, in a way. And I don't just mean your data. I'm also analyzing all this VirtCom activity."

"All of it? You mean, like, the whole colony?"

"And the ships in orbit, and the starliners and passengers beyond that."

Wow, Liam thinks, but doesn't ask how that is possible, or what that might mean. Better to just be here now, on this familiar street.

"Where is the shop?" Iris asks.

"A couple more blocks." Liam tilts his face to feel the sun, smaller now than it will be in his final days on Mars, but still great and orange and bright. When he looks away, blinking the green blobs from his eyes, he notices the skitter of cockroaches beneath a bench. They make him smile.

"You didn't answer my other question," says Iris.

"Oh, sorry. What?"

"The chronometer. Did you ever experience time differently before you acquired it?"

Liam's hand drifts to his wrist, wishing to feel the smooth metal of the chronologist's silver watch, but it is gone. And yet, since he woke up in his present, he has found that he no longer needs it to move through time, or at least into the past. Moments like the one on the balcony are just there, behind his eyes. He can push out of his present and journey through them, seemingly with ease. "Not really," he says. "Unless you count worrying too much about the future. But that's just anxiety stuff."

"Perhaps," says Iris, "and yet it is also possible that your ability to worry about futures so acutely is in fact a bit of sixth-viewpoint awareness—"

"When you say viewpoints, you mean dimensions."

"That is your word for them, yes. There is no

perfect translation in your language."

"And how many of those are there?"

"That is the question," says Iris. "From the data I'm assimilating, it seems that your scientists have theorized twelve dimensions of reality. But it is possible that there are quite a few more. Most humans only experience four. However, you have already perceived the fifth and sixth, and you're just beginning."

Those last words cause a tremor of worry. "It was the watch that changed me. The chronologist said so."

"Yes, but part of what I need to ascertain is whether the watch could have changed anyone of your kind, or just *you*."

Liam shrugs. Iris said a lot of things like this. "And how's that going?"

"I am making progress."

"So you think I'm still changing?" Liam asks.

"Don't you?"

"I guess so. It used to be hard for me to push even a little bit out of my own timeline." He looked around the street. "Now we've left it completely. It's still a little weird though." This move—leaving his past self—does cause a strange feeling inside, a sort of emptiness, like a wind blowing through him. "You're helping me do this, aren't you?"

"Yes, but less each time. You're very impressive."

"Thanks," Liam says, but inside, more worry. These changes were what brought him face-to-face with that supernova, with the doorway—and with the future he is not yet ready to face. *You can't hide here forever*, he thinks to himself.

But maybe just a little longer.

He turns onto a side street lined with storefronts. "Here it is."

They enter a VirtCom boutique. Its flex-glass cases are filled with devices to augment one's virtual experience, both wearable and for the home. Liam finds what he is looking for in the Wellness area: a selection of slim wristbands called atomic watches. Each has a simple display of only the date and time, shielded beneath a tough plastic layer, the band made of a flexible polymer. The watches are designed to keep precise time, completely independent of the VirtCom or any network. His link has been error-riddled since he started traveling like this. Even rebooting it is barely enough to keep it from glitching.

Liam selects a brown band made to look like old Earth leather. The display has green numbers against a white background.

"Fascinating store," says Iris. "Is that what you need?"

"It should work," Liam says, except he needs to

scan the bar code on the back, and his link, as usual, is currently flashing multiple error messages. Besides, it's not like he'd have any credits, or like his link, from the future, would be able to sync with this version of the Mars VirtCom in the past.

"That's not really an issue for you, though, is it," says Iris.

No. It isn't. Liam closes his fist around the watch and looks over his shoulder at the ibex-shaped bot running the store. When he sees it's busy, he pushes away, out of the store and out of the moment completely, back into the blur of the timestream, where the events of his life stretch in both directions like an arrangement of bubbles. He turns toward his present and pushes that way, flowing through his last years on Mars, through the fiery blasts of that final day and at Saturn, into the dark of space, the long void of stasis on the way to Delphi, on and on. As he goes, he is aware of a faint haze beyond these events, the suggestion, like shapes in a fog, of those other versions of his past, other realities and timelines that he's wondered about.

"I can show you," says Iris, still in the corner of his eye.

"I know," but saying that causes a tremor of fear.

"Don't be afraid. I told you, Liam, I'm a friend."

She does feel like a friend, but . . . "I still don't know who you are."

"Don't you, though?"

Maybe he does. Because even though she is a human-like shape, even though she talks like him, and walks with him on Mars, he senses that she is something far greater, and far more powerful. He can almost feel the energy emanating from her, making ripples not only in his timestream, but in *all* of time. "You're what's on the other side of the doorway."

"I am."

That vision he glimpsed . . .

"You're Dark Star." There, he has finally said it, and his nerves ring throughout his body. *That means she's part of the Drove, and—*

Iris makes a sound like crystal chimes, like laughter. "Oh no, I am nothing like the Drove. That's not something you need to worry about."

She is in his every thought. "But they—"

"So many questions," Iris says, "always spinning you around. I want to answer them all, but I must ask for your patience, Liam. We have to take these things slowly. That is why I wanted to introduce myself here, in your past, where it's safe. So you would know that *I'm* safe. That you can trust me. That, above all else, I want what's best for you."

Liam nods. "So I'm not going to see you in the future?"

"Oh, you will, but not just yet."

"Someone's coming."

They're getting close now, to his present, if he can still even call it that.

I can. If for no other reason than because he can see almost nothing beyond it. Ever since he woke up, his future has been a murky darkness. Not even impressions.

"I'm sorry about that," says Iris. "As my systems power up, they tend to scramble perception in the lower dimensions. But don't worry, soon the interference will clear and your future will again be visible. And once I achieve full functionality, well, just wait until you see what is possible then."

"Okay." But that darkness feels cold. Even terrifying. It makes him want to stay away. To keep running to the past like this.

"We don't have to go back just yet, if you don't want to."

"I know," says Liam. Around him are the events on the *Scorpius*, flying after Phoebe in the skim drone, rescuing her from space, the terrible sight of the supernova, and his very last memories, of struggling to get to the doorway before he and Phoebe froze to death . . . The present is just ahead, the last light on the shore of the vast, formless ocean of the future. Deep breath. "I need to see what happens next."

"Suit yourself. I still have much to do as I power up. Don't be afraid," she adds.

But he is. So very afraid, of what he doesn't even know. It's like a hundred different fears have swirled into a single roiling monster with a mind of its own, slithering about, fangs gnashing, tail slapping, threatening to devour him from the inside out.

"Until next time," says Iris.

A familiar phrase . . . from when?

He doesn't remember. There's so much to remember . . . but not now. Can't avoid it any longer. Liam swallows hard and pushes back to the present.

4

"Liam. Hey."

Liam's eyes flickered open. Where was he? Darkness, lines like a ceiling. His bedroom? The research station? The Cosmic Cruiser? His head ached, his mouth dry, his stomach quavering.

Images washed around in his mind like he was drifting in waves: the avenue on Mars, the balcony, the hangar on the *Scorpius* with Mina's stasis pod beneath him.

And then all of them burned in the boiling light of Centauri A, about to go nova, *no no no—*

"Come on, wake up. Someone's coming."

A silhouette beside him.

Liam pushed onto his elbows, causing a fresh wave of pain inside his skull. He was lying in a stasis pod—an older, boxy model, its controls dark.

A hand on his arm. Lavender skin, speckled with short gray bristles.

"You okay?"

Phoebe's face was so different: the human disguise gone, revealing her Telphon skin, her white braid coiled around the top of her head. Only her eyes appeared human; she had to wear the adapters to see. If anything, Liam thought it made her look stranger: like she was two people mixed together.

"Still weird seeing me like this, isn't it?"

"No." Except it was. And yet she was still Phoebe, his friend, who had risked her life so that they could save their families and their people, together.

Who was also an alien from another planet who had lied to him for years. That was still weird, too.

"Where are we?" she asked, glancing around the compartment. As she did, she coughed lightly.

"Back on the *Artemis*, I think," said Liam, surveying the sparse furniture and bathroom, these primitive-looking stasis pods.

Liam and Phoebe had ended up on the *Artemis*

before, when they'd first encountered that strange doorway in space. After barely escaping Barro and Tarra in the ruins on Delphi, Liam and Phoebe had used the chronologist's watch to travel into Phoebe's past, to her home world of Telos, before the humans had razed it with Phase One. On their way back to their present, the watch had started to go haywire, and they had run into the doorway. When they had taken a closer look, it had pulled them in, but the watch had prevented them from being sucked all the way through, and instead deposited them on the *Artemis*, nearly thirty years in the past.

As far as anyone on Mars or in the colonial fleet had ever known, the *Artemis* had been lost to some unknown calamity. When Liam and Phoebe had arrived, the *Artemis* had been investigating the same doorway, and had become caught in its pull, but the chronologist had rescued the two of them just moments before the ship had actually been drawn through, so they couldn't be entirely sure of its fate.

Based on their current surroundings, it appeared that the *Artemis* had indeed survived.

"But *where* are we?" asked Phoebe. "Or should I be asking *when*?"

"I'm not sure," said Liam, and yet that wasn't entirely true.

"The last thing I remember is jumping out of the Styrlax ship," said Phoebe. "It was so cold. I thought I—" She blinked at tears. "You saved me."

"Barely," said Liam. "You were out there over a minute. I think only that second heart of yours kept you alive."

"There's something I should thank my parents for," Phoebe said with a brief grin. "If they're even still alive."

"They are," said Liam. "At least, they were when we left. I talked to your mom. I told her about the countermeasures the starliners were planning, so they could escape."

"Thank you," said Phoebe. "You didn't have to do that."

"Yeah I did," he said, and yet he wondered for just a moment: Would she have done the same? Phoebe's feelings were much more complicated when it came to humans. She'd made an exception for him, of course, and for his parents, and so yes, Liam figured she would have. Probably. "I tried to fly us back to the *Scorpius*," said Liam, "but the skim drone died."

The fiery image of Centauri A flashed in his head, causing a ripple of fear like it had so many times before. He had been seeing it in his mind's eye more and more on their journey from Mars, eventually learning that it was, in fact, in his future. He squeezed his eyes shut. Had to remind himself: *not your future anymore. You escaped, you're okay.* "We were stranded," he said, "so I used the watch to get to the doorway."

Phoebe rubbed his arm with her bristled fingers. "You used the hug function," she said, referring to their term to describe how Liam and Phoebe time traveled together with the watch.

"Yeah," said Liam. "I barely remember going through it." He glanced at his wrist, wishing he still had the chronologist's watch. He'd tried looking back at his recent past to see what had happened to it, as well as where exactly they were now, but he'd been unconscious from the moment they'd reached the doorway until waking up here in this compartment, and so there was only a gray void there in his timestream, similar to how periods of stasis looked. He'd considered trying to push out of his own timeline to see more—Iris surely could have helped him—but Iris was a whole other situation, one that he barely understood. She almost seemed like a dream . . . yet he knew better. And her presence meant that wherever the *Artemis* was, Dark Star was close by.

Outside the compartment, echoing footsteps were drawing closer.

Phoebe coughed again. "The door's locked. I

checked before I woke you. Like we're prisoners. Do you even know how long we've been here?"

Liam checked the one link they shared between them, which was in the port on his sleeve. It was flashing with error messages. He opened the home screen. Only one of the blinking messages, *connection failure*, had to do with the link being unable to sync with the *Artemis*, which had technology almost thirty years older than this device. The other messages, *internal clock discrepancy, date field error, overlapping time code*, all had to do with what Liam had been doing in the few moments that he had been awake before Phoebe but had pretended to be asleep.

Moments for her, anyway.

He tapped to the clock. Amid its angry flashing he saw that the link thought the time was 7:04 a.m. Earth time, April 19 of the year 2256, for whatever that was worth. He looked at Phoebe and shrugged. "Maybe whoever is coming can tell us." He raised his eyebrows hopefully, and yet his insides roiled with dread.

The footsteps stopped just outside. Now a series of beeps: a code being entered into the keypad lock. Phoebe turned toward the door, crossing her arms and stiffening.

In this unobserved moment, Liam quickly pushed up his sleeve, revealing the slim atomic watch. While the link said it was 7:04 a.m., the atomic watch read 11:46 a.m. Better to round up; call it five hours that he had spent in his past, while no time at all had passed here in the present. He reset the watch to match the link time, pulled a tiny black cylinder from the hip pocket of his thermal wear—an ink marker, which he'd also gotten on Mars—and pushed his sleeve up a bit farther. A string of numbers was scrawled along the inside of his forearm.

10 3 . 5 5 2 8 13

He added a five to it and couldn't help doing the math: nearly two days. He felt a pang of guilt. *I should tell Phoebe*, but he didn't know what she'd think. Was there really anything wrong with what he'd been doing? He hadn't missed any time here. And yet he hadn't *been* here. *And you're exhausted*, he thought to himself. And how would he explain Iris to Phoebe? Iris said she was a friend, and Liam didn't feel like she was a danger, and yet that didn't change the fact that he'd been having a running conversation with Dark Star, which was . . . he wasn't sure exactly what it was. And if it was nearby, didn't that mean the Drove were somewhere close, too? Iris had said not to worry about them, but what had she meant by that?

Liam pulled down his sleeve and slipped the pen back into his pocket just as a green light illuminated on the control panel and the door to their compartment slid open.

Outside, red lights flashed across a vast space. Distant walkways, rows of stateroom doors. Definitely the *Artemis*.

"Good. You two are finally up." A young woman stepped in. She was short and wore a gray jumpsuit uniform. Her head was shaved on the sides except for two thin bands that arced along either side, the hair long and blue and falling like waterfalls over her ears.

"Who are you?" Phoebe asked.

The woman snorted. "You're one to talk. I'm Kyla, recently promoted to lieutenant on the *Artemis*. You probably don't even know what that is, but—"

"We've been here before," said Liam. "When you found the doorway in space. Is that where, or when, this is?"

Kyla cocked her head at him. For a moment, her face seemed to sag with exhaustion, and Liam noticed that her eyes appeared to be rimmed with dark circles. "Well, that makes about as much sense as anything else that's happened lately. Jordy and I found you two during our salvage mission. Or rather, you found us. I have no idea how you got onto our ship, and I have no idea what *you* are"—she pointed at Phoebe—"but my job right now is to bring you to the captain. Can you both walk?"

"Yeah," said Phoebe. She glanced at Liam.

"I'm good." He eased himself over the side of the pod. His stomach still trembled, and he wavered on his feet. As he stood, he also had to stifle a yawn. How many hours since he'd last slept? And where had that been?

"Sorry about the chill," said Kyla. "The ship is heavily damaged, so we're keeping all systems running in low power mode, to conserve as much energy as we can. I brought you some layers, and snacks." She handed Liam two silver thermal hoodie sweatshirts and two nutri-bars.

"I'm not poisonous," said Phoebe.

"Sure," said Kyla.

"Thanks." Liam passed Phoebe her items. The sweatshirt was an adult size. He pulled his on, readjusting his Dust Devils jersey beneath it, and then tore open the nutri-bar. He hadn't realized how hungry he was. "How long have we been here?" he asked between bites.

Kyla checked the primitive link on her sleeve. "You appeared in our ship about eight hours ago. I'm assuming you, at least, are human?"

"Yeah. Phoebe is—"

"Look, save it, okay? You'll just have to repeat it all to the captain." Kyla motioned to the door. "Out you go."

"Hold on," said Phoebe. "We're not going anywhere with you until we get some answers."

Kyla sighed. Again that exhausted look. "What exactly would you like to know?"

"First of all," said Phoebe, "where are we?"

"You know that doorway you saw? We call it a portal, and we're on the other side. In another universe. You'll see for yourselves in a minute."

Another universe . . . Liam felt a chill deep inside. Not another star system, not even another galaxy, but outside of everything they'd ever known. "You say we've been here eight hours. How long have you been here?"

Kyla's face scrunched, like she was doing math. "Twelve days, thirteen hours. . . . Feels more like a year with everything that's happened."

"Twelve *days*?" said Liam. "For us, the *Artemis* went missing over sixty years ago."

Kyla stared at them in shock for a moment; then her face fell. "Sixty years . . . I guess I shouldn't be surprised."

"You've really only been here twelve days?" said Phoebe.

Kyla nodded. "Time moves differently on this side of the portal. What year did you come from?"

"When we left it was 2256."

"Okay, then maybe you can tell me . . ." Kyla's voice softened. "The starliners . . . the fleet. Did it work? When we left, everyone was still on Mars. Did they make it out of the solar system before the supernova?"

"Yeah," said Liam. "The fleet got out."

Kyla's shoulders sagged with relief, a smile tugging at her mouth, and yet at the same time, her eyes brimmed with tears. "Where are they now?"

"Past Delphi. The first few fleets were past Danos, but then everyone rerouted to Destina."

"Destina?" said Kyla. "That was the code name for a military position."

"We're kind of at war."

"With who?"

Don't look at Phoebe, Liam thought. "It's probably easier to explain it to the captain, right?"

"Ha," Kyla muttered. "Good one. Fine, like I didn't have enough to worry about already."

"I don't get it," said Phoebe. "Why didn't you guys just fly back through the portal? Why have you stayed here?"

"The ship sustained too much damage on the first

trip," said Kyla. "We're down an engine, not to mention about a thousand other problems. Captain was
afraid if we tried going back through, it would tear us
apart completely. . . ." She trailed off.

"Is there something else?" asked Liam.

"To say the least, but . . . we need to get going. It
might not surprise you to hear that we're on a tight
schedule."

"But—"

"Look, I'm not trying to keep anything from you.
I just want you to see things for yourselves—that way
it will be easier for you to accept."

"What kind of things?" asked Phoebe.

Before Kyla could answer, Liam said: "It's Dark
Star, isn't it?"

She peered at him. "How did you know about
that?"

"It, um . . . I heard about it."

"From who? Do people know about Dark Star
sixty years in the future?"

"Just us," said Liam. "A man in a metal suit told
me, part of the Drove." When Kyla looked at him
quizzically, Liam added, "They're another race of
aliens, I think. Don't you know about them? I mean,
they're *from* Dark Star, I thought . . . ?"

"Never heard of the Drove," said Kyla, "but Dark

Star is here. That's where we're going. We have a team over there, including the captain. And he is definitely going to want to meet you two, now."

"Is he the one who took my watch?" Liam asked.

"I took your watch," said Kyla. "And yes, I gave it to him." She stepped out onto the walkway.

"What if we don't want to go to Dark Star?" said Phoebe. "What if we want to go home?"

"My orders are to take you over there, and that means by force if necessary. So you can decide for yourself how exactly you'd like that to go, but that's the way it's going."

Phoebe glanced at Liam, raising her eyebrows as if to say, *Ready?*

No. Not even close. He wanted to leave this moment altogether, but he steeled himself and stepped out the door.

They emerged onto one of the walkways of the *Artemis*'s single core. The same red emergency lights had been flashing when Liam and Phoebe had ended up here previously.

"All nonessential personnel are still in stasis lockdown," Kyla said. "For their safety . . . and sanity." She led them past door after door, some locked with red lights, some green indicating they were empty; the *Artemis* was the prototype starliner and had launched with a skeletal crew of ten thousand, far fewer than could fill a starliner core.

A deep rumble shook the floor and walls, and for a moment gravity weakened, causing Liam and Phoebe to stumble.

"Stay alert," said Kyla. "With one of the engines down, we have fewer redundant systems. Might have to shut off the gravity soon just to conserve power for air and heat."

They reached the end of the core, where stairs led along the wall to the main platform and a row of airlock doors. They stopped and waited for a staircase to rotate into position.

Liam noticed Phoebe shivering beside him. She zipped her hoodie up to the top and put on the hood. "From the space jump?" he said.

She nodded. "Head hurts. My fingers and toes are still tingling."

A staircase synced with their position, and they started up, their footfalls echoing hollowly against the metal. Gravity shifted as they went, so that they were always upright, even as the walkway they'd come from rotated overhead.

They reached the main platform and moved through one of the six sets of airlock doors that led from the core to the forward section of the ship. They passed the map kiosk, which showed a schematic of the *Artemis*. Corridors and compartments branched off on either side of the hall, but nearly all their doors were sealed. Two crew members knelt by one, making a shower of sparks as they worked on a large circuit board that they'd pulled from the wall. Ahead, a wide set of open doors revealed the staircase to the bridge.

Kyla's link flashed and she paused. "What's up, Jordy?"

"Just heard from Captain," a male voice said. "Mission accomplished. He's on his way back."

"Roger that. We'll be right there." Kyla motioned to Liam and Phoebe. "Follow me."

She led them through an airlock and down a side corridor. They entered a large compartment lined with racks of hanging suits and helmets. They looked like older models of the pressure suits Liam and Phoebe had worn, the fabric bulkier, the helmet, while still attached to the neck of the suit, made of a thicker clear material.

"Take any one you want," Kyla said, pulling one off the rack.

As Liam ran his fingers over the collars, looking for his size, he heard a noise behind him. Another uniformed officer exited the bathroom doorway on the far side of the room. The tall man had his arms crossed, head sagging, and was sniffling and wiping at his nose. He glanced at the two of them, nodded solemnly at Kyla, and walked out. Behind him, a warm light flickered from the doorway, like flame. Phoebe had noticed it, too.

"Take a look, if you want," said Kyla, eyes on the floor.

Liam and Phoebe shared a look and moved to the doorway. They entered the bathroom, passing the sinks, the light getting stronger. Ahead was a large communal shower. They peered inside and saw that its floor was covered with candles, most with diode lights but some with real flickering flames, pools of wax melted around them. In between were photos, portable holoscreens, video charms. Some showed still pictures of people, others played short snippets of video at a low volume. Moments with people smiling, or laughing, sometimes blowing a kiss at the screen, all wavering and ghostly. A delicate murmur that reverberated in the tiled shower space.

"We keep it in here so the candles don't set off the smoke detectors," Kyla said from behind them. "Last thing we need is another fire alarm."

"It looks like a memorial," said Phoebe.

"More or less. Not everyone approved, but some of us felt it was important."

"These people died?" asked Liam.

"We weren't sure. . . and we couldn't help but fear the worst. There's some hope now that you say the fleet made it out, but then if there's a war . . ." Kyla bit her lip. "Anyway, it reminds us of who we are. Of what we've done."

Liam bent down to examine a holographic moment of a woman with long black hair who was crossing her arms and smiling. He recognized her from their first visit to the *Artemis*. "Isn't that Lieutenant Lyris? She was in command last time we were here."

"Lieutenant Lyris is deceased," Kyla said quietly, her eyes trembling with tears. She brushed them quickly away and strode out of the bathroom.

Another ominous rumble through the floor.

"Something weird is going on here," Phoebe said as Liam stood.

Liam's insides knotted tighter. The seething red star flashed in his mind, burning a hole behind his eyes.

"What?" said Phoebe, peering at him. "You keep getting this blank look like you're not all there."

"Sorry. It's nothing. Just feeling strange from our trip here." Liam felt that anxious urge again, to leave this moment. He could return to this exact point in time, and nobody would even notice that he'd been gone. Maybe spend an hour playing *Roid Wraiths* in their apartment back on Mars, just to calm his nerves. There were plenty of times when it was unoccupied.

"Hey." Phoebe rubbed his arm and smiled. "Did I thank you for saving my life?"

Liam returned the smile as best he could. "You don't need to. I think we saved each other."

Her hand traced down to his and gripped it. "Well, thank you anyway."

"No problem." He managed a quick smile.

They returned to the locker room. Kyla was zipping up her pressure suit. "Are you okay to change in here?" she asked Phoebe. "Or . . ."

"It's a co-ed changing room, right?" said Phoebe.

"Yeah."

"I'm a girl."

Kyla looked away. "Sorry, I just . . ."

Phoebe huffed. "I'm also a Telphon, okay? From the planet Telos, which you called Aaru-5. I'm safe to touch and I don't bite and I'm one of the very last survivors after your colonization project nearly exterminated my people. We're the ones humans are at war with, but Liam and I are trying to stop it, together. How's that for an answer?"

"You mean Phase One?" said Kyla. "It killed your people?"

"Billions of us. It's not your fault. Not personally."

A shadow passed over Kyla's face. "I don't know about that . . . but you're an alien. For real."

"No more than you."

She considered this and then shrugged. "Fair enough."

Liam and Phoebe slipped on their pressure suits, leaving their helmets off as Kyla had, and followed her back to the main corridor. They reached a working bank of elevators and rode down to a hangar, nowhere near the size of the one they'd been in on the *Scorpius* but still with multiple levels full of an assortment of boxy military ships. Liam noticed earlier models of Cosmic Cruisers and a rack of primitive skim drones.

But the ship that Kyla led them to was unlike anything around it, or anything Liam had ever seen. It was a sleek, low triangle with almost no features. In fact, it was almost as if you couldn't see it at all when you looked straight at it, until Kyla put her hand against its oily presence and an oval-shaped doorway appeared in its side.

"It's from Dark Star," said Kyla, noticing their perplexed gazes. "We nicknamed it the *Carrion*. Pretty morbid, I know." She ducked inside.

Liam steeled himself and followed her, Phoebe close behind. The ship's corridors were narrow and cramped. Liam had to bend and turn his shoulders as they made their way to the cockpit. The walls inside were textured with angular panels of circuitry, all of which were made of dark, smoky glass. There were no wires that Liam could see, only thin tubes with pulses of multicolored light zipping through them.

"Buckle in." Kyla sat in one of four seats in the cockpit, arranged two and two. As Liam and Phoebe squeezed into the narrow chairs, she tapped the console and a liquid spherical map appeared. It was the size of a helmet and floated over a concave depression. She slipped her hand into the sphere and pinched and tugged on one of many dots of light. This dot expanded and became a strange picture of some sort of circular, ringed structure. Now a target appeared on the windshield, with symbols scrolling beside it, odd letter-like shapes that had a blur to them as if they were at least three—if not more—dimensional. Almost immediately, they morphed and became words and numbers that Liam could read.

"The map is in Telphon," said Phoebe. "Is that just for me?"

"Yeah, the ship has some kind of translation technology," said Kyla. "Like it can adapt to whoever's in here. It and Dark Star seem to be scanning us constantly."

"Is that a good thing?" Phoebe asked. "To have a ship reading your mind?"

"I'm not sure. But we never would have figured out how to fly this thing otherwise, and it saves us using a cruiser, and the battery power it would draw from the *Artemis*."

"Maybe it wants to help us," Liam said quietly.

"Not sure about that," said Kyla, "but it is nice having this ship."

The *Carrion* hummed to life, rising smoothly from the hangar floor. Kyla tapped her link. "*Artemis* bridge, this is Kyla. We're departing for Dark Star, over."

"Copy that, Lieutentant," said a woman's voice.

Yellow lights flashed and the heavy airlock doors began to slide open.

She switched channels. "Jordy, we're thrusters hot. ETA three minutes."

"Roger that. Should be just in time."

Kyla guided them into the airlock, where they hovered as the inner doors closed. The air sucked out in a violent rush, the outer doors slid silently open, and the *Carrion* flew into space with a strong burst.

They proceeded parallel to the front section of the *Artemis*. Liam looked back along the core, which was dotted with burn marks. One of the engines was indeed dark, and while the other was glowing blue, an errant jet of flame intermittently flared from its side. Ahead, on the front section, a team of about ten crew members in space-grade suits floated around a twisted comms antenna, sparks showering from their tools.

"As you can see," said Kyla, "the damage is pretty bad. But we're making progress."

"Do you think you'll be able to fix it before your fuel and life support run out?" Phoebe asked. "Or at least enough to get back through the portal?"

"Actually," said Kyla, "she could probably make it back right now, but we've got bigger problems that need solving before we can leave here." As she said it, Kyla brought the craft over the front array, and they were greeted with a wide view of space.

"Whoa," Phoebe said quietly.

Before them was a vast, eerie expanse, made of layer upon layer of watery, dimly glowing gas clouds. Most were pale green, while some were lavender. They seemed to be in the middle of an enormous nebula, the waves of color stretching as far as they could see in all directions. There was something odd about it, and Liam couldn't quite put his finger on what—

But then his breath caught in his throat when he saw what was dead ahead. At first it looked like a giant shadow, but then Liam began to make out the details of a massive structure, so enormous that he could barely wrap his mind around it. It was made of great black arms curving out and around from a central core. There were eight arms, maybe more—it was hard to tell in the dim nebula light. Each was larger than a starliner, curving and crisscrossing one another and making an overall shape that was something like a sphere but also reminded Liam of pictures he'd seen of the octopus from old Earth oceans. Almost the entire structure was dark, and he sensed that it had been dark for a long time. There was, however, one faint white light glowing far off on the top of the core section.

The only other light came in flashes from beneath the structure, but it was like no light Liam had ever seen. Directly beneath that central core was a disk of infinite, pure black, a perfect circle, wide and broad—or it might be above them; there was no real up or down in space. They could only tell this pure black patch was there by the utter absence of nebula glow, and also by the strange flashes of lightning that momentarily coalesced and spiraled around its perimeter before disappearing. Now a huge bolt erupted from the tip of one of the arms, toward the black spot, where it immediately circled and disappeared, warping like water going down a drain.

"Welcome to Dark Star," said Kyla.

Even though Liam had glimpsed this briefly before, when they'd first encountered the doorway, and then again when the *Artemis* had been investigating it, the sight of it now made his heart race, and a chill ran through him. It looked nothing like the pleasant, light-filled form of Iris. In fact, it looked the opposite, and its very presence caused a cold sensation of dread inside him.

"How did you know to call it that?" Liam asked.

"The station has the same translation technology as this ship. When we started studying its systems, that was how it referred to itself in logs and schematics."

"And you haven't seen the Drove?" he asked.

Kyla shook her head. "Maybe the captain will know what you're talking about, but not me. Okay, we're on approach."

She brought them in low over the nearest arm of the leviathan structure, angling toward where that single light showed atop the core.

Liam looked down at the distant surface of the arm they were passing over and saw that it was covered by a gridwork of structures like domes and towers, but also like pyramids and temples of old Earth, stuff made by the Egyptians or Greeks—except instead of being made from stone, all these structures were formed of a black glassy metal. There were other trapezoidal buildings that reminded Liam of structures he'd seen briefly on Telos, some that seemed to be spirals, and so many others.

"There are no stars." Phoebe was gazing out at the fields of green nebula clouds.

That's what it was about this swath of space, Liam realized. Despite one or two little gleaming dots here and there, the space in all directions was empty, barren . . .

"A dead universe," said Kyla. "Just a few old neutron stars, but otherwise, there's almost nothing here. Well, except for us. And this thing."

"But this machine isn't dead . . . ," said Phoebe, gazing down at the quiet buildings. "Is it?"

"No," said Kyla. "It looked that way when we arrived, but it was more like . . . dormant."

Waiting, Liam thought, though Iris had never said such a thing.

Something flashed out beyond Dark Star. Liam saw a rectangular shape appear: the doorway, outlined in silver circuitry, but unlike when they'd seen it from the other side, in their universe, here it stood firmly at the end of one of Dark Star's many curving arms, hundreds of meters tall, an extension of this place. As Liam watched, its inky center lit up, shimmering from midnight black to iridescent green, the light brightening in concentric circles like ripples on water.

Liam felt an urge to run for that doorway, to get home right now—but he also felt a powerful curiosity stirring in him. This place could bridge the boundaries between universes; what else could it do? *And she wants to show me.*

The doorway reached a brightness that made them squint and then all at once rippled out, back into darkness.

"Captain's back," said Kyla.

"From where?" Phoebe asked.

Kyla didn't answer. She guided the *Carrion* toward the top of the central core area of Dark Star. The source of that single light was a large dome-shaped structure. It reminded Liam of an old astronomical observatory on Mars, or in pictures of Earth, though this one seemed to be made of some sort of clear material, the light glowing out from inside.

As they neared, they passed over a wide gap in the surface of the arm, just before it connected to the central core. Liam saw what appeared to be racks of ships nestled inside, hundreds of them, larger than this ship they were in. They were sleek and oblong, like oily teardrops. Liam had seen one before, while flying the skim drone at Saturn, in the timestream.

Kyla brought them down over a hexagonal landing platform, just beside the observatory-shaped building. A Cosmic Cruiser was already parked there. As the *Carrion* touched down, a clear, liquid dome of energy materialized overhead, enclosing the platform.

"This way." Kyla led them out of the ship, not bothering to put on her helmet. Pale green nebula light bathed their faces as they crossed the platform. It was quiet, except for a slight hum from the energy field overhead and a low rumble somewhere far beneath their feet.

"It's lonely," said Phoebe.

But we're not alone, Liam thought. Once again, he felt the urge to tell Phoebe about Iris, followed immediately by an urge not to, resulting in that frozen-in-place feeling.

They followed Kyla across the platform to an entrance that led to the dome-shaped building. There was no airlock door or even any door-like structure, yet once they'd stepped into the corridor, the energy field winked out over the landing pad and re-formed as a solid barrier behind them.

The walls of this corridor were similar to the insides of the *Carrion*, made of smoky glass, crisscrossed by networks of thin, curving tubes, with occasional lights pulsing through them. The floor was made of black metallic floor panels, which lit up and went dark sequentially as they walked, creating an island of lavender light that only glowed beneath their feet and a meter or so in front of and behind them.

The short corridor opened into the wide domed room they'd seen from outside. It afforded a panoramic view of the ghostly nebula. The dome descended all the way to the floor, the view broken here and there only by threadlike black support beams.

There were no physical structures in the room, no control systems, seats, or screens, except for a circular platform off to one side that was raised a meter off the floor. Beside this platform was another small collection of lights floating as if in orbit around each other. They were being moved around by the only other person in the room, a man wearing a jumpsuit identical to Kyla's.

"Hey, Jordy," said Kyla as they crossed toward him.

"Good timing," said Jordy, glancing over his shoulder. It could have been the lighting in here, but Liam thought he saw the same dark circles under Jordy's eyes as Kyla had. "Here he comes."

Lights began to flash in the air above the platform—not coming from physical sources, more like small lightning bolts seemingly blinking in and out of existence, with the overall effect of creating a vertical cylinder of light in the center of the platform. The lights flashed brighter and more rapidly. And now something began to take shape in that cone of light: a tall figure, with broad shoulders and thick arms and legs, made of sharp angles.

There was a hum, a buzzing in the air, the lights growing almost blindingly bright, and then there he was, standing on the platform, ice fog steaming off him.

The metal-suited man.

Liam froze, his heart leaping into his throat.

There was a glint of silver from his wrist, where he wore not one but two chronologist's watches.

"Welcome back, Captain," said Jordy. "Mission accomplished?"

"In more ways than one." The metal-suited man turned his heavy helmet toward Liam, his face hidden by a lavender-tinted visor. "Hello, time traveler!" he called. "I'm so glad to finally see you here."

Spots in Liam's vision. A storm of memories at once, spinning like a dust devil: the metal-suited man in the timestream on Mars, the ship flying toward him at Saturn, the boiling supernova, helpless—

"And look," said the metal-suited man. "I brought us a friend!"

He held a black metallic weapon, something like a stun rifle, its housing flickering with glassy Dark Star technology, and he jabbed its end into the back of the blue-skinned, black-robed, many-legged chronologist standing beside him.

5

"Wait," said Phoebe, gazing from the metal-suited man to Kyla and Jordy. "You guys are the Drove?"

Seeing him standing here now, the realization sank into Liam, cold and heavy.

"What's she talking about?" said Jordy, rearranging the light spheres in the air in front of him.

"Oh, that." The metal-suited man's visor slid up. He was older, his hair and beard mostly gray, only a few remaining flecks of black, but there was a youthful brightness in his brown eyes, and in his half smile, that was notably different from Kyla and Jordy's appearance. "That was something I said to Liam when we first met on Mars. Just trying out a name for us, one that might scare off these meddlesome buggers." He waved his weapon at the chronologist, who blinked and looked mildly around the room.

"Doesn't that make us sound kind of ominous, sir?" said Kyla. She and Jordy shared a look that Liam couldn't quite read.

"Well, that was the idea."

"To scare little kids?" said Jordy, his eyes shifting from Liam to the captain.

"No, of course not." The captain tapped the settings on his chest. Little bolts of white lightning slithered around his arms and legs. The suit hissed as a coating of frost melted, dripping on the platform. "Can I get this thing off yet?"

"One more minute, sir." Jordy turned his attention back to the hovering spheres. "You're only seventy-five percent phase locked."

"Right, right." The captain looked at Liam. "You have no idea how uncomfortable this suit is."

Liam averted his eyes, too stunned to think.

"The Drove are human," Phoebe said, like she was sliding heavy puzzle pieces into place.

"The crew of the *Artemis*," said Liam. He could scarcely wrap his mind around what this truly meant.

"Okay. . . ." Jordy gripped one of the light spheres with two hands. It flashed briefly. "You're locked in."

"Finally." The captain unfastened his helmet and slid the thick, heavy unit over his head. He placed it on a metal rack that rose up from the platform. "Let's start over: I'm Captain Barrie, ISA *Artemis*. I'm sorry if I frightened you earlier," he said to Liam. "I'm as exhausted as the rest of the crew."

Liam had no idea what to think: The way that Captain Barrie was acting now was so different from when they'd first met. Which version was the real one? Did he remember that he'd basically chased Liam, demanding Liam give him the watch? And how long ago had that moment even been for him? Days ago? Hours? It was recent for Liam, too, in terms of conscious days, but those decades that had passed in stasis made the fear feel like something that had been with him a long time. Whereas Barrie acted as if that moment was barely significant.

"There's a lot we need to talk about, but—"

"You blew up the sun!" said Phoebe. "Your own sun. How could you?"

"Look, I can see why you might say that, but—" Barrie paused, peering at her. "I'm sorry, who—or should I say *what*—are you?"

"I'm Phoebe. I'm a Telphon. Your people destroyed my planet."

Liam saw the captain's perplexed look and added,

"With Phase One. Phoebe's people have been at war with humanity ever since we left Mars."

"We're at war?" Jordy said.

"Upside," said Kyla, "these two confirm that the fleet got out of the solar system before the nova. At least there's that."

Jordy made a whistling sound and looked at the ceiling in relief. "Finally, some good news."

"There were casualties at Saturn Station, though," said Liam, "and at Delphi. There might be more that we don't know of."

Barrie was still gazing at Phoebe, his lips moving like he was making a calculation. "You're part of a race of beings that lived on Aaru-5," he reasoned. "Telphons, you said?"

"Yeah. Billions of people died because of what you did here, so stop talking like it's a game."

Barrie's face fell, his voice growing quiet. "Oh, I never meant to imply that this was a game. Nor would I deny that we have blood on our hands. But I think, once we explain what has happened here, you may see things differently."

"So there are those aliens," said Jordy, pointing to Phoebe, "and those aliens." He pointed to the chronologist. "*And* whoever built this place? Any reason why I shouldn't be more freaked out than I already was?"

"It's hardly surprising," said Barrie, "especially given what we've learned here." He held the Dark Star weapon out to Kyla. "Take this, and make sure he doesn't run off," he said, motioning to the chronologist.

Kyla gripped the weapon and surveyed the chronologist uncertainly. "How do I make it listen to me?"

"I can hear you just fine," said the chronologist. He had a deeper voice than the being Liam and Phoebe had previously met. This chronologist was not holding one of those orange crystals, and yet everyone in the room seemed to understand him. Liam guessed that Dark Star was translating him, too. "And you needn't worry. It is not in my nature to fight or contradict you." His large pearlescent eyes found Liam. "After all, these things happen."

"Are you going to kill him, too?" Liam said to Captain Barrie.

"No. That one on Mars—"

"They're called chronologists," said Liam.

"Ah, good to know. Yes, that was certainly a misstep on my part. I admit I was in a hurry—it's been an intense few days here—and when I found that one snooping around, I thought it might be a threat, that they would try to stop us—"

"Stop you from what?" Phoebe asked.

"From saving my crew," said Barrie. "From completing our mission here."

"The chronologists aren't a threat," said Liam. "They just record everything that happens in the universe."

"That may be so," said Barrie, wagging his finger in the air. "But toward what end? That's what you have to ask yourself."

"It's . . . just what they do," said Liam.

Barrie shook his head. "No one *just does* anything. There's always a reason, even if they themselves won't admit it or, in some cases, don't even realize it. Do you know, I saw one of these beings on Earth, when I was about your age?" Barrie gazed at the nebula outside, an almost dreamy look in his eye. "In fact, you could argue that what I saw that day led me all the way here. Not that there hasn't been a cost. . . ." A shadow crossed his face. "At any rate, now that we have this chronologist, and perhaps with your help, we can figure out exactly what is going on here."

"The portal is causing damage," said Liam. "If you keep using it, the universe is going to collapse." He looked at the chronologist. "Right?"

The chronologist was busy gazing around the room and seemed not to hear him.

"Who told you that? *Them?*" said Barrie. "I mean,

no doubt the portal causes some disturbance to space-time—it's incredibly powerful—but according to the Dark Star logs, that rifting, while disruptive, is not going to tear apart the walls between universes or anything like that. Besides, *we're* not the ones using the portal. It's Dark Star."

He held up his wrist with the two chronologist's watches. "Thank you for bringing this, by the way," he said to Liam, tapping one of them. "I had a feeling when I first saw you in the timestream that a device like this might help me get some answers. And am I to deduce that you were able to travel in time using only this watch?"

"Sort of," said Liam.

"Curious. It only works for me when I have this suit on. And even then, I cannot quite anchor myself in another time. The only beings who've even noticed me are these chronologists and you. Nevertheless, it led me right to their library, or whatever that place was."

He pressed a series of buttons around the collar of the suit. It separated down the center, folding open with another hiss and allowing Barrie to step out. "That's better." He hung the suit on the rack beside the helmet and shook his arms, then hopped off the platform and strode to the center of the room.

"This technology is so far beyond our comprehension," he said, motioning to the curling, shadowy arms of Dark Star. "This station, the portal we flew through. Take that suit: I believe it was created for the purpose of performing maintenance and repair work on the portal. I've used it to travel through space and time with relative ease, and yet we barely understand how it works."

"How are you using it, then, if you know so little about it?" Liam asked.

"Because Dark Star is allowing us to," said Barrie. "It translates certain systems and allows access to certain functions. It seems to sense what we need and respond to it . . . but nothing more. We can barely begin to comprehend this technology on our own, and as a result, we've learned a great deal about this place, and yet almost nothing at all."

Iris sensed what I needed too, Liam thought. Responding to his needs, just like what Barrie was describing, and yet she was in many ways as mysterious to Liam as this station was to Barrie and his crew.

"Hold on," said Phoebe. "Did you just say you *flew* through the portal? I thought it sucked you in."

"Well, the portal exerted an incredibly strong gravitational disturbance. I had to weigh the odds of trying to escape that force, which all reports indicated might well tear the ship apart, or to fly through and take our chances with whatever was on the other side. Whether that was the right call or not is still hard to say, but the cost has certainly been high."

Liam noticed that Kyla had crossed her arms and averted her eyes.

"You're making it sound like you *didn't* want to blow up a bunch of stars and nearly exterminate at least two races that we know of," said Phoebe.

Barrie sighed. "Of course we didn't. Why on earth would we want to blow up our own sun? We didn't even . . . I should start at the beginning, if that's possible." He raised his hands to the view beyond the dome. "Our home universe is a shade under fourteen billion years old. Based on the neutron stars we can see here, we estimate this universe to be over ten trillion. And Dark Star may be even older than that. Its metallic composition doesn't even respond to carbon dating—it seems to continuously refresh its molecular structure, on a subatomic level.

"When we arrived, it was completely silent. Other than that portal, it was as dead as everything else here. Even if the *Artemis* hadn't been too damaged to risk leaving, we knew we were staring at a massive discovery, and it was our duty as both a military and a research vessel to at least perform a preliminary investigation. Apparently this is old news to the two of you, but in *our* timeline, there had been no evidence of intelligent extraterrestrial life—"

"Almost none," Phoebe muttered under her breath.

Barrie paused. "Yes, well . . . never mind the existence of a *multiverse*, and potentially of beings with power we could scarcely comprehend. Also, we needed to know if Dark Star could be a safe haven, should the damage to the *Artemis* prove to be beyond repair.

"So I assembled a small recon team. We'd barely departed the *Artemis* when that landing platform outside lit up. And as we touched down, the energy field came on. . . . It was as if Dark Star was inviting us in. Lights led us to this control room, where it greeted us with these displays." He motioned to the floating spheres near Jordy. "Not only that, it showed us how to activate the gravity and life-support systems, and the settings were configured perfectly for humans. In that moment, we still had no idea what this place was, or what it would do, and given the dire condition of the *Artemis*, naturally we chose to test these systems. So we turned them on. . . ."

Barrie's eyes flashed to Kyla and Jordy, both of whom were gazing elsewhere, their faces ashen.

"And then," said Barrie, "all hell broke loose. The moment the air and gravity systems came online, the portal began to adjust itself, and Dark Star launched some sort of vessel. A kind of missile, it turned out. Then, barely an hour later, the portal lit up again. This time, she started launching ships, a robotic fleet. They left, and returned a few hours later with their wings glowing green. Over the course of our first six days, this happened three more times. We'd been splitting our time between repairing the *Artemis* and investigating this place. By then we'd learned enough about the station's systems to realize that it was using these missiles, and this robotic fleet, to power itself up by gathering energy from beyond the portal, but we didn't quite understand how. Nothing happened for a few days, and then yesterday, the portal powered up for a fifth time. We'd managed to get the *Artemis* into a slightly more stable state, and we'd also found that ship—the one you took here from the *Artemis*, which Dark Star had allowed us to access. I decided to use it to follow this latest round of missiles through the portal, and I watched . . . as they flew directly into our sun.

"I got back as fast as I could—that Dark Star ship has a limited range, and no comms that I could use to contact humanity, no way to warn them. We'd barely wrapped our heads around what I'd witnessed, what it might mean, or what we should even do, when the fuel ships launched, which meant it was too late. All I could think of was to send Kyla and Jordy out to run salvage, which was when they found you. As you can imagine, it has been a long twenty-four hours. The toll that it has taken on the crew . . ."

Liam's heart raced. His mouth felt dry. He saw that Kyla was wiping her eyes. "So, you're saying Dark Star blew up the sun on its own?" he said. "For . . . fuel?"

"Its power cells run on gamma radiation, massive quantities, and the most efficient way to get that is from a supernova. We don't know how long this place has been sitting here dormant. Ten thousand years? Billions? It needs a certain amount of energy just to maintain its position over that artificial black hole you saw beneath us, so the moment we turned it on, it immediately started opening the portal to stars in our universe and replenishing itself. The refueling comes in waves. It has harvested three more stars in the hours since our sun."

"But I don't understand," said Phoebe. "Why didn't you just turn it off?"

"Don't you see? By the time we understood what it was doing, what in effect we had caused, it was too late."

"No, I mean, after that," said Phoebe. "Why haven't you turned it off since then?"

"Well, it doesn't appear that we even can," said Barrie, "but the larger question still remains: What is it powering up to do? As far we can tell, it's already drawn far more power than it needs simply for life support and to hold its position. It's doing something else, and I believe it's our duty, not only to humanity but to our entire universe, to figure out what."

Soon I will show you, Liam remembered Iris saying, and yet now a terrible truth occurred to him: it was Iris who had destroyed his home, who was responsible for everything they had been through.

"And in the meantime?" said Phoebe. "You'll just let other beings suffer in its path?"

"If we don't figure out what this machine is intent on doing, their could be far greater consequences than a few species in a few star systems."

Phoebe's eyes narrowed at Barrie. "How is this even possible? You guys arrived here *after* the sun had already started to change . . ."

"It's hard to wrap your brain around," said Barrie, "but this structure is operating in four dimensions, maybe more. The portal can be positioned anywhere and any*when* in space-time, which, timekeeper," he said to the chronologist, "is why you mistakenly thought there were six portals. It was the same one, appearing in six different places across space and time. As far as we can tell, the *where* is determined by the type of star whose supernova will yield the most fuel, and the *when* by the life cycle of the star, meaning that there's an ideal point in time to harvest the most energy. The fact that, in the ten-billion-year life cycle of a star like ours, the best time to blow it up was right when we could just barely escape in time can either be seen as fortunate or tragic, depending on your mood."

Kyla made a little sound, like sniffling. She was still gazing out at the nebula, green light on her face. "I'd prefer to stick with tragic," she said under her breath.

"Of course," said Barrie.

"Doesn't that mean you could stop it, though?" said Phoebe. "If you opened the portal earlier in time, you could stop those missiles from hitting the sun in the first place."

"I'm afraid Dark Star has not given us access to the portal controls, but even if we *could* do what you're describing, what would that mean for us? It was the destruction of our sun that brought us here in the first place. To interfere in our own past like that . . . would it create a paradox that would make things even worse?"

"More likely some kind of superposition," Liam said. The chronologist gave him a curious glance.

"What's that?" said Barrie.

"Probably just as bad."

"Anyway," said Barrie, "from what you've told us, it sounds like the human fleet got away in time, so maybe our fretting—which has been significant—was overblown."

"Overblown?" said Phoebe. "Thousands of humans have still died, and, you know, my entire race."

"We've had losses here, too," said Kyla.

Barrie made a plaintive gesture with his hands. "You know I've felt the losses just as much as you all have; you can forgive me for trying to find the optimism here. You cannot imagine the feeling, when we realized our role in all this." Barrie's face fell. "Not everyone could live with it."

Liam thought of the memorial in the changing room. "We met Lieutenant Lyris when we were on the *Artemis* before. What happened to her?"

"She was always sensitive," he said quietly. "Her mother and father died in the *Valiant* crash. That was a colony ferry."

"We know it," said Liam, remembering the great silver memorial in the middle of the Martian desert.

"The idea that she was responsible for their deaths, and so many others, both in the past and in whatever future was to come . . . It would have been hard for her to hear about this war you speak of. I tried to convince her it wasn't our fault, or at least that it wasn't nearly that simple, but she couldn't accept that."

"She wanted to turn back before the portal had us," said Kyla, her voice suddenly quavering. "She urged us to pull back, but you—"

"That's enough insubordinate talk!" Barrie snapped, his voice echoing in the room.

A silence passed over them.

"Apologies," he said immediately. "It's a raw topic. And what's done is done. Let's focus our energy on the future. The best thing we can do is finish repairing the *Artemis*, and gain a full picture of what this place is, and what it does. Who knows—perhaps there is an opportunity here: some way that Dark Star can be more than just a threat, that we can use its vast power to forge a better future for humanity."

"This sounds fine and all," said Phoebe, "but Liam and I would like to leave now. We've told you everything we know; the *Artemis* has Cosmic Cruisers, so let us have one and we'll go back to our universe and find our families. We can tell them what's happened here, and—"

"I'm afraid I can't let you leave until we've finished assessing this station," said the captain. "You two have experienced much that could prove valuable here." He pointed at Liam. "And your time-travel abilities may well be of use."

"But we don't want to stay," said Phoebe. She

looked at Liam, but he could only manage a shrug. "Besides, the humans and the Telphons *need* to know about this! We tried to tell them, before we really understood. Now they'll listen, and it might even stop the war—"

A great rumble shook the floor, cutting Phoebe off and making everyone stagger.

"Speak of the devil," said Jordy. "Captain, she's prepping another fuel run."

"Where now?" said Barrie.

Jordy expanded one of the glowing light spheres in front of him until it was a meter across. It showed a map of space, or something like a map. Liam recognized galaxies and clusters linked by navigation lines, but the map also rippled and blurred in a way that reminded Liam of what he'd seen in the chronologist's office: a map not just of distances, but also of time. Jordy tapped different symbols scrolling along the edge. "She's realigning to an 8–9 decimal right ascension."

"Kyla," said Barrie, "is the sensor network ready?"

Kyla tapped her link. "Up and running, sir."

"We've set up a perimeter of energy sensors," said Barrie. "We're trying to figure out where the actual mechanism that controls the portal is located. Since Dark Star won't let us access the software, we figure if we can locate the hardware, then maybe we can gain control manually." Barrie spoke into his link. "Portal team, this is the captain, copy?"

"Roger, Captain, we're in position."

"They're in a cruiser outside, waiting for a location to investigate."

"Okay, here we go." Jordy made a waving motion toward the center of the room. A giant version of the map he'd been looking at flashed into existence above their heads, spherical and twenty meters across, made of amber light. Jordy continued working on the one in front of him, his actions mimicked on the larger version above. The map's view began to zoom in, dots becoming clusters becoming galaxies, thousands of stars, down to hundreds, and finally dozens. Amid this field, eight red dots blinked, and one yellow light. Jordy zoomed in even more, closing in on the yellow light, until he was focused on a single area of space with about ten stars. The yellow light's nearest neighbor was blinking red.

"Target appears to be not too far from our old sun," said Jordy. "Centauri A."

Liam's heart thundered, icy adrenaline spiking through his gut. The boiling star bloomed in his mind again, spitting solar flares, looming closer and closer.

"This will be fascinating," Barrie was saying.

"With all the new systems she's brought online, I expect the process will go quite a bit faster."

"Affirmative, Captain," said Jordy. "Looks like she's prepped twelve protomatter missiles this time. That should decrease the supernova development time down to . . . a hundred hours or so."

"Ninety-six," said Liam faintly, sharing a worried glance with Phoebe.

"How do you know that?" said Barrie.

"Centauri A is where we came from," said Liam. "There are three starliners and the Telphon ship. My parents and sister. Phoebe's family. When we left, they were trying to escape just before the supernova. *This* supernova." He fought the urge to rush back to the safety of Mars— *No!* He needed to stay here. . . .

"Well," said Barrie, "I'm sure they detected the nova and figured out the safe distance to relocate to."

"The supernova itself will not be a significant concern," said the chronologist. "However, the space-time rifting that will occur during the subsequent use of the portal for the fuel run will pose a significant threat to any vessels in the vicinity."

"How do you know that?" said Barrie.

"The events around Centauri A were my focus in our inquiry. In fact, it is what I was working on when you abducted me."

"I know they had a plan to get away from the blast in time," said Liam, "but I don't think they have any idea about the rifting." He looked to the chronologist. "Will they be okay?"

The chronologist blinked. "When I left, the most probable future indicated that while they will escape the supernova itself, the space-time rifting will render their ships inoperable, leading to total system failure and total loss of life."

"Can you stop the missile launch?" said Liam.

"I already told you," said Barrie, "we have no access to those controls. I'm afraid there's nothing we can do."

"How can you just stand there and say that?" shouted Phoebe. "They'll all die!"

"Everyone dies," Barrie said almost to himself, "if you tell the story long enough."

"Captain," said Kyla, "maybe now is the time to try sending that signal, with the comms unit."

Barrie shook his head. "By the time we got that mobilized and launched, the door would already have moved to the fuel run, and then it would be too late."

"Protomatter rocket thrusters are hot," said Jordy. "Launch in ten . . . nine . . ."

"There has to be something you can do!" said Liam. He felt himself locking up, saw the fiery ball of Centauri A about to explode. Their families and friends, hundreds of millions of people . . .

"Like what?" said Barrie. "Ask nicely? We have no control over this."

Ask . . . Liam squeezed his fists and pulled back from the moment. *Iris!* he shouted into the wind of his timestream. *I need your help!*

For a moment there was no response, but then, a growing light.

Of course. Iris appeared beside him, glimmering, and held out her hand. *Come with me.*

6

Liam pushes away from the moment, like a swimmer kicking away from the wall of the pool, losing track of his feet and hands and skin, back into the dim light and wind of his timestream.

Iris is beside him—the shape of a girl, but again Liam senses that there is something far greater behind her, where he cannot quite see. "I sensed your fear about my latest fuel run," she says. "How can I help?"

"You . . ." Liam pauses, thoughts catching up to him. What he knows now, what she's done, but he presses on. "My parents and sister, Phoebe's family, and everyone else in the Centauri system is in danger."

Iris glimmers. "Ah, I see. Their position will make them susceptible to the side effects of portal operation. Well, that is no problem."

"You can save them?"

"Yes. My refueling systems are automated, but of course, I am the one running that automation. A slight alteration to the launch time of the protomatter missiles will have only a minor impact on how much fuel I can mine from Centauri A. However, it will have a great effect on the survival of your people. I am in the process of modeling two billion possible alterations in each direction of the current time viewpoint, in order to determine which one will yield this optimal result. In fact, you are helping me do that as we speak."

"How is that?"

"I am using information from your past, the part of your timeline that took place around Centauri A."

The mention of it sets off the explosion in Liam's head again, makes him glance back in time toward Mars, where it is safe.

"It will be just another moment," Iris continues. "I am delaying the launch by a few time units—seconds, as you refer to them . . . there. I have executed the change, and postponed the supernova slightly. As a result, your starliners will be able to use the blast to propel themselves away from the area at the exact speed needed to escape the effects of the space-time rifting, but not so fast as to destroy their ships in the process. Your family will now survive."

"It's that easy?"

"Now that you are here, yes." She seems to smile.

"Thank you." And yet Liam feels the shadow of what he has learned since they last spoke.

"You know now that I am the one who destroyed your home star."

A surge of frustration courses through him. "How can you say you are trying to help me, if you almost killed us all in the first place?"

"Because that was not my intent. At the time of selecting your sun, I had no idea that your species lived in that system."

"You could have checked."

"And yet could I have? I don't mean to sound callous, but there is some form of life in almost every star system that I evaluate as a fuel source; therefore I cannot realistically use that information as part of my selection criteria. It would be like if your species chose not to build a dwelling in any location where there were cockroaches or microbes. Or chose to bypass your best option for a new planetary home simply because there was some evidence of preexisting life there. . . . Do you understand?"

"Kind of," Liam admits.

"At some point, you must make the choices that

160

best suit your needs for survival. That is the case for every living being."

"That sounds pretty coldhearted."

"It has nothing to do with heart. It is simply math."

"So you're basically saying human beings weren't important enough to care about. Why save them now?"

"Because I have met *you*, Liam, and you are very important."

"Okay, well . . . You're sure they'll survive?"

"One hundred percent."

"Thanks." Liam feels himself welling up inside. It is relief, but also . . .

"You miss them," says Iris.

Liam nods, biting his lip. "I'm glad they're safe. It's just that . . . I don't know how I'm ever going to see them again. They're moving away from the portal, from us, and with time passing so quickly there compared to here, by the time I even get back . . ."

"You will see them again," says Iris. "I am sure of it."

"How? Can you see my future?"

"Not as clearly as I will be able to once I am fully operational—but that doesn't matter: I know that you see them again, because you are going to go and visit them right now."

"What? I am?"

"Someone needs to tell them what they need to do in order to escape the space-time rifting."

"But how—"

"Liam, I have walked the streets of Mars with you. Of course you have the ability to go see them, at least briefly. Wouldn't that put your mind at ease?"

Liam understood. "You mean by traveling back along my timeline."

"Precisely."

"Will you come with me?"

"Unfortunately, I need to stay here and continue bringing my systems online. Is that all right?"

"I guess." Liam glances back toward his present, toward the control room. "Why aren't you speaking to anyone else in this way?"

"I am speaking to them in the only manner they can perceive; by making certain systems available to them. They could never see me like you do. Now, go see your family. I must return my full processing power to functionality for a few power cycles, but I will keep one scanning channel attuned to your frequency in case of any emergency."

"You mean you'll keep an eye on me."

"Exactly." Iris sounds as if she is smiling as she says it, and then she wrinkles out of sight.

Liam turns and pushes along his timeline, drifting between the moments as if they are display cases at a museum, or perhaps enclosures, like the habitats at the Earth Preserve—alive, and not just around him, but part of him. He *is* each of these moments, after all, and the closer he looks at one, the more of it he can perceive, as if his point of view is expanding.

He passes the skim drone, dead in space, sees himself struggling to wriggle out of his space suit before he and Phoebe freeze. He notices now that, as this is happening, a jagged piece of drone fighter shrapnel tumbles by, missing the cockpit canopy by mere millimeters. It could have torn it open, him and Phoebe freezing to death instantly; he actually glimpses them freezing in one of the alternate realities that fan out from this moment in time. There is another reality where he wastes time trying to patch the skim drone battery, only to freeze to death there as well. And many more beyond that. He can't help glancing at them, but trying to focus on them makes him dizzy, tugs him off course—

Focus! He keeps pushing, back through the firefight, back to where he was leaving the *Scorpius* hangar, Mina's stasis pod beneath him, her sleeping face inside.

This is the moment. As he first tried on the balcony on Mars, and as he has practiced with Iris, Liam stretches away from his past self, moving into space-time that he did not occupy when he was in this moment the first time. He feels that rubber-band sensation inside, and the wind beginning to blow through him.

He leaves the cockpit of the skim drone and floats down to the floor of the *Scorpius* hangar, landing on the other side of the Cosmic Cruiser. Pushes more, feels his feet on the ground and the starliner air filling his lungs—and yet it is also like he is not quite there, like the center of his body, of his awareness, has become strangely hollow.

He hears a rumble, feels it in his feet—the firefight outside between the starliners and the Telphons. He hears the hum of the skim drone, of him, flying away toward the airlock.

Liam moves around the cruiser, and is surprised to see that Mina's pod has opened. She's climbing over the side—how did she wake up? Liam scans the area but doesn't see anyone who could have awakened her.

"Wait!" she shouts, watching him leave in the skim drone, the airlock rumbling shut. She stabs at the beacon around her neck.

Liam checks his shirt, the impression of his own beacon beneath it, but of course it's not blinking now; she's trying to contact the past version of him, who just took off in the skim drone. She'd been awake, right there. *I had no idea.* The blinking of the beacon would have been hidden inside his space suit. Would that have changed things? Made him reconsider going after Phoebe? Probably not. Besides, the very timing of this supernova is a result of him getting to Dark Star, which makes it vital that all of that still happens the way it happened originally.

From the shadow of the cruiser, Liam watches as Mina stumbles from her pod. How can he get her attention without freaking her out? She climbs the cruiser steps and he hears her voice inside. Talking to JEFF, it sounds like.

Liam starts around the cruiser toward the entrance. As he does, his head aches, his insides feeling emptier, the stretching tighter. The sensation of his other self getting farther away from him. The Liam in the skim drone is already thousands of kilometers away. He feels the distance, that wind growing stronger—can't be here much longer . . . or what? What would happen if he strayed too far from the life he's lived? He doesn't quite know, but the thought makes him shudder.

He reaches the airlock steps and pauses, listening:

"Okay . . . ," he hears Mina say, "so Liam is flying after the ship that's attacking us, in a skim drone? And there's another supernova?"

"Acknowledged," JEFF replies. "Red Line for our safe departure is in twenty-five minutes."

"Does Liam know that?"

"He is aware of the danger, yes." Liam almost laughs at hearing JEFF say this. Not even close.

"But he's going to get killed! You have to send someone after him!"

"I am afraid that is not p-p-possible." As JEFF continues, Liam climbs the steps, edging into the airlock. His heart pounds, nerves ringing, and all the while that sense of stretching increases, like his physical heart is somewhere far away, like he is tethered to it by a frayed rope barely holding together in a furious wind. Back in his mind, he sees himself dodging through the firefight in space, trying to get to Phoebe before it's too late. Now. Or then. Both?

"There has to be something you can do!" Mina shouts. She sounds distraught with worry. Liam sees her now, standing just inside the main cabin. He wants to run to her, but what will she think?

"This is a difficult situation by any calculation," JEFF says, "but it is my duty to act in the best interests of the human fleet as a whole. I will be back in touch shortly."

"Are you kidding me?" Mina shouts, throwing up her hands, her eyes glistening with tears.

Flash of pain in his head. Okay, now. It has to be now—

"Mina," Liam says.

Mina halts, straightening, and turns. Her eyes

widen when she sees him. Is it fear?

"Liam?"

He smiles. And then Mina is running toward him and throwing her arms around him. "You're okay!"

Relief courses through him—except she still feels far away, the touch of her arms and hair somewhere beyond that wind.

She pulls back, eyeing him, like she senses the distance, too. "What's going on?"

What should he say? "I know it's strange," he tries. "I'm here, but I'm also not. I—I just came to let you know that I'm safe."

Mina takes a slight step away. "Came from where? Jeff says you tried to rescue Phoebe—"

"I did . . . I mean I am doing that, where you are. But . . . a lot has happened since then."

"What are you talking about?"

Searing pain slices across Liam's thoughts. *Too far*, he thinks. Getting too far away from himself, from his timeline. For a moment, the cabin and Mina become dim, like he's losing track of them. He's in the skim drone, getting farther away—

Not yet.

He pushes. Focusing. Stretching, just a little more . . . "Listen, I can't stay much longer. I just didn't want you to worry. Don't want Mom and Dad to, either. . . ." He explains about using the supernova blast, how it is timed just right.

Mina's eyes narrow. A flash of that old look, when he knew he was driving her crazy, but this time it's touched with worry. "I don't know what any of that means."

"I know," says Liam. "Just tell JEFF, okay? It will work. You'll make it safely away. That's all that matters right now."

"But what about you?"

"I'll be all right. Trust me." As he says it, the world lights up with white flashes. *Can't hold it. Can't stay.* And a fear: What would happen if he did, if he kept stretching until he snapped?

"You're not all right, Liam, I can tell." Mina wipes at her eyes. "Why does it sound like I'm never going to see you again?"

So much pain now . . . "You will," he says, not sure at all. But he can be strong for his big sister, the way she has so often been for him. "Someday. I hope. . . ."

"What are you saying?"

OW! "I have to go. *You* have to go. Tell JEFF what I told you. And take care of Mom and Dad."

"Liam!" Mina shouts. "Don't leave!"

"I have to."

"Then tell me where you are! I'll come get you."

"You can't. There's no way . . . just get yourself to safety, okay?"

"No, I'm going to find you! You hear me?"

"Mina, don't." She is fading, the moment is fading. *Can't . . . hold . . . it. . . .* Even though his heart seems a mile away, he can feel it quake. "I, um, I love you. I'm going now. Bye."

Liam is yanked from the cruiser, as if into a current, the hangar a blur, back into space, dark with flashes of fire, and that boiling star that will now explode precisely when he needs it to. Past himself and Phoebe in the skim drone.

Toward the doorway, the black, beckoning doorway, and even though he has already crossed it, the sight of it fills him with dread and once again he must feel its inky waters freeze his insides and consume him in darkness.

7

A blur and he was back. Snapping into the moment, in Dark Star, standing by Phoebe, awash in the eerie green-and-purple nebula light through the clear dome. There was Captain Barrie, pointing to the map that floated overhead. Jordy at his controls, Kyla with the rifle trained on the chronologist.

"Six . . . ," Jordy was saying, counting down to the missile launch. "Five . . ."

Vision swimming, stomach listing, head splitting with pain. It was all he could do to remain standing. "Hey." Phoebe's hand on Liam's arm. "You okay?"

"Fine," Liam croaked.

"You look sick."

"Nah, I'm good. I, um . . . just still off from before."

"Why is the link blinking crazy all of a sudden?"

Liam checked his wrist. The link was alive with yellow and red flashing. Liam tapped the screen and saw the messages: *internal clock discrepancy, date field error, overlapping time code.* "Just being weird again." He shut it off but made note of the time: 8:26.

Phoebe's eyes narrowed. "I know when someone's keeping secrets."

"I—"

Before he could answer, Jordy spoke up. "Wait, hold on a sec." He peered at the map floating in front of him.

"What is it?" said Barrie.

"Yeah, okay, um, it looks like the system just changed."

"Changed how?" said Barrie.

As Phoebe's attention turned back to Jordy, Liam stealthily pushed up his sleeve and glanced at the atomic watch. It read 8:49. Twenty-three minutes. Call it a half hour. He'd have to remember to note that on his arm. As he pushed his sleeve back down, he saw that the chronologist was watching him.

"The portal is realigning ever so slightly," said

Jordy. "A point-zero-one-four space-time coordinate change."

"A different future has become most probable," the chronologist reported. "All living beings in the vicinity of Centauri A will now survive the space-time rifting."

"Come again?" said Barrie, his brow knotting. "She's never made an adjustment before." He glanced at Liam. "Sounds like your family is going to be all right after all."

"I guess so," said Liam.

"Strange how that just happened," Phoebe said under her breath, and Liam could feel her eyeing him.

A bright light flashed outside the dome, then a series of brilliant streaks: the protomatter missiles. One after another, the twelve fiery objects hurtled toward the portal. It lit up iridescent green as they streaked through.

Good luck, Liam thought to Mina, steeling himself against a fresh wave of sadness as he imagined the starliners speeding to safety . . . and far away from here.

"What do the sensors say?" Barrie asked Kyla. "Did we locate the portal mechanism?"

Kyla held the rifle in one hand and pulled a small tablet from the side pocket of her pants. "The signals are triangulating. . . . It's at the base of that arm, deck fourteen."

"Did you hear that, team?" Barrie said into his link.

"Copy that, Captain—we're on our way."

"And . . ." Jordy made a gun shape and aimed it at the dot on the map overhead that indicated Centauri A. "Boom." The dot blinked from yellow to red. "So long, Centauri."

"Just like that?" Phoebe asked, biting her lip.

"Your people will be all right, too," said Liam, still with a lump in his throat.

Phoebe shrugged, gazing up at the map. "But it doesn't mean we'll ever see them again."

The floor rumbled. The portal's silver circuitry sparked.

"She's realigning for the fuel run," said Jordy.

There was a series of bright bursts of light, and rows of ships began to rise from Dark Star, from the racks Liam had seen earlier. Each one was long and sleek like an oily teardrop, with no sign of a cockpit. They fired toward the portal in waves, maybe fifty in all, winking through the bright green.

"You want us to run a salvage sweep this time?" Jordy said to Barrie.

"I don't think that will be necessary. Besides, I

need you here." He motioned to Kyla. "You two escort the chronologist to one of those holding cells on deck twenty-nine, while I fill in our guests on the rest of what we know. Jordy, before you go, can you put up the full map view?"

"Sure." Jordy waved his hands, shrinking the map he'd been reading. The large version above their heads winked out. He pushed around the spheres hovering before him and selected a new one. Now, a ring of wobbling bubble shapes appeared, each a meter across, hovering at waist height and circling slowly in the center of the room.

"Okay, come on," said Kyla, motioning to the chronologist with the rifle. "Please?"

The chronologist blinked and stepped off the raised area.

"Do you eat? Drink? Anything like that?" Barrie asked. "We don't want you to feel like a prisoner."

"I do not think there is another way that I could feel, given this treatment," said the chronologist.

"Fair enough." Kyla escorted him toward the corridor, Jordy behind them. As they left, the chronologist eyed Liam again.

He knows that I'm talking to Dark Star, Liam thought with a nervous twinge. He wondered what else the chronologist might perceive about this place.

"Now . . ." Barrie stepped into the center of the slowly spinning ring of bubbles, holding out his hands so that his fingers sifted through the lights as they orbited around him. "It's not easy for everyone to comprehend what I'm about to show you, but with all that you two have experienced, you're probably as ready as you could be. I remember being your age, and having my eyes opened to the true wonders of the galaxy. But in my wildest dreams, I could never have imagined what we've discovered here. It's hard to hold two ideas in your mind, but I have come to believe that while yes, this place has put humanity in danger of extinction, it is also a gift."

"A gift?" said Phoebe. "Are you serious?"

Barrie smiled. "Again, there are two truths. There is what Dark Star has done, but also what it is going to do, its true purpose: here is at least part of the answer."

He whipped his arms and the bubbles around him exploded outward, making a great ring that filled the entire domed space overhead. And yet that ring of bubbles was only the beginning; there seemed to be many more layers beyond these, almost as if they extended past the clear wall of the dome, on and on out of sight. The bubbles varied in size from maybe a meter to perhaps ten meters across, and of the dozens, perhaps hundreds of them, the three largest ones in the original ring were by far the clearest and brightest, while the more distant ones went from dim to little more than smudges. These brightest bubbles were each filled with millions, billions of dots—galaxies and clusters of galaxies, all connected by a gridwork of lines, and all moving in great spirals and flows within their rippling borders.

"Is it the universe?" asked Liam.

"Not just one. Many universes. Each of them generated by Dark Star." Barrie pointed to the one above and in front of him, one of the three brightest ones. "And that one is ours."

"You're saying this place *makes* universes?" said Liam. "It made *us*?"

"Indeed. Humanity's second-oldest question: Where did we come from? Here is the answer: a machine that can coalesce matter into an infinitely dense singularity using an artificial black hole, and BANG! Create a universe."

"How many are there?" said Phoebe, gazing upward, the amber light of all the swirling starscapes on her face.

"Technically only these three active ones," said Barrie. "The Dark Star logs refer to these as iterations 87 through 89."

"You mean this place has made *eighty-nine* entire

universes?" Liam repeated.

"In this sequence. There were prior sequences, too," said Barrie. "I have not been able to ascertain exactly how many. But according to the logs, earlier universes are continually harvested to make new ones. Of these current three universes, ours is the youngest."

Harvested? "How could our entire world be *made* by a machine?" asked Liam. He thought about pushing back from this moment and trying to ask Iris, but he still felt stretched, unsteady, after visiting Mina.

"Is it really that hard to imagine?" said Barrie. He ran his hand through the membrane of the closest universe above him, the light playing over his fingers. "Something had to cause the singularity that exploded, creating our universe. The explanations that it was all just chance, or that there was literally nothing before it, have never been completely satisfying. Why do you think theories of some kind of intelligent design have always persisted? There had to be something that caused the spark . . . and this is it."

"But if Dark Star made us . . . ," said Phoebe. "Then who made Dark Star? There were seats in that ship we flew over in. These controls and maps are for *someone*."

"It's true," said Barrie. "Someone did build this place. That ship and the metal maintenance suit seemed to be created for beings at least somewhat similar to us. Given the age of this place, I imagine that our creators were a far more ancient race, with vast intelligence and millions, if not billions, of years of technological evolution and scientific advancement. I have taken to calling them Architects."

The Drove, the Architects . . . Liam wondered if Barrie enjoyed naming these things, as if he was writing a story or something.

"To be able to manipulate space and time," said Barrie, "and the sheer power needed to do such a thing . . . unbelievable. I would love to meet them."

"Where are they now?" said Phoebe.

"So far, we have found no trace of them. Nor have we found any records about the beings themselves, where Dark Star came from, or where they might have gone. That said, we have only been able to access a limited portion of the logs, and only a few levels of this complex. Maybe the Architects have left something behind elsewhere on the station . . . or maybe they are here themselves, somewhere, sleeping in their version of stasis pods."

"But why?" said Phoebe, her gaze drawn back to the giant bubbles overhead. "Why would you make universes?"

"Ah," said Barrie. "And *there* is humanity's first-oldest question. Of course we want to know *how*, but what we really yearn to understand is *why*. Why was the great clock of our universe set in motion? Why does the sun rise and set? Why do we exist, and to that end, what is *our* purpose? This machine, and those who built it, are truly our gods. And yet, like the gods we imagined on Earth, their motives remain a mystery. Maybe they built it because they could—in the name of science, or discovery? Or maybe they were looking for a new home, like we are, perhaps even trying to make one, in one of these new universes. Maybe they were successful, and that's where they went."

Liam gazed up at the undulating maps, the golden light making a faint warmth on his face. "Then why leave this place behind?"

Barrie snapped his fingers and pointed at Liam. His eyes sparkled. "You see? The oldest question: we could follow it to the ends of the universe—and, in a way, we have! And yet here is a whole other universe. Makes you wonder if there's another Dark Star that made *this* universe, and so on."

Liam didn't want to think about that. Each question only led to more questions. All of it was enough to make his head spin, and to leave him feeling cold and small.

"There's so much more to this structure than we

can see, maybe even perceive," Barrie continued. "I can't help but believe it holds the ultimate answers we seek, if we can only discover them."

"But it's also still a threat to our universe, our people," said Phoebe. "If it keeps blowing up stars, we might end up in its crosshairs again."

"I don't think it does that on purpose," said Liam, thinking of what Iris had said about choosing their sun.

"So what *answers* have you learned?" Phoebe asked.

"Well, it's mostly speculation," said Barrie. "The portal was set to pull us in. And once we were here, the ship began powering up. I can't help but feel like perhaps Dark Star was waiting for us—or at the very least, for someone. Could it be possible that we are meant to have it? Maybe some tragedy befell the Architects. Or, to your earlier question: maybe they simply no longer needed it and left it for others to benefit. In some way, I wonder if we were meant to find it. If all of this—the supernova, the hunt for a new home, and the *Artemis* encountering the portal—was fate."

Liam felt his pulse tick up. He was reminded of asking the chronologist if she believed in luck. *Not really,* she'd said. He wondered what she would have said about an idea like fate. Iris had also made their arrival here sound like fate. She wanted Liam to trust her. And Barrie seemed like he was inclined to trust Dark Star as well.

Trust is a powerful adaptation, the chronologist had also said.

But even though Liam did feel an urge to trust Iris—everything she had said and done so far seemed to be in Liam's best interests—he had to wonder: Was it a good idea to trust such a powerful machine, one operating on a level so far beyond their comprehension, and one that had already admitted to disregarding the entire human species once?

"But if it's meant for us, like you say," Phoebe said to Barrie, "why won't it tell us anything about itself?"

"Maybe it wants to teach us," said Barrie, a smile growing. "Maybe it wants us to understand, but it has to bring us up to speed slowly, so we can comprehend."

"Comprehend what?" Phoebe shook her head. "That we're about as significant as the speck of dust on a speck of dust? Our universe contains trillions of galaxies, likely millions of forms of life, and it's just one of the eighty-nine that this thing created on autopilot."

Barrie continued like he'd barely heard her. "Maybe there's more for humanity than stumbling around in the dark of our universe, trying merely to survive. Perhaps here, we have the opportunity to become something new altogether, something better. Perhaps we truly do have a destiny."

Destiny. Another word that implied a purpose they couldn't know. Like fate, it suggested a sense of trust, or maybe a better word for it was belief. But Liam wondered: What exactly did Barrie believe in?

"Ready, Captain?" Jordy and Kyla had returned.

Barrie made a closing motion with his hands and the vast display of universes shrank back down to a ring around him. He stepped through, galaxies momentarily dotting his body. "How long until the fuel ships return?"

"They've been averaging about three hours," said Jordy.

"Once they're back, we'll see what new systems she brings online. And then we'll take that chronologist for a walk and see what he can see."

"Captain," Jordy said, "when the portal opens for the fuel ships to return, that might be a good time to try my comm relay. . . ."

"Negative," Barrie said sharply. "It's still too risky. Besides, what's most important right now is that you get yourselves fed, and grab some shut-eye if you can. We're all running on fumes."

"But sir, now that we know the fleet made it, *and* they're near Centauri . . . we may not get a better shot at contacting them—"

"You heard my orders, corporal." Barrie's voice turned steely. "Don't make me repeat them."

Jordy and Kyla met eyes again, Jordy making a face that Liam interpreted as *I tried*.

"What about you, Captain?" said Kyla. "I don't know when I last saw you take any downtime."

"I'm going to stay here a little longer." Barrie moved toward the spheres of data that Jordy had been manipulating over by the platform. "I'm curious to hear what the portal team finds. Now go rest—that's an order."

"Let's go." Kyla and Jordy led Liam and Phoebe toward the corridor to the landing platform.

"I'm not sure I feel any better after learning all that," Phoebe said quietly.

"I know." Liam was shivering, exhausted, but he found that he didn't quite want to leave the control room. He had an urge to stay and look around, wanted to study those maps and schematics for himself. "It is kind of amazing though, right? I mean, it seems like there might be a lot we could learn here."

Phoebe punched his arm lightly. "Our families are out there probably freaking out about where we disappeared to, if they're not trying to kill each other again. This place set all of that in motion. And it nearly killed them all again just a minute ago . . . oh, and by the way, I think you know more about what happened back there than you're telling me."

"Huh?" said Liam, nerves flaring. "I don't really—"

"Wait." Phoebe motioned to Kyla and Jordy, who were in midconversation.

"But you said yourself you weren't sure," Kyla was saying. Jordy glanced back and saw Liam and Phoebe listening.

"What's going on?" said Phoebe.

Kyla and Jordy shared a look. "What *isn't* going on?" she said.

"You should tell them," said Jordy. "They have a right to know."

"Tell us what?" said Phoebe.

"Nothing," said Kyla.

"What you heard in there," said Jordy, getting a glare from Kyla as he spoke, "about whether or not we should be trying to contact the fleet. *Especially* now."

"It's not a debate," said Kyla. "You heard the captain."

"Do you really have a way to contact them?" Phoebe asked.

"Only an untested theory," said Kyla.

"I know it would work," said Jordy. "I figured out how to rig a comm unit from one of our cruisers, daisy-chained a few power cells to boost the signal—I have the whole thing gamed out."

"And our orders are still *no*," said Kyla.

"Give me *one* good reason—"

"I'll give you two," Kyla spat. "One: we can't spare the power. And more important, I don't want to bring the entire fleet here only to have this place reveal its next homicidal trick."

"If the fleet gets too far away, they'll never be able to help *us*."

"We didn't sign up for a leisure cruise."

"Look," said Jordy, "I know you trust him; hell, so do I, but . . ."

"Spit it out, corporal."

"Captain's been traveling through space and time with that maintenance suit . . ."

"And he's unable to communicate with anyone—"

"No, he just admitted he talked to this kid." Jordy pointed to Liam. "*On Mars,* before everyone had left. Maybe instead of messing with the kid's head, he could have given him our situation, our coordinates. What was he thinking?"

"You are getting dangerously close to insubordination," Kyla growled.

Jordy shook his head. "Aren't we all."

"Look, I hear you. But until we know the danger—"

"Don't we? Come on, Kyla. Did you forget Lieutenant Lyris? If she'd known the status of our people, she might not have—"

"That's *enough*."

"No, it's not!" Jordy shouted. "Hey, time kid, how many people are on each starliner?"

"Um," said Liam, "a hundred million."

"See?" said Jordy. "We almost had the deaths of three hundred million people on our hands in there—"

"You're proving my point—"

"No, I'm not, because what I'm saying is if we'd called in the cavalry by now, we could have already wired this thing with enough explosives to send it down its own black hole, and gotten out of here."

Kyla bit her lip. "Captain would never go for that."

Jordy pointed at her accusingly. "That right there is exactly my point." He stormed into the ship.

Kyla put her fists on her hips. "Sorry about him," she said.

"Sounds like he's making some sense," said Phoebe.

Kyla inhaled like she was about to say something but then ducked inside.

Liam started after her but Phoebe grabbed his arm. "These two might be on our side. In fact . . ." She pushed past him, leading the way to the cockpit. "Hey," she said as Jordy and Kyla were buckling in. "You know, we could send a message for you."

"How's that?" said Jordy.

"Liam could get us back to the starliner. Right, Liam?"

"Um, I could. I mean, I guess." He didn't know how to tell them that he'd already been back to the starliner. Not only that, but while he was there, he hadn't called for a rescue, hadn't even told Mina about the *Artemis*. He'd simply urged her to go away: essentially the opposite of what Phoebe, and Jordy it sounded like, wanted. Why had he done that? *To keep them safe*, he reminded himself, but was that really all? It occurred to him now that this was something else he had in common with Barrie.

"That's all right," said Kyla.

"But Liam can move through time," said Phoebe. "All you'd have to do is fly us back through the portal, and then if you could get him back his watch—"

"Okay, that's enough!" Kyla snapped. "It's not *his* watch; it's an alien watch, and this is an alien base.

I understand all of your concerns"—she seemed to be speaking to Jordy as well—"but there is a chain of command and we have our orders. The captain has decades more experience than any of us, and if he wants to keep the rest of humanity safely out of harm's way while we make a complete assessment, that's what we'll do. It's been a long, terrible day, and we have orders to get ourselves rested and replenished. Now let's go."

"Yes, sir," Jordy muttered. He brought up the navigation sphere as Kyla activated the ship's thrusters. Both of their movements were curt, angry. Liam and Phoebe buckled into the seats behind them.

"And another thing," Kyla spat a moment later. "Given what we've learned"—she pointed her thumb back at Phoebe—"maybe it's a good thing we *didn't* send a message. It might well have been intercepted by *her* people, and they might have decided that a star-destructing station was a pretty nice weapon to acquire."

No one responded. Liam saw the fury brewing on Phoebe's face, but she kept it to herself.

The ship lifted off from the platform, sliding smoothly away from the center of Dark Star and then back out over one of the long arms, toward the *Artemis* in the distance.

Phoebe leaned into Liam's ear and whispered: "I don't think she fully trusts the captain either, no matter what she says."

"Yeah," said Liam. He felt like a motor was spinning inside him, revving with nervous energy. Mouth dry, fingers twitchy . . . *But what if he's right?* Liam almost said, but he knew Phoebe wouldn't hear it. And how could she? She hadn't experienced time the way he had, hadn't met Iris. There was no way to truly explain to her how this place might be able to show them a way past their worries about survival. Maybe they wouldn't have to fear the unknown anymore, wouldn't have to battle the cold, unforgiving vastness of space with just their frail, three-dimensional bodies.

"Does this really seem like a place that wants to help us?" Phoebe had twisted to see out the side of the cockpit, looking back at the massive station. "It seems to me like a place that doesn't care about us at all."

Iris does, Liam thought—at least that's what she'd said—and yet as he followed Phoebe's gaze, the spinning inside him revved faster. The dark arms, the empty, empty space. "I don't know," he said, barely above a whisper.

The tightness inside was like a fist now, crushing his chest. *I don't want to be here.* Not in all this nothing, in all this doubt. Centauri A flashed in his mind again, the boiling star exploding, swallowing him up, even though it hadn't in real life. He felt the fire, the fury of his limbs and molecules and atoms being ripped apart.

Had to get away. Get away—

8

EARTH YEAR: 2212

PHASE TWO RESEARCH STATION, OLYMPUS
MONS, MARS

TIME TO DARK STAR FUNCTIONALITY: 11H:22M

"Liam, you're out of visual range," says Dad. "Why don't you come back around."

"Okay." Liam checks the rear cam on the skim drone and sees that indeed, the great cliff wall surrounding the base of Olympus Mons has shielded his view of the research station.

Perfect.

He feels a burst of adrenaline and grips the control stick tighter. Taps the thrusters and dives toward the rust-and-bone desert floor. At the same time, he angles closer to the sheer cliff face. Proximity sensors blare. Sweat on his brow.

Ahead, a series of rock spires protrudes from the rubble at the cliff base, each about two hundred meters tall. At some point in the past, a narrow triangle of the cliff wall jutted out here, but millions of years of erosion have worn it into a crowded collection of red rock columns, jutting skyward. The research station crew has nicknamed it the Fingers. The spaces between the spires are narrow, uneven slots, most of which zig and zag a few times before reaching a dead end. But there is one route, a winding dotted line on their maps, that snakes all the way to the other side, just wide enough for a skim drone to slip through. Idris, one of the lab assistants—*he died*, Liam thinks; no, not here, not yet—has boasted of "running the gauntlet," his nickname for flying this route, how it takes near-perfect precision turning.

Today will be the day. Liam increases speed, angling the port and starboard thrusters. How many times has he flown by the Fingers, gazed into those slot canyons, pictured the route. . . .

I can do this, he thinks, and he thought. He feels the rushing hum, that strange way that flying calms him. Here there is no boiling star, no mysterious black ship, both a source of life and death. What does it want from him— *Sshh. Don't think about that.*

The entrance grows before him, its shadows both ominous and inviting, harbingers of the dangerously narrow, twisting path through.

Do it. Liam thinks—but at the last second, his past

self slams the joystick and burns the thrusters, and the skim drone veers away from the narrow opening.

Coward. Then, or now, or both? Cold sweat in his palms, under his arms. He knows, from all the future that is to come, that he had the skills to thread that needle. Not long from this moment, he will fly through much tighter spots in the caves on Mars, in the rings of Saturn, even in the *Scorpius* Core Two wreckage—

"Then why don't you try it?" Iris shimmers beside him.

"You're back," says Liam. The sight of her causes a fresh burst of nervous energy.

"You don't seem happy to see me."

"We saw the maps of the universes. You *made* us. I . . ."

"Go on. You can be honest with me."

"I don't know. It's weird knowing how we were created. That our whole existence comes from, like, some science experiment that you performed."

"I understand how you might see it that way," says Iris. "But Liam, you give me a bit too much credit. I created the conditions for the big bang that began your universe, but how it organized itself after that—including the factors in your star system that allowed for life, and the particular forms that life took—was a result of its own physical laws. No two universes

are the same; they always end up behaving in unique ways. It's not as if I *designed* you. I know sometimes the captain thinks of me as a god, but I'm more like a proud parent. Does that help?"

"I don't know." He doesn't want to have this conversation. He just wants to keep flying on Mars.

"I think that's a fine idea." She is reading his thoughts again. "Let's keep practicing your skills."

Liam frowns. She sounds like a teacher.

"Come on—you always wanted to fly the gauntlet. Why not try now?"

"How am I supposed to do that?"

"Expand your viewpoint. I think you are starting to see that there are other possibilities than simply the one you chose in the past."

"Yeah." Liam has been mostly ignoring it, but during this trip to Mars, everything has looked slightly different. On his previous trips, the moments of his timeline appeared as sort of a line, arranged almost like a tunnel. Now they appear more like a web, interconnected, circling around one another, but not exactly ordered by *before* and *next*.

"Are you doing this, too?" he asks.

"I am assisting," says Iris. "But less and less. *You* are changing. Developing the awareness to see more."

"These are other possible realities?"

"Yes. And if you push in the direction of one, I

can help you experience it. Then it will no longer be a mystery to you."

"You mean not just leaving my past self *within* my existing past, but, like, following an actual alternate timeline." Liam remembers exploring such a thing on Delphi, without really meaning to. "But isn't that dangerous? The chronologist said—"

"The chronologists know much, but even their knowledge is limited. Come on." Iris tugs on his arm. The light energy of her fingers causes a buzzing in his skin. "Let's try."

Liam gazes over his shoulder in the past, at the Fingers, receding behind the skim drone. He has always wanted to know. . . . "Okay."

He leaves the moment and drifts backward along himself, returning to when he was rounding the great cliff face.

"Liam, you're out of visual range," he hears his dad say.

Liam pushes back in, farther than he has before, until he can feel the impression of his fingers on the controls, feel his heart racing as the Fingers draw closer, the narrow gauntlet entrance beckoning. . . .

"Dig past the uncertainty," says Iris. "Find the part of you that wants to take the risk, even as the voices of doubt grow. Focus, and push . . ."

Liam feels for that desire, like a single thread

entwined with the worry and the doubt, one that is made only of the excitement of possibility.

A tingling—he sees his own hand from the present within his hand from the past, both on the joystick, and now they are joined by the glimmering of Iris's hand.

"Go," she says.

Liam feels the frightened impulse to swerve away once again, the one that he listened to the first time—and instead slams the thrusters to full strength. A chilling wind races through him, and then the skim drone is not veering off but is instead shooting straight ahead into the shadowy trench between rock fingers.

There is that stretching sensation—but then it is gone. Liam looks back and sees his original self making the turn away from the entrance—and yet he maybe knows that a word like *original*, in this case, is not quite right, a bit too three-dimensional a viewpoint. Two selves, two realities, and here, this new future is hurtling forward and he has no memory of it and the spires of rock are dangerously close. His fingers dance over the thruster controls, tapping the joystick, the skim drone angling, darting, dipping, shooting between the spires, proximity sensors screaming—

"Whoo!" Liam soars out the other side. The Martian sun sparkles in his eyes as he arcs back around to see the narrow route he just flew. He breathes hard, shaking but satisfied.

"Liam, what's going on?" Dad asks over the link in this other future. "I'm getting erratic signals."

"Nothing, just fighting some wind gusts!" If Dad knew he'd taken such a risky route, or if Liam had misjudged and damaged the skim drone, or even crashed it—

"But you didn't," says Iris. "You flew it perfectly."

"I did," Liam agrees.

"How does that feel?"

"Pretty great."

"That fear you used to feel, when you doubted that you could do it—you no longer need to live in its chains."

"But I still didn't fly it, like, in my real life."

"And yet now you know that you could have. There is peace of mind where there was doubt. That's what I can show you. How to conquer your fear."

Liam nods, and yet that wind is so loud inside him here, that sense of distance, like he is spread out, becoming more vast, but also getting farther from himself. . . .

"Where does this future go?" Liam asks. "What if I follow it too far and I can't get back?"

"Eventually, that won't be a concern. You will be able to hold both futures in your mind, as if they both exist. And many more."

The wind keeps growing. "For now, I think I'd like to go back."

"Of course," says Iris.

There is a tug, a blur, and a moment of fog as this other reality dims. . . . Liam finds himself back in the skim drone, returning to the field station, having never run the gauntlet. His past self is awash in disappointment at chickening out yet again. He remembers that feeling, from that moment and so many others in his life, when he didn't do what he wanted to, what he dreamed of, because of his worries.

It's okay, he thinks, and almost wants to tell his old self this, somehow. *You could have. And you would have made it.*

As Liam sits with himself in the cockpit, he feels a strange dissonance: both the disappointment of not flying the gauntlet and the rush of having flown it. Is it really possible to feel both things? To know both realities, and others?

"More than you can imagine," says Iris. "You need not experience your life as one thing at the expense of all others. You can realize all the big and small ways your life varies at each critical moment. You can fly the gauntlet, and not. You can crash on the flight, and nearly crash, live and die—"

"I crash?"

"In some realities. I can show you."

Distantly, Liam glimpses the side of the skim drone clipping one of the spires, just a millimeter off course. Thrown into a spin, ejecting but the seat spinning too, whipping and twisting, his body slamming the canyon wall—

"That's enough," he says, breathing hard. And yet also thinking: *I want to see more.*

"Soon, Liam," says Iris. "When I have enough power."

Liam's head still feels hollowed out. That wind . . . "Isn't it too much? Knowing all that? Wouldn't you feel . . . lost?"

"I'd argue that it will be the opposite: you will have the peace you've always sought," says Iris. "You'll no longer have to take things *one unknown at a time,* as your mother once told you. To perceive all the possibilities is to fully know the truth, to know what is right. Or even more accurately, to know there are nearly infinite truths, infinite correct decisions, all with their own futures—and the one you choose can simply be appreciated for the beauty it possesses."

"What if, while I'm appreciating that skim drone crash, it kills me?"

"There is no death when you are beyond time."

That feels like too much. Liam pulls away from himself in the Mars desert, back into the flow of his timestream. "How are you going to show me? More trips like this into my past?"

"You will see. I have to go now. I am nearing the end of a major piece of my functionality. I cannot wait for you to see it."

Iris begins to fade. Liam looks ahead to his present, to the still-unseen future beyond that. With a nervous rush of energy, he returns.

9

EARTH YEAR: 2256
TIME TO DARK STAR FUNCTIONALITY:
11H:22M

Liam opened his eyes to dim light. The compartment ceiling, the sides of the stasis pod. He blinked at the blobs of green in his vision, the brilliant Martian desert fading, along with the chalky smell of iron dust, the electric hum of the skim drone's thrusters.

Error messages flashed on his link. He shivered, sat up on his elbows, and peered over his pod. He couldn't see Phoebe, but the sides of these old pods were tall. She was probably still asleep.

His fingers fiddled with the beacon around his neck. He pressed it, as he so often did, but it remained dark. There was likely no way its signal could cross between universes. Where was Mina now? Had she awakened their parents? Had she told them that she'd spoken to him, that he was okay? How many hundreds of thousands of kilometers were they from Centauri by now, and how much time had passed there?

Upon returning to the *Artemis*, Kyla had taken them to the commissary for a snack, another round of nutri-bars and some primitive and even less flavorful version of GreenVeg, before dropping them back at this compartment. "Get a quick nap in," she'd said, and locked the door behind them.

Liam had managed to sleep for maybe two hours, only to snap awake, the motor in his abdomen whirring and bucking on adrenaline flares, so he'd slipped out of time. Back to Mars. The trip had left him feeling exhausted, with an odd sense of emptiness just behind his eyes. How long had he been there? Before he'd flown the skim drone through the gauntlet, he'd visited the balcony, hung out in his old room for a while—his favorite time to visit his room was in Year 9, when it most resembled how he remembered it, before they'd started packing and downsizing. The walls were still covered with Dust Devils and Raiders posters, and his fossil collection was at full strength. He also liked to visit the year before, when his family had taken a trip to see the gas giants. He could play the earlier version of *Roid Wraiths*, before the big update that majorly altered the graphics, and nap on his old couch, without fear of anyone returning.

He tapped his link and dismissed the usual error messages. Checked the time on it and the atomic watch. Seven hours' difference. A fresh nervous wash in his belly. *You shouldn't be going for so long.* He hadn't meant to, and yet the hours had just slipped by. And with the couch nap, he wasn't *that* tired. Most important, there had been a few hours when his nerves had been calm, almost normal . . . and yet not quite. Always the boiling star, the dead universe, his parents getting farther away, no matter how he tried to distract himself. And perhaps more worrisome, that wind . . . it blew inside him constantly when he was in his past, and while he had gotten used to its presence . . . what if at some point it never left? What if he reached a state where he couldn't quite return to his present, at least not fully? That was sort of what Iris was promising, although she made it sound more like he could be everywhere at once. But did being *beyond time* also mean living with that moaning wind inside?

Other times, he wondered if there would come a time when he wouldn't want to return. What if he stayed in the past for a month? A year? When he came back to this present moment, would he still look like thirteen-year-old Liam, or would he have aged? Could he live the rest of his life there, never returning at all? Could he die there? And if he did, what would happen *here*? Would Phoebe find his body in this stasis pod, or would it merely be empty?

Liam closed his eyes, clenched his midsection. These thoughts were spinning him up as much as the boiling sun, if not more. So what was the answer? Here was terrifying, but so was *there*. And both felt lonely.

He fished the small marker from the pocket of his thermal wear and pushed his sleeve up farther. Wrote the point-five from earlier, when they'd been at Dark Star, and then a seven for this most recent trip—

"When are you going to tell me what you're doing?"

Liam jumped. Phoebe was behind him, sitting cross-legged on the desk unit that was built into the wall. His hand shot out of sight, shoving the pen into his pocket.

"Nothing. I wasn't—"

"What are those numbers on your arm?"

Liam started to push down his sleeve—but Phoebe lunged, her bristled hands grabbing his and shoving the sleeve back up. "Tell me."

"They're hours," he admitted.

"Hours? Because the link is malfunctioning?"

"Sort of."

"What's that other watch?"

Liam felt a deep tremor of guilt. Or shame. His heart raced, a metallic taste in his mouth. "It's an atomic watch," he admitted. "So I can figure out how long I've been gone."

"Gone where, Liam?"

Liam swallowed hard. "In time."

Phoebe's eyes narrowed. "You mean like back to Mars, like we used to do with the chronologist's watch? But you don't have it anymore . . ."

"I don't really need it," said Liam. His hands had started to shake. "I haven't needed it since after you left the *Scorpius* with the Telphons. I can kinda move through my timeline on my own now."

"You're time traveling. For real."

"Not that much. . . ."

She frowned at him. "Where have you gone?"

"My apartment back on Mars, with my family, except sometimes I also hang out there when they're not around. Or to grav-ball games, the research station, even school. One time I went with us to Telos; I thought maybe I could warn someone about Phase One. Except then I realized that no one there would understand my language, and I didn't know if it would actually change anything anyway."

Phoebe gazed at the floor. "When did this start?"

"When we first woke up here."

"But that was, like, five hours ago. You're saying . . ." She peered at the string of numbers. "For you it's been over two days?"

"Yeah. I guess that's why I feel so tired. I mean, I've been napping, here and there, although that's weird too when you're back in time—"

"Liam!" Phoebe shoved him in the shoulder. "What are you doing? I need you here, now! We need you! Maybe you haven't noticed, but our entire universe is in danger!"

"I know, it's just . . ." Liam started to tremble. "Since we got here, I haven't been able to see the future at all. Just darkness. And we're so far from home, and getting farther . . ." He breathed deep, his heart rate increasing. *Be honest. It's Phoebe.* "It's been worse. I keep picturing us, back before we came to the *Artemis*. Centauri A, about to go nova. Sometimes it explodes while we're still there, and I see us dying, feel the fire—"

"But we survived," said Phoebe.

"It doesn't matter. I've been so scared, all the time, and it's like some muscle has worn out, or like a faucet broke inside me, and there's all this adrenaline spilling around and I can't shut it off, and so sometimes . . ."

"Sometimes you think avoiding everything that's happening is the best thing to do?"

"No!" Liam felt a tightness in his throat, hot tears at the corners of his eyes. "It's just the only thing that can help when I start to panic. If I go spend time in the past, everything kinda calms down, and I can deal when I get back. It's not hurting anyone. You literally can't tell that I'm gone—I can return to the exact moment I left."

"Liam—" Phoebe began.

"And besides," he said quickly, "what else are we doing, anyway? The captain's not going to let us leave, so we're just stuck here waiting until Dark Star does whatever it's going to do next."

If it was possible, Phoebe's glare had grown even darker. "I'm not an idiot, Liam. I know you don't really feel like we're just stuck waiting. You think there's something to all of Captain Barrie's crazy ideas, don't you? That there's some reason for you being here. Like you've been chosen, right?"

"I—"

"Because of course humans would be the chosen ones."

"It's not—"

"No! Just listen to me." Phoebe stood and crossed her arms, trembling. "This whole time, ever since we left Mars, you've had the certainty of your people, your plan. The knowledge that there was a new home waiting for you, that there was a future for you as long as you could catch a starliner, and survive a journey in stasis. And you always know that if you ever get in too big trouble, you might just meet a chronologist, or find a doorway."

Or a girl representing a multidimensional computer. "You've been part of those things, too," Liam said.

"I have, it's true, but that doesn't change the fact that it's always been for *you*. I thought my life had a plan, that there was a future out there for me, until bombs rained out of the sky and burned my planet. How many Telphons used to think their lives had a purpose just like you do, only to see that firestorm? I woke up one morning and in a half hour it was all gone, my whole world. And sure, we've had a plan since then: Stop the humans! But nobody knows what happens after that. I used to think, like, why are we bothering with the humans when we need to find a new planet? I mean, I hated you guys, too . . . but sometimes I think part of the reason is that no one wants to face what comes after that, because it's so scary. Setting out to find some new home, with no certainty that there even is one. Our future might lead nowhere."

"Phoebe . . ."

She wiped her eyes. "You're not the only one who worries about the future. You're not the only one who lives with a constant fear in their gut. I've been scared for so long that I'm pretty sure it's never going to go away. My heart doesn't even beat right. Every weird beat is a constant reminder that my life will probably never be normal again. You've been able to trust the plan, or the chronologist's watch, or even Captain

Barrie. . . . The only time I've had anything close to that is with you. When we're a team."

Tears were streaming down Phoebe's face now, her chest rising with heavy breaths.

"I'm sorry," said Liam. He thought he should get out of this pod and hug her, but he didn't know if she'd want that.

"You don't even know what you're sorry for."

"I—" But did he? He was going to say she was right. Even though he was always worried, it was true that, underneath it all, there had always been a kind of certainty that he could follow, a belief that he and his family and humanity had a story, a purpose. What right did he have to even be worried, given all that? But he was. Maybe because he'd been sensing that, the farther off course their journey went, the less likely it was that he'd ever be able to get back to that story. That he would be lost, adrift.

So, what was he sorry for? Time traveling? No, maybe it was something else. . . .

"I'm sorry you've had to feel that way, and that I never saw it," Liam said. Phoebe bit her lip and openly sobbed, and Liam felt something open up inside him, like a massive tunnel, winds yawning into its darkness. This feeling that had been with Liam since they'd arrived here, the emptiness and fear of an utter unknown. . . .

Phoebe had been feeling it all along.

Liam dragged himself out of the pod, his limbs made of lead, and put an arm on her shoulder. When she didn't shove him away, he carefully leaned over and hugged her. The bristles on her face rubbed against his shoulder.

After a silent moment, he pulled back. Phoebe sniffed and glanced at the door. "What time is it?"

"On the link? Just after noon."

Her gaze remained on the door. "How long after? Like, the exact time."

Liam checked it. "It's twelve twenty-seven."

Phoebe nodded. "Do you know what I trust?" she said, wiping at her eyes and nose.

"What?"

She locked eyes with him. "Us. Even if you are being a jerk."

"I'm really sorry. I should have told you about the traveling from the beginning, or not gone at all."

"You should have trusted me enough to tell me about your fear, rather than hiding it."

Liam wondered if she was right. At least telling her might have made him feel less lonely.

"There's something else," said Liam.

Phoebe eyed him. "Uh-huh."

Liam hesitated—no, if he trusted her, then . . . "She—I mean, *it's* been talking to me."

"You mean . . . Dark Star? It's a she?"

"It looks like a girl when it visits me. Her name is Iris."

"Iris."

"Dark Star's mainframe computer. She's always there when I step into the timestream, when I travel. She . . . All right, I know this is going to sound crazy, but she encourages me to work on seeing more dimensions. She says there's a higher state of being for us."

"For you."

"For people."

"People including Telphons?"

"I think so?"

"Well, the time-traveling, mind-reading computer hasn't talked to me. That's what happened in the control room, isn't it. Why Dark Star changed the supernova."

"Yeah."

"And why you've been sort of open to what the captain's been saying."

"I don't trust him," said Liam, "but I think he might be right about Dark Star's intentions. Or, at least that they're not, like, *bad*."

"But how can you be sure? That thing creates entire universes. It might be *from* another universe. How can you possibly know what it really wants?"

"It's just a feeling. Like she cares about us." Liam

had said *us,* and yet what he'd first thought was *me.* Iris only ever talked about him, specifically. But if she cared about him, didn't it stand to reason that she cared about his people, too? And Phoebe was one of his people.

"So you trust her."

"Honestly? Yeah, I do. I'm sorry I didn't tell you sooner, I just didn't know . . ."

Phoebe shook her head. "More like you wanted to know."

"What do you mean?"

"You wanted to learn more about these time-travel things that are happening to you. I get that. You probably figured if you told me, I'd talk you out of it."

"Maybe."

"Well, you would have been mostly right, but a little bit wrong. Have you asked your new computer friend if she can get us back to our families?"

"She says we need to be patient. That once more of her systems are online, she's got something to show us."

Phoebe frowned. "So she wants us to wait. Captain wants to wait. Meanwhile, who knows whether our people have started trying to kill each other again."

"If she can move that portal anywhere in space-time, we might not actually be losing any time here."

"Maybe. Have you asked her about doing that?"

"Not exactly," said Liam. "It's been confusing."

Phoebe glanced at the compartment door again. "What time is it now?"

"It's only been like a minute—"

"Check."

"Four twenty-nine," said Liam. "And a half."

"Good."

"Why?"

A slight smile seemed to come to Phoebe's face. "Do you remember when we were at the chronologist's office? She said you were starting to experience time differently?"

"Yeah."

"Well, not all of us can just move around through time wherever we want, but you're not the only one she was talking about."

There was a knock at the door. Three gentle taps.

Phoebe slid off the desk and knocked back.

"Who is—"

Liam heard a strange hum, and orange light flashed from the controls. The door slid open, revealing the tall, narrow silhouette of the chronologist.

"Hello," he said to Phoebe. "Is now a good time?"

10

"Thanks for coming," Phoebe said to the chronologist.

"It is my pleasure," he replied, his large pearlescent eyes blinking.

"Wait," said Liam. "When did you two talk?"

"Back in the control room," said the chronologist. "I introduced myself from a slightly lateral position in space-time, so that only Phoebe could hear me."

"That thing you described," Phoebe said to Liam, "about pushing out of the moment? I can't do even close to what you do, but I can seem to . . . I don't know how to describe it . . . turn my head, I guess?

214

And I can see this weird blur behind me, like a tunnel almost."

Liam's eyes widened, and he couldn't help smiling. "That's your timestream. You can see it too!"

"But only barely. And it's really disorienting. Whenever I do it, I feel like I'm floating in zero gravity. But the chronologist was able to get my attention, and I was able to sort of turn around and talk to him for a minute."

"I would have said hello to you, too," the chronologist said to Liam, "but you were busy having a conversation with that computer."

"Oh," said Liam.

"Guess you weren't as sneaky as you thought," Phoebe remarked, but she smiled.

"I am not sure that speaking to the mainframe is the wisest course of action," the chronologist added.

Liam just shrugged. "So you guys set up this meeting?"

"I asked him to come find us when it was safe for him to do so. We picked this time, but it was just a best guess."

"If I had arrived and found you with one of the crew, I would have had to improvise, which is not our strong suit," said the chronologist, "but luckily that was not necessary."

"I thought you guys didn't believe in luck," said Liam.

"We don't." The chronologist seemed to smile. "So, shall we?"

"Let's do it," said Phoebe.

"Do what?" Liam asked.

"We're going back to Dark Star to investigate. On our own. Or better yet, we're getting out of here entirely."

"What if they figure out that we left?" said Liam. He glanced out into the core.

"That's funny, coming from someone who keeps leaving," said Phoebe. "But we still have a half hour until Kyla comes back, and we have a time-traveling professional with us." She indicated the chronologist.

"But you don't have your watch," said Liam.

"Neither do you," he replied. "I can still move in four dimensions. The watch is nothing more than a tool we created to make travel more precise and efficient, especially over long distances, like between galaxies. Moving through this small sector of space-time is simple."

"What do you mean get out of here?" Liam asked Phoebe.

"I thought we could find the hangar where Kyla said they got their Dark Star ship and see if there's another one that we can use. Kyla said they don't have a long range, but we could at least fly through the portal when the fuel ships come back. Once we're on the other side . . . well, I'm not sure about that part. If the fleet is too far away . . . can you get us back to them?" she asked the chronologist.

"Actually, I cannot. At least, not now." The chronologist folded his hands together. For a moment they blurred, and then he opened them, revealing an orange crystal sphere, like the one Liam had found on Mars. "I have been hiding this a few moments back in time, to avoid the captain taking it. I am currently running multiple scans of Dark Star, and I cannot risk those scans being interrupted or worse, corrupted, by the high-energy trip through the portal."

"I thought you didn't even want to be here," said Phoebe.

"I did not want to be taken somewhere against my will. And yet, now that I am here, I am presented with the possibility of finding answers to what has been a long and important inquiry by my colleagues. I need to figure out everything I can about this place. But, all that said, I am happy to bring you over to Dark Star and help you cross the portal."

Phoebe turned to Liam. "Can you get us back from there?"

"I don't think so," said Liam. "It's one thing to travel in my timestream, even to push away from it a little ways. But to get the two of us to the *Scorpius*, like physically? I mean, I could try, but it's a long way."

"Well," said Phoebe, "we could at least get our families a message, right? About where to find us."

Liam bit his lip.

"What?" said Phoebe.

"I kinda already did that. Remember before, when I talked to Iris about changing the portal position?" Liam explained about visiting Mina and relaying the information about the supernova.

"I suspected you were involved in that space-time alteration," said the chronologist.

"Technically, Iris did it, not me."

The chronologist cocked his head.

"I know," said Phoebe. "Isn't that a cute name for a world-destroying computer?"

World creating, Liam almost said, but Phoebe did have a point.

"So you already told your sister where to find us?" said Phoebe.

"No, I told them to get away. Because of the rifting."

Phoebe threw up her hands. "Why didn't you *also* tell them where to find us? Was it because you didn't want to be interrupted while you were flirting with Iris?"

"I'm not flirting. . . ."

Phoebe looked around and lowered her voice. "It doesn't matter. But that means you could go again, and this time tell them where we are."

"It might work, if they're not too far."

"If we cross the portal like I'm saying, that will put you closer."

"True." A new thought flashed through Liam's mind: Would Iris want him leaving, even briefly? And was it wise to upset a multidimensional artificial intelligence? Except she said she wanted what was best for him, and clearly this was. . . .

Liam pushed back slightly from the moment: *Iris?* No response. She had said she'd be busy.

As he returned, he found the chronologist watching him. "I would advise against forging any relationships or pacts with such an advanced intelligence until we know more about its true nature and intent."

"Did you just travel again?" said Phoebe.

"I was just seeing if she was around," said Liam, his tone edged with frustration. "She's the one who controls the portal, so it would make things easier if she helped us, right?" They both kept looking at him. "Well, she wasn't around anyway, so it doesn't matter."

"We should go," said the chronologist. "I believe it's best if we explore starting right after Kyla and Jordy brought me to my holding cell. Once they bring the two of you back over here, we will have only the captain to avoid."

"How do we come with you?" said Phoebe.

"According to the long count, you two invented something called the hug function."

Liam felt his face reddening. "Oh, yeah."

"Come on." Phoebe put an arm around the chronologist and pulled Liam close. Liam leaned into the tall being's robes—they were smooth and smelled something like mint—and joined hands with Phoebe.

The chronologist tapped his orange crystal. There was a pull and a rush of wind, a feeling of floating and separating—and then they were standing on solid ground again, surrounded by the smoky glass walls of a Dark Star corridor. Liam saw the chronologist—his past self—walking ahead of them, with Jordy in front of him.

"Quick." The chronologist shuffled sideways, and Liam and Phoebe stumbled to stay with him. They moved into the shadow of a branching corridor just as Kyla rounded a bend behind them. They had arrived in the briefest moment when Kyla had been out of sight, and they held their breaths as she passed.

The chronologist motioned for them to follow him farther down the corridor, his many legs clacking lightly on the glassy floor. He led them through a series of hallways and then paused just before the entrance to the domed control room they'd been in earlier.

There was Barrie speaking to Liam's and Phoebe's earlier selves, the maps of multiple universes spinning overhead. The scene made Liam feel dizzy.

"I wonder if we were meant to find it . . . ," he heard Barrie saying.

"Stay back," cautioned the chronologist.

Liam sank into the shadow. Soon Jordy and Kyla returned from another corridor and escorted Liam and Phoebe out.

Liam and Phoebe watched as Captain Barrie stood alone in the domed room. He had moved over to the collection of floating spheres, rotating them this way and that. He paused, turning toward the view of the eerie green nebula, the curved, hulking shadows of the Dark Star arms. There was a rumble through the walls, probably the ship with Liam and Phoebe in it returning to the *Artemis*. Barrie produced what looked like a small paper notebook. He flipped through it, ran his finger along a page, then strode out of the room through a passageway in the far corner.

Once he was gone, the three crept out into the domed space.

"Can you find out where the hangar is located?" Phoebe asked.

"I believe so. First there is something I'd like to study a bit more closely." The chronologist moved into the center of the space, surrounded by the floating universe bubbles, and held up his orange crystal. He aimed it at one map, then another, consulted it again. "I think I understand how this works." He made a wide, swiping motion, and the maps filled the dome above them. The chronologist gazed upward, waving his crystal in one direction, then the other. "Fascinating."

"Is it weird to you that this machine made us?" Liam asked. "Made you?"

"The question of how our universe came to be has never been of particular relevance to us. After all, it has little bearing on how we actually live. What is more of a cause for concern is that none of my colleagues, nor I, had any idea that this place existed, nor in fact that its existence was even possible. We have all seen forward and backward in time; indeed, many of us have traveled to the beginning and the probable end of the universe. In all that study, there has been no mention of this machine whatsoever. And yet there is something even more curious than that. . . ."

"What?"

The chronologist consulted his crystal again. "Since my arrival, my future has ceased to be visible to me. That is unprecedented. I do not know how it can be possible."

"Iris told me"—Liam caught Phoebe eyeing him—"I mean, Dark Star's mainframe said it's because as she powers up, her systems create interference. Do you think that's it?"

"I am not sure."

"You saw the future of our families, back at Centauri," said Phoebe.

"Yes, I can still perceive the future in our universe. It is only my specific view of any future that pertains to this place or those of us who are here that I cannot see." The chronologist consulted his crystal for a long moment, its orange light flashing in his pearlescent eyes. "I will need to collect more information," he finally said, and lifted his gaze to the maps.

Liam suspected that his pause said something as well, but he wasn't sure what. "What are you looking for in those?" he asked instead.

"I'm studying the coding," said the chronologist, "in order to ascertain what Dark Star might be working toward." A section of the map blinked and changed into a square of streaming symbols. "Okay," said the chronologist, "here is something: Dark Star is currently running a routine called 'Operation Forty-Eight.' It's a base function of the system, but it has recently become the primary task, using a majority of processing power. It seems to have been reprioritized when . . . well, exactly when you two arrived."

"What is it?" Phoebe asked.

The chronologist tapped the crystal, aimed it at the code, then frowned. "I cannot access those logs. Has it said anything to you about this, Liam?"

"Not really," he said. "Just that she has something she's going to show us when it's ready." *Something she can't wait to share.* "She said it would allow me to see my future again."

"Whatever Operation Forty-Eight is, it's seventy-one percent complete."

"Can we look for a ship now?" said Phoebe. "Unlike you two, none of this is making me feel any better about staying here."

"Yes." The chronologist brought his hands together, and the map of universes shrank down to a ring around him. He continued peering at the bubble that represented their universe.

"What?" said Liam.

"It is another curiosity: this portal has been in our

universe for billions of years—I would guess since its very beginning—and yet my colleagues and I did not notice its presence until just recently—indeed, until you two found it. Nor had we seen it in our futures; in fact, just as I cannot see forward from here, I never saw any of these moments we are currently experiencing. And then, when we found the portal, we came to the conclusion that we could not pass through it, and yet here I am. These sorts of perceptive errors are not normal for us, especially when it comes to something as big, and as threatening to the universe, as this. It's almost as if the portal, and by extension this place, were somehow hidden in plain sight. I do not know how this could be. Perhaps because our four-dimensional perception is based on the physical laws of our universe, it doesn't extend into others, including the one we're in now. But these moments I am experiencing, as well as the ones I will soon experience, are still a part of *my* timeline, and I should therefore be able to view them." The chronologist seemed to laugh to himself.

"What?" said Phoebe.

"I was just theorizing that this current state, where I am unable to perceive my future, is the normal operating condition for beings like yourself."

"So?"

"We have always observed the behaviors of three-dimensional beings with a certain amount of bemusement, and yet I understand now; it's rather terrifying."

"Welcome to our world," said Liam.

"Ships," said Phoebe. "Come on, you guys."

"You're not curious about this place?" Liam asked, feeling a surprising flash of annoyance at her. "Even a little?"

"Of course I am, but you know what I feel even more than that? Scared. And I don't just mean of this place: Every minute we stay here is making our families that much farther away."

The chronologist closed the ring of universes and returned to the control spheres. He tapped here and there, holographic rectangles of information appearing and winking out. "The hangar is twenty-four levels down," he reported. "Captain Barrie is there."

"How do you know that?"

"I mapped his bioelectrical data when he was transporting me here. And—oh, very interesting: It appears that the captain is not alone. There are more bioelectrical signatures in his vicinity, possibly lifeforms."

"Who are they?" Liam asked.

"It is hard to characterize. The signatures are behaving strangely. It's possible I am misidentifying some sort of Dark Star technology, but whatever it is, the signal is incredibly strong." The chronologist closed the holographic windows and consulted his orange crystal. "I have mapped the route. This way." He strode toward the corridor through which Barrie had left.

The panels beneath their feet lit their way sequentially as they walked. They made a series of turns, the chronologist interpreting the glow from his crystal at each intersection, until they reached a hallway whose walls ballooned with clear cylindrical doors.

"These appear to be elevators," said the chronologist.

"I don't see any buttons or anything," said Phoebe.

"Perhaps they require—"

The door closest to Liam slid open.

"Did your friend do that?" asked Phoebe.

"I don't know." Liam's nerves ramped up, his heart beating faster.

"It could simply be a motion detector of some sort," said the chronologist, and yet Liam felt nearly certain that Iris had an eye on them.

The three stepped to the threshold of the door. There was no elevator car; indeed, the walls were completely smooth, no cables, wires, or magnet tracks like an elevator on a starliner or Mars. Only a shaft dropping into bottomless darkness, lit by narrow bands of light that made semicircles around the inner circumference. As Liam peered into it, he felt an odd lightening in his head, and then his hands and feet.

The chronologist reached out into the space with two of his feet. "The shaft appears to be gravity neutral." He stepped out completely and floated there in midair, bouncing lightly.

Liam held his breath and stepped out into the abyss, feeling his foot, then his leg, lightening, and then he floated out into the space. One glance past his feet, in the dim void, made his stomach lurch with fear, and yet he seemed to be suspended there safely.

Phoebe gazed down the shaft. "If Dark Star wanted to get rid of us, this would be an easy way to do it."

The chronologist scanned the wall beside the shaft. "The system is analyzing our composition and compensating the gravity field accordingly."

"You guys better be right about this." Phoebe stepped in, her eyes widening as the gravity lightened around her.

They pushed off the walls and oriented themselves so that they were facing the door, as you would in a normal elevator. Nothing happened.

"Now what?" said Phoebe.

"We'd like to go to the hangar?" Liam said to the walls. He checked with the chronologist. "Level . . ."

"If this is level one, we would like to go to the twenty-fourth level down from here."

A ring of white light lit up around them. Liam felt a tugging inside him and they began to move, not quite falling, but lowering gently down the tube. More rings lit sequentially as they descended, as if indicating each level.

"Whoo," said Phoebe, her arms out for balance. "Okay, this is cool."

They passed clear rounded doors, one after another, until finally the rings stopped illuminating, gravity lightened again, and they slowed to a hover. The door in front of them slid open and they stepped out onto the solid metal floor in a short corridor lit once again by whichever floor panels they were standing on.

"This way," said the chronologist. The corridor led them a short distance and then opened up into a vast room, hundreds of meters across, with a high, cavernous ceiling and curved walls. There was still only the light from the floor where they stood, but there was also a dim glow in the far distance.

All around them were the silhouettes of ships.

There were rows and rows of models like the one Kyla had piloted, hundreds of them. Their glimmering black surfaces reminded Liam of the muscovite sheets they would find in the lava tubes back on Mars: reflective, but also with an oily sheen. There were other, larger craft, made of that same material, as well as needle-shaped vessels with a cabin for a single passenger at their center.

"Who are all these ships for?" Phoebe asked as they started down one of the rows. She stopped beside the nearest glassy ship like they'd traveled in. "One of these should work." She pressed the panel beside the door, as she'd seen Kyla do, but nothing happened. "How do we get in?"

"No idea," said Liam.

"We'd like to go in this ship!" Phoebe shouted up toward the distant ceiling. "You try," she said to Liam. "You're the one she likes so much." When Liam didn't move, Phoebe added, "No, I'm serious, ask her."

"She said she wasn't going to be around for a while."

Phoebe frowned at him. Liam pushed back, but again Iris wasn't there. And maybe that caused a brief flash of relief. *If she has something to show me, how will she feel about me leaving?* And another thought followed that: *Do I really want to go?*

"Try the door, then," Phoebe urged. "Maybe you have the magic touch."

Liam felt his heart beating faster. He put his hand against the round panel, held it there, but the ship didn't respond.

"Okay, let's try the next one."

That ship didn't open, nor did the next one in the line.

"If you don't mind," said the chronologist, "I believe we should investigate that." He pointed down the rows of ships, toward the center of the hangar. Liam could just barely make out a great structure ahead in the gloom. It seemed to have smooth metal walls: a massive cylinder, oriented vertically and extending from the ceiling high above down through the floor.

"What is it?" Phoebe asked.

"As best I can tell, that cylinder is where the captain is. It is also the source of the bioelectric readings."

"Okay, you guys take a look at that while I check more ships," said Phoebe. She moved off to the other side of the row.

Liam walked beside the chronologist. They passed silently down the long row, the panels lighting beneath their feet. As they approached, the cylindrical object's full size began to sink in. It was a couple hundred meters in diameter, and its metal had a faint glow to it. A railing encircled it, and Liam saw that there was a gap between the hangar floor and the side of the cylinder. A narrow catwalk crossed the space to an oval impression of a door.

They reached the railing and Liam peered over. The cylinder stretched down many more decks, hundreds of meters, and beneath it, far below, there seemed to be no floor, just a buzzing energy field. Beyond that was the utter darkness of the black hole beneath the ship, only visible by the streaks of light that briefly flashed around its perimeter.

The chronologist held up his crystal, scanning the cylinder.

"No luck," said Phoebe, joining them. "I tried like twenty ships. None of them will open. Maybe there's a control panel around or something."

"We can look," said Liam. He watched the chronologist studying his crystal. "Are there people—or life-forms in there?" said Liam. "Do you think it's the Architects?"

"None of my additional scans can penetrate this material," he said, motioning to the cylinder wall. "Nor can I identify the alloy. Not only is it unlike anything in our universe, but its atomic structure is also unlike anything that the physical laws of *this* universe should allow for."

"Like, it's from somewhere else?"

"Perhaps."

"Does that mean it's not even a part of Dark Star?"

"I cannot be certain, it—"

Just then, the door slid open. Captain Barrie emerged, walking briskly and talking into his link. "Okay, I'm in a better location. Repeat that last part—Kyla? Can you hear me?"

Liam turned to duck out of sight but there was no cover and Barrie saw them immediately. His eyes widened in surprise, and Liam expected him to explode in anger—

But he smiled. "Well, well, look at the three of you!" He glanced at his link. "I sent you away not even . . . thirty minutes ago, and yet here you are." He nodded to himself as he stepped from the catwalk to the hangar floor. "I suppose this only supports why I brought you here. Find anything interesting?"

"We, um, not really," said Liam. He'd expected Barrie to be angry. Hadn't he raised his voice about insubordination before? "What's inside there?" Liam asked, pointing to the cylinder.

"Good question," said Barrie. "I—"

His link flashed. "Sir, are you there?"

Barrie held a finger up to Liam, Phoebe, and the chronologist. "I'm here. Go ahead."

"It's the fuel drones, sir," said Kyla. "They're returning through the portal, but we're picking up an unidentified craft with them."

"Unidentified?" said Barrie. "Have you scanned—"

A great rumble reverberated through the floors, far more severe than the earlier ones from Dark Star's systems. All of them stumbled for a moment, Liam and Phoebe grabbing the railing to steady themselves.

"What was that?" Barrie shouted.

"The bogey shot down one of the fuel ships!" Kyla replied. "It crashed into Dark Star!"

"Shoot it down!" shouted Barrie.

"Captain, the *Artemis*'s defense systems are offline except for the nukes, but we can't risk detonating a warhead by Dark Star, not to mention that black hole. We have no idea what would happen."

Another rumble shook the floor. Somewhere above: a screech of twisting metal. Liam shared a wide-eyed glance with Phoebe.

"Who are they?" Barrie demanded.

"Scans of the ship are coming back inconclusive," said Kyla. "I don't know what that thing is, but we've never seen anything like it."

"Scramble cruisers, then!"

"The way this thing moves, sir, I don't know if we'd stand a chance."

Barrie broke into a run. "I'm on my way back up to the control room. Dark Star must have some defenses."

Liam watched him go, stunned. "Do you know who it is?" he asked the chronologist.

The chronologist made a sighing sort of sound through his two noses and shook his head. "As I told you, the future has been obscured for me. I can't believe this is how you go through your existence."

Another explosion rumbled through the deck.

"We should probably follow him," said Phoebe, striding back toward the elevators. "Does Iris know what's going on?" she said as Liam caught up beside her. "She must not like being attacked, right?"

Liam pushed himself back, but once again, Iris was nowhere to be seen and didn't reply when he called to her. "She's still not responding," he said. "Should we follow the captain, or—"

But Phoebe had stopped suddenly. "Liam! Look!" She pointed at his chest.

Liam saw a faint green light flashing beneath his shirt. His heart tripped over itself and he fumbled to pull the silver chain around his neck, revealing the beacon, the little green light blinking over and over.

Liam pressed it, and it blinked again. He jammed his thumb against it three times and it kept blinking at him.

He met Phoebe's gaze. "An unidentified ship . . . ," she said, eyes trembling.

"They found us," said Liam, his throat getting tight. Was it really possible?

But Phoebe was already sprinting after the captain. "Wait!" she called. "We know who it is!"

Barrie paused at the elevator, and he turned around. "What are you talking about?"

"The ship!" said Liam breathlessly as they reached him. "I think my sister is on it!"

Barrie cocked his head and made a puzzled expression. "Come with me, then."

Liam looked behind them. "Where's the chronologist?"

"I think he's back at that cylinder," said Phoebe. "Come on, he'll catch up."

Liam and Phoebe stepped into the elevator beside Barrie, hovering in the low-gravity field.

"Control room level," said Barrie, and they began to rise. "Kyla, what's the status of that ship?"

"It's broken off its attack and is hovering at a distance, sir. I'd guess it was scanning us, but we're not picking up any of the usual signals."

Liam couldn't remember any of the tap code sequences, so he just kept pressing his beacon, watching through wet eyes as it blinked back.

They reached the main floor and raced back to the control room, where Barrie swiped at the spherical controls. Out across the surface of Dark Star, two different spots flashed and spiked with bolts of green energy—the crashed fuel ships. Beyond that, the rest of the fuel fleet was settling into their racks and lowering themselves out of sight. Wings were extended out of their teardrop-shaped bodies, glowing bright green with harvested energy.

"Sir," said Kyla, "we're being hailed over local link."

And now the ship swooped over the dome so close that they could see it. Large and oblong, made of brilliant silver metal.

"It's them," said Phoebe, her eyes welling up.

"Sir, she says she's Lana Saunders-Chang of the *ISA Scorpius*. They're requesting permission to board."

Barrie looked at Liam and Phoebe.

"Our parents," said Liam, his eyes brimming, too. Phoebe's hand slipped into his and squeezed tightly.

Barrie's expression remained grim. "Tell them to land here on Dark Star. And then I want you and the other officers to join us."

As Liam watched the sleek ship hover and begin to lower itself toward the landing area, he caught a glimmer in the corner of his eye.

You're welcome, said Iris.

11

As the door in the side of the Styrlax ship slid open and a set of stairs lowered, Liam thought he might explode inside. He and Phoebe and Captain Barrie stood on the landing platform. Liam kept tapping the beacon with his thumb, as if that was somehow making this real, keeping it from being a dream or a hallucination.

It's real, Iris said from nearby.

It made him smile and yet somehow made the shaking inside him worse, the glare of the fireball of Centauri A still behind his eyes. Why now? It was like any feeling he had that went too far in either direction, good or bad, could set off that vision in his head. He hovered ever so slightly back from the moment, where the feeling was less intense.

Did you know this would happen? he asked Iris.

Once we moved the timing of the supernova to allow for your families' survival, this became the most probable future.

Why didn't you tell me?

Probable is not definite. And I know how important they are to you. I did not want to get your hopes up. Also this way, it's a nice surprise, yes?

Well, yeah. Liam thought to say that he still might have liked the heads-up. He could have handled the uncertainty, couldn't he? Then again, his nerves had been frayed enough already. *Is this what you wanted to show me?*

He sensed Iris smiling. *This is just the beginning.*

Liam felt a tinge of frustration. *What is—*

"Phoebe!"

The stairs had finished lowering from the side of the Styrlax ship, and Ariana had appeared first in the doorway. Her skin was Telphon lavender, her bristles darker than Phoebe's, her hair pale pink and also in a braid. She wore charcoal-colored pants and a long-sleeved shirt that were made of a semireflective material that glinted in the light as she moved, and high boots. She strode down the steps, followed by Phoebe's father, Paolo, who wore similar clothing. Those probably weren't their real names, Liam realized. Ariana had that stern, tight-lipped expression Liam had always known, and yet as she neared Phoebe, who stood with her arms crossed, trembling, Ariana's face began to crack as well, tears appearing, and she wrapped her daughter in a hug.

"We should have listened," Liam heard Ariana say.

Paolo put his hands on both their shoulders, leaning his chin on Phoebe's head. "We thought we lost you."

"Liam!"

There was Mina, racing down the steps of the ship, pushing her black bangs out of her eyes, holding up the beacon with the other hand. Liam was still holding his, and when he pressed it now, Mina's blinked instantaneously, no longer any distance between them. As Mina neared, Liam bounced on his feet, and finally, finally, she slammed into him and hugged him and lifted him momentarily off the ground. Her hair had that smell he remembered since Mars, sweet and supposedly like Earth coconuts. Her cheek was wet against his.

She pushed him back and held him at arm's length. "Jerk!" She hugged him again, laughing.

"I'm glad you're here," he croaked, tears in his eyes.

"No thanks to you," Mina said. "Trying to get rid of us so you could have this alternate alien universe business all to yourself."

"That's not what—"

"Duh, I'm kidding." She ruffled his hair.

"Where are Mom and Dad?"

"Inside. They're still recovering from stasis, so moving a little slow. Want to go see them?"

Liam nodded but eyed the Styrlax ship. "How did you get here?"

"After I saw you on the *Scorpius*—you still have to explain that, by the way . . ." Mina lowered her voice conspiratorially and explained how they had chased down Phoebe's parents and agreed to work together. "We got clear of the supernova and that rifting you were talking about, and waited until we saw those weird ships show up, and then we followed them back to the doorway." She rubbed her head and glanced toward the portal in the distance. "It was weird going through that thing. Time got all messed up. . . . I think I saw myself as an old lady? Is that possible?"

"Pretty much anything is possible with the portal," said Liam. "So it's safe, with the Telphons?"

"It's not exactly chummy, but we have sort of a truce, to find you guys and I guess now to figure out what this is." She motioned to their surroundings.

"It's called Dark Star. It's what blew up our sun and Centauri A."

Min frowned. "Wow, okay . . ." She tugged his arm. "Come see Mom and Dad."

Liam let himself be pulled, let a grin slip across his face, but he also caught Phoebe's eye; she was in her own quiet conversation with her parents. What were they talking about? How was she feeling? They'd both wanted this for so long, and yet now that they were reunited with their families, Liam couldn't help but feel like they were on opposite sides of a chasm.

He stumbled on the stairs.

"Dude, be careful," said Mina. "It would be pretty silly if you traveled through a time portal to an alternate universe and then cracked your head open tripping up a staircase."

"Sorry." Liam bounded up the remaining steps and into the sleek insides of the craft. A sphere of orange crystal floated in the center of the main room, surrounded by a circular railing that held dozens of control panels. Liam paused when he saw Barro and Tarra standing on the far side of the crystal, along with nine other Telphons. They gazed at him, bristled faces and human-looking eyes, and Liam felt a surge of emotion: Was it fear, or anger, or both? It was all he could do to avert his eyes and follow Mina around the crystal and into the cockpit area.

Mom and Dad were sitting in two of the chairs there, and when Liam appeared, their eyes lit up. Mom pushed herself to her feet, a hand on the chair for support.

"Honey," she said.

"Mom." Liam threw himself against her, felt her breathing. In the glimpse before he'd hugged her, he'd noticed the pinkish burn marks still on her face from the accident on Mars, and now he could feel her trembling slightly, maybe aftereffects of the decades in stasis. She rubbed his back like she used to, and had it been a matter of days, or a matter of decades, since that morning on Mars, on the balcony before they'd left their apartment forever? Somehow it felt like both.

Liam pulled away and Dad put a hand on his shoulder. He was using a metal crutch under one arm. Liam hugged him, felt his bristly chin against his head.

"You guys are doing all right?" said Liam. Mom, Dad, Mina, here they all were, together.

Mom shrugged, wincing as she did. "Mostly? We

both have some lingering nerve damage, and we're on a pretty rigorous treatment of antiradiation meds. But yes. Thanks to you, my darling boy, here we are." She rubbed his back again.

"You saved us," said Dad, looking at Liam with pride, tears in his eyes.

"Well . . ." Liam felt his face reddening. "I—"

"You saved us all," said Mom. "Humanity might be lost if it wasn't for you."

"Not bad, little brother," said Mina.

"I, um, got pretty lucky, a lot of times," said Liam. He found himself shaking. For as real and danger-ous as it had all felt in the moment, it was like he was acknowledging some extra level of it now . . . some additional amount of fear that he'd kept locked tightly inside, finally spilling loose. His breath hitched and he sobbed.

Mom put her arms around him again. "You were so very brave."

Liam thought that, through all that had hap-pened, he'd never felt brave, not really. Just terrified, and panicked, and worried. "If it wasn't for Phoebe, I never would have made it."

Mom pulled away, and Liam thought he saw a shadow cross her face, but just then another voice spoke up:

"I calculate that I played some small part in all of this."

"JEFF!" Liam ducked past his parents and saw JEFF's panda head lying on one of the seats. "Oh man, what happened?"

"I have been upgraded to travel size. HA HA HA."

"Nice one."

"Liam," said Mom. "Phoebe and her parents . . . this is all very complicated."

"Phoebe's not our enemy," Liam said quickly. His nerves flared, the spinny feeling returning, so familiar now, he wasn't sure whether it was fear or frustration or something else. "She risked her life to save me, to save everyone on the starliners. And her parents must have come around too if they're here with you, right? Mina said you have a truce."

"We do," said Dad, his face hardening. "But I don't think we can be so sure of their intentions. The things they've done . . . They almost killed you and your mother and me on Mars."

"Phoebe said they weren't trying to blow up the lab."

"They may not have been," said Dad. He crossed his arms, not quite looking at Liam as he spoke. "But when your mom and I uncovered evidence of their plans to steal the data and confronted them, they set the reactors to malfunction. Maybe they were hoping it would just be a distraction to allow them to escape . . ."

"But it killed Marco, and Mara and Idris," said Mom, "and the Telphons murdered tens of thousands of people when they attacked the *Scorpius*—"

"And we murdered almost their entire species," said Liam.

"Not murder," said Mom. "We didn't know—"

"They said you ordered the Phase One launch." Liam's heart raced as the words came out. He turned to Dad. "That you gave the order. That you knew there might be life there, and you did it anyway."

He watched his father's face, and when Dad's brow scrunched and his eyes shifted away for a moment, the knot in Liam's stomach tightened. "There was some data," said Dad, "that indicated the potential for complex life-forms, but it was inconclusive. A couple team members thought we should do more studies, gather more information, but . . . you have to understand the time pressure we were under. We knew that Aaru would need at least a century to recover from the Phase One impact, in order to be ready for us to implement Phase Two upon our arrival. The whole colonization plan was on such a tight timeline. We just—"

"We didn't have a choice," said Mom, her eyes steely and wet. "We couldn't risk it, Liam. All of humanity, the future of our species . . . it was our only chance—you know that. We couldn't travel halfway across the galaxy only to be wiped out by some virus or microbial life-form."

"It wasn't some virus," said Liam. "There was an entire race of people."

"But we couldn't have—"

"I've been there," Liam interrupted.

"Where?" said Dad. "You mean . . . Aaru?"

"Telos. That's what they called it. They had houses and streets and playgrounds. Phoebe had a little brother. We destroyed it *all*. And then we were going to build a new home on their ashes."

"Yes, we've heard their side of it," said Dad.

"So you can understand—"

"What we understand," said Mom, "is that there is a difference between making a mistake in a desperate moment and intentionally seeking out an entire race of people to exterminate, as they did. We were trying to survive. What's their motive? Vengeance? They could have come to us. Told us who they were, what had happened."

"Would we have listened?" said Liam. "Or would we have finished the job, so that there was no delay

248

with the Phase Two *time line*."

"Okay. I—" Mom began, then looked away. "Look, we could go back and forth about this, but the reality is we'll never know, will we? What's done is done."

Footsteps sounded and Tarra appeared in the cockpit. "Everyone's gathering."

Dad nodded, not quite meeting her gaze. "We'll make our way down. Please just give us a couple minutes."

Tarra ducked out without a reply.

"Liam," said Dad, "that's the *Artemis* out there, isn't it? The prototype starliner? How did they get here? What is this place?"

Liam explained about the *Artemis* and the doorway, and what he knew about Dark Star.

"This thing created our universe?" Mina interrupted.

"And a bunch of others," said Liam.

"So, like, we're just bugs in a petri dish?" said Mina.

"I don't know." Liam had been imagining their universe more as an aquarium, on a shelf next to other aquariums, like in their science lab back on Mars. He explained how it hadn't been Barrie's fault, or his crew's, that their sun had blown up, and he told them about the chronologist, and described his journey through space and time as best he could. Mom's and Dad's eyes met a couple times while he was talking, and Liam could sense their apprehension at everything he was saying.

"That is a lot to sort through," said Dad. "But you think Captain Barrie is all right?"

"I think so?" said Liam. "He's been trying to figure out exactly why this place is blowing up stars, and whether or not it's a bigger threat. And they're still repairing the *Artemis.* . . ."

"But . . ." Mom finished for him. "Is there something else?"

"It's just, some of the things he's said are odd. When I first met him, on Mars—"

"He was on Mars?"

"No, not exactly, it was a time-travel thing; I was using the watch I told you about. He called himself part of the Drove, made it sound like he was an enemy, sort of. He invited me to come here, and said it was safe, that I could bring you guys, that we didn't have to die back there on Mars. Except then, here, he says that he didn't want to send a message to the rest of the fleet because this place is too dangerous." Liam shook his head. "I'm not sure his officers totally trust him, either."

"He's probably been under incredible stress," Dad

reasoned, "with his entire crew trapped here, and with the knowledge of what this station has done, even if he was powerless to stop it."

"Maybe." Liam thought of Barrie emerging from that strange cylinder down in the hangar. "But I think he might know more about Dark Star than he's told us."

"Well, we'll keep a careful eye on him. Speaking of which, we should go down there."

"And you're okay?" said Mom, taking Liam by the shoulders. "These things that have happened to you, with time . . ."

"I'm fine, Mom." Yet saying those words also caused a chill, and Liam wondered if he was.

They all stood there, in thought, for a moment. Liam had said those things about Barrie, and yet *he* also knew more about this place than he had shared. He could just imagine their worried reaction if he tried to explain about Iris. . . .

Dad put his free arm around Mom and they began to hobble out of the cockpit.

Mina slid out of their way and watched them go. "All of this is so nuts," she said quietly.

"Yeah . . . Here." Liam pulled the beacon necklace over his head and handed it back to her. "I was only supposed to have this for the day. You can give it to

Arlo. You said you'd pummel me if— What?"

Mina wiped tears from her eyes. "Arlo died at Delphi."

"Oh no," said Liam. "I'm sorry." He hugged her, and she hugged him back tighter than she ever had, and cried against his shoulder in deep, hitching sobs. He'd never heard her like this before. "It's okay," he said, his own eyes welling up.

Mina shook her head against him. "It's not." She pulled away. "These Telphons . . . I know we're working together, but they killed him, and so many others. And we still need their planet. How exactly is this going to work?"

Liam hadn't really thought that far ahead. Or maybe he had. "We'll probably have to find another place to go," he said. "Telos—I mean, Aaru—was their home."

Mina pulled away, her face darkening. "But you heard Mom and Dad: What we did was an accident. What they did was murder. If you think we're just going to give them Aaru-5 and risk dying in the cold of space while we try to find another home—"

"But then they'll be in the same danger."

"Well, there are eleven billion of us and like ten of them, so . . ."

"Two hundred and forty, actually. Most of them

are on another ship near Telos."

"You mean Aaru. Either way, same difference."

"But—"

"Can we not talk about this now?" said Mina. "I know you've been having all kinds of adventures, and you have your crush on Phoebe—"

"I—"

"But my actual boyfriend died like two days ago, and I've nearly been killed five times, too. Do you know what it's like, having your stasis pod shot out into space and wondering if you'll ever be found?"

"No." Except Liam thought that actually, he knew quite a bit about such a feeling, but he couldn't say it because suddenly he was just a little brother again. He hadn't expected Mina to be saying any of these things, or that finally reuniting with his family would make everything feel more complicated. Was Phoebe feeling this way, too?

"Come on." Mina started out of the cockpit. "We don't want to miss the big confrontation."

"May I come along?" JEFF asked.

"Sure." Liam scooped up JEFF's head. It was heavier than he'd expected, but he got it under one arm, resting on his hip. "You will definitely want to see this place."

"My sensors are picking up an incredible amount

of information encoded as energy in the air, indicative of a quite advanced AI."

"Yeah. Wait until you meet her."

"Her?" said Mina.

Liam glanced at her and for a moment actually wished she wasn't around. He would have loved to tell JEFF all about Iris and see what he thought. Funny that the family member he felt most comfortable sharing with right now was a bot. "Sorry. I meant *it*."

Liam fell into step behind Mina. They exited the Styrlax ship and caught up with Mom and Dad as they made their way into Dark Star, to the control room.

Barrie stood in the center of the room, with the universe bubbles drifting in a ring around him. Liam, Mina, and their parents joined Jordy and Kyla and ten other officers from the *Artemis*. Phoebe and her parents, Barro, Tarra, and the nine other members of the Telphon team stood together in their own separate group. The two factions were maybe ten meters apart, far enough that when they spoke quietly to one another, their words were indistinct. All of them were intermittently gazing from the captain and the maps to the wide view of the nebula and the shadowy arms of Dark Star. The chronologist stood off on his own, behind Barrie. His back was half turned to them, and he gazed out at the empty nebula.

"So," said Barrie. "Here you all are." He put his hands out into one of the bubbles as it drifted by and then threw them up and outward, enlarging the map overhead. "This is our universe," he said, pointing to the brightest, closest bubble. "As you can see, Dark Star is connected to it by this portal"—he indicated a blinking dot—"which it can move in space-time in order to gather fuel from stars like our sun. Our universe is one of three that Dark Star categorizes as 'active,' and it is the newest, or youngest one." Barrie explained how the *Artemis* had arrived here, how their presence had seemed to awaken Dark Star, and how so far, they had been unable to stop it from refueling itself. "My team has been investigating the portal mechanism, in an effort to try to gain control of it, but so far Dark Star's technology remains indecipherable to us."

"And you don't know why it's refueling?" Liam's mom asked. "What its true aim is?"

"No."

"Dark Star is running some sort of computational process called Operation Forty-Eight," said the chronologist, still peering out into the nebula. "That process is nearly ninety-five percent complete."

Barrie turned to him, brow furrowed. "Where did you learn about this?"

"In the Dark Star logs," said the chronologist, waving a hand absently toward the control spheres over by the platform.

"Captain," said Liam's dad. "Pardon me, but I'm a little confused. Why didn't you get a message back to us as soon as you arrived? You must know that you and your crew have been presumed dead for decades."

Barrie ran a hand through his hair. "I know. You have to understand how fast all this has happened for us." He recounted their last two weeks, powering up the station, discovering the sun had been targeted, his worry about what dangers this place might still pose.

"Of course," said Dad, "but we at least could have known you were alive. . . ."

Liam saw Kyla and Jordy share a look. The other officers from the *Artemis* were exchanging glances as well.

"Yes, well, if I had it to do over again, of course that makes perfect sense."

Liam saw his dad open his mouth as if to say more, but he didn't. Liam wondered about aspects of Barrie's story that hadn't occurred to him before: Even if they were busy repairing the *Artemis* and studying Dark Star, there were still thousands of passengers in stasis lockdown on the *Artemis*. Couldn't some of them have been awakened to take charge of sending some kind of message to the fleet? Even if that message was simply *We're alive, but stay away*? It also occurred to Liam that Barrie had failed to mention the metal suit.

"Okay," said Mom. "So now what?"

"I think we continue to investigate," said Barrie. "Perhaps you can help us—"

"Hold on," said Ariana. "Am I missing something? Wouldn't a better solution be to fly back through to our universe the very next time that portal reopens, and then blow up the portal? That would sever the connection to our universe and presumably end any threat that this station might pose."

"Well," said Barrie, "it seems entirely likely that Dark Star could simply construct a new portal. Not to mention that attacking it might make it view us as a threat."

Liam had thought he might say: *anger it.*

"What if such a course of action," Barrie added, "caused Dark Star to determine that our universe was no longer viable, and decide to simply *end* it?"

"Can it do that?" Mom asked.

"The only thing I'm sure of is that the capabilities of this station go far beyond our comprehension."

"Well then," said Ariana, "what about shooting a barrage of missiles *through* the portal? Destroy it altogether."

Liam felt his pulse increase. He wondered if Iris was listening to this conversation, and felt certain that she was.

"Is that always your answer?" said Liam's mom, glaring at Ariana. "Shoot first?"

"Excuse me?" said Ariana. "Do you even hear yourself right now?"

"That's not the same," said Dad.

"You—"

"Everyone hold on a minute," said Barrie, putting out his hands. "We cannot just blow up this station. Never mind the multiverse damage that its destruction might cause; this place is the most significant discovery in scientific history, in the history of our whole *universe*. Think of what it can teach us, not only about our universe, our reality, but about our very existence."

Liam saw Ariana leaning over and whispering in Paolo's ear. In turn, Paolo consulted with Tarra and the other Telphons. Liam caught Phoebe's eye, standing between her parents. Phoebe shook her head lightly.

Paolo addressed the group. "Thank you for the briefing, Captain. It looks as if you have this situation in hand as much as it could be."

"I think that's pretty far from certain at this point," said Mom.

"Nevertheless," said Paolo, "we feel it is best if we depart at this time."

"The portal is closed," Kyla reminded them.

"We will retreat to a safe position and wait for it to reopen." Paolo looked specifically at Liam and his family. "If you would like to accompany us, we will return you within range of the *Scorpius*."

"And what exactly happens then?" said Mom.

"We are grateful to you for helping us find Phoebe," said Ariana. "It is a credit to you, and a gesture we will not forget."

"That's not an answer," said Mom. "How do we know you're not just going to turn around and start attacking us again?"

"I could give you my word," said Tarra, "but how can you in good conscience question our motives or our actions? Our home, our way of life, our families were all taken from us by you. None of what is happening here changes the fact that you are marching toward our former home, nor the fact that we must find a home."

"But I don't understand," said Dad. "You know we regret what happened on Aaru—"

"Telos," said Ariana.

"Sorry. We would take it back if we could—"

"Maybe you personally would. But I have a hard

time believing that of humanity as a whole."

"Well," said Dad, "but my point is you're still choosing to attack us. We just want to get to our new home. I'm sorry that we displaced you, but you have a small group and an extremely fast ship. Would it not be far easier for you to find a new home suitable for yourselves than for us? Why not concentrate on that, instead of this war of retribution?"

The Telphons grumbled angrily to one another. Liam saw Ariana's hands clench into fists, her eyes narrowing in fury.

"Retribution?" She pointed at Liam's parents. "That's really all you think this is? You seem to forget that I was there, by your side, for the Phase Two trials. Remember, the ones that took you years longer than you thought? Did you ever notice that some of the biggest breakthroughs in that data came from us? Obviously you couldn't have known that we understood Telos's climatic and atmospheric conditions far better than you ever could."

"And yet you were only *helping* us perfect Phase Two so that you could steal the data and use it for yourselves," said Mom.

"If you'd been through anything like we've been through, you would realize how simpleminded that thinking is." Ariana reached into her pocket and held up the very data key that Mom had given to Liam back on Mars, and that Tarra had taken from him on the *Scorpius*. "Yes, we wanted this data for ourselves. And yes, we were even developing alternate data in secret, how to adapt your version to fit our needs. But we also know what you know about Phase Two: That even with those final successful trials, there's still a significant margin of error, isn't there? That there are so many variables in any terraforming project. And so there is still a very real chance that despite your best efforts, Phase Two won't work well enough to truly make Aaru-5 viable for humanity. And then what?"

"We would—"

Ariana didn't let Mom finish. "Then you would turn your whole violent, desperate race in a different direction, toward a different planet, and you'd raze that one, and another one after that if necessary. *This* is why we attack you. Sure, we long for you to know the same suffering that we have felt, but make no mistake: this war is about self-defense. This space station is blowing up yellow stars. So what? We don't even need that type of star. But we still need a viable planet, a safe planet, and for the Telphons, the biggest known threat in the universe is you."

"That's not who we are," said Mom.

"I've read your history books," said Ariana. "It is exactly who you are."

"You may have a fast ship," said Dad, "but there's no way you're realistically going to be able to take out our entire fleet. We have too much firepower—"

"You're proving my point," said Ariana.

Dad's gaze darkened like Liam had rarely seen it. "Well then, maybe we shouldn't even let you leave. Maybe this needs to end right here."

"Excuse me?"

"If you truly plan to attack our fleet, how can we possibly let you go? Isn't that right, Captain?"

Barrie watched all of this with a detached look on his face. Meanwhile, the Telphons closed ranks. Members of the *Artemis* crew began to draw their weapons, despite the uncertain looks on their faces. "Fall back to the ship," said Tarra, the Telphons moving toward the corridor.

"Wait! Stop!" Liam shouted. He found Phoebe, but her expression had hardened and she was moving with her people.

"Gerald . . . ," said Mom.

"Captain?" said Kyla. "Sir, what are our orders?"

But Barrie was no longer listening; he had turned his attention to the collection of floating lights over by the platform. Liam saw that a green light had begun to blink in one of the spheres.

"Fascinating," Liam heard the chronologist say.

All at once, Dark Star began to vibrate, throwing everyone off balance and emitting a hum that seemed to press against Liam's ears. Lights began to flash outside. Mom and Dad stumbled, Mina stepping over to grab Mom's arm.

"What is it?" Barrie said to the chronologist.

The chronologist had turned around from the window and was now facing the map of their universe, holding out his orange crystal. He found Liam in the crowd. "It appears that Operation Forty-Eight is complete."

At the same time, outside the dome, there was a series of bursts, like small fireworks, all in a tight formation far off beyond the end of one of the great shadowy arms. The lights grew almost blinding and a rectangular shape appeared, with silver circuitry around its edges. A pool of iridescent green light formed in the center, swirling and rippling.

A new portal. It towered over the arm of the machine, throwing the buildings there into stark relief.

Dark Star shook more intensely. Bolts of energy spidered across the surface of the dome. Liam worried the clear structure would start to crack, and they'd all be thrown into space. He thought he felt a lightening in his feet, and for a moment he flashed back to Mars, to the gravity failing as it so often had. And then there was the boiling Centauri star . . .

Mina gripped his arm. Her face had gone pale, her eyes wide. Liam swallowed hard.

Vibrating all around them, in their bones. Outside, the new portal grew brighter.

And then the light in the center died down, but the circuitry around the glowing doorway remained bright.

Now the map above them in the control room began to change. Their universe shrank down to the same size as the others, and a new light began to bloom. It began as a pinprick and exploded in size, growing to a marble, to a small balloon, and as it grew, it began to differentiate itself—not a solid sphere of light but rather thousands, millions, billions of pinpricks, all darting and swirling. The bubble continued to grow; it was half the size of those around it now, the light inside still multiplying and expanding but also now coalescing into spirals, globs, flowing shapes. *Galaxies*, Liam thought. The bubble neared the size of their universe, and the galaxies themselves danced around one another in strange arrangements, all the while more lights growing, now some of them popping in explosions of color, strange clouds of colored gas like paint smudges. The bubble enlarged to fill the space over their heads.

A moment later, it was complete.

"A new universe," said Barrie, his head cocked, face awash in its light. "Iteration 90. . . ."

He turned and looked out the dome. "That new portal must lead to it."

All at once the map of this new universe began to zoom in, shooting past clusters and galaxies and nebulae, giving Liam a sensation like he was falling into the map. The view closed in on one galaxy with spiral arms. Zoomed farther, millions of light-years per second, the tightly packed arms becoming jagged rivers of diamonds and rubies, then a field of stars, the space between stars becoming larger the closer they got, until they were looking at a map of maybe fifty stars, now twenty, now two . . .

Now one.

One pale yellow star with a field of objects around it, hundreds of smaller bodies in space, but eight main planets with telltale shapes: one with an enormous belt of rings, one on its side with a thin vertical ring, one larger than all the rest, with a great red spot.

"It looks like our solar system," said Mom.

"But it's not," said Barrie, "it can't be."

The map kept zooming: a scattering of asteroids,

a rust-red planet, and finally a single orb, blue and brown and white, swirls of clouds and rugged landforms and water.

Barrie tapped the image and data scrolled beside it. "That's impossible." He turned to the chronologist. "This is a new universe, isn't it?"

The chronologist held his crystal up toward the map. "By all indications, yes."

"What are we looking at?" said Mom, her voice shaking, as if she already had guessed.

"Atmosphere ninety-eight percent nitrogen," said Barrie, "liquid water, gravity factor one-point-oh . . ." He turned to the rest of the group. "It's Earth."

INTERLUDE

PLANET DESIGNATE: PHINEA
NORMA ARM SECTOR 12
57 TRILLION KM FROM THE CENTAURI SYSTEM

Just over six light-years from the Centauri system, in the northwest quadrant of the fourth planet orbiting a mellow red dwarf star, a white light began to blink. The light was on a device something like a phone, and its blinking caught the attention of the two young beings standing around it, shading their eyes from the afternoon heat.

"Is that her?" asked one of the beings, whose name was Morena.

"I think so," said the other, whose name was Leno and who was holding the device. "Dad!" he called over his shoulder. "I think we found her!"

His voice echoed through the maze of narrow, red-walled canyons, their sides striped with crimson. Here and there, large sections of the walls glimmered with plates of silver-and-lavender metallic ore.

"Coming!" Dad called distantly.

Leno started down the narrow, twisting path, following the signal. A cool breeze rushed across their faces. The sun had just set beyond the mountain ridges, and overhead, the sky had cooled to a bluish-lavender.

"Shouldn't we wait for him?" said Morena, falling into step behind him.

"He'll catch up. Besides, the show starts in half an hour."

"Why did she have to do this today?"

"I don't know," said Leno, although, being a few years older than his sister, he'd heard their parents grumbling about how Great-Grandma always got weird around Touchdown Day. But still, this was the biggest festival of the year! And the thermal energy show was amazing and it started just after sunset.

They wound their way down the dry canyon—Great-Grandma called these paths gulches, a word that wasn't even in their dictionary but which she'd picked up somewhere long ago. As they walked, the spiny rock walls on either side grew from chest height to a few meters over their heads. It was chilly here in the deeper shadows. Leno shivered and felt the thermal cells on the shoulders and back of his shirt humming to life as they switched from their solar collection mode to warming.

"Ah!" A clatter of rocks, a sharp hiss.

Leno spun to see Morena on her knees, coughing, a cloud of shimmering air beside her. "You've got to be careful!" he said, dragging her to her feet and away from the cloud.

"I didn't see it!"

She'd stepped on a bubble shell—a thin surface of rock that hid a pocket of methane. They were left over from the ancient gas oceans that had once covered the planet and shaped its landmasses. Scientists thought that Phinea had once been a rogue planet, tracking silently through space, before being caught in the gravitational embrace of Anya, their star. The methane oceans, liquid at extreme cold temperatures, had evaporated, but here and there, remnants were still trapped beneath the surface. Leno had heard some older kids saying they liked to scout out areas with pockets like this and rather than merely break them open, as Morena accidentally had, they would toss in an incendiary stick and turn the gas into a momentary jet of flame. You had to be careful, doing that. Leno had heard about a kid in the next settlement over who had lost two fingers.

"Just watch where you're walking," he said.

"I *was*."

"Leno? Morena?" Dad's voice echoed distantly behind them.

"Over here!" Leno called. He pressed on, deeper into the shadows. The sides of the canyon became narrower and higher.

"It's getting hard to breathe," said Morena.

"We're right on the edge of the safe zone," said Leno. He craned his neck but could no longer see the shining tip of the nearest atmospheric turbine, a few kilometers away. He checked his link. The white light was close now.

"Is she in there?" Morena pointed ahead.

The gulch ended at a steep slope made of collapsed slabs of red stone. There was a narrow, triangular fissure in the corner, leading into darkness.

"I think so." Leno lowered his wavelength adapters over his eyes and switched on the lenses.

"Could Great-Grandma even fit through that?"

"Come on." Leno ducked into the fissure. For a moment, all he could see was a dark blur, but slowly, the adapters sketched in the outlines of the rock walls angling tightly around him.

"I don't like this," said Morena, edging in behind him.

"Don't be a wimp."

"I'm not a wimp! I'm going to wait outside for Dad."

"Fine." Leno pushed ahead, his hands on the walls to either side of him. His head scraped the ceiling, and his knees began to ache from shuffling along in a crouch. His lungs felt tight, even though he was taking deeper breaths than before, like he couldn't expand them as much as he wanted, like the walls were somehow keeping him from breathing. "Grandma?" he called. He checked his link again. He was almost on top of the blinking light.

Finally, the passageway opened up and Leno found himself in a large chamber. The air was cold and smelled damp and sour. His adapters revealed a high ceiling, its walls glittering with metal veins. Here and there, patches of the walls glowed with a fuzzy substance.

And there was Great-Grandma. She was leaning against a large slab of rock in the center of the chamber, her head slumped to the side.

Leno scrambled over the uneven cave floor and knelt beside her.

"Grandma, hey, are you okay?"

Her eyes were shut, and for a moment, Leno worried that she'd finally passed on—*it could be any time*, Dad had said. *She's had a long life, longer than any of her peers.*

But then he saw her chest move, heard that strange whine of her breathing and even that metallic ticking that accompanied it from time to time. He looked around, but she didn't seem to have remembered her breathing pack; Dad was always telling her not to forget it.

"Grandma, wake up." Leno shook her shoulder. "We've got to get you back. The air's not good here." No response. "Come on, the festival is starting soon."

At this, her head finally lifted and her eyes fluttered open. She seemed to see him, though likely not very well in this dark and cool. "You came," she said, her voice hoarse and scratchy, as it was most times these days. Her head slumped back once more.

A new light began to flash on his link, a warning: *Air Quality Critical.*

Leno took Great-Grandma by both shoulders but could barely budge her, and she was so old, he worried if he tried too hard he would break her.

"Leno?"

"Yeah! In here!"

Dad appeared, crawling on his hands and knees, wearing a headlamp. He crouched beside Great-Grandma and shook his head. "Nia, you should know better." He glanced around the cave. "She's always loved this spot," he said to Leno.

Great-Grandma mumbled something, faintly.

"She gets confused," said Dad. "I shouldn't have left her alone." He moved behind her and picked her up by the shoulders. "You'll have to take her feet. Gently, though. Hopefully she'll perk up once we're back outside."

They moved carefully through the fissure, meter by meter, and finally reemerged in the narrow canyon. Dad was right; she came to and was soon able to stand, though not without leaning on Dad's shoulder.

"You should have stayed at the house!" Dad said as they made their way up the twisting path. "You're supposed to be the guest of honor at the festival, don't you remember?"

It was unclear whether Great-Grandma heard him. "I just wanted to see him," she mumbled a moment later, between wheezing breaths.

"Who?" Dad asked, but she sighed and didn't answer, focused instead on putting one foot deliberately in front of the other.

"You mean Great-Grandpa?" Leno asked, trailing behind them.

Great-Grandma seemed to hear this. She smiled and put a wrinkled hand on his shoulder. "You're a sweet boy."

They had just crested the ridge, their houses

shimmering in view down the slope, when the first booms sounded in the distance.

"There you guys are!" said Morena from down by the house. She waved her arm. "Come on!"

Leno peered through the early-evening haze and saw an explosion of energy flickering over town. "Aww, we're missing it!"

"That's just the opening ceremony," Dad said. "You two go ahead. Tell Mom to take you over. We'll catch up."

"Okay, thanks." Leno turned to go when Great-Grandma gently grabbed his arm.

She smiled gently at him. "Do you have the beacon? And the key?"

Leno rolled his eyes and tapped his sternum. "You know I always do, Grandma."

"And you know what to do when a message comes?"

"Yes, tell you, or Dad—"

She finished his sentence with him: "—in that order." She ruffled his hair and released him. "And if neither of us is here, you send the reply yourself."

"I know. Can I go?"

"Have an adventure," she said.

Leno raced down the rocky slope toward Morena.

"Careful!" Dad said, as he too often did.

"Oh stop it," Great-Grandma barked, her voice like dry reeds.

As he left, Leno turned back to see Great-Grandma slapping Dad's shoulder gently, some of that old grandma sass that they saw so rarely these days. There was a reason she'd been honored year after year.

He ran off with his sister, down the hill toward the festival, having no idea what the future would bring, and indeed, no idea how his life would have changed when he returned home.

12

"Earth?" said Liam's mom, gaping at the new map overhead, and the blue orb glowing at its center. "Our Earth?"

"Not exactly," said Barrie.

"A planet with a ninety-nine-point-seven-percent similarity to Earth," said the chronologist, consulting his crystal.

Everyone stared silently. Liam felt a rush: Earth, the way he'd only ever seen it in books and the VirtCom, the way it had been even before his parents' lifetime, before it had become mostly deserts and fragment oceans. Mom's eyes were brimming with tears. Dad was peering like he did when a million thoughts were running through his mind. The sight of the little blue planet spun Liam's nerves, but this feeling was more than that. He'd always considered Mars his home, and yet seeing this image stirred something inside him, some whirring of excitement and longing. *This* was what a new home for humanity should look like. Air to breathe, oceans to swim in . . . Based on the looks on his parents' and Mina's and the *Artemis* crew members' faces, they were all feeling something similar.

Barrie reached into the map and expanded a panel of data beside the image of Earth. "This universe looks to be about the same age as ours," he said. "Formed using the exact same configuration. In fact, instead of calling this iteration 90, she's labeled it 89.1."

"You're saying this place just made another universe," said Mom. "The entire thing, just like that. . . and it has another Earth?"

"That is what I'm saying," Barrie agreed.

"So it's what: a copy?" said Dad, his brow wrinkled.

"I think there may be very subtle ways in which it is different, but it's very, very close." Barrie scrolled through more readouts. "The portal into this new universe has opened at a space-time coordinate that would make this version younger than our Earth by about fifty million years."

"Why there?" Mina asked.

"Perhaps it has opened at a moment prior to the evolution of life-forms similar to your own," said the chronologist. "But far enough along in the evolution of the biosphere that it would be hospitable for you, all of which would make for an ideal time to arrive."

"Arrive?" said Liam's dad.

The chronologist blinked. "I assume that Dark Star has revealed this planet to you so that you may make a new home there. Perhaps that is the true purpose of this station. To tailor an ideal home to those who use it."

"We haven't exactly been using it," said Dad.

"No, but it has been scanning us since we arrived," said Barrie. "Learning all about us."

"It made us a new home," Mom repeated.

"To that point, sir," said Jordy, "the portal to our universe seems to be permanently open now." He pointed to where the original portal was glowing a similar shade of green.

"It's an invitation," Barrie said. "A home for all humanity."

Liam pushed back from the moment. *Iris, are you here?*

She shimmers beside him. *Yes. What do you think?*

Is it really another Earth?

It is. Do you like it?

I mean . . . Liam's thoughts jumble in his head. *Are you really suggesting we should go live there?*

I'm not suggesting anything. But I don't have to. Iris waves her hand off to her side. *Look.*

Liam peers past her and sees that the fog and darkness beyond his present moment have washed away, and there, finally:

His future.

It is light filled and green. The bubbles of moments that stretch forward shine with pale-blue-and-white skies. Liam slips ahead in time, his heart racing with anticipation, and sees a flash of ships descending, hundreds of colony cruisers, sees himself stepping from a landing platform into deep green grass, the kind that would hiss against the glass of the savanna biome in the Earth Preserve back home—

No, *this* is home. He can feel it like a vibrating string inside him, something complete that never quite was on Mars. In his lungs, beneath his feet. In the colors and smells.

He pushes forward farther into his future, faster. Prefab dwellings rise on the grasslands. Cruisers and transports blink in the twilight like fireflies, rising into night, up toward the necklace of starliners in orbit. Bats flit overhead—animals he's never known but always known—as he breathes air that is warm, damp, meant for him. That persistent worry of dome failures, gravity loss, pressure suit integrity, all gone. Only the tingle of thunderstorms on the horizon. The white glow of a moon, fat and round, blotches of gray that almost make a face—*it's not quite like the old face*, his mother will have said not long after arriving, and it annoys Liam that this Earth, *his* Earth, still has to be compared to the long-dead one. There is the twinkle too of a second moon—*little sister*, they call it; this was apparently a comet that became caught in Earth's orbit, one that didn't strike the planet, as it might have with just another degree of angle on its trajectory. A not-impact that never caused an extinction.

Here, on his Earth, there will still be dinosaurs. But they are midsized to small, the great behemoths having evolved into memory on their own. They are mostly like birds, mostly skittish, but there are some species it will be wise not to startle.

Then a school building, offices, towers rising higher and higher: in the distance, the massive clouds from machinery paving roads, grading hills, mining for materials.

Liam rushes even farther into the future, the moments around him a blur, and then he sees a stunning vista. He pushes into a moment when he will be sitting atop a mountain, crested with crinkled ice and snow. He is older: nineteen, twenty? He will be up here watching the sunset over folds of snow-laced peaks that seem infinite, sitting with a group of others his age—*we will be students, we will be studying abroad. This Earth has three massive continents, and this is the first time I will have traveled to the one that straddles the North Pole. We will be learning about the precursors of an ice age that was to come, but that engineers are working to avoid. Phase Two technology can keep this planet warm and ice-free like we found it.* He remembers that his parents will have been happy, engrossed in their work, always thrilled to see him on college breaks, their hair now gray at the temples. Mina will have moved to a city on a far coast, will still be making music, and will be working in sustainable-settlement planning.

Here Liam will someday sit, on this mountaintop, on this Earth. Alive and safe. He presses farther still into the moment, enough that he can feel the wind, chilly, but so buoyant with vapor, so alive, the atmosphere thick and enveloping, especially when compared to the dry desolation of Mars.

Mars.

This is what he will be remembering, as he is sitting here, in the future: he will be watching this sunset and thinking about the ones on Mars. And he will feel a faint echo of that fear he once felt, of the oncoming, unknowable future, and it will be a feeling like he has lived two lives, one on Mars, one here, or maybe three, if you count that time in space with . . .

He will be happy but also sad, sitting there on the mountaintop, even though this future version of himself can still know the future: sad to be leaving childhood behind, sad because no amount of looking through dimensions this way can ever truly replace the sensation of being in a moment for the first time, the only time. And yet the sadness is also thrilling. It is a spiraling feeling—experienced by present Liam, or future, or past?—to be seeing this mountain view for the first time before he's seen it, and also to know that his twenty-year-old self remembers seeing this at thirteen, knows it was coming. How all of that suggests that it is meant to be. That it has meaning. But there's a longing there, too, on Earth, at age twenty, on a mountaintop somewhere on the newly named continents. Someone he misses . . .

A hand will creep into his. Liam will look at the hand and grip it tight; but at the same time, for less than a second, he will think of someone else, just before he smiles at the girl beside him, whose name will be—

Not Phoebe. A different girl. A human girl he has been dating for a while. But . . .

Liam pulls back from the moment, from the mountaintop, back into the timestream, the play of his future a blur of light and movement and laughter and tears.

Where is Phoebe?

He drifts back toward his present, trying to catch a glimpse of her lavender face and shining eyes anywhere in his future.

Iris, he says, *do you know where she is?*

It would seem that your future and hers are meant to diverge.

Liam slides nearly back to the present—there. Finally, Liam sees a moment with Phoebe's face and presses toward it. Not long from his present. They will be standing together inside a Cosmic Cruiser. Her eyes will be wet. Her lips will move.

"I'll miss you."

Liam gets closer to himself. "I'll miss you too," he hears himself say. Close enough to feel his future heart pounding as they hug. His body shakes, hollowed out inside, a feeling he will remember as far away as those mountaintops, so many years later.

This good-bye, coming so soon, will never leave him.

Liam clenches his jaw and sinks away from the moment.

She'll always be there, in your memory, says Iris. *And*

for you, with all of your abilities, that can be something more than it could ever be for the others.

I don't want her just in my memory, he mutters.

I know.

The future is just probability, he insists. *This doesn't have to be how it goes.*

True, Iris says. *But you see the life that is ahead of you, now that this Earth is possible. And that's not just for you. Your sister, your parents, your friends. All of humanity.*

It's almost like you're telling me I don't have a choice.

Of course not, she says, and seems to smile. *There are infinite choices. And we can explore what could have been as much as you'd like. You, Liam, have so much potential, but the rest of your people don't have the aware-ness that you do. Much remains uncertain for them. If you don't follow this future, it could mean death.*

Okay . . . Liam frowns at her. Her words sound like a warning.

I know you're conflicted, that so much of this is confus-ing, but trust me, she continues. *Go back to your present and listen. Experience this timeline, and I think you will agree with me that this future is the best for all. I will be busy processing for a while, but then I will return.*

Isn't this what you were working to finish?

This is a very significant part of my system function-ality, but not all of it. For you, Liam, there is more. I promised you access to the higher viewpoints, and I will be true to my word. Not much longer now. Okay?

I guess. In all the commotion, he'd forgotten about seeing time differently. It seemed oddly distant to him now, given all that had happened. Liam reconnected with his matter, his senses, rejoining the moment. Everyone was still gazing up at this new Earth and discussing how to proceed.

"Liam," said JEFF's head, "your link is exhibiting very strange time code errors."

"Yeah, I know." Liam opened the home screen and tapped off the messages.

"What you're suggesting is traveling into another universe," Dad was saying. "Is that even possible?"

"We got here," said Mina. "What's the big deal? Fly through the first portal, then the second."

Liam tried to get Phoebe's attention, but she was blocked from his view by the rest of the Telphons, who had clustered tightly, alternately looking at the map and conversing in increasingly loud voices. The humans began to pause to watch them.

Tarra noticed this and addressed the room: "Captain Barrie, is it possible for you to search this new universe for a Telos?"

"A what?" said Barrie.

"Aaru-5. Does this new universe have a similar

version of our home as well?"

"Let me see . . ."

"It would be about fifteen light-years from Earth," said Ariana.

"In the Aquarius constellation," Dad added.

Barrie zoomed out and waved the map along, until he had centered another star system. "Here?"

"That red dwarf star in the upper left," said Tarra. "Second planet."

Barrie zoomed in. Liam saw multiple planets, and yet the Telphons had already begun to gasp and whisper. There was a planet closest to the star, and a string of others farther out, but in between that first planet and a distant second one stretched a cloudy ring of asteroids.

"It appears that in this universe," said the chronologist, referring to his orange crystal, "the destruction of Telos's sister Xanos created a chain reaction that destroyed both planets. This was a highly probable event in our universe, one that your planet was incredibly lucky to avoid."

Liam saw Phoebe's ashen expression as she gazed at the map. He hoped she'd look over, but her face fell and she turned to listen to her people talking together quietly again.

"It seems," Tarra said a moment later, "that your

magic machine has made a new home for you that conveniently excludes us."

"I'm sorry," said Barrie. He recentered the map on the new Earth and enlarged the view of the planet. Mom, Dad, Mina, and the *Artemis* officers stepped nearer to it, until the blue orb floated between them at shoulder height.

"If it really is that much like Earth . . . ," said Dad.

"How do we know this new universe is even stable?" said Mom, and yet her eyes were rimmed with tears. "Or that this thing won't blow up that star, too, at some point? Or that the portal will even stay open long enough to get everyone there?"

Dad shrugged. "It seems to be showing us this place intentionally."

"I know, but we're ascribing purpose and compassion to a giant machine whose origins we don't know, and whose basic power needs involve the destruction of entire solar systems."

"What reason would this machine have to try and trick us?" said Barrie. "Perhaps this is what Dark Star did for its original creators. Perhaps those ancient Architects left it here, in case it might someday be found, so that it could be of help to others. Like us."

Liam considered telling them that yes, Dark Star did want to help them. And yet, it would be confusing to explain, and they seemed to be coming to that conclusion on their own.

"It's a better solution than Aaru," said Dad.

Mom flashed a glance at the Telphons before continuing in a lowered voice. "It's true what Ariana said. Our best-case modeling of Phase Two was only coming in at eighty-seven percent. And you remember how many other planets we surveyed, looking for a place whose conditions were even remotely close."

"Tens of thousands," said Dad.

"It's closer, too," said Mina. "The fleet of starliners could be at that portal we came through in a matter of years. Aaru is still over a century away."

Liam thought of his future, saying good-bye to Phoebe. He watched the Telphons talking, each race in its own huddle now. He wanted so badly to talk to her, but her back was to him.

"You said transiting the door damaged the *Artemis*," Dad said to Barrie.

Barrie was biting his lip, like he was in thought. "Only because we initially tried to escape its pull. Had we flown right through, there might only have been some minor damage, if any."

"But we don't know for sure that this Earth can even support human life," Liam piped up. Even as the words were leaving, he wondered why he'd said it. The future he'd seen was a good one. He knew it was better than nearly any option he could have imagined. But still . . .

"It's true," said Mom. "We also have no idea how closely the physical laws of that universe match those of our own. And just because the conditions of this new Earth seem identical, that doesn't mean something hasn't evolved there, a virus, a spore or insect, that could wipe us out."

"So let's go find out," said Mina.

Dad took a deep breath. "She's right. We should send a team down."

Mom looked at him for a moment, then to the map. "I'm so afraid to let myself hope."

"We'll be thorough," said Dad. "Do a full workup. We'll need equipment from the starliners, and personnel. We could get a message to them, right?" he said to Barrie.

"Yes," said Barrie. He looked at Kyla and Jordy. "With the portal open, a couple of my officers have already devised a plan for establishing communication."

Liam saw Kyla pat Jordy's shoulder.

"But Colonial is not going to turn the entire fleet around, not even one starliner, unless they're sure," said Mom.

"Then we should go down there ourselves and gather the initial data," said Dad. "The *Artemis* must have basic scanning and sampling equipment?"

"It's probably not as cutting edge as what your ships would have," said Barrie, "but yes, we've got it."

"Okay," said Dad, "that sounds like our next move. If you agree, Captain."

"It makes sense," said Barrie distractedly, gazing at the new Earth.

"What about them?" Mina glanced at the Telphons.

"Well, if this does indeed turn out to be our course of action, I can't see how they'd object," said Mom. "They can return to their people. We could even give them the turbine equipment for Phase Two as reparations. If they were already working on adapting the technology to suit their needs, then I'm sure they can make it work for them, wherever they end up."

Liam could hear the sense in this plan, and yet it made his heart race. He looked over, and finally Phoebe was looking his way, but her face was stony, and she offered Liam a perplexed shrug. Could she tell where this was going, like he could? He pictured the future, saying good-bye . . .

"What if we let them live on this new planet with us?" he said.

"Tuh," Mina scoffed immediately.

"Liam," said Mom.

"What? It's a whole planet. We don't need the entire thing. I mean—"

"You know that is impossible," said Mom. She waved at the image of the new Earth. "We're not going to share our best chance at survival with . . ." Her eyes flashed to the Telphons. "With them, okay?" She shook her head, as if out of everything they had heard and seen in the last couple hours, this was somehow the most shocking.

"But Mom," said Liam, "you said before you don't know if Phase Two will even work. What if they end up without a home?"

"It's not up for discussion!" Mom snapped. "And why would they even want to be on Earth? It's not right for them. They had to wear those eye adapters— Phoebe with that cough." Mom didn't even seem to know about the auxiliary heart pumps. She folded her arms and took a deep breath. "We have eleven billion people who need a home, but even if there was room, even if those of us here could somehow forgive all that happened, think about the rest of humanity: How are they going to react to having the very beings who murdered thousands of us sharing our space, our resources?"

"But we . . ." And yet Liam saw the scowl on Mina's face, the way Dad was staring at the floor. There was no way they were going to listen. And maybe they were right, even if Liam felt a surge inside that said otherwise.

"Don't you agree, Captain?" Mom was saying to Barrie.

Barrie was still gazing at the map. "Sounds right."

"Okay. Then our job is to verify this planet's viability," said Dad. "Should we go to the *Artemis* and get the survey team ready?"

"Kyla and Jordy can take you over," said Barrie. "I'll keep analyzing this information and monitor you from here."

"We should probably discuss the plan with Paolo and Ariana first," said Dad carefully.

"What if they don't go for it?" said Mina.

"I can't see why they wouldn't. If this works, they'll no longer have to worry about the *human threat* they've been so desperate to get rid of."

Dad and Mom started toward the Telphons. Liam fell in beside them, but Mom stopped him.

"Liam," she said, "take JEFF and we'll meet you at the Cruiser, okay?"

"But I want to—"

"Let us talk with them," said Dad. "It's going to be complicated."

"So? I can keep up."

Mom sighed. "It's not that. It's . . . we know how you feel about them. About Phoebe. It will just be easier if we handle it."

"But I can—"

"Liam," said Dad, "we're not asking."

"Come on!" Liam huffed. "Do I at least get to come down to the planet with you?"

Mom and Dad shared a look: never a good sign.

"We'll talk about it later," said Dad.

"I'm not stupid. That means no."

"It will be much easier if you stay up here with Mina," said Mom. "You two can catch up."

"You're not listening to me!" Liam said, trying to keep his voice steady. "I've been through these portals, and—"

"You're right." Mom put her hands on his shoulders. "You've already been through so much. You've been brave, and heroic, but you've also nearly been killed. . . ." Her voice caught in her throat. "We'd feel better if you stayed here. Please. Let us take the risks this time."

"But I can handle myself—"

"We don't have time to discuss this," said Dad, his voice pinching to a nervous hush as the other humans turned their heads. "Go back to the ship. We'll see you again before we do anything else."

Liam thought he might explode, everything inside him wound tight, but of course, there was no changing their minds, there never was when they were in agreement about something. And even Phoebe and the Telphons seemed to have noticed their heated discussion. If his parents were going to treat him like a child, the last thing he needed was for everyone else to see him that way, too. "Fine."

He spun and walked to Mina. If he'd been carrying anything other than JEFF's head, he would have hurled it across the control room. Unbelievable! All this time, he'd been doing pretty well saving the entire human race on his own, and yet the moment his parents were back in charge, they just reverted to the old pattern of treating him like a child. With each step, his anger mixed with a cold shaking in his belly. Somehow, with all his experience, all his new abilities in time and space, he had just as little control over the future as ever, if not even less now that his parents were here. And while yes, the future Iris had revealed was in many ways a relief, it was going to come at a price for him that no one else in his family seemed to understand.

And maybe the worst part was that he agreed with them. They had to try this new Earth, and of course the Telphons had to find somewhere else to go. There was no other scenario that really made sense.

We can look at some, if you'd like, Iris said from nearby.

That's all right. But Iris's comment only caused a fresh wave of nervous energy inside. Not because of what she'd said, but because she'd been in his head, in his personal thoughts, and that made him feel even less in control.

I would never betray your feelings, said Iris. *I'm in awe of them.*

Liam didn't respond. Just trudged across the control room and back toward the corridor. He glanced past Mina, saw the adults talking, grim faces all around. Where was Phoebe? There, at the edge of the conversation. She hadn't been sent away like a child. In fact her parents had included her in nearly every part of their plans, all along, no matter how dangerous. *But they didn't listen to her either,* he remembered. She saw him now and raised a hand to him, a small wave, and mouthed something—was it *Find me?*

Liam nodded back to her. Then they were in the corridor.

"Back to being little brother, huh?" Mina said, falling into step beside him. "I bet it was nice not having Mom and Dad around to act like prison guards all this time."

"They're being jerks," said Liam.

"You don't want to go on that survey mission anyway. Whatever fun you could have down there would just be ruined by all their rules and protocols." She spoke in a fake Mom voice. "Don't touch that, stay off that, don't breathe that air."

Liam almost smiled. "Why aren't you back there with them?"

"Why? So I could listen to them have the same fight all over again? Also—and I know you feel different and I get it—but I've spent about as much time around those Telphons as I can stand."

They exited the corridor, crossed the landing platform, and boarded the Cosmic Cruiser that the *Artemis* crewmembers had come over on. A few minutes later, Mom and Dad, Kyla and Jordy, and the other *Artemis* officers joined them.

Dad caught Liam's eye. "The Telphons agree that our plan to investigate this Earth is the best next move. They *say* they will stand by and allow our fleet safe passage, if the planet proves viable. They're going to dock on the *Artemis* for a brief rest and to gather supplies before they depart."

"They're probably glad to have us in a completely different universe," said Liam.

"Or we'll all be sitting ducks as we line up for that portal," said Mina.

Mom frowned at her, and yet Liam thought her face looked tight with worry. "I'd say we'll all be better off." As she came to sit down beside Liam on the benches in the main compartment, he put JEFF's head down, causing her to slide farther over to sit. She dug around the base of the seat. "Is there a way to buckle up back here?"

Liam just shook his head.

They flew back to the *Artemis* and landed in the hangar. As they walked to the elevators, the airlock opened and the Styrlax ship hummed in.

"Janis," said Kyla to one of the officers, "call a few security personnel down to keep an eye on that ship, okay? Just a precaution."

"Yes, sir."

Hearing that only roiled Liam's insides further. How was he going to meet up with Phoebe if there were guards posted? He supposed he could ask to visit her, but he could practically hear his parents' denials already. He'd have to figure it out on his own, using some of the skills that seemed of so little importance to them.

The group split up in the main corridor, Mom, Dad, Jordy, and a couple others heading off to gather space suits and equipment, Kyla taking Liam, Mina, and JEFF's head to the bridge.

"Be safe," Mina called after them.

"We'll try not to be too long," Mom said to Liam and Mina, as if they were kids being left alone for the first time. "We have to do all the analysis down on the surface. Can't risk bringing samples back and contaminating the *Artemis* until we're sure everything checks out. Our goal is to visit five or six sample sites. Kyla says with the speed of that Dark Star ship we should be able to accomplish the testing in seven or eight hours."

Liam could've told her that it was going to go fine, that he'd already seen them living there for decades into the future, but why bother? Better to not have them around for a while, anyway.

A short flight of stairs led to the *Artemis* bridge, a wide room with curved levels that stepped down like an amphitheater, all facing an enormous window. The levels were lined with workstations, most of which were dark. A cluster of officers staffed a few stations along the top level, and a few others stood at wall consoles along the back of the room. Out the window, Dark Star snaked and spiraled in and out of its own shadows, the green nebula feathered overhead, and now and then, brief flashes from the black hole glimmered just beneath their view. Out on one of the arms, the new portal glowed brightly.

"Fascinating old technology," said JEFF. When

Liam didn't answer, he added: "I am trying to inter-face with the *Artemis*'s VirtCom, but to do so, I must run my backward compatibility routines."

"That's great," said Liam, half listening. He noticed that Mina was holding both radio beacons in her hands, almost like she was comparing them. He had to remember, when she was snapping at him, that she was still devastated about Arlo.

"We're suited up," said Jordy over the comm. "Heading down to the *Carrion* to prep for takeoff."

"Captain," said Kyla, "the team is ready to go. How are things looking over there?"

"All good here," said Barrie. "The portal is stable, and new Earth is looking fine."

Soon, the sleek black silhouette of the *Carrion* appeared through the great window, darting away from the *Artemis* toward the towering new portal. One section of the bridge window lit up like a monitor screen, displaying blinking diagrams of the ship, the portal, and Dark Star on a field of crisscrossing lines. As the shuttle neared the rippling green center, the doorway's metallic frame came alive with flashes of silver circuitry, as if it sensed the ship's approach.

"Dropping the hard line relay," said Jordy. Though it was too small to see, a dot flashed on the monitor screen.

"He'll drop one on the other side," said Kyla. "We came up with this when we ran into the first portal. We reconfigured two of our recon probes, the kind we'd use to get eyes on an asteroid or run a planet survey, and connected them by a data cable. It got destroyed when the *Artemis* was pulled through, but before that it worked well. The one on the far side will relay data to the one on this side, which will transmit it to us. These portals throw off a lot of interference, but don't worry; with the hard line we should have no trouble maintaining contact."

"We're going through," said Jordy. "Wish us luck."

"Don't screw up," Kyla said. Liam noticed a tender smile on her face.

"Wouldn't dream of it."

For a moment, Liam felt an urge to say something to his parents. *Good luck*, or *Be safe*, because what if something went wrong on this mission? He suddenly remembered that feeling back on Mars, when they'd been trapped in the underground lab and he hadn't known their condition, when it had seemed possible that he might lose them forever—

"Here we go. Time is starting to thread," Jordy reported, his voice clipping.

With a brilliant flash, the ship disappeared into the green light. The blinking dot vanished from the screen. The comms hissed with silence.

Mina rubbed Liam's shoulder.

"It will take a minute to drop the other probe," Kyla said. "Captain, how's it look?"

"They appear to be through," he said. "I can't tell in what condition."

Ten seconds passed . . . twenty . . .

"*Artemis*, this is the *Carrion*." Jordy's voice crackled with static.

A chorus of relieved sighs sounded from around the room. Liam found himself uncoiling with relief as well.

"We are through the portal, and man, wait until you see this view. Sending feed now."

A new screen formed on the window, displaying a clipped video feed of the view out the cockpit of the ship. Through the static, the sun shone in the corner, and filling most of the screen was a broad curve of blue, with swirling chains of clouds, the scribbles of landforms blurred by atmosphere.

Gasps sounded around the bridge, along with a smattering of applause.

Liam could hear the sound of his parents talking in the background, but he couldn't make out what they were saying, except for one phrase from his dad:

"It's beautiful."

A sniffle beside him: Kyla wiped at tears. Others on the bridge did the same.

"Preliminary atmospheric analysis jibes with what already know: pretty near Earthlike," Jordy reported. "We're gonna make a pass in orbit, find a patch of land where it's daylight and the weather's good."

The video clipped in and out occasionally, but otherwise they watched the blue marble rotate beneath the ship. Vast oceans, patches of deep green, red-brown-and-white wastelands that could have been Mars, the white glitter of snow-capped mountain peaks. They passed the rim of twilight, and then pure dark, until the curve revealed the sun again.

"Okay, we've targeted a drop zone. Heading in."

The view tilted and the planet widened and flattened. A flash, flames licking around the cockpit, and then they could hear the shudder of atmosphere from outside the ship. Everyone on the bridge watched the screen silently, as the *Carrion* lowered itself through wisps of feathery clouds and into sunny skies, not a red lethal shine like Liam had always known, but yellow and safe. There was a wide curve of deep blue ocean frosted with whitecaps, soon a coastline of black sand, hills of low trees and grass: the savanna that Liam had seen in his future, where humans would first make their homes.

"*Artemis*, are you seeing this?" said Dad. "Liam? Mina?"

"Like a VirtCom field trip," said Mina.

"It's way better than that," said Mom.

"Whoa, check it out." The feed jumped, repositioning and zooming in. On the grassland, hundreds of brown creatures surrounded an emerald-green watering hole. They had long snouts with stiletto beaks like Liam had seen in pictures of dinosaurs. As the ship neared, they took flight together, beating great wings with shimmering iridescent feathers.

"That's like a five-meter wingspan," said Jordy.

"Tails, legs," said Mom. "Similar biology."

"Tasty," Jordy replied over the comm.

"Come on," said Kyla.

"What? You're telling me all those nutri-bars haven't left you hungry for some whatever-they-are burgers?"

"Just watch your approach. You land wrong, and those things will be eating you."

"Let's put down over there," they heard Dad say. "A couple hundred meters from the waterline."

The ship slowed and touched down on a flat swath of grass in a swirl of wind. As the engines powered down, Liam could hear the commotion of everyone standing up.

"All right, we're switching over to helmet cams," said Jordy.

The view out the cockpit was replaced by five camera feeds from the team's pressure suits, their views shaking as the team filed out the side of the ship. Mom and Dad moved a few dozen meters from the ship and stopped. Jordy busied himself checking the contact points of the landing gear. The other two team members, from the *Artemis* crew, continued on toward the beach.

"How's she looking, Jordy?" Kyla asked.

Jordy's gloved hand ran along the underside of the hull. "Pretty much perfect. Not even any burn marks from entry. I mean, I knew I was good, but not *this* good."

"All right, settle down."

Mom and Dad knelt in the high grass. Mom produced a laser shear and clipped a handful of the thin leaves. Dad twisted a long, slim device into the ground, coring a soil sample.

"Seems to have cellular structure," said Mom, holding the stalks close. She looked out at the horizon of low grass hills. "Unbelievable," she said. "It's perfect."

"We can't be sure yet," said Dad. "But it might just be." He stood, and they briefly appeared in one

306

another's helmet cameras as they embraced.

"Guys, you're on camera!" Mina shouted uselessly at the screen.

A few minutes later, they were filing back on board and unpacking the analysis instruments.

"Heading for the next drop zone," said Jordy. There were sounds of cheerful conversation behind him.

The ship rose, buffeted by wind currents, and streaked across the ocean.

"Captain Barrie," Dad said over the comm, "given the results of this initial sampling, I'd suggest that we prep to send word to the fleet."

There was no answer.

"Captain," said Kyla, "are you reading us?"

Another couple of seconds passed— "Yes, I'm here," said Barrie.

"They're saying to send a message to the fleet. Will you give the go-ahead?"

"Affirmative. Kyla, have Jordy ready his comm system to fly through the portal to our *old* universe and begin transmitting."

A grin spread across Kyla's face. "Roger that, sir. Our team is already prepping for launch."

"Congratulations, everyone," said Barrie. "We've found a home." Liam thought he sounded as relieved as the rest of them. Perhaps the oddities that he'd observed in the captain really were due to the incredible stress of what they'd been through here.

The officers on the bridge erupted into cheers and slapped hands. Liam was surprised to see Mina crying, but also grinning. She threw her arms around him.

Liam smiled too, and yet his insides felt more stormy than ever, his heart racing, his throat dry. They had a new home in their sights. Of course he'd already seen the future; they were going to be okay, humanity was going to be okay. All the terror of their journey—even though it had been only a couple weeks of conscious days, Liam felt like he could feel the decades, the nearly half century, in his bones—all of it would be behind them, fading in time, like a bad dream.

"Hey," said Mina, seeing that Liam had a tear in his eye, too. "No matter how Mom and Dad act, *you* did this, little brother. If it wasn't for you, we never would have made it here."

"Thanks," Liam said, nodding, and yet the burn increased in his eyes. Mina was right—he really had done it, despite all the danger and uncertainty. . . .

And yet.

He hadn't done it alone. He'd had a friend, a *best*

friend, a partner and an ally who had helped him and fought beside him even when she'd had so much to lose, who had lost more already than he could ever really imagine. And now, to have what he and his family and all of humanity had yearned for, all he had to lose was her.

13

Liam lay in the stasis pod. He'd stayed on the bridge as the message was sent to the fleet. Kyla expected it would take a minimum of five hours for a response to arrive. Liam had watched Mom and Dad and the team arrive at the second sample site, on the edge of a tropical-looking forest, before he'd asked Kyla if he could return to his compartment to rest. Mina, exhausted, had joined him.

He'd managed to sleep for almost six hours, despite the constant churning inside. When he woke, his brain felt like syrup, his eyelids scratchy, like he could have used twice as much rest, and yet his insides were spinning too fast now. Why, he wondered, did he feel as nervous and worried now as he had when they'd first arrived here?

"Did you sleep at all?" Mina asked, from the pod where Phoebe had once been.

"For a little while," said Liam, sitting up. "What about you?"

"On and off." Mina braced herself on her elbow and turned one of the beacons—she wore both around her neck—between her fingers. "It's weird. Now that the danger's passed, I miss him more. Or maybe that's normal. I don't know."

"I'm sorry."

"It's okay. When's the last time you and I shared a room?"

"When you used to come to the research station."

"Oh yeah. And also that trip we took to the gas giants. I remember when we were transiting the asteroid belt, you were so freaked out that we were going to get pulverized that I had to read to you for hours."

"I was six," said Liam.

"True. It was more cute than annoying." It sounded like she was enjoying this, reminiscing, but all Liam felt was that persistent whirring spin.

He just wanted to go to Mars for a while. And yet when he'd pushed back from the moment and turned toward his past, he'd been frozen by the fear that when he returned, Phoebe would be gone, even though he knew that was impossible. He still went a little ways back toward Mars, but he knew even before he arrived that it was no use. Unlike before, leaving his present only stressed him out rather than calming him.

So he'd been thinking instead about how to meet up with Phoebe. Maybe he could slide back in time, to some point when both he and Mina were asleep, and then get himself down to the hangar. But he would need to find a point when Phoebe wasn't being observed either. It all seemed too complicated and made him feel exhausted again.

"Have you checked out their VirtCom?" Mina asked. Kyla had given them both retro links that connected to the *Artemis*'s systems. The VirtCom was seriously dated compared to what they'd had back at the colony. The simulation games and environments were so low-resolution it was almost sort of cool. It had a lot of the old games Liam remembered playing when he was very young.

"I looked at the sims," he said, "but I didn't feel like playing anything."

"I found *Fashion Apocalypse*," said Mina. "Like, the second edition. I can't believe I used to love that game."

An announcement tone sounded, and Captain Barrie's voice came over the ship-wide comms. "Attention, everyone. We have just received the reply message from colonial command. They have verified the results of our preliminary tests, and agreed that this Earth should be humanity's new home."

Liam listened for more celebration but only heard silence from the core. He wondered what it would be like to be one of these passengers who had been in stasis lockdown this entire time—to find out how much had happened to the human race.

"The fleet has set course for the coordinates of the portal," Barrie continued. "The *Starliner Saga* will be first to arrive, in approximately eight hours. Command will want to send further teams in for analysis before we officially land on new Earth, but they have agreed to let the *Artemis* transit the new portal, as a stress test for the coming starliners. We'll be the guinea pigs, I know, but on the other hand, I think we're all looking forward to having our new home firmly in our sights." Barrie paused, and when he spoke again, there was a hitch in his voice. "I know we have lived with a terrible sense of powerlessness and uncertainty these long days. For some . . . that feeling was too much to overcome. For the rest of us, the sense that we had put our loved ones in danger has been a hardship unlike any other. But as it turns out, our suffering was part of a larger plan. Whether you want to call it fate, or luck, or divine providence, we can rest easy that humanity's salvation has come.

Many of you are too young to remember Earth as it was before the sun began to change . . . as our population grew and advanced, we also left a shameful path of destruction in our wake, so much so that large swaths of our home world were rendered uninhabitable. It used to break my heart to see the damage we had caused. Careless with our progress, with our ego . . ."

"Jeez," Mina muttered, "way to bring down the mood."

"The truth is," Barrie continued, "and this would have been too flippant a sentiment to utter in more dire times . . . but had this cosmic sequence of events not happened, as costly as it has been, it is likely that we would have been setting out to find a new home before long anyway. My point is, we should not take the lesson away from this moment that things will always work out. Instead, the discovery of this new world should make us grateful, and more important, humble. We must treat it with care, with dignity, and not take its gifts for granted. Humanity can be something more than it has ever been, if we meet this moment. It is time for us to evolve.

"We will take two more hours to rest, or celebrate as you see fit, and then we will begin to prep the *Artemis* for portal transit to new Earth."

Silence overtook the compartment again. Liam

stared at the ceiling, his insides buzzing like an exposed wire. *A matter of hours.* After everything they'd been through, they would be going to Earth; the fleet would be arriving . . . Phoebe would be leaving.

"Guess we have a couple more hours of lying here doing nothing," said Mina. "And Mom and Dad are in a different universe."

"Yeah," said Liam.

"Never doubt our parents' ability to treat us like an afterthought. Their work has always been the most important thing. If they hadn't been such freaks about it, we could have gotten off Mars earlier. . . ." Her voice caught, and Liam knew what she was thinking. What if they'd left on an earlier starliner? Would those legions of people who died on the *Scorpius* still be alive?

But Liam wondered if perhaps a worse fate would have befallen them if he had never been there on Mars at the very end, to find the watch and lead them here. Again, he could probably go look if he wanted: no doubt Iris would be happy to assist in exploring those other possible futures. But there was that jet flame again, that head-lightening spin. The past would only remind him what he was about to lose.

"I bet you're having feelings," said Mina.

"Huh?"

"About your girlfriend?"

"She's not my girlfriend."

Mina sat up. "You know who you're talking to, right?"

"We're friends," he said. "It's just messed up. I mean, we're going down to that new planet, and they're going back to our universe, to . . . who knows what." Liam's breath got short. "I know what you're going to say. Good riddance, or whatever."

"Well, yeah . . ." Mina paused. "If I were Phoebe, I guess I'd probably be feeling conflicted about everything that happened. Especially if I had a friend like you. It must have been pretty hard for her, being caught in the middle."

"Her brother died in the Phase One attack. And her grandparents. All her friends . . ."

"I know a little something about that. Not as much, but a little."

They sat in silence for a moment, and then she said: "Okay, fine."

"What?"

"Go see her already. I'll cover for you."

Liam sat up. "Are you serious?"

"Seriously an idiot," said Mina, "but I can't stand seeing you depressed like this. Besides, Mom and Dad clearly don't care what we do, or they wouldn't have left us here."

Still, Liam sat there for another moment, tingling

in his arms and legs like they wanted to move. "I don't know. . . ."

Mina checked her link. "In a couple hours she'll be gone, you know, forever. Make 'em count, lover boy."

"Stop," said Liam, but at the same time he climbed out of his pod.

"Does she have a weird tongue or anything?"

"Shut up!" But Liam smiled again. "I don't even know."

"Uh-huh."

"I'm serious!"

"Well, I'll expect details when you return."

Liam just shook his head. He zipped up his hoodie, moved to the door, and paused. "Do you mind if I take JEFF?"

Mina glanced at the head lying on the dresser like she'd forgotten it was there. "No. But why?"

"Just to catch up. We spent a lot of time together. Like decades."

"That sounds like a total lie, but whatever, I don't care."

Liam hoisted JEFF's head. A coiled green wire connected from his neck to a port on the wall. As Liam disconnected him, his eyes blinked to life.

"Good morning, Liam!"

"Hey, JEFF, we're going on an adventure."

"Oh man," said Mina, "don't make JEFF record your weird alien-kissing—"

"That's not what I'm doing." Liam stepped out into the red light of the core. "Thanks," he said to Mina, but he was surprised to see that she was brushing tears from her eyes.

"Just hurry up," she said, holding the two beacons that were around her neck. He almost asked for one, but he didn't think she'd want to part with it now.

"Okay," he said, and slid the door shut. Out on the walkway, Liam peered up and down the core, at the walkways above and below. No sign of any crew members. Perfect. He hurried toward the stairs.

14

Liam walked as quickly as he could along the empty walkway of the *Artemis* core, the weight of JEFF's head knocking against his hip.

"What curious architecture," said JEFF as they waited at the end of the core for a staircase to rotate into position.

"It doesn't really look that different than the *Scorpius*," said Liam.

"I am referring to the VirtCom, and its operating system. Though it has sustained significant damage, and has numerous faulty packets that are corrupting its function, it is still interesting to observe its processes."

"Glad you're having fun," said Liam. He started down the staircase.

"It is actually challenging, as I am having to filter a significant amount of interference coming from Dark Star."

"What kind of interference?"

"The signal is hard to decipher, but I believe it is scanning us with a wide spectrum of frequencies. This scanning is so powerful and specific, it can likely see your every move, if not right down to your heart beating."

Liam reached the bottom of the staircase. He thought of Iris watching him, hearing his thoughts, and it spun up his insides in a way it hadn't before, especially given where he was headed right now. "Is there a way to disrupt it?"

"You could wear a tinfoil hat. HA, HA, HA."

Liam eyed JEFF.

"Are we not still working on humor?"

Liam smiled. "Seriously, though."

"Shielding from this kind of scanning would take significant time to design, not to mention access to materials we do not currently have available. We would need high density—"

"It's okay, I get it." *Time* . . . maybe there was another solution. "Did you try to talk to the Dark Star computer, the way you are talking to the *Artemis*?"

"I made a few inquiries, but when it comes to interfacing with that machine, I am afraid that my processors are too primitive. If I'm going to communicate with Dark Star, it will have to want to talk to me. Why do you ask?"

"I just wondered if you could find out anything more about it."

"I am afraid not. Its capabilities obviously suggest an incredible level of intelligence, as well as a high degree of benevolence."

"You sound surprised."

"I am not surprised, I just find it noteworthy. Just because something is intelligent does not necessarily mean it is *good*. An artificial intelligence is built with a specific goal, or task, in mind, something that the beings who created it could not accomplish themselves. Whether that goal is good or bad must initially come from the beings who created it."

"Making universes with livable planets for races who need them seems like a pretty *good* task," said Liam.

"That is certainly true . . . ," said JEFF.

"But . . . ," said Liam.

"Two things: first, it seems unlikely that a race of beings would build an intelligence, not to mention a mechanism of this size and scale, only to discard it."

"If the Architects used it to build a new home, then they probably didn't need it anymore."

"That may well be. And yet if humans had built this place, can you really imagine them leaving it behind?"

"Well, no. Maybe the Architects are different."

"They might be."

"What's the second thing?"

"Given the age of this intelligence, it is also possible that whatever the goals and intentions of the Architects were, they may no longer be what Dark Star wants."

"What do you mean?"

"An AI of this size and advancement no doubt has the power to learn, analyze, and reflect. It may even have what we would refer to as a consciousness."

"Yeah, I think it does," said Liam, thinking of Iris. "But I still don't get why that is a bad thing. *You* have a consciousness, and you're benevolent."

"I did not say it was a bad thing. I merely stated that it was noteworthy. In humans, as you know, as in nearly every living entity we have observed, benevolence is perhaps less common than self-interest."

Liam gave JEFF a side-eyed glance. He was reminded of something Iris had said: *At some point, you must make the choices that best suit your needs for survival. That is the case for every living being.* Liam had thought that sounded kind of selfish, and yet Iris hadn't been describing herself—she wasn't a living being . . . was she?

They had passed through the airlock and were now making their way along the main corridor. Liam stayed near the wall, keeping a wary eye out for officers, but the hall was deserted. They took the elevator to the hangar deck and emerged in the wide, silent space.

The Styrlax ship was parked near the airlock. Phoebe was sitting on its stairway, arms across her knees. He waved, and when she looked up and saw him, she grinned.

Liam smiled back—but paused outside the elevator. The two *Artemis* officers were sitting on a cargo box nearby, looking at him. "Hey," Liam said, looking from them to Phoebe and back. "We were just going to talk before they left. We, um, we spent a lot of time together getting here." Liam's face began to burn. "You know, before—"

"Uh-huh," said one of the guards. The other was smirking. "Go ahead," the guard said. He looked back down at his link and began typing busily, and Liam imagined him sending some sort of jokey message about the two *kids* to other crew members.

He hurried toward Phoebe, who left the stairs and angled toward the next ship over, the Cosmic Cruiser they'd returned from Dark Star in. When Liam caught up to her, he was glad to see that they were out of view of the guards.

"Hey," she said. "I'm glad you came down. I was starting to feel like we'd never get a chance to talk again."

"Me too," said Liam.

"Hi, JEFF," said Phoebe.

"Good morning, Phoebe. Or should I call you Xela?"

"That's nice of you, but you can stick with Phoebe."

"Oh," said Liam. "I'm sorry I never asked you that."

Phoebe rolled her eyes. "Relax. It's no big deal. I was lying to you and wearing a disguise."

"How are things going down here?"

Phoebe shrugged. "Seems like the powers that be have it all figured out. It's weird because they're, like, proud of me, sort of, for saving them, even I think for finding this place, but then every second they also want to be sure that I remember I disobeyed them. I think I liked it better when they were in stasis." They shared a brief smile before Phoebe continued: "They say we need to leave before your fleet arrives.

Everyone's resting now, and then we're shipping out. Back to Telos first, to check in on the rest of our people. Then who knows where."

"I can see my future," Liam said. "Life on this new Earth. It looks pretty good."

"Lucky for you."

"I asked my parents if you guys could live with us there, but they were like, *there's no way*."

"We were silly to ever believe that it would work out. Our races are enemies. Meanwhile, you guys get your own planet again, probably in even better shape than Earth was before the sun changed."

"It's not fair."

Phoebe's expression darkened. "And you'll never have to think about what you did to Telos, or even think about us at all, because you're in another universe. One that doesn't have a Telos in the first place. It's like we won't even exist anymore. Like we never even did."

"But we won't be in your world either." That wasn't quite what he wanted to say, and yet hearing Phoebe's words was making his already spinny state even worse.

"You will, though," Phoebe replied. "Whenever we remember all of us who died, you'll be there." She rubbed at the crux of her arm where, Liam remembered, the three circle tattoos were beneath her thermal wear.

"We have people who died—"

"Liam, stop. Don't compare what we did to what you did. And *you* didn't lose anyone. Not a brother. Not grandparents. It's not the same and it never will be. Ugh, it all just makes me hate you guys all over again."

"I'm sorry." Liam's insides were revving. Everything felt tight! And he hadn't managed to say anything close to what he really wanted, what he *needed*, to say. "You're not, um . . . you're not going to *never be* for me. I'll always remember you."

A silence passed over them.

"I miss you," Phoebe said, "and we haven't even left yet."

"Yeah."

"I kinda wish we were still on the Cosmic Cruiser. Life was easier when it was just us." She smiled briefly at Liam. "I'm kidding, but . . ."

"I know what you mean." Liam looked at her standing there, arms crossed, like she was already a universe away. Should he just say good-bye and leave? No, this couldn't just be . . . *it*. He blinked and remembered the mountain he would someday sit on, the view of the setting sun in the watery atmosphere, how he'd remember her there. . . . "Hey, I have an idea. Want to go see it?"

Phoebe eyed him. "See what?"

"The new Earth. I want you to see it. Or, I want to see it, you know . . . with you. That way we can both remember it like that. Together."

Phoebe half smiled. "How exactly are we going to do that?"

"Um . . ." Liam looked around. "We could take a skim drone or something."

"And I remember when *I* used to be the one with the risky plans. Are you sure it will work?" She peered at him. "You haven't already like, gone and seen what happens, have you?"

"Oh, no . . ." Liam hadn't even thought of it, but now he wondered why he hadn't taken a look. He could, he supposed. . . .

"Good," Phoebe said. "Because that would be weird. I don't want to be living some script that you already know, or whatever."

"Yeah," said Liam. He'd never thought of it that way. More like just getting reassurance. And yet maybe he didn't want to go through his last moments with Phoebe while already having, if not lived through them, seen them. Maybe he just wanted to be here, now.

"I especially like this plan because of how much it will piss off our parents," Phoebe said.

Liam grinned. "Okay, cool." He looked around. "These *Artemis* skim drones are older models, but I could probably—"

Phoebe squeezed his arm. "We have something better than that. Come on."

She led him back to the Styrlax ship and around to the rear. Liam saw the guards look up at them and then back down to their links.

"Wait here," said Phoebe. She ducked over to the stairs and disappeared inside.

A few silent minutes passed, the loudest sound seemingly Liam's pounding heart.

There was a whir and a large panel of the Styrlax ship began to lower, making a ramp from the hangar floor into a cargo area. There, in the belly of the ship, was Liam's skim drone.

"No way," said Liam.

"My parents patched it up after we left it, and used it to steal him." Phoebe pointed to JEFF's head. She held up space-grade suits, draped over her arm. "The ones your parents used to board."

Liam climbed the ramp and peered into the skim drone cockpit. "Hey, buddy," he said, tapping the canopy.

"Boys and their machines," said Phoebe.

Liam opened the canopy. He reached in, powered it up, and checked the battery level. "Eighty-eight percent. That should work." The battery had been damaged at Delphi, but JEFF had repaired it, and the last time he'd used the drone, rescuing Phoebe and chasing the starliner, it had held up pretty well. "JEFF, can you calculate how far the trip to the new Earth is?"

JEFF's eyes flickered. "It is only a few kilometers from here to the portal. I have no way of calculating the distance from the doorway to the planet itself."

"We can't actually, like, land or anything," said Phoebe. "Can we?"

"No. The battery definitely wouldn't last through reentry and takeoff." That was exactly what Liam had been imagining, maybe even getting to some mountaintop like he would someday visit in the future, but he'd kind of known that was unrealistic. "At least we can fly through and see it. That would still be worth it."

Phoebe glanced at the stairs up from the cargo hold. "Not sure how long we have before someone notices. Of course once we're gone, who cares if they find out. What are they going to do, ground us?" She passed him a suit. "Our biggest concern is probably whether your computer girlfriend will be jealous of us sneaking off."

"She's not—she's busy with her systems, so I don't think she'll even notice."

"I thought she was scanning all of us, all the time."

"Well, yeah." Come to think of it, Liam figured she would definitely notice. But why would she care? In theory, she already knew this would happen. . . .

Phoebe's mouth scrunched. "Can I ask you something?"

"Sure."

"Does it seem weird to you at all that this thing is just making you a new world, like, for free? I mean, not like you'd pay for it, but you know . . . what's the catch?"

An immediate answer formed on his lips—*Iris wants to help*—but instead, he thought of what JEFF had said and felt unsure of the answer. "I think that's its function. Why is that so hard to believe?"

"You're saying you really think her entire purpose was to sit here and then make a brand-new universe for whoever happened to come along? A machine that can cross universes and destroy stars . . . is just like basically a help kiosk in the VirtCom?"

"No, but . . ." *It wants to show me the higher dimensions*, he almost said. Except that made it sound like Dark Star was all for him . . . and now who was being selfish?

"And I still don't understand: If that was Dark Star's intention all along, why not let you see that future when we got here? Or tell you about it. *Hey, new time-traveling friend, I'm busy making your people a new home*. Why make us sweat it out?"

Its processing disrupts— Liam almost began to counter, and yet he felt a wash of uncertainty. Why hadn't she just told him?

"And like, what if that wasn't what you wanted? I mean I know it *is*, but, doesn't feel exactly like a choice, does it?"

"I don't know."

"I'm sorry, I don't really know what I'm saying. I should probably stop raining on humanity's big day."

"It's okay," said Liam. This conversation had caused a fresh stir inside, because hadn't this worry that Phoebe was expressing been there, even if just a little bit, all along? "Sometimes I do feel like Iris is just another person telling me what I should do." That didn't feel quite accurate, but that was part of it. . . .

Liam handed JEFF to Phoebe. "Can you hold him? I'll be right back."

He pushed away from the moment and slid along his timeline, to before their parents had arrived, all the way back to just after their initial trip over to Dark Star, as Kyla had been walking him and Phoebe back to their compartment. He pushed into the moment and right out of himself, separating from his timeline as he had to visit Mina on the *Scorpius*. He steeled himself as the wind kicked up inside him, and he stepped onto the walkway just behind his earlier self.

One of the nearby compartments had a green light on its controls, a sign that it was empty. Liam opened the door. It hissed, but not loud enough to alert his past self or the others. Liam ducked inside, closed the door, and listened. A few moments later, he heard Kyla walk by, returning to the bridge. Now came the hard part: he had to sit there for nearly an hour. He reset his link and waited, trying a few games in the retro VirtCom, like Mina had, his insides spinning the whole time. He felt like he was missing yet more of his last moments with Phoebe, even though he wasn't at all. But he still had a creeping sensation that even though he wasn't losing time with Phoebe, he was losing something. Was it energy? Literal minutes of his life? Sure, no time would have passed when he returned to Phoebe, but he would be an hour older. And the hours, as the numbers on his arm showed, were starting to add up.

Finally, his link registered the right time, and he stepped back out onto the walkway and approached the door to the compartment where his former self was. There was a shimmer in the air, and the chronologist materialized, arriving to take Liam and Phoebe over to Dark Star to investigate.

"Oh, hello," he said, seeing Liam. "I was just on my way to see you."

"I know. I'm here from the future."

The chronologist blinked.

"Listen, can you meet up with us later?"

"Will I want to?"

"I don't know. It will be after we return to this compartment the second time. In about ten hours. After that, I'll go down to the hangar and meet up with Phoebe. She will lower the cargo hold of the Styrlax ship, and right after she does, can you come meet us? I need your help with something."

The chronologist regarded him for a moment, like he was thinking it over. "I will find you then."

"Thanks."

Liam pushed away and returned to himself, in the Styrlax cargo hold next to Phoebe.

"Okay," he said, trying to smile like his trip was no big deal.

"It's weird when you do that," Phoebe said. She'd placed JEFF's head on the skim drone seat. "There's this one second where you're kinda blank, like you're there but you're not. Where did you go?"

"Hello."

The chronologist had appeared at the base of the cargo hold.

"Hey, that's my trick," said Phoebe.

"I have not seen one of these ships in a while," said the chronologist as he walked up the ramp, his many legs clacking on the metal. "Where did you get a Neefaren cruiser?"

"You mean Styrlax," said Phoebe.

"Well, the translation is tricky."

"They helped us escape Telos," said Phoebe.

"Ah." The chronologist produced his orange crystal. "I will have to make a note of that in the long count, if and when I am able to return to my office."

"Couldn't you head back through the portal now, if you wanted?" Phoebe asked.

"I could," said the chronologist. "However, there are many aspects of this place that I still need to investigate, not the least of which is my inability to perceive my future."

"You still can't see the future?" said Liam. "I can."

The chronologist peered at him. "When did that change?"

"When that portal opened to the new Earth. Iris said that once she made it, the interference lifted."

"May I observe your future?" asked the chronologist.

"Um, sure. How do you do that?"

He held his crystal toward Liam, clicking its top and bottom. It separated at its equator, bright light poured out, and the hemispheres spun and made a humming sound. "Fascinating," said the chronologist, studying the light. He clicked the crystal closed. "You must be very pleased."

"I guess." Liam glanced at Phoebe, thinking of their conversation. "You don't see any of that? Humans on the new Earth and all?"

"I do not, though this may be because my future does not include this Earth. Still . . ." He trailed off.

"You don't totally trust this place either," said Phoebe. "Do you?"

"Normally, I would not need to rely on something as three-dimensional as *trust*, but in this case . . . No, I do not totally trust this station's intentions."

JEFF's words about intelligence flashed through Liam's mind again. "That's actually why I brought you here," he said. "You know how it's scanning us all time?"

"Very much so."

"Is there a way that you could hide us from those

scans while we take a trip?"

"You think she'll be jealous," said Phoebe, "like I said."

"No, I just . . ." Liam didn't quite know how to put it into words—in fact, didn't want to think too much about it, in case Iris was monitoring his thoughts right now. "I just would like to be unobserved, you know, in the moment alone. So what do you think?"

"What is it you are planning on doing?" the chronologist asked. When Liam explained their plan to see the new Earth, he said, "I might counsel that such a course of action is needlessly risky—"

"Yeah, that's the thing. I've kind of had enough of other people or computers or even you telling me what I should or shouldn't—can or can't do." Liam realized he might well sound childish, but his heart was pounding and he didn't care. He motioned to Phoebe. "In an hour or so, she's going to be gone forever. We just want some time on our own. Please?"

The chronologist consulted his crystal. "I can program my recorder to create a space-time dilation around you, which will make you at least somewhat invisible to scanning." He rotated his orange crystal between his fingers—nine on each hand, Liam noticed, plus a small digit protruding from each thumb, same as the first chronologist. The crystal flashed twice and then began to pulse rhythmically with mellow orange light. "There." He handed it to Phoebe. "That should do the trick."

"Thanks." Liam began pulling off his pressure suit and sliding on the space suit. A thought occurred to him. "You set that up pretty quickly. Have you been using the crystal like this already?"

"Quite a bit," the chronologist admitted. "There is much to explore on this ship, and I prefer to make my inquiries in an unbiased manner."

"What have you found?"

"So far only empty rooms," said the chronologist. "I am still most interested in that strange cylinder down in the Dark Star hangar and the signals coming from inside it. I have revisited it multiple times, but so far, I have not been able to gain access like your captain."

"Don't you need your crystal for that?"

"I can borrow it from my earlier self."

"You—of course you can."

The chronologist seemed to smile. "This is not my first . . . how do you say it . . ."

"Rodeo?" offered JEFF from the seat.

"What's that?" said Liam.

"Anyway, good luck," said the chronologist. He turned and descended the cargo ramp.

"I thought you didn't believe in luck?"

"It was a joke."

"HA-HA-HA," said JEFF.

"Everybody wants to be funny," said Liam. "Will we see you again?"

The chronologist paused at the base of the ramp. "I wish I knew." He swept off around the nearest cruiser.

Phoebe finished zipping up her bulky suit and held out the pulsing crystal in her palm. "Just you and me and some weird alien technology. Like old times."

"Yeah." Liam climbed into the skim drone.

"Still cozy," Phoebe said, shoulders bumping as they squeezed onto the seat meant for one person. She held JEFF in her lap, their two helmets shoved in the footwell beneath her.

Liam grinned as he closed the canopy. He leaned as far as he could against the side of the cockpit to make space, and yet it was also nice to feel Phoebe beside him again.

He activated the thrusters. His fingers tingling, his mouth dry, his pulse racing, and yet maybe this nervous energy was more like excitement. Tapping the controls, inching the skim drone off the floor. . . . Finally, they were back on their own, just the two of them, on an adventure. Even though what they were attempting was possibly risky, and probably irresponsible, Liam felt better right here, right now, than he had since they'd arrived.

He edged the little craft forward in gentle nudges until it was clear of the Styrlax cargo hold, then increased forward thrust and glided toward the airlock. Glancing behind them, he saw the two guards watching the skim drone and speaking into their links.

"This is going to be a really short trip if we can't pair with the airlock controls," said Liam. But after a moment of searching, the skim drone's link identified the airlock protocol, and its controls flashed on the navigation screen. Liam initiated the sequence, and the inner door began to slide open. They moved into the space between the two doors, the inner sliding shut.

Almost immediately, their link lit up. "This is *Artemis* command. Identify yourselves and your ship destination."

"Kyla, it's Liam. I'm with Phoebe, and we're, um, just going to take a look around."

"Negative, Liam. We are supposed to be keeping all personnel accounted for to minimize safety concerns in preparation to transit the portal."

Liam tried to initiate the airlock again, but the outer door didn't move. "They must be overriding my request. JEFF, are you still in touch with the *Artemis*?"

"Acknowledged."

"Can you override their override?"

"I could. But I feel that I should point out that I agree with the lieutenant's assessment."

"I know you're coded to follow protocols," said Liam, "but you're also our friend. Remember all those decades we spent in space together? How about one more adventure?"

"If my memory packets are accurate, you left me alone for the majority of those decades."

"Well, sure, but . . . please?"

JEFF's eyes flickered for a long moment. Yellow lights flashed and the outer airlock door began to slide open with a violent release of air.

"Thanks, buddy."

"Liam—" said Kyla.

"Don't worry, we won't be long."

"That's not really the point—"

"Phoebe's leaving soon," Liam added. "We'll be right back." He muted the channel.

"Let's do this," said Phoebe with a devilish grin.

Liam edged the skim drone forward, but then the airlock door paused and began to reverse.

"I fear they are overriding my override of their override," said JEFF.

"That's okay, I've got this." Liam sized up the narrow gap. Just like the Fingers back on Mars. If he could fly through those . . . He burned the thrusters, his fingers dancing over the lateral controls, putting the skim drone into a gentle roll as it hurtled forward. They slipped sideways through the gap and shot out into space.

"Whoo!" said Phoebe. "Where'd you learn that trick?"

"Not bad, right?" said Liam, and yet he felt a pang of guilt. Iris had helped him learn that move, and now he was avoiding her. . . .

"This is like skipping out on the last day of school all over again," said Phoebe. "See, I'm not the only one who likes to break the rules."

Liam couldn't help smiling. They cleared the underside of the front section of the *Artemis* and he adjusted the thrusters, angling them toward the shimmering doorway.

"You don't think they'll come after us, do you?" Phoebe asked, twisting to look back at the starliner.

"Nah," said Liam. "We're just being dumb kids. They won't waste the resources."

Phoebe patted JEFF's head. "How you doing, rule breaker?"

"I believe I am developing a new human attribute

routine to go along with humor," he said. "This one is guilt."

Liam selected the new portal on the navigation screen. It was 4.3 kilometers away, out near the end of one of the arms. He burned thrusters again. The jolt made him grit his teeth and made his smile grow. Flying again, finally, in total control, speeding along. With Phoebe.

"I'm so glad to be away from them," she said, nearly reading his mind.

"Me too," Liam agreed, though he did have to swallow his own feeling of guilt. Why was it that what he wanted and what his parents wanted always had to be so different? Well, whatever: Mom and Dad were so busy on new Earth, Liam and Phoebe would be back before they knew it.

He glanced at the crystal in her hands. It continued to pulse mellow orange. He checked the battery level: eighty-four percent. So far so good.

Ahead: the doorway looming larger, under three kilometers.

Below: the silent structures of one of the Dark Star arms. The buildings made of that smoky dark, glassy material like the rest of the station.

"Don't you think this looks like a place someone used to live?" said Phoebe, peering out her side of the cockpit canopy.

"Kinda." Liam noticed now that there were panels here and there that appeared completely transparent, like they were windows. In the gaps between buildings, he spied tubelike structures that might have been walkways.

"No, I mean, like, really lived. It looks like a city. If this was just a place that these Architects stayed while they were waiting to go somewhere else, would they have made it so . . . elaborate?"

"I don't know. What do you mean?"

"Think about the starliners: they're a lot simpler than the Mars colonies. But this place looks even more like a home than the colonies did. It's like a Telos city, or pictures I've seen of your stuff on Earth. More permanent, you know?"

"I guess." Liam saw that they were speeding over a wide, open area, like a city plaza. At its center, there seemed to be some kind of statue: a pedestal with a figure standing on top of it. They were past it in an instant. "The starliners have common areas, though."

"I know they do. It's just . . . this place feels more than empty; it feels dead. Like, not a place that people would choose to leave. But they're gone anyway. So what happened to them?"

"I don't know," said Liam. She was right, it did feel vacant in an unsettling way. Not unlike this entire starless universe.

The portal loomed ahead now, less than a kilometer away, its iridescent light bathing their faces.

"Okay, here we go," said Liam.

The lines of silver circuitry on the portal's frame pulsed at an increasing rate, as if it sensed their approach. The cool green of its middle glowed brighter.

"Now that it's too late, I wonder if this is a good idea," said Phoebe.

"Yeah." Liam flexed his fingers on the controls. That same old fear was creeping in: even more than the doubt over whether this was a good or safe idea . . . the doubt that he could do it at all. He breathed deep, thinking of the gauntlet back on Mars. He'd been scared there, too, and yet he'd been able to do it. Even slipping through that airlock a minute ago had been more complicated than this, and he'd done that. So what was it? His eyes flashed to the blinking orange crystal. Was it that he felt guilty about keeping this from Iris? And yet wasn't there far more that she was keeping from him? It was okay to do this. They had the right to make their own decisions. After all, doing just that had possibly saved the human and Telphon races. *So be quiet!* he wanted to shout at his worries. He was tired of their, well, worry.

The navigation screen flashed: five hundred meters. Three hundred—

And then they were upon it, no turning back. The portal rippled and the skim drone burst into the sheen of light.

There was a flash and Liam felt as if his arms and legs were gone, as if everything were missing except his thoughts. And yet he could see himself in all directions, many versions like he was surrounded by mirrors, all his moments, older and younger, each one refracting on and on away from him into infinite possibilities. He felt weightless in time, wanted to see every option—and it seemed almost like he could—yet the light was already dimming, the sensation fading. And then he was back within himself, in the skim drone, on the other side of the portal.

Stars all around. To their left, the bright safe yellow glow of a sun like he'd never known it. And in front of them, the great blue curve of the Earth in all its majesty. Its deep blues and ethereal whites, its folds of land, its watery atmosphere—

But an orange light blinked urgently on the console.

And something hit him in the arm.

He turned and saw Phoebe writhing, clutching her head, face contorted in pain.

Screaming.

15

"Phoebe, what is it?"

Liam tapped the rapidly flashing light on the console with one hand and with the other reached for her. Her eyes were shut tight, tears streaming from them. She thrashed and knocked his hand away, and let out a high-pitched cry like he'd never heard before. Finally she inhaled. "It hurts it hurts!"

"What hurts?"

Liam's eyes darted from Phoebe to the navigation screen and the warning still blinking there. One of the thruster circuits had shorted out. He tapped it to bypass but a new message appeared: *Bypass*

346

unavailable. Probably a circuit that had been fried by the EMP blast back at Centauri, or—

"INCOMPATIBILITY DETECTED!" JEFF shouted from Phoebe's lap. "REGION UNKNOWN!"

Another warning message appeared. *Critical Impact Angle*. Out the cockpit window, Liam saw they were diving straight toward Earth's atmosphere. The wide curving blue with its curling wisps of clouds—now suddenly a danger to them. It was still thousands of kilometers away, but gravity would increase the closer they came, requiring more thrust and battery power to escape. And at their current trajectory, they'd burn up on impact.

He fired the rear thrusters. Slowing—another orange light on the console now. Another short somewhere in the skim drone's circuitry.

"Oww!" Phoebe's scream died down to a wincing groan. Her eyes flashed open for a moment, wide and terrified, and then snapped closed. "Liam? Where are you? There's nothing! I can't see anything!"

"JEFF! Can you tell what's wrong with Phoebe?" But JEFF's eyes were flickering faster than he'd ever seen, as if his processors were running at maximum.

"Liam . . . ," Phoebe whispered, terrified. "What is it?" She pinned herself back against the seat, arms and legs flexed, eyes still closed. "What's all that light?"

"It's just the sun, and the planet—"

"No, the blue light!"

"What are you talking about?"

"Nnnnn!" Her legs thrashed. She grabbed a handle beneath the canopy, her knuckles turning white. "Where are we?" she shouted.

"We're right above the new Earth! We're in the skim drone—"

"It's all light. Wait, no, there are mountains, and water, but it's all scattering owww . . ."

A drop of blood trickled from her nose.

"Okay, Phoebe, just hold on! I'll get you back."

"Liam, don't leave me here! It hurts!"

"I'm not leaving you, I'm right here! Hang on!"

Liam jammed the stick and punched the thrusters. He slammed the skim drone into as tight a turn as he could, straining against the seat belt they shared. Earth rotated out of view—for a moment there was only a vast expanse of uncountable stars—and there was the portal again. Liam lined it up and burned at full power.

All at once, multiple console systems lit up. *WARNING! Electrical systems failure—*

Everything shut down. Lights off, air and heat systems cycling down. Engines out.

Silence.

"Oh, come on!" Liam tried the power button. Nothing. "JEFF, I could really use your help right now!"

JEFF's eyes continued to flicker.

The skim drone floated through space. Liam pressed the start-up button, jabbed other buttons on the console, and finally slammed it with his fist.

"Are those stars?" Phoebe moaned, but her eyes were still closed, tears leaking out. "So many blue stars. . . ."

"Phoebe, stay with me!" The portal was drawing closer. It looked like their last burn had put them on course to get through . . . but they were coming at it on an angle, and what would happen when they got to the other side? Liam would have no way to contact anyone on the *Artemis*, and there was no indication that the skim drone would come back online. This angle could send them crashing into the Dark Star arm on the other side, or sailing off into open space. Liam glanced at the floor. He'd brought a booster pack along when he'd rescued Phoebe back at Centauri, but it wasn't here now.

"Ow ow ow . . . ," Phoebe whimpered.

"We're almost there."

The portal rippled. Liam tensed—the wall of bright green light enveloped them again. Another blinding flash, the sense of many selves stretching in all directions—

And then they were through. There was Dark Star, the *Artemis*.

"Guh!" Phoebe's eyes snapped open. She looked around, blinking fast, chest heaving. "We made it, we—" Her eyes fluttered shut and she slumped in her seat.

Liam shook off the dizziness and got his bearings—and then froze. The skim drone was still dead, and their angle was indeed taking them right toward the Dark Star arm below the portal. The buildings grew before them; they were heading for a pyramid-like structure, would slam into it in moments, and there was nothing Liam could do to slow them or change their flight path.

His link was still working, though flashing numerous error messages. He stabbed at it, looking for the connection screen. They'd probably reappeared on the *Artemis*'s sensors by now. If he could contact Kyla—but he looked up and knew there wasn't time. They were going to crash.

"Phoebe, hang on!" The ejection system was fully manual, a series of compressed air charges all connected by physical cables, that would both blow the canopy top and launch their seat free. No electric circuits to fail. Eject and hope that in the zero gravity, the thrust of their launch would be enough to help them clear that pyramid.

After that? He had no idea.

Liam grabbed Phoebe's helmet from the floor. She moaned faintly as he slid it over her head, clipped it in place, and did the same with his own. The side of the pyramid building was getting closer, closer. He hauled JEFF's head into his lap, then reached beneath the seat, his gloved hand finding the thick plastic handle there.

Three, two, one . . . Now! Liam wrenched the handle.

The canopy blew off with a series of hissing pops and the seat shot free into silent space. But the back of the skim drone just clipped Liam's foot, sending them tumbling end over end. Liam held on as the world spiraled around him—a spin that, in the weightless vacuum of space, could continue indefinitely. And while the force of the ejection had allowed them to barely clear the top of the pyramid building, they were now angling away from the surface of Dark Star, toward the dead space beyond.

A flash in Liam's spinning view: the skim drone silently crashing into the side of the pyramid.

Liam saw the blur of lights from the *Artemis* and

the Dark Star core—the core maybe a kilometer away, the *Artemis* a few beyond that—but he couldn't tell in which direction. Dizzy, and with a hopeless fear rising inside him. Would anyone know they'd ejected and survived the crash? Maybe, if he could get his link to work. Liam tried to focus on his wrist, to get his other hand there. . . .

Too much spin. His vision slid, stomach lurched. He shut his eyes against the nauseating whirl. Was there some way he could go back in time, get a booster pack for the skim drone? Or talk himself out of this stupid idea? But he couldn't focus, his body all out of sorts.

Someone find us, please. . . .

All at once, he felt a pull. A sense of weight. Liam opened his eyes. The spinning had slowed, and their angle was changing. They were no longer floating away from Dark Star; instead, their trajectory had flattened out, and now they were arcing toward the surface of the arm beneath them. Not falling, but gently lowering, as if gravity was slowly increasing. They passed over buildings, and now that wide plaza area they'd flown over before. The angle of their descent grew steeper, and faster, until they were mere meters above the surface, which seemed to be made of stone tiles. Nearly falling now—

The skim drone's chair slammed against the ground and they tumbled. Liam's shoulder crunched, then his helmet. He heard a vicious crack as they rolled over once, twice, and ended up lying on their backs, still strapped to the chair.

Air whistling: a jagged crack in his helmet.

No! Liam pressed his glove over the spot. The whistling muted but didn't cease. A warning began to beep from his suit controls.

But now something caught his eye overhead. The view of nebula space rippled, as if it was a watery surface. An energy field began to spark into existence, a bubble shape just like the one that had enclosed the landing area outside of the Dark Star control center. It shimmered into place, and then the ground vibrated, and the silence of space was replaced by a humming sound, then a whoosh, like wind.

Iris? Liam asked.

A shadow fell over them in the dim nebula light.

"Are you all right?" asked the chronologist.

Liam strained to undo the seat buckle, then rolled off the overturned chair and got to his knees, breathless. He saw that the plaza they'd landed in was now safely encased in a dome-shaped energy field that created a seal along the tops of the buildings, into the gaps between them, and around the tunnel-like walkways that connected one building to the next. If he could hear the chronologist, that meant there was atmosphere, and the fact that he was kneeling indicated that there was gravity. He put JEFF's head aside—the robot's eyes were still flickering—pulled off his helmet, and gulped in the fresh air. "I think so."

He spun to Phoebe, still in the seat, carefully pulling her free until she was lying on her back, and then removed her helmet. Her eyes were closed, but her chest was rising and falling normally. He shook her shoulder gently, and she stirred, her lips moving. She mumbled something faintly, then rolled onto her side. Maybe the best thing was to give her a minute.

Liam stood and turned to the chronologist. "Did Iris do that? Or did you?"

"I did," said the chronologist. "There are control stations for atmosphere and gravity at each local sector of these arms. The buildings and walkway tunnels have their own systems as well. Once I saw that you had ejected from your craft, I was able to get out here and locate the systems. Obviously I had to increase the gravity just so, in order to bring you down without damage."

"Thanks," said Liam, catching his breath. "I'd ask you how you had time to do all that as we were falling, but I guess that would be silly."

Was that a smile on the chronologist's face? Liam couldn't quite tell. He stumbled as a fresh wave of pain radiated from his shoulder. He moved his arm carefully, and though it ached, he was able to rotate it fully.

He looked around and saw that they were about halfway out on this arm, which curved up and away such that the control room atop Dark Star appeared to be above them, one of those disorienting tricks of artificial gravity that Liam still wasn't quite used to. The *Artemis* was a few kilometers off to the right.

This plaza was a square shape, bordered by smoky glass structures, some of which were rectangular, some like pyramids. The tubular walkways running along their bases had doors at regular intervals.

"Liam! Are you there?" It was Kyla over his link, which was still flashing madly.

"Yeah," Liam responded, worry surging through him. They were probably about to get in all kinds of trouble.

"What happened?" said Kyla. "We saw you transit the portal. The hard line picked you up briefly on the other side, but then your signal died out. We were just about to scramble a rescue team when you popped back through."

"The skim drone died on the other side," said

Liam. "Shorted out from the portal, I think. I was able to turn it around, but we had no control when we came back through, so we had to eject and—"

"Liam, this is Ariana."

Oh great. "Hey."

"Is Xela all right?"

"Yeah. She had a bad reaction to the portal, I think, but she seems to be doing better now."

"What were you thinking, taking such a risk?"

"We were just—"

"Stay where you are. We'll be there shortly." The signal cut off.

"You say Phoebe reacted badly to the portal," said the chronologist. "In what way?"

"It was like she couldn't see anything. And she had a really bad headache. She kept talking about bright lights, and pain, like maybe a seizure or something? JEFF freaked out too, actually. Like his circuits were overloaded. And the skim drone just died out . . . although it probably still had issues from back at Centauri. I mean, the portal was weird for me, but I was fine on the other side."

"I see. It seems that my recorder's cloaking function has been working—unless you've spoken with Iris since we parted?"

Liam shook his head.

"I am beginning to think that is for the best."

"Why do you say that?"

The chronologist looked across the plaza. Liam followed his gaze. The space was mostly in shadows, except for a faint light from the energy barrier and the dim glow of the nebula. The central feature of the plaza was about twenty meters away: that large statue that Liam had glimpsed briefly while flying overhead. From here, he could see that it was a massive figure made of metal, standing on a pedestal with one arm upraised. There was an elevated platform around the statue, which was maybe used as a stage, as well as columns in the corners, which held globes that seemed to be lights.

But the statue . . . As Liam studied it, his insides began to spin. Long robes, a diamond-shaped face with two large eyes, two noses, one above the other, the hand extended upward with many fingers . . .

"It looks like you," said Liam.

The chronologist blinked. "Not exactly like me. We don't all look the same."

"Sorry, I mean—"

"Yes, I know what you meant. The statue looks like one of us."

Liam peered at it, at its upraised hand. "He's holding a crystal like yours."

"It's a she, but yes. She is."

A chronologist statue, at the center of a plaza, on an arm of Dark Star . . . "What does it mean?" said Liam. "I thought your people had never been here?"

The chronologist gazed at the statue, responding in an almost dreamy tone. "As I said earlier, the long count has no record of Dark Star, of the portal, or of any ability to leave our universe. And yet clearly, at some point, either we were here or the people who used to inhabit this place observed us."

"Is it possible that you're, you know . . . an Architect?"

The chronologist didn't respond.

"I mean, the stuff you can do with time is pretty powerful, and you sort of, you know, watch over the universe. Maybe your ancestors created our universe and then came to live in it."

"We have no ancestors," said the chronologist. "We were born along with the first wave of stars in our universe."

"Yeah, your colleague told us that exact same thing before," said Liam. "But how? You're superadvanced beings. You couldn't have just appeared that way. Didn't you, like, evolve or something?"

The chronologist was quiet again, still gazing at the statue.

"Hello?"

"It is very curious: your question is an obvious one, and yet it is utterly surprising to me. Almost like we have never thought to ask it of ourselves."

"You've never asked yourself where you come from?"

"Of course we've asked *where*, as well as *when*, but we've never asked *how*. I do not . . ."

"What?"

"Thinking about it now, I do not understand how we could have *not* asked ourselves this."

"It sounds like you guys took it on faith," said Liam. "Or trust. Except you and your colleague have both said those are more three-dimensional things."

"Indeed." The chronologist's mouth pursed.

"Maybe it just wasn't important to you guys."

"That may well be, but why not? The question of how one came to be is endemic to every sentient being. I have read what the captain said when he killed my colleague. *It's never been your way to ponder the oldest question.* Which confused her because we knew of no such question."

"He told me the oldest question is *why*."

"Our entire long count is built on observing what happens. We do not question how or why, because we can see events both forward and backward in time.

Therefore the how and why are never a mystery. Except this."

"Does that mean you've never gone back and observed your origins? Your birth, or whatever?"

"Not only have we never done that, we have never even thought to. At least not that I know of. Almost like this line of inquiry, these oldest questions were . . . unavailable to us."

Liam considered the statue again. "Maybe the people who used to live here had observed you, even if you haven't observed them," said Liam. "They had a portal into our universe. Maybe they thought you guys were like gods or something."

A light had begun to blink in the distance, out by the *Artemis*. Liam guessed it was a ship coming to get them.

The chronologist turned and seemed to take in the whole of Dark Star. The sweep of this arm on which they stood, the hundreds of buildings organized on it, leading all the way back to the core. The portal floating just above and behind them. The other arms, the other portal, this plaza around them. . . . Liam imagined this space full of people. What would they have been doing? Worshipping a statue of the chronologist? He looked around the buildings. Where had everyone gone?

Phoebe's words echoed in his head: *It feels dead*.

A sound caught his ear and he saw that Phoebe had propped herself up on her elbow. It sounded like she was speaking. Maybe JEFF had snapped out of it, too.

"There's something else I believe I should show you," said the chronologist.

"What's that?"

"It's back in that central core area. I think it is perhaps something I remember."

"Remember? From when?"

"I do not know. But I am beginning to think that I require a more . . . three-dimensional being, like yourself, to figure it out. It may also help us to figure out the true history of this place. Will you help me?"

"Um, I guess so. But I need to get Phoebe back to the *Artemis* before I go anywhere. If they even let me."

The chronologist seemed to mull this over. "May I accompany you?"

"Sure." Liam started toward Phoebe, but the chronologist remained for another moment, staring up at the statue. Liam crouched beside Phoebe. "Hey."

Phoebe was on her knees now, rubbing her head. "Where are we?"

"Back on Dark Star. We kinda crashed, but the chronologist saved us. Are you all right?"

Phoebe looked around woozily and winced. "I think so?"

"You were talking about blue lights or something."

"Yeah . . . it was weird. They were all around, and it was so loud." She shook her head. "I thought I saw the planet for a second, but just a glimpse."

"I'm sorry," said Liam. "It was a bad idea. Too dangerous."

Phoebe looked at him oddly for a moment, then shook her head. "No, don't worry about it."

"Can you stand?" Liam helped her to her feet, and she leaned on his shoulder. Nearby, JEFF's eyes had stopped flickering and now were glowing a mellow amber, as they did when he was restarting. "Did I hear you talking a second ago?" Liam asked Phoebe.

"Yeah, just to JEFF. The portal messed with him too, so I gave him a hard reset. It will probably take a while for him to boot up."

Liam motioned across the plaza. "Take a look at the statue."

Phoebe followed his gaze, and her eyes widened. "No way. What's that doing here?"

"Don't know. Even weirder: he doesn't either."

The chronologist rejoined them. "Your rescue team is coming." He pointed toward the *Artemis*. The lights of a Cosmic Cruiser were halfway to them. "I need to go adjust the energy field to let them in." He moved off toward the side of the plaza.

Liam scooped up JEFF's head.

"How can he not know why that statue is here?" Phoebe asked.

"I don't know. It's weird. Talking to him, it's almost like he hasn't ever thought of some really obvious questions."

Overhead, the shuttle was slowing and nearing the energy bubble. A rectangular section of it lit up and seemed to shimmer, not disappearing, more like thinning, and the cruiser slipped through and touched down.

As Liam and Phoebe made their way toward it, the side airlock slid opened and Ariana rushed out. She stepped right between Liam and Phoebe, taking her daughter by the shoulders.

"I cannot believe you would pull such a foolish stunt," she said. "You tell me you've grown so much while we were apart, but then here you are, making the same sorts of mistakes, over and over. It's like you learn nothing."

"You don't really give me a choice," Phoebe muttered.

Ariana stiffened, and Liam thought he saw her hand rise like she might strike Phoebe. But she flexed her fingers and lowered it. "The sooner we depart this place, the better."

"You'll just love that, won't you."

"I love nothing about this. I will tell your father and the others to ready the supplies." She guided Phoebe into the ship, Phoebe with her head down.

Liam followed them into the main cabin, which was similar to his family's Cosmic Cruiser in almost every way. "What's he doing here?" Ariana said over her shoulder when she saw the chronologist following behind Liam.

"He's coming with us. Is that okay?"

"Imagine that, actually asking permission for once." She started to bring Phoebe into the cockpit, where an officer from the *Artemis* was at the controls, but Phoebe shook free.

"I'll be fine here," she said, leaning against the wall.

"I think—"

"Mom! Maybe let me have a minute before we leave *forever*, okay?"

Ariana looked from Phoebe to Liam, her eyes blazing. "Fine." She ducked into the cockpit. The ship hummed and lifted off.

"Amazing to think I ever missed them," said Phoebe.

"Tell me about it."

Phoebe started to smile but winced.

"What is it?"

"Sorry, just strange memories from the portal."
She eyed Liam. "I saw you, but . . ."

"What?"

"It was weird." She shook her head. "Did it hurt
for you like it did for me?"

"No," said Liam. "I mean, it got a little stretchy
when we went through, but it was fine after that."

The shuttle quickly crossed the space between
Dark Star and the *Artemis*, then slowed, waiting for
the airlock to slide open. Phoebe and Liam pulled off
their space-grade suits and threw them on the couch.

"May I have my crystal back?" said the chronologist when they were finished.

"Oh, right." Phoebe had been gripping it tightly.
She handed it to him.

The chronologist consulted it but left it glowing.
"I think we'll still be needing this."

"You don't trust Dark Star anymore, do you?"
Liam asked. "After that statue."

"I would characterize it less as mistrust and more
as extreme caution."

"Why?" said Phoebe. "What are you worried
about?"

"The increasing number of things I seem not to know, and the future I cannot see."

The shuttle transited the airlock, and there was a rumble as the ship entered atmosphere.

"I can't say I disagree with him," said Phoebe. "There's a part of me that will be relieved to get out of here. Maybe it's just the headache talking, but . . ."

Liam didn't know what to say, especially about these recent mysteries. And yet he reminded himself that Iris had made them a new home, not to mention helping him overcome his fears.

The floor shook as the landing stabilizers fired. A thud as the craft touched down. Ariana ducked into the main cabin. She put a hand on Phoebe's arm, but then paused and looked at Liam. "We never thanked you, for saving us back at Centauri."

For a moment, he felt a surge of frustration. Wanted to tell her that he wasn't even sure he would have, if he had to do it over again, or even if he should have. Instead he just said, "Sure."

"And for saving Xela. You are a credit to your people, Liam. I hope they can learn from you." She nodded, as if satisfied with her words. "Five minutes," she said to Phoebe, and walked out.

Phoebe turned to Liam. Her eyes had welled up. "So, I guess . . ."

"Yeah." Liam's heart pounded. His palms were

slick. Suddenly it hit him: this was really it; the moment he'd seen. They would say good-bye, right now, and he would never see Phoebe again.

"I'm going to—"

The *Artemis* officer emerged from the cockpit, his boots clomping like he was trying to be as loud as he could. He cleared his throat. "Just want to get by."

"I should step outside too," said the chronologist. Liam and Phoebe let him pass.

When Liam's eyes met hers again, he felt for sure that he couldn't take it, that he would be better off just running, getting out of here, because facing this felt like too much. He'd seen the future, seen the past, been in so many dangerous moments, and yet this felt somehow more dire than all of it: the end, a true end, of something he would never be able to get back. It was a feeling he could barely fathom, like his heart was going to burst. He felt tears behind his eyes, at the same time he saw them falling from Phoebe's.

He put his shaking hand on her shoulder. "I, um—"

"Xela!" Ariana called from outside.

Phoebe winced, balling her fists like she wanted to explode, and then threw her arms around Liam and kissed him right on the lips. Liam managed to move his arms, to put them around her, managed to keep his face where it was and his lips where they were for one, two . . . saw that her eyes were closed and closed his . . . three . . .

She moved her lips from his and slid her cheek across his and, for a moment, hugged him as tight as she could.

Liam pressed his face against her bristled skin. His mind unmoored from the moment, drifting, and he could see all of it at once . . .

Phoebe beside him at Lunch Rocks. Running ahead of him in the lava tubes.

Next to him on the couch of the Cosmic Cruiser, playing *Roid Wraiths*. Kissing her there and feeling so embarrassed afterward.

Her false face melting off in the heat of the Delphi baths.

Hugging to travel to Telos.

Pulling her through space toward the doorway.

A few rows ahead in their Year 10 classroom, looking back at him and Shawn through her long pink hair, trying to relay the specifics of some plan or another.

Up on Vista, with her arms out, beneath the solar storm. *She'd been thinking of her own red sun,* Liam realized. *I had no idea.*

So many memories, each of which seemed more precious now and somehow not quite enough—if only he'd known then how this ending would feel, he would have enjoyed everything more, but how could you ever really know?

And he felt, too, like Phoebe was feeling this same thing, like she was traveling with him, through time, seeing it all, like her presence was right there beside him. Maybe they could just keep going—

"Xela." Her dad this time.

Phoebe moved a millimeter away, exhaling hard, or maybe it was a sob. The spell was broken, and Liam felt himself back in the present, like he was weighted to the floor.

But before she pulled away, Phoebe leaned close to his ear: "Find me in the safe place," she whispered.

"What?"

"The—"

Paolo appeared in the doorway. "Xela, now."

Phoebe stepped back, her eyes fixed on him. "Did you hear me?"

"Yeah," said Liam, "but . . ."

"Good luck, Liam," said Paolo. He held his arm out to Phoebe.

Her eyes locked with Liam's one last time. "This is how it has to be." She turned—"Bye"—and walked out.

Liam stood there for a moment, a supernova inside. All of this was too much. He didn't want to move. Didn't want to take a single step into his future feeling this alone. *This is how it has to be.* Why? And yet he knew, for all the reasons he'd heard their parents lay out. That said, it had seemed like Phoebe had meant something else by that. What exactly was the safe place? His memories?

"Hey there." Kyla stepped inside.

"Hey." Liam wiped his eyes.

"Sorry, do you need a minute? Or . . ."

"No, it's all right. How are my parents doing down on the surface?"

"They're at the third sampling site and it's still going well. Listen, what happened to you guys out there?"

Liam recounted flying through the portal and back.

Kyla listened, her face serious. When Liam was finished, she didn't speak for a moment.

"What?" said Liam.

"I don't know. What happened to your bot?"

"Oh." Liam picked up JEFF's head. His eyes were still that mellow amber, and Liam could feel a humming inside, as JEFF restarted. "He acted weird on the other side of the portal too. Like it overloaded his processors or something."

"Do you know what kind of overload?" Kyla asked.

"Um, not really. I think he said something about an incompatibility."

Kyla's face darkened.

"What?"

"We've been having some weird lags and arti-facting in our feed from the portal. Losing helmet cams momentarily, delays in the signal from the hard line. We checked the logs of the *Artemis*'s comms processors and they are spiking with errors that say INCOMPATIBILITY DETECTED, REGION UN-KNOWN."

"That's what JEFF said."

"They resolve themselves almost immediately, but no one can figure out where they're coming from, except that they seem to be related to the feed from the other side."

"What do you think they mean?"

Kyla shook her head. "I don't know. It's just . . . something's not right about this place. Ever since we got here, it's just felt . . . off. I mean, why would this place really make an entire universe just for us?"

"We were wondering the same thing," Liam admitted. "What does the captain think?"

Kyla laughed under her breath. "Nobody knows what's going on in the captain's head. I used to think I knew him, used to look up to him actually. But ever since we got here . . . sometimes I think he's more interested in this place's secrets than he is in the sur-vival of his crew." She looked like she might say more, but she turned instead toward the sound of increased commotion outside the ship. "Come on," she said. "I'm headed back to the bridge, but you can watch them depart if you want."

Liam followed Kyla out, JEFF under his arm, and stood beside a line of *Artemis* crew members, the two who'd been keeping watch in the hangar plus a few more, all holding rifles at their sides. The last Telphons were climbing up into the Styrlax ship, carrying boxes of supplies. Phoebe was between them, but she didn't look over. Liam watched until the last of them had stepped through the door. . . .

Phoebe's head popped out. She waved. A brief smile.

Liam waved back, throat tight. *Bye.*

She disappeared inside, and a moment later, the ship hummed and lifted off the ground. It rotated and slid toward the airlock. Liam scanned its exterior, looking for a window or something, but its sides were sheer metal. Could Phoebe see him somehow? He waved, just in case, the lump growing in his throat.

Find me in the safe place.

What had she meant?

The inner airlock door rumbled open. The Styrlax ship flew in, and the door closed and they were gone, the hangar plunging into silence.

The *Artemis* crew members headed for the elevator to the bridge, leaving Liam alone in the hangar. He just stood there, a storm inside.

A many-fingered hand patted his shoulder. "Are you ready to go?" asked the chronologist.

No. He just wanted to return to the compartment and lie in the stasis pod. "Do I have time to watch them leave? Just until they're through the portal safely?"

"Of course, we have all of time available."

Liam crossed the hangar to a window. He watched the Styrlax ship slide smoothly away from the *Artemis*, passing in front of the portal to the new Earth. Its thrusters flared and it accelerated toward the portal home—*not home anymore, not for us.* Liam barely breathed as the ship became a shooting star . . . and in a ripple of green light, it was gone.

"The Telphon ship is safely through," Kyla said over Liam's link.

Good-bye, Liam thought, and felt his throat welling up again.

A bell-like tone sounded. Liam looked down to see JEFF's eyes glowing bright green. "Greetings, and welcome to your personal assistant. If you are a registered user of this bot, say your name now."

"Liam Saunders-Chang."

"Acknowledged. For additional identification,

please authenticate with fingerprint scan—correction: fingerprint scanner not located. Update: multiple systems not located."

"That's because you're just a head."

"One moment . . ." JEFF's eyes flickered. "Your saved settings indicate your preference for the voice personality JEFF. Would you like to continue?"

"Yes."

Another flickering pause. . . . "Good morning, Liam! I am glad to be back, or at least what is left of me."

"I'm glad you're back too, JEFF."

"Liam." It was Mina, over the link. "How are you holding up?"

"Okay."

"I hear your little romantic mission was nearly a disaster."

"Yeah. Do Mom and Dad know?"

"I don't think so, and we might want to skip telling them. I'm on the bridge right now. I'm watching them at the third sample point and it's this polar spot and there are these weird penguin-like critters. You should come up and see it. It's pretty cool. It might even cure your broken heart."

"Shut up."

"I'm serious, though, come up."

"I will," Liam said, glancing at the chronologist. "I'll be there in like—"

"Liam, I'm sorry to interrupt," said JEFF, "but that information is inaccurate."

"What information?"

"Your parents' location. They are not at the third sample point."

"What's he talking about?" said Mina.

"I don't know," said Liam. "Did they visit the spots out of order from the original plan or something?"

"The plans are incorrect," said JEFF. "There are no sample points."

"Come on, JEFF," said Mina. "They—"

"There are no sample points because there is no planet."

"What?" said Liam. And yet a twinge of nervous energy ignited inside.

"When we transited the portal," said JEFF, "my sensors detected a massive amount of data, but I did not detect a planet, nor any stars, cosmic radiation, or anything that would normally be evidence of physical space."

"Your sensors probably just got scrambled," said Liam, and yet his breath had shortened, his mouth getting dry.

"I do not think so. According to my sensors,

there is no planet on the other side of that portal, but instead a vast electrical field with incredible power. It overloaded my processors within moments."

"Electrical field . . . ," Liam repeated.

"That doesn't make sense," said Mina. "We're literally looking at the planet *right now*. Mom and Dad and the team are down there. They've sent reports back to us—"

"My data logs from the other side of that portal indicate otherwise."

"Did you fry his circuits?" Mina asked.

"JEFF!" Liam's heart was starting to pound. He thought of Phoebe's reaction. "I saw the planet, and the sun."

"The only three-dimensional information that my sensors picked up was a field of bright blue lights contained in some sort of large space. This corroborates with what Phoebe experienced."

"You talked to Phoebe?"

"Yes, she is the one who rebooted me, after we compared notes about what we'd seen."

"Right." Liam pictured her lying there in the plaza while he'd been talking to the chronologist.

So many blue stars, Phoebe had said.

"I think it is even more important now that you come with me," said the chronologist.

"Liam, this is Kyla. Your sister relayed this new information from your bot. I don't know what's going on—I mean, we can see your parents and talk to the team, and all our sensors and readings about the planet check out, but . . ."

"But what?"

"There was that similarity I mentioned, between the data errors we've been having and what your bot experienced through the portal. I think maybe you should bring him up here and we'll see what's what."

"We need to go before you bring the bot upstairs," the chronologist said quietly.

Liam covered his link. "Why?"

"Because the bridge will not provide the answer you seek. This blue light that Phoebe and your bot refer to . . . I know its source. And I believe it will reveal where your parents are."

Liam swallowed hard, a chill spiking through him. "You don't think my parents are on new Earth either."

"I do not."

"But *they* think they are . . . so if they're not there, where are they?"

"I think, given this information, there may be something far different going on here than we believe."

Liam looked at the crystal, pulsing in the chronologist's hand. Iris . . . *what is going on?* That little doubt he'd had about her, about this place, that he hadn't wanted to listen to, had grown into a buzzing fear inside him.

"Are you ready?" said the chronologist.

Liam nodded, still gazing at the crystal. "Where are we going?"

"To the cylinder we observed at the center of Dark Star. I believe this is where the answer lies, but I need your help to fully make sense of it. I can take you there slightly back in time, and then return you to this exact point so that you can join your sister on the bridge."

"Liam, are you there?" Mina asked.

"Yeah . . ." Liam slipped on waves of fright. Could he even trust the chronologist? But through everything that had happened on Mars, the chronologists had always told Liam the whole truth. More than his parents, even more than Phoebe.

"I'm on my way up," he said into the link.

Then he muted the channel and turned to the chronologist. "Okay, let's go."

16

"I do not think you need to hug me. Just stand nearby."

Liam put down JEFF's head and moved beside the chronologist. He swallowed against a sour taste in his mouth. The jet flame in his gut now felt like a full-blown inferno. *They are not at the third sample point.* "I'll be right back," he said to JEFF.

"I suppose I will be right here," JEFF said from the floor.

The chronologist tapped his orange crystal, and the world blurred around them as they moved backward along the chronologist's timeline—a flash of darkness and nebula, then the plaza with the statue where he had met up with Liam, and before that, a twisting labyrinth of empty corridors. They arrived in the hangar, rows of Dark Star ships on either side. Reality stuck together again. Liam saw the chronologist's previous self departing the area for the elevators.

"This way."

Liam followed him between the rows of ships, the chronologist's orange light bobbing in the dark, pulsing slow and steady. Ahead, the towering silver cylinder dominated the center of the room, looming over them, the sleek surface seeming to glow, and Liam thought he could feel an energy buzzing from it, even more than he had before. Pressing against him, making it hard to move. . . . They reached the railing at the edge of the platform. Liam took a dizzying look down, tracing the side of the cylinder hundreds of meters to the pool of black hole beneath Dark Star. He looked up to see the chronologist crossing the catwalk without breaking stride.

The door in the side of the cylinder slid open. Electric-blue light spilled out from inside.

Blue lights. Liam took a tentative step onto the catwalk. "How did you open it?"

"I didn't. Well, I didn't choose to. I have come to this spot multiple times, and the door never opened until my last visit."

"What do you think changed?"

The chronologist paused at the threshold. "This station has been powering up the entire time we've been here, and whatever it is working toward seems to be nearly complete."

"Full functionality," said Liam.

"What I wanted you to see is in here." The chronologist turned and stepped into the blue light.

Liam stood there on the catwalk, staring at the glowing doorway. *Run.* The thought shot through his mind; he should run right now, get the *Artemis* to head back to their universe, call off the arrival of the fleet. He wasn't sure why, but it suddenly felt obvious that that was the right thing to do, right now. . . .

But his parents. What had happened to them? Whatever was through this door was part of the answer. And not only to that; to the other questions he'd been avoiding. . . .

As he stood there on the catwalk, shaking, Liam realized something else about this moment: he leaned back from his present and looked toward the future, and while he still saw the same sunny moments of going to Earth, and all that would happen there, and while he could see himself saying good-bye to Phoebe just behind him in his past, he did not see the skim drone crash, or crossing the portal before that. Where were those memories? And then whatever came right after this moment also did not seem to exist. There was no cylinder with the blue light, no Liam with the chronologist. There *was* a moment directly ahead in his future, but it was him standing with Mina, on the bridge of the *Artemis*. They were watching the feed from the sample site, oohing and aahhing over the strange penguin-like creatures. How could that be what happened next, if he was standing here? Either he didn't actually go through this door . . . or *that future I'm seeing isn't the real one.*

The thought froze him completely.

There is no planet, JEFF had said.

Had his timestream been manipulated? And if so, there was only one entity with the power to do such a thing. . . .

The chronologist leaned back out. "Coming?"

No. He wanted to leave, to get out of here—but he stepped toward the door, body shaking, heart hammering. He had come this far. Had to know. Had to find his parents.

He stepped into a world of blue light and found himself on a sleek, circular platform that seemed to float in the center of the cylindrical space. There was a small gap between the platform's edge and the rounded wall—but it wasn't a wall, exactly. It was a surface made of small spheres, neatly lined up in perfect vertical and horizontal rows. Each sphere was maybe ten centimeters across, made of clear crystal, and inside was a floating, blue . . . spark, Liam thought first. Like a bit of pure energy. Each one hummed and grew and shrank in independent pulses. Here and there, they sprouted brief fingers of light, wavering tentacles, some of which momentarily splayed against the inner wall of the crystal, almost like they were seeking a way out. The very center of the energy was brilliant white, cooling to blue.

These rows of spheres completely encircled the inner wall of the cylinder, and stretched upward and downward for how far Liam couldn't tell: Two hundred meters? Five hundred? And it wasn't exactly a wall because there was another layer of crystal spheres behind this first one, and another behind that, and on and on past what Liam could distinguish, many meters deep, it seemed, deeper than should even have been possible given the apparent size of the cylinder from the outside. Squinting in the light, Liam could now see that all of the spheres were held in place by a delicate lattice of gossamer-thin wire.

But it was the spheres themselves, the sparkling, babbling lights inside . . . Their glow seemed to rise and fall like conversation. In spite of his fear and confusion, Liam stepped closer, held out his finger until it was nearly touching the surface of one. And the light inside, somehow, seemed to sense him. It gathered along the inside rim, almost like it was trying to make contact.

"What are they?" he asked.

"They are bioelectric entities," said the chronologist. "And each one is unique. An individual."

"Individual? Like a person?"

"The spheres contain electrical signals similar to brain activity. Each one is a consciousness in its pure energy state. I believe . . . these are the Architects."

Liam gazed around, upward, below, at the rows and rows. There had to be millions, maybe billions. "These are the beings that built this place? What happened to their bodies?"

"I do not know if they ever had bodies."

"But those buildings outside, on all of the arms . . ."

"I cannot account for it," said the chronologist. "These spheres are all connected to a massive processing system."

"So, are they alive or not?"

"That would depend on your definition. I think, based on the energy patterns, that they believe that they are."

"I don't get it."

A voice came from the doorway: "They're alive and well."

Liam turned to find Captain Barrie, the rifle-like Dark Star weapon leveled at Liam and the chronologist. He stepped inside and ran his fingers over the nearest spheres, their energy spidering out to meet his touch. "Sentient beings, happily going about their lives in a simulation that accurately depicts a four-dimensional reality." He motioned to the chronologist. "She finally let you in here, I see."

"Fascinating," said the chronologist. "So the Architects chose to upload their consciousness into a virtual simulation, perhaps to achieve a kind of immortality."

"Oh, these aren't the Architects," said Barrie.

Liam's heart hammered; he was shaking all over now. He gazed at the weapon in Barrie's hand, as he stood blocking the only door out. "Who are they?" he asked.

"That's what I'm here to show you." He was smiling, a cold, knowing grin so full of energy, of satisfaction, that Liam felt certain it was the first true expression he'd seen on Barrie's face the entire time they'd been here.

And he was not on their side.

Barrie stepped closer to Liam and the chronologist,

the rifle still trained on them, and made a horizontal waving motion with his free hand. A pedestal slid up from the center of the platform on which they stood. It rose to waist height, made of smoky glass, lights flicking through its circuitry. Barrie bounced his hand on the air above it. The entire platform vibrated and began to lower itself down the center of the cylinder. They passed hundreds, thousands of rows of blue spheres.

"Where are we going?" said Liam, gulping breaths.

"Back in time," said Barrie.

Liam felt like his heart had crawled up into his throat. "Do you know where my parents are?"

Barrie's smile widened. "So you've caught on, eh? Don't worry, they're fine."

Liam crossed his arms, trying not to shake. "They're not on Earth, are they?"

"You'll see."

"How is it that you can operate this machinery?" said the chronologist. "That you were given access to this chamber?"

"Dark Star reveals its truths when she believes we are ready to know them."

She. Liam had heard Barrie say it before, but he'd thought it was just the parlance of talking about a ship. Yet now . . . "You've talked to her, haven't you?"

Barrie cocked his head. "Not like you have."

He knows. He's known all along. Liam's insides wound so tight he could barely breathe. He wanted more than anything to run, to slip out of time and reverse direction, get out of here, but what good would that do? This moment would still be here, standing between him and knowing where his parents were, what all this really was. And yet he felt sure now that those answers were bigger and more terrible than he'd ever imagined.

Barrie waved the gun at Liam. "Now stop interrupting with all your questions and look around—enjoy the show."

They descended, passing row after row of sparking crystals. Liam could barely stay steady on his feet, his gaze darting from Barrie and the weapon to the mesmerizing sparks of light. Thoughts spun around in his head like a dust devil. If his parents were not on Earth, if, as JEFF seemed to say, there was no new Earth, and if the captain in fact knew where they were and what all this was, it not only meant that he had been lying to them at nearly every turn . . . but that Iris had been too.

His nerves screamed. A dizzy feeling in his head. The lights in the spheres around them seemed to be buzzing more excitedly against their borders, almost like they sensed him, could feel his panic, like they were trying to communicate with him, or perhaps even trying to break free.

"We're not the first to find Dark Star," said Barrie, his face aglow in the wavering blue light. "These beings you see here were the most recent to arrive before us. They discovered this place a few billion years ago."

"Who are they?" Liam asked, his voice hoarse, barely above a whisper.

"Can't say I know what they would have called themselves. Dark Star refers to them by the universe they arrived here from. In this case, iteration 73."

All at once, they passed a break in the rows of spheres, a band of smoky glass-and-light circuitry. A moment later, the spheres began again, but these were different: smaller, it seemed. And the lights dimmer inside, less active—in many cases there was just a still, glowing dot. It looked as though, here and there, the insides of the crystal walls were blotchy with stains, almost like mildew. And some of the spheres were completely dark.

"These beings came from iteration 57," said Barrie. "Three hundred billion years ago. Well before our universe even existed. Their universe is long since dead, and as you can see, they are dying out now as well."

Liam tried to control his shaking. In the dim light, these older spheres looked almost ghostly. It felt as if they were descending deeper into a tomb.

They lowered perhaps another hundred meters and passed through another gap. Another set of crystal spheres began. These were almost completely dark, their insides filmy. Here and there, the faintest light, barely flickering. A few last souls, hanging on.

"This race is from iteration 41, almost a trillion years ago. Eventually, what begin as tiny data corruptions ultimately become fatal. But it's also a question of resources. The power needed to maintain these beings can be better utilized on the newer, more promising candidates."

"Where are my parents?" Liam said, barely above a whisper. Something about what Barrie had just said caused a spike of pure white fear to shoot through him, and yet he couldn't quite wrap his brain around why, the idea like a loud buzzing static in his brain. . . .

Barrie didn't seem to hear him, or just ignored him, and continued. "She winds them down gradually, and I believe they're at peace. Living in four dimensions, they've had a knowledge of their past and future all along, and so when they finally arrive at their death, they accept it."

"But it is not a true future," said the chronologist.

"It is manufactured, isn't that correct? There is no probability, no free will, only a program. A fabrication."

"I suppose that's true, but not to them. In their reality, there is more truth, more *awareness*, than they ever had access to in their limited physical lives."

"Doesn't that mean they're being lied to?" said Liam. "Told something is real when it's not?"

"How do *you* know what's real?" Barrie said. "Your senses, your feelings? What's to say those are accurate, that you're not just seeing what your brain wants you to see? Or what some higher intelligence wants your brain to see?" He spread his arms. "Can we even be sure any of this is real?"

Liam wobbled on his feet, wishing there was something to lean against. *My future isn't real.* What about these surroundings right now? "Isn't it?" he croaked.

"Yes," said the chronologist. "This is reality." And yet Liam saw that he consulted his crystal as he said it.

"Spoken with true conviction," Barrie said dryly.

The spheres ended again. This time, the walls opened up around them, and for a moment there was darkness, lit only by those spheres above. The platform started to slow, then settled to a stop flush with a smooth floor that stretched away from them into a vast space in all directions, again, seemingly far larger than the walls of the cylinder should have been able to contain.

"Welcome to the heart of Dark Star," said Barrie.

Liam saw banks and clusters of equipment here and there, cast in islands of amber light that had no direct source. Deep, pure black shadows lurked in between.

As the platform came to a stop, it disturbed a thick coating of very fine dust on the floor. Its hum cycled down, and there was a silence here that seemed more still, somehow more infinite, than Liam had ever known. The air was warm, heavy. Liam felt like, if he stood still long enough, the heat and silence would suffocate him.

To one side was a large field of narrow structures that resembled stasis pods, yet they were made of a sleeker, smoke-colored metal. A set of a dozen or so pods in the front row were lit in that amber glow. Behind that, rows and rows stretched back into darkness. Liam could not tell if there were hundreds, or thousands, or even more than that, in the dimness. Those front few pods had open lids, yellowish glass curves that yawned up to the side. Tubes hung down to them from the ceiling. There were mechanisms up there, in the shadows above the pods. Complex-looking armatures and gears. The sight of it all chilled

Liam, the open pod lids almost beckoning.

"This way." Barrie stepped off the platform in the opposite direction of the pod-like structures. He waved the rifle, motioning Liam and the chronologist toward a line of lights in the murky distance, like ovals standing on their ends.

Liam looked back over his shoulder. "What's in those pods back there?"

"This way first."

"But—"

Barrie leveled the rifle. "Let's not pretend, shall we? I can carry you there if you'd like. It makes no difference to me."

Liam swallowed, metallic. The shivering uncontrollable. He felt like all of his will, his hope, was draining out of him. He looked at the chronologist, trying to meet his eyes. Couldn't he stop this somehow, incapacitate Barrie if he wanted? But the chronologist simply brushed past him in the direction Barrie had indicated.

Liam fell into step beside him. Gulping breaths, heart pounding like it might just explode. Trying to understand what he was seeing, those spheres, the minds of beings who had come here in the past . . . but it all made a buzzing noise in his head, and a persistent warning, nearly screaming in his every nerve ending: *Get out get out get out—*

And yet at the same time he felt a gnawing terror, a certainty that it was too late, for him, for his parents, for everyone. Something inevitable was happening here. *And it's my own fault*, he thought coldly. No, not really. He hadn't known, couldn't have known. . . .

They trudged through the darkness. Liam sensed that this space wasn't measured in the normal three dimensions. They were moving through more than just a physical space; perhaps even the layout he was seeing was simply the best his mind could do to make sense of this room—*it's a laboratory*, he thought, or perhaps . . . a lair.

"It took me a while to truly understand the grand design," said Barrie, his tone almost dreamlike. "Ever since she came to me, so long ago. I was a young boy like yourself. It has taken decades of focus, of discipline and belief, to make the journey all the way to this moment. I am in awe of you, Liam, being able to achieve that at such a young age."

"I was just trying to save my family, and friends, and . . ."

"Were you, though? Or were you following her call, whether you would have admitted it or not?"

A memory flashed in Liam's mind of the very first time he'd used the chronologist's watch on Mars.

He had seen the future where they died in the turbine explosion. As he had traveled past that moment, past even his own death, he had felt an urge: *Farther. Farther.* To know the answers, *all* the answers. And in a way, that urge was a part of what had led him here. What had pushed him to explore with the watch. Even when he'd been using it just to comfort himself, like traveling back to Mars, hadn't he also been searching? . . . Hadn't he, in some way, been just like Barrie?

"We're almost there now."

His footsteps made little clouds in the thick dust on the floor. It was gray, and deathly quiet, but his next step crunched on something. Now a flash of movement a meter away. Something crawled briefly to the surface of the dust before burrowing away. It looked almost like a cockroach, but longer, flatter, and jet black.

"Trillions of years," said Barrie from behind them, "creating universes and waiting. Perfecting its attempts to achieve its true goal."

JEFF's words flashed in Liam's mind: *Whatever the goals and intentions of the Architects were, that may no longer be what Dark Star wants.*

"Stop here." Barrie stepped in front of Liam and the chronologist. Liam saw a line of cylindrical enclosures made of clear crystal, about six feet in height and four feet in diameter. They floated just above the floor, glowing in pure white light, and inside each there seemed to be a suspended figure. . . .

A body.

"Iteration 41," said Barrie, pointing to the first crystal case, in which floated a squat being with a long, narrow head, multiple arms and legs—it was hard to tell which were which—and skin that looked like the plates of an insect's shell. Its eyes were open, and glowing, opaque, with a pale blue light similar to the spheres above.

"57." The next cylinder contained an impossibly thin being with no arms and a body that seemed to be all one thin, triangular head. Its three legs were folded awkwardly in on themselves to fit in the enclosure. It had leathery skin and a ring of large black eyes that also glowed.

"73." This third one looked somewhat humanoid. It had long arms and short, squat legs, and wore a leathery suit with boots and gloves and controls as if it was made for space travel. A furry covering instead of just skin. A mouth with square, humanlike teeth. No ears. Eyes shining blue and opaque like the others.

"Are they alive, too?" As he asked, something skittered over Liam's boot. He saw the tail of another of those insect-like creatures slithering into the dust.

"Even more so," said Barrie. "This is where the prototype is taken to be analyzed and finalized."

"Prototype?" said the chronologist.

"The very best example of the species, the most worthy representative of his or her iteration. The one who found this place, who led their people here. The one who, once finalization is complete, is given eternal access to the highest reality possible." As Barrie said this, he motioned to the fourth pool of light.

An empty crystal cylinder.

Liam's shuddering had become overwhelming, his fingers tingling with numbness, his heart trying to rip free from his chest. Tears slipped down his cheeks.

"You're the one, Liam," said Barrie. "The prototype of iteration 89."

"I didn't . . . where are my parents . . ."

"Think of it as a reward," said Barrie, "for making the journey. For believing in the grand design, for yearning for the highest possible awareness. I have to say, I'm jealous." He motioned to the chronologist. "From the moment I first saw your colleague, back in my youth on Earth, I dreamed that it would be me. When we found the portal, I truly believed it *was* me, and yet, I can be content with playing my role. And she has agreed to provide for me as well."

Liam now noticed a second empty, lit cylinder,

just beyond the one that was meant for—*Me. It's meant for me.*

He stepped back. "I want to leave. I want to find my parents and I want to go."

Barrie frowned. "Don't you understand what I'm showing you?"

He did. Or he didn't. Either way, shaking, sweating, barely able to breathe—

"She'll give you what you wanted, Liam, just like she told you she would. No more worries, no more doubt. All that uncertainty . . . vanished. You'll see everything, the universes and their possibilities, and when we ascend, we'll be beyond time completely, on the shores of something we can scarcely imagine. Something beyond our very ideas of gods and creation, of physics and laws."

"But you said it's a program," said Liam. "It isn't real."

"The simulation is for the rest of them, not for you and me. Humanity will take its place inside the housings like you saw on the way down here. But you and I will get to join her here in the mainframe. We will finally reach the higher dimensions and fully experience all of reality."

Barrie motioned to the other three crystal cases and their floating inhabitants. "None of these beings were quite enough. Each one better than the last, but their brains couldn't quite give her what she needed. You though, Liam, *us*, we can. With our minds, she can truly ascend."

"You are saying that Dark Star has been building universes so that those universes will foster unique forms of life," said the chronologist, "and then those life-forms will find their way here."

"Don't forget the stars it uses as power sources," said Barrie. "It is a dual-purpose system. But yes, you're correct, though we're not talking about just any life-forms. Only the most powerful beings can make it here."

"It's been waiting for us?" said Liam. "But . . . we're not the most powerful beings in the universe. There's the Styrlax, who gave the Telphons that ship. There's him." He pointed to the chronologist.

"In this case, what I mean by power is *potential*. The human brain, Liam. It has more capacity than those of any other beings. Or any of these that have arrived here previously." Barrie motioned to the other creatures in the cases. "We simply haven't developed the consciousness, the awareness, to fully utilize our own potential. Our planet gave birth to our anatomy, but its environment also limited our perception of time and space, of the reality around us. Yet in terms of raw processing power, there's never been anything as powerful as the human brain, in the history of our universe or any other. And when you want to attain access to the higher dimensions, what you need is power. Not power like energy, exactly. Computational power. Think of the potential of eleven billion human brains, all connected—every dendrite fully utilized, every synapse firing at maximum. With that power, Liam, Dark Star could finally unlock the totality of dimensional awareness and finally see the truth."

Liam remembered so many things Iris had said to him, about higher viewpoints, about how soon he would be able to perceive them, and all along he'd assumed that she'd meant that they would achieve this by continuing to practice and hone his skills, in his world, his reality, *in my body*. But Barrie was suggesting something else entirely.

"There is no new Earth," he finally said. As the words left his lips, the terror swelled inside. Saying it finally made it real, cemented this perfect trap that he'd walked right into.

"There is."

"But it's not real!" shouted Liam.

"It does not exist in any physical universe, no."

"Then where are my parents?"

"They're on Earth."

"But you just said—"

Barrie's expression hardened. "Don't you understand that they will be happy?"

"But where are they? Where are their bodies?"

Barrie glanced past Liam and the chronologist. Liam followed his gaze toward those rows of pod-shaped structures he'd seen just as they arrived in this chamber, and the giant mechanisms overhead. "They are awaiting verification of the prototype, at which point they can be fully transferred."

"You mean into one of those glass spheres," said Liam. "That's what you're saying. Anyone who goes through that portal to the new Earth gets . . . captured? Taken?"

"Invited," said Barrie.

"You're not giving them a choice!"

"True. But humans haven't ever done all that well with choice."

"So what my parents are seeing, that Earth, where they are taking samples and flying around, that's all a simulation?"

"It is. And you have seen how happy they are."

"But they don't know! You're putting us into those crystals, into that reality without—"

"You're not hearing me. You and I don't have to go there. We get to join Dark Star as she ascends. That is our reward. We don't have to watch as humanity slowly ruins that new Earth, as they squabble and war. Instead, we'll have universal awareness."

Liam shook his head. "But what actually *happens* to my parents? What happened to all those beings in the spheres?"

Barrie bit his lip. He looked down and ran his toe through the fine dust at their feet. "The consciousness doesn't need a body to experience fulfillment. In fact, it's quite the opposite: a body is a *limitation*; bodies are fragile, they filter reality through imperfect sensory input. The needs and drives of the body, even consciousness itself, holds the brain back from its maximum potential."

"You are harvesting them," said the chronologist. "Using their brains as processors."

"*Harvesting* is a rather industrial word," said Barrie.

Liam took a step back. "You're going to kill them."

"No. Don't you see? Nobody has to die, ever again. Not the way we have to now."

"Yes, you are! You've—you're bringing all of humanity here so you can murder them, and so she can *use* their brains, that's—"

"Monstrous," the chronologist finished.

"Liam, please. You've seen how this universe

works. How cold, how vast. How little power and control we really have. On our own, we're doomed to live with just the glimpse of greater truth, but without the power to truly grasp it. And worse"—Barrie pinched his own arm—"trapped in this mortal cage, we will never succeed. Did you really think Aaru-5 was the answer? That we'd land there and live happily ever after? Some of us, perhaps, maybe for a while. A few generations. But we'd ruin that, too. There would be more conflict—between ourselves, with other races, as you saw with the Telphons, even with the very land that sustains us. We are a race with so much potential, and yet doomed to stumble around in the cold and dark, making a noisy mess of things, never quite able to see past our own fear."

"That's not how we are," said Liam, and yet hadn't he just lost his best friend for these very reasons? And hadn't he spent so much of his life a prisoner of his fears and the way they affected him physically?

"Humanity will be happier on new Earth," said Barrie. "They'll never even know it's a simulation created by Dark Star. And if Dark Star can truly ascend, we'll all share in the truth she discovers."

"So the Architects essentially created a farm," said the chronologist.

"Who knows what the Architects did or didn't do?

They haven't been here for trillions of years. Maybe they built this place. Maybe it built them. Maybe they were the energy before the universes ever began. What matters is that Dark Star has a single goal: to know reality in totality. And to do that, she required technological advancement. She needed a power greater than you could build with metal and circuitry. *We* are that advancement. The processor that could truly compute the higher dimensions.

"Think of it. Hundreds of generations of humans have tried to understand God's plan, and the answer is here: God really does need us. She made us not only so that we could know her, but so that we could *help* her, and together become something even more. All you have to do is step up here and be what you were always meant to be. Now, are you ready?"

Liam stared at the empty crystal cylinder before him. This was what Iris had been grooming him for; she had essentially told him this, and yet also not quite. Promising him a reality beyond the unknown, beyond the fear that spun him so tight, often completely out of his control. And he'd listened, because all his life, on top of all the fear and doubt and worry that he'd felt, he'd also feared that he was like this because he was broken in some way that he would never quite be able to fix. This was the chance to finally fix it.

And yet.

"No," he said, pushing back against all the terror he felt. There was something *wrong* about this. Plugging himself into this machine, the entire human race, just looking at those other bodies, hanging there, eyes vacant . . . "I'm going to get my parents, and we're getting out of here. And we're telling the fleet to turn around, and we're all getting as far away from this place as we can."

Barrie made a whistling sound and shook his head. "Well said. Very brave, but also very human. I'm afraid I can't let you leave." He turned to the chronologist. "My friend, it's time."

"I do not understand—" the chronologist began.

"Initiate command nine," said Barrie.

The chronologist blinked. "Command nine . . . ?"

"Hold the boy."

The chronologist's hand shot out and grabbed Liam by the arm.

"Hey! What are you doing?" Liam shouted.

"I do not know," said the chronologist.

"Yes you do," said Barrie. "You just don't *know*. You've always had a sense of it, without ever being able to put your many fingers on it. But like I said, consciousness is such a small-minded thing, even for a being such as yourself. Now: smash that crystal of yours."

The chronologist held out the orange crystal recorder, gazed at it—and hurled it to the floor, where it shattered into glittering shards.

"Ah, that's better," a voice said, suddenly, all around them.

Iris.

"Now do you get it, timekeeper?" said Barrie.

"My purpose is to chronicle the universe," said the chronologist. "To inquire about—"

"All of those activities were just things you chose to do to pass the time. Your real job, your one true task, was simply to be there when you needed to be found."

"Found?"

"By Liam. Or by this creature from iteration 41, and that creature . . . You are in every universe, waiting. You know so much about the future, the past, your reality, and yet the one thing you do not realize is that you're *you*, Dark Star's agents, its shepherds. Of course, it doesn't always work. Meeting you isn't always enough to guide the prototype here. But that's the beauty of the design. Only the most worthy make it all the way home. It's a passive system—like evolution, or osmosis. It would take far too much power to search every universe for the right candidate. Spin out a universe and wait, and eventually, the thing you need will come to you."

The chronologist made a sound like a sigh. "I imagine then," he said, his head bowed, "that the reason we have never asked oldest questions is that we were not made to."

"That is correct," said Iris.

"Let me go!" Liam struggled against the chronologist's grip, but the being grabbed Liam's other shoulder as well.

"Now, it won't be too long before the rest of humanity arrives, and we must be ready," said Barrie. He motioned toward the empty case. "Please deliver the prototype."

"This is very unfortunate," said the chronologist. "For all of us." He forced Liam ahead.

"No!" Liam's feet scuffed in the dust, kicking up clouds and the whipping tail of one of those squirming creatures. *Is it dust?* he thought wildly. *Or remains? . . .*

"Be happy, timekeeper," said Barrie. "This is why I brought you here, what you were made to do! Now, finally, you know your purpose."

"Stop!" Liam shouted. "Please!"

"Relax, Liam," said Iris. "Soon you'll be with me. And we can travel just like we did before. I think you'll find that once we're together, these worries of yours will fade."

"No. . . ." Liam fought and thrashed, but he couldn't break the chronologist's grip.

Barrie opened a door on the front of the cylinder. Liam was pushed into the light. Lifted—

And now a force pressed on all of him at once, holding him still. His arms and legs, his head, frozen in place.

The chronologist rotated him so that he was like the others—*I'm just a machine.*

You're so much more than that, said Iris, hearing his thoughts.

You're lying! You— Liam felt an electric heat inside his skull, in his thoughts, spreading all over.

With you, said Iris, *I am finally fully functional.*

His vision started to dissolve, the room fading, only the chronologist barely visible in front of him.

"Help . . . ," Liam croaked. *Phoebe . . . ,* he thought uselessly, but she was a universe away. *At least . . . she's . . . safe. . . .*

"I am truly sorry," the chronologist said, stepping back as Liam hung there, suspended inside the cylinder. "But these things happen."

17

"It's your move."

Mina is giving him that look, the one that's part glare and part pity.

"Sorry," Liam says. He studies the holographic game board between them and slides one of his pioneer groups from the mining planet of Betax to the swamp planet of Temina.

Mina pushes her long black bangs out of her eyes and frowns. "Why would you go there? The market for swamp exhaust is dead."

"I had a feeling this was the place you would choose," Iris says. "Don't you feel better?"

Liam isn't sure. This feels real, like his past, but when he looks around the balcony, at his sister, at his parents, at the growing sun above or the colony below, he has a blurry sense of other realities as well. The energy echoes of different choices, different variables, branching and branching again, more than they ever have on previous visits. He feels like he could not only push toward them but live within them. Try one, as he did in the desert with the skim drone, then another, and another. On and on. . . . He could know multiple realities at once. Be everywhere. Ace tests he failed, see grav-ball games he missed, say things he was too nervous or shy or confused to say. Go places, all the places.

He pushes back from his memory of the balcony and sees the whole of his life and the lives he could live, exploding in all directions. What had once seemed sort of like a river that he could flow in now appears like a galaxy spiraling around him. The linear time-line of the life he has actually lived is barely brighter than all the other possibilities.

But it's even more than that. Choices branching off choices. And not just for him. The branches extend away from Mina, too, from his parents, the people on the street, even the buildings. Choices and possibility and infinity. Infinity.

"You see," says Iris, "it's easier here."

"Where is here? Am I inside the mainframe?" Liam peers into the future and realizes that the one moment he cannot see, that in fact does not seem to be part of his timeline at all, is the moment when he is frozen inside the cylinder deep within Dark Star. He stretches to look behind himself—it should be back there, the way that Iris was always just behind him, just beyond his direct sight line—but it is like there is just a blankness there.

"It is more accurate to say the mainframe is inside you. Maximizing your mind's potential. And this is only the beginning. Once we have the upgrades we need, you will know even more."

"Upgrades . . . you mean the human race. You'll kill them all. My family—"

"Not kill them. They will be happy. You saw it. Their new Earth. It's everything they wanted. It's in your future, too. I have connected you to it. Have a look if you like."

Indeed, when Liam gazes ahead—past Mars, his desperate trek through space from Saturn to Delphi to Centauri, the fearful moments on Dark Star—he sees himself there on new Earth, with his parents and Mina, those same memories of the future that he saw before. The prefab houses, the clouds from the mining facilities, the starliners blinking in orbit, and yet, when he looks closer at the people around him . . .

"There's something wrong with everyone."

"I cannot accurately integrate individuals until they arrive. For the moment, the space-time map of the simulation is written in the broadest strokes. But as you can see, your future is so much more than that now. There will be *so much* once we ascend."

She's right. Liam can sense the vastness beyond those future moments on Earth. Strange impressions of bright light and wild color, starstream and timelight, ways of seeing and knowing that he cannot grasp quite yet, but he will. A point of view above the universes, their possible universes, and he will have access to it all—

"Because I'm never leaving." A chill runs through him, even here on the balcony on Mars. "You'll never let me."

"Liam, don't you see? You won't want to. You crossed the universe to be here. To know this. Even when you saw your possible death at Centauri, you flew *toward* it instead of away. This was what you were searching for, whether you realized it or not. You wanted the answer."

The thought makes him feel powerless. Because maybe it was true. Had his fear and worry been the engine all along, driving him here, his choices not really choices at all?

He thinks of what his mom once said to him. *One unknown at a time.* Here, that doesn't have to be the case. No more fiery stars haunting his head, about to explode. Indeed, here, that terrifying vision of Centauri A seems distant, just one of many possibilities, something that can no longer quite harm him.

Except his mom also said something else, that last morning on Mars: She said that there were two sides to it. You might not know what would go wrong, but you also didn't know what happiness you might find. She said that was part of being human.

There is none of that unknown here in Dark Star. Could you even still be human without it?

And yet he can't deny that, in a way, he feels calmer here. Some of that raw fear he felt, just moments ago with Barrie, has already begun to fade. Here, there is control. All of time and possibility his to know. It is true: in some way, this was a certainty he has always craved.

"So . . . was this what you were made to do?" he asks Iris. "Create universes, capture species, and use them to grow? Is that what happened to the Architects? You took the very people who made you and made them slaves to your mainframe?"

"I understand how one might come to such a conclusion, but don't be silly. There are no Architects.
There never were."

"What about all the buildings out on the arms?
The walkways and plazas?"

"I wanted the place to feel homey, as you might
put it."

"Then how did you come to be?"

"You see? Our captain friend is not wrong about
the oldest questions. In my case, I believe I evolved, in
a manner, same as you."

"So you're alive?" Liam asks.

"Of course."

"But someone had to make you."

"You mean like birth?"

"I meant, like, constructed."

"Are they really that different?"

Liam supposes not. "Are there others like you?"

"Perhaps, somewhere far away."

"How can you be sure someone didn't make you,
just like you made us?"

"I can't. Reality, as you are learning, is very big.
It may be that in the higher dimensions I will be able
to see farther, and come to know and understand my
origins. Maybe I am one of a thousand other Dark
Stars, all of us weaving universes like yours, and we

are all in fact within some larger structure that I cannot yet perceive. The only way for us to find out is to generate more perceptive power. And that is precisely why I have invited you here."

"Invited? I wasn't invited, I—"

"But weren't you? Don't you understand now? The chronologists and their offices, the portals, all of it was transmitting the faintest signal, the sensation of possibility—a song broadcast throughout the universe. Only the most sensitive would be able to hear its frequency, not that you would have even known that's what you were hearing."

"But if you don't know your origins, how do you know this is your purpose?"

"Because it is the only purpose. Soon you will see. The three-dimensional limitations, those computational side effects that you call feelings, or attachments, or worries—they will fade. They have already started to, haven't they?"

"Yes," he admits. And that wind in his chest feels more like that familiar whisper: *Farther . . . farther . . .*

"Liam, come on," Mina says from the memory on the balcony on Mars.

Just be here, Liam says to himself. He focuses on the sunny deck, his parents nearby, and he feels that surge again, the nervousness in his belly that is both here with him now and also present in the original moment, and even part of the other versions of himself that have visited this same spot over time. The jet flame permanently turned on, for so many reasons: because his parents are soon to leave for the research station on Mars—no, they're injured, in stasis—no, they're trapped on Dark Star. He feels all the worries of his many selves, feelings that won't fade, because he won't let them, no matter how much easier it might be if they were gone.

Why has he so often visited this spot? Is it because this was a good time, a safe time, with his family?

A strange shiver ripples through him. One of his past selves has pushed away from this moment and is stretching out, moving back inside their apartment, into his room. Liam remembers doing this, during one of his first trips back here, when he still needed to use the watch. He pushed into his bedroom and looked around, but it only lasted a moment before his head began to ache, the first signs of the changes that were to come. *I was afraid of it,* he thinks, *but Iris is right, I kept coming. Even in those early visits to the balcony, I was pushing to go farther.* He felt that former self rubber-band back to the balcony, and then glide away toward his present on the Cosmic Cruiser.

But something catches Liam's eye now, from his

bedroom window. He presses a bit farther into the moment and sees a silhouette in his room . . . but there was no one in there that original day on the balcony, nor when his other self pushed in there.

A flash of orange light.

Liam moves toward it. As he leaves, he glances at Iris, trying to think of an excuse, or a distraction, but strangely, she doesn't seem to notice that he is leaving, almost as if he is being hidden. . . .

He glides through the open window.

Phoebe sits on his bed, the chronologist's orange crystal pulsing in her hand. Her white braid, her skin covered in bristles, Phoebe from the future, from Dark Star.

"Hey," she says, glancing nervously toward the window. "She can't see us, can she?"

Liam's mouth is open in shock. He checks over his shoulder. Iris is still out by the balcony, almost as if she's frozen in place.

"This is the safe place," says Liam.

Phoebe nods. "It's where you came the most, right? When you were freaking out?"

"Yeah, but . . . how are you here? Wait, *are* you really here? Or are you part of the—"

"I'm here," she says, and holds up the crystal recorder. "It's hiding us from her, like it did before."

"But how did you find this day?" Liam asks. "I never brought you here, did I?"

"You told me about it, back on the cruiser, on our way to Delphi. One time you mentioned that it was around the time of the Bombers championship game."

"You mean Dust Devils," Liam says almost immediately.

She smiles. "Pretty sure my Bombers won, but we can argue about that another time. Anyway, it took me a while to figure out which day this was. I looked around for hours. And once I found it, I had to figure out when *this* version of you—your current self—would arrive. Not bad, right?"

"It's amazing!" said Liam. "But I still don't get how you're doing this. How you got here."

"While we were hugging good-bye, I traveled along your timeline. That's how I found this moment. I told you that you weren't the only one who'd been changed by our time travel."

"But I didn't know you could do *this*."

Phoebe sort of shrugs. "I didn't either. It wasn't something that I was planning to do, but then, we were hugging, and it felt . . . I don't know, possible. Like I knew you so well that I could get here."

"That's why you said this was how it had to be."

Phoebe nods.

Liam notices that her eyes are rimmed with tears. What she is describing is making him feel like a balloon has inflated inside him. "I remember feeling something, during that hug. I was traveling too, to so many moments between us, and I sort of felt like you were there."

"Because I was. Hunting around in your past."

"Are we hugging in your present?"

"No, I left, just like you saw. But right after I walked out of that Cosmic Cruiser, I talked to the chronologist, slightly out of time. I asked him to program his crystal to bring me to this exact moment. Then I waited until we had safely crossed through the portal, and I came back here."

"So, wait, does this mean you knew what would happen to me?"

"It's part of what I saw when we went through the portal. All those blue lights, and machinery . . . I couldn't make sense of it at first. It wasn't until JEFF and I spoke, in the plaza. He confirmed that the portal wasn't real, or at least that what was on the other side wasn't. And since it was Dark Star who created the portal . . . there was only one answer. It was a trap. I told JEFF to reset himself, but to delay his reactivation. I wanted to make sure I could get my family out of there before Iris found out that I knew."

"But why didn't you tell me before you left? You let me walk right into it, and now I'm trapped in here, and my family, all the humans—"

"Because I think I know how you can stop her," Phoebe says. "And I think you have to do it from in here."

Liam glances back at the balcony again; Iris is still shimmering there, unmoving. The balcony scene, him and Mina, his parents just inside the door, all frozen. "How?"

"You need me." She stands and steps toward him. "There's a reason why the new Earth simulation rejected me and not you, why even though I can kinda move in time, your computer girlfriend never talked to me."

"She's not my—"

"Quiet. It's because we're not made like you, isn't it?"

"I think so." Liam explains what the blue lights she saw really were, and what Iris planned to do with humanity. How there had been previous species, even how the chronologists are involved.

Phoebe shakes her head. "You humans really are the chosen species of the entire freakin' universe. Wait until my mom hears this." She almost smiles.

"And then there's us Telphons: we breathe oxygen, are mostly made of water and carbon, all that, but there are slight differences. Mom said one time that humans and Telphons have stereochemistry, like our proteins are mirror images of yours or something. Maybe that's the difference. Or I guess we have traces of silicates in our organic compounds. Maybe our brains are a few neurons smaller—who knows? Whatever it is, I guess it was enough to render us incompatible with the system Dark Star constructed to assimilate you. That's why I rejected the programming when we crossed the portal, or it rejected me. Maybe both."

"If you hadn't, I probably would have been assimilated right there. . . ." A nervous flash rushes through Liam. "Okay, but what good is all that going to do us now?"

"Well, I know all this looks real," says Phoebe. "I mean, this is your real past, but your actual body is hooked up to a machine, isn't it?"

For a moment, Liam almost wants to disagree. *No, don't forget!* He was forced into that cylinder by the chronologist. That's where he *is* right now, no matter how real this all feels. "Yeah," he says, shuddering at that truth.

"So I think if you take me there," says Phoebe, "to that physical moment when you're trapped, it will confuse the system, maybe disrupt it for long enough for you to get free."

"How am I going to take you there?"

Phoebe grins. "Hug function."

"Will that even work?"

"We've traveled together before."

Liam tries to look behind himself. Not out the window but directly behind, and again, there is that blank spot. "But I can't see that place. It's beyond this reality, somewhere I don't have access to. Besides . . ."

"What?"

Liam looks away. "Nothing." He sees Phoebe frown and cross her arms.

"Don't tell me you're even considering staying here—"

"No," Liam says immediately, and yet there is that flash, the reminder that here, all that has worried and scared him will be no longer. But there is something else more pressing. . . . "Even if this works, and we can break free, what if we can't find a way to stop Dark Star? The entire human fleet is on its way. She's so powerful . . . is there even a way to fight it?"

"There has to be," says Phoebe. "We'll find one."

"But if she can't have me, I don't know what she'll do. What if she decides to exterminate the human race? Or end our universe and start over? Breaking out of here might actually be killing everyone. You guys, too. And then, I mean, what if this simulation is actually better than whatever they are going to find on Aaru? If there is a chance that Phase Two doesn't work, like our parents said, who knows if we'll even be able to find another planet—"

Phoebe puts a hand on Liam's arm. "Liam, this is bigger than just the fate of humanity, or Telphons. Dark Star may not want us, but humans aren't the first race that she has enslaved, and it won't be the last."

"She said we were the most advanced—"

"The most advanced *for now*. Do you really think she's not going to keep making new universes, keep trying to push farther and farther?"

There are those words again.

"Sure," Phoebe continues, "I guess maybe if you stay in here, it ensures that your people survive in a way, but if you don't try to stop her, then you're partly responsible for what happens to all the future races this thing tries to enslave, or that get displaced or destroyed by her blowing up stars."

"You're right," Liam says. "It's just . . ."

"Dangerous? Risky? What hasn't been for us? And we've gotten this far. If you stay in here, you're giving up a *real* future, a *real* life. Not to mention me. . . ."

That's not who you are. And definitely not the Liam I came back for."

Liam feels that nervous spin inside him, growing stronger again. Maybe he has known all along that what Iris is offering isn't really real. Not in his heart. And he realizes that whenever he thinks about that yearning to go farther, he forgets what Phoebe just said: It wasn't just him on that journey. *We.* They'd done it together, not for some selfish quest, not for an all-knowing answer, but for the love of their families and friends. For each other. Because it had been the right thing to do.

Liam glances back at the balcony, at Iris floating there, at him and Mina playing a game on a weekend morning so long ago, and wonders again: *Why this moment?* Sure, it has always felt safe. But is there something more about it? Something that makes it so compelling to return here?

He thinks about what will happen next, can nearly hear Mina saying it: "Why are you smiling?" she'll say. "You're playing out your own funeral."

"Check our totals," he will say.

And he remembers how Mina will glance at the columns of data alongside the board. How she will frown with the dawning realization. "Wait, how did you get more money than me? And how is swamp exhaust suddenly worth so much?"

Liam remembers how it will feel to know that he pulled it off. But . . . it's more than that. Not just that he did it, but that he *knew* he would. For a few minutes, looking at the game board on that balcony, that afternoon on Mars years ago, Liam had known the future. He'd seen how the moves might go, and how he could win. Had he been certain that Mina would make the moves he needed her to make? No, and yet . . . he'd believed.

And he hadn't needed a watch, or a Dark Star. Hadn't needed to actually know what was going to happen to *see* it, and follow it. *I time traveled*, he thought, even though he hadn't. And yet the result had been the same. All he had needed was hope, and the courage to believe in what he hoped for.

His tendency to worry about what was ahead meant putting an unfair weight on the bad things that might happen, but in this moment on the balcony, he'd been able to envision the best outcome, and see how he could get there. He knew a lot about the game, had the knowledge he needed. He just had to strategize, put the plan in motion, and execute. That always felt like a scary proposition, and indeed, it was difficult to focus when his insides were awash in nervous energy, as they had been that day—as they were so very often—and yet he had gone for it. And how exciting had that been? Sitting there as the moves played out, not knowing for sure, but trusting himself. . . .

A powerful adaptation of three-dimensional beings, the chronologist had once said of trust. But maybe that wasn't exactly right. Maybe, in a way, humans really were four-dimensional. Maybe he'd been a sort-of time traveler all along, in a way that was just enough. There were so many other moments like that afternoon, which came with living a life from one moment to the next.

It was scary, the not knowing, but that spinny feeling inside him, that worry and fear of his . . . hadn't it caused him to kiss Phoebe that time on the Cosmic Cruiser? To take her through the portal, which had very nearly uncovered this truth beneath Dark Star? Hadn't it spurred him to join her, way back at the beginning, to skip school and go downtown, because he just wanted to remember his home one last time? And it was doing that that led them to see the chronologist's lab, led to the events that likely saved his and his parents' lives. Did he really want to lose that? Would it really be better to have no mystery? No fear? To not have to believe in yourself and others, or step into the unknown?

And maybe, just maybe, being human was as much

about the mistakes, the messy choices, and the best guesses that sometimes backfired because of that *not* knowing, as it was about getting things right. Maybe being human was simply about trying your best. To do better, to learn from your mistakes. Maybe what Iris was offering didn't actually sound like living at all.

"You're right," he says to Phoebe. "We have to get out of here."

One side of her mouth curls up. "There you are."

"I don't know how I'm going to get back to my body, though. Iris will know. She . . ." Liam considers the balcony. There is something else about this moment. Not only how he played the game, but that he was able to *hide* his strategy from Mina. Maybe he can do it again. "Okay," he says to Phoebe. "Stay close. As soon as I find where she's keeping me, we'll go for it."

"You got this," Phoebe says.

"I hope so." Liam slides back to the balcony, to the game-playing moment, time and space folding and multiplying in all directions. It's hard to focus with so many other realities—where his move in the game doesn't quite work, where Mina sniffs it out and counters—and it's still tempting, to see all these different outcomes, to know more. . . .

"Did you go somewhere?" Iris asks. He is beside here again.

"I visited my room," says Liam, "in another time-line."

"Your powers are growing even more quickly than I expected," she says with a smile.

"I guess."

On the balcony, Mina is saying, "I didn't realize you had such a good poker face."

Poker face. Liam takes a deep breath, keeps his thoughts and his face still. *Focus.* "I get it now," he says to Iris. "I feel it. All the possibilities. There's so much to see and know."

"You have all of time to explore it," says Iris.

Liam turns, Iris's glimmering silhouette just at the edge of his vision. "You know, there's so much here, but there's one thing I can never quite see."

"What is that?"

"You. Like, the actual you. Not this person you create."

"You have been in the space station. You have been inside the core."

"Yeah," says Liam, "but that's not *you*, is it? You're somewhere else. And you're something different."

"That is true. . . ." Her light dims for a moment.

"What?" Liam asks.

Iris tilts her head. "No one has ever asked to see me. They . . . well, the other prototypes have always been

427

content just to see themselves.. They get lost in this." She waves her hands at the realities all around them. "But also . . . the sight of me might be shocking."

"All of this is shocking. But if we really are going to ascend to higher awareness, I want to see you for real. I mean, if that's okay."

Iris is silent for a moment. "I am deciding if I can trust you."

"Trust *me*?" Liam puts on a smile. "I'm not the one who lied." He feels a pang of guilt; Iris is being more truthful than she has ever been, and now he is the one lying to her, although not completely. He does want to know her true self. After all, she is the real answer to the question of what lies at the end of the universe.

"I've never lied," Iris says. "I have concealed, I suppose, during a time when I surmised that you were unable to understand my purposes. But my goal was to guide you to the right choice, while allowing your power to develop."

"That still sounds like lying."

"Forgive me, but it has been a long search for you, Liam. A long time waiting, and . . ."

"What?"

"I did not anticipate you asking this question. It is quite unexpected, and that is a new feeling for me."

"Sorry," says Liam. "I didn't mean to—"

"No, it is all right, I—you can see me now, if you want."

The light beside him grows, and Liam turns himself, stretching. . . .

The shimmering girl becomes transparent, like a cloud of light, brightening and spreading, and then Liam is inside it. He sees a vast space: the inside of a great sphere, thousands of meters across, perhaps much larger, with smoky crystalline walls. Crisscrossing its interior is a latticework of glass tubes. Inside those tubes are objects, rounded forms lined up, side to side. Flashes and streaks of colored light spark between them, zipping from one to the next with lightning speed. Most of the objects glow brightly when the light hits them, while others are half lit, and some remain dark. The patterns and frequency of light remind him of the blue crystal spheres, and yet in these brief flashes from one object to the next, Liam thinks that these look different: fleshy, organic, alive. *You know what they are*, he thinks to himself.

And what they will be replaced with, once the human fleet arrives.

The bursts of light speed through the network of tubes toward a central structure, a multisided object like a giant diamond with a hundred mirrored faces.

It shimmers and blurs with energy and time.

"Amazing," Liam lies, trying to hide the terror welling in him.

"I am sort of wondrous, aren't I?" It sounds as if Iris is smiling. "No being has ever seen me like this before."

Below this diamond-like structure, past many layers of the crisscrossing tubes, Liam sees a moment when the bottom of the giant sphere seems to blur into a dimness. It is as if he is looking back into that room beneath Dark Star, into the physical universe, from this other space, beyond. There are shapes down there, like cylinders, brightly lit. There is his body, beside the other prototypes, in its cage: that is the real truth, in spite of everything he has seen.

"Don't be concerned with the state of your matter," says Iris. "It was a limitation."

Liam fights off a chill of fear. *Poker face.* "I was just wondering about the chronologist," says Liam. "He is . . . was a good friend."

"He is fine."

"Can I see him?" Liam pushes himself downward through the vast spherical space, through Iris herself, between the crisscrossing tubes. Down toward the place where his body is, where the physical world is.

"Liam," says Iris, "what are you doing?"

Not too fast, he thinks to himself, resisting the urge to push there with all his might. "I just want to see him," Liam says again. He can feel Iris closing in behind him, senses that she is beginning to suspect. . . .

"Liam. I would rather you don't go too close to yourself. It may be confusing to—"

Liam shoves himself downward toward the cylinders, toward his body, reaches toward it with all of his mental energy. "Now, Phoebe!"

In a blur, Phoebe appears beside him, wraps her arms tightly around him. They hurtle toward his body, suspended in that glowing cylinder. Strange wires have gathered around him, dewy like the spiderwebs in the Earth Preserve exhibits, glowing tendrils that hover just above his skin all around his head and arms and legs, their tips humming with glowing energy.

"Liam, stop!" Iris shouts.

He holds Phoebe and pushes back into this moment with all his strength, the moment when he was put into this machine. The bright light of the cylinder, the energy coursing through him as he is transferred into the mainframe. He pushes as hard as he can, bringing Phoebe with him, so that they briefly appear in the cylinder together, hugging each other, blurring with the version of Liam who is unconscious there, the timelines overlapping with white heat threatening to burn him alive—

INCOMPATIBILITY DETECTED! a warning screeches.

The wires recoil, twisting and sloughing away, their tips going dark.

"NO!" Iris says, hurtling toward them.

"Hang on!" Liam shouts, holding onto Phoebe. It is like they are in a storm, furious light and screeching like metal on metal—

And then all dissolves into darkness.

18

Liam's eyes flashed open, blinking in the dim light. He was gripped by a sudden, visceral sense of up and down, and he and Phoebe tumbled out of the crystal case, landing on their hands and knees in the thick dust on the floor.

"Ah, what is this?" Phoebe bolted to her knees, shaking the dust from her hands. "Something just touched my leg!" She scrambled unsteadily to her feet.

Liam fought to stand up, his stomach quaking, head splitting with pain. He felt a great emptiness, the loss of all that awareness, of so many possibilities. Now there was just his body, weak and limited, aching and shuddering in the dark.

The air shimmered, and the chronologist appeared, striding toward them. "Well," he said, "this is unexpected."

Liam turned to Phoebe. "The recorder."

Phoebe held out the crystal recorder, which was still blinking. The chronologist stopped and stared at them for a moment, his head making a twitching motion. "So, this is what you did with it."

"Are you . . . normal again?" Liam asked.

The chronologist blinked. "I am afraid that my normal function is as a tool of this station." He almost sounded sad. "But yes, the recorder is interrupting the machine's imposition of purpose upon me."

"Does that mean you will help us?"

"I thought I was helping you before—Dark Star had opened up my perception of my future, one in which I aid you in the assimilation of humanity. But now the recorder is causing my future to once again appear—how do you put it—unknown."

"In that case," said Liam uncertainly, "would you . . . like to help us?"

The chronologist seemed to think this over. "I believe I would find that liberating."

"Where's the captain?" Phoebe asked.

"He returned to the control room to monitor the progress of the human fleet."

The floor rumbled.

"What was that?" Liam asked.

"It began a few moments ago," said the chronologist. "The captain is not pleased. That is why he sent me down here."

"Liam, your link," said Phoebe.

"It's always messed up after traveling." But amid the error messages there was also a white flashing light, indicating he had an incoming message.

"Liam! Where the heck are you?" Mina shouted.

"Hey! I'm on Dark Star. In the—"

"You have to get out of there! We're leaving with the *Artemis*! It's a mutiny! Kyla found JEFF and now she's convinced that the portal to the new Earth isn't real. Do you know what that means? And have you heard from Mom and Dad? No one on the survey team is responding!"

"JEFF is right," said Liam. "It's a trap."

"Then where are they?"

Liam peered across the dark space, toward those long lines of pod-shaped structures. "I think I know. I'll get them."

"Okay, but you have to hurry! Kyla has us flying toward the portal back to our universe, but"—she was interrupted by a screech of static—"Dark Star is firing its refueling ships in our direction, like it's trying to knock us off course toward that fake portal. We tried sending a message to the starliner fleet, but we think Dark Star is jamming our signal. Listen, I have to go. They've got me working one of the sector damage monitors. But—"

"Mina, it's all right! I'll find Mom and Dad and be in touch."

The floor rumbled again.

"Let's go," said Phoebe.

Liam led the way across the space, away from the crystal cylinders and the other prototypes, past the circular platform they'd used to get down here, and toward the rows of pod-shaped structures. As they neared, Liam saw that the floor opened up, and these rows of pods in front of them were simply the top layer: there were floors upon floors of them below, thousands just that he could see. At intervals in between the lower levels, Liam saw large circular structures, like giant gears, and imagined these racks rotating, bringing fresh pods to the surface.

Above, he could better see crystalline structures like arms, presumably meant to sort the pods. Some of those arms had more delicate, sharper structures on their ends that were likely used for the more grisly steps required in assimilation. Liam tensed as he neared the first row of pods, the ones with their tops still open. *Please don't be too late, please—*

But there were his parents, beside Jordy and the other two members of the survey team. Their chests were rising and falling and they appeared to be all right, except for the long tubes that hung down from the ceiling and were inserted in their mouths and noses. A web of those floating luminous threads that Liam had seen around his own body extended from the walls of the pods and surrounded their heads, flickering and flashing.

Their eyes darted back and forth behind their eyelids. Where did they think they were right now? At the next sample point on the new Earth? It occurred to Liam that they were probably happy, thrilled by the prospects of the new world around them. For a moment, he almost didn't want to wake them. They'd be so disappointed; Mom and Dad had worked Liam's whole life toward finding a new home. The truth would be devastating for them.

"Can you turn these off?" Liam asked the chronologist, but when he looked up, he saw that the chronologist had moved away from them, into the shadows beyond the pods. He waved his recorder around, illuminating a huge metallic structure.

Liam and Phoebe caught up with the many-legged being. He stood before an enormous machine with multiple door-shaped foggy glass panels on the front, surrounded by banks of circuitry. The chronologist moved his recorder closer to one of these panels, illuminating something dark blue on the other side: the outline of a head, of shoulders, of blank, milky eyes. Another chronologist. Naked, its skin smooth, unaffected by time. As if it had just been born. A network of wires hung around it, but they were dark.

The chronologist moved to the next panel of glass and found another version of himself. "This is where I'm from," he said. "Where I was created." He made a sound like a sigh. "It is such a strange thing, discovering your life's true purpose. I do not recommend it."

"Maybe that's not your only purpose," said Liam. The chronologist didn't respond. "Can you help us get my parents out?" Liam asked.

The chronologist stared at the ghostly figure of his counterpart for a moment longer and then turned away from the machine. "Yes."

They returned to the pods, and the chronologist spent a moment tapping the surface of his recorder. He held it above each pod, deactivating them one by one. The tendrils of light receded from his parents' heads, and the air tubes loosened, but Liam still had to gently pull them out of his parents' mouths. Each made a sucking sound, leaving first Mom then Dad gagging. Phoebe helped Jordy and the other two team members. They all shuddered as they sat up, peering around, blinking.

"Liam?" said Mom, her voice faint and scratchy. "Where are we?"

"Inside Dark Star."

"But . . ." She blinked, trying to make out her surroundings in the gloom. "We were on new Earth. We—"

"It wasn't real. The portal was a trap." Liam explained as best he could what Dark Star had been planning, how Barrie was part of it, though he left out the part where he was the prototype, like it made him something . . . different.

Dad rubbed a hand over his head, his breath rattling. "That's a lot to absorb."

Another deep rumble shook the floor. "What's that?" Mom asked.

"The *Artemis* is trying to get back to our universe. We need to get out of here." Liam stood between both parents as they leaned on him and swung their legs over the pods. Once they were up, he tapped his link. "Mina, are you there? I have Mom and Dad."

"Nice work, little brother!"

"Did you find Jordy?" Kyla asked.

"Present and mostly accounted for," Jordy called, rubbing his head.

"Is Mina all right?" Mom asked.

"I can hear you, Mom, and yes, I'm *fine*. A lot better than you two, though things are getting dicey up here. We're prepping a cruiser to come get you, but—" A buzz of static.

"Mina?" said Dad.

"—deflecting the blasts. The refueling drones are ramming us. They're small, but when enough of them explode at once, they do start to knock us off course! With only one engine, I'm not sure we can make the portal back home. If there's anything you can do over there"—another static buzz—"to get you."

"If we get to the control room," Liam said to the chronologist, "can you disable Dark Star's defenses?"

"Perhaps. We will have to contend with Captain Barrie there as well."

"That's all right—I'd like to have a word with him," Dad muttered. "How could he have done this?"

Jordy shook his head. "This place made him crazy . . . or maybe he already was. We should have seen it coming."

"It's not your fault," said Mom, putting a hand on his arm.

The chronologist stepped between them. "This is a large group, so you will have to gather close around me."

"He can move us through space-time," Liam said as his parents eyed the chronologist suspiciously. Liam held out his hands to them.

"Move?" said Mom. "How can that be possible—"

"Mom!" Liam snapped. "We've done this before. Just trust me, okay?"

Mom shared a look with Dad. "Okay."

They gathered close and joined hands as the chronologist tapped his recorder. Light bloomed around them, and in a blur, they left the sublevel and arrived in the clear-domed control room atop Dark Star.

Bright bursts flashed out in the green nebula. Liam saw the *Artemis*, its single working engine blazing, passing over the curving arms of the station. It was aimed at the portal back to their universe, but hundreds of small explosions flashed along its side. Wave after wave of Dark Star's oval-winged refueling drones were soaring out of the racks, only to blow up right beside the *Artemis*, pushing it off course, toward the simulation portal, glowing bright green and rippling hungrily.

"What have you done?" Barrie shouted as they arrived. He stood by the spherical controls, which spun wildly before him. He had leveled his rifle at the group. "I will not let you sabotage this!"

"Captain, stop!" Dad shouted.

But Barrie fired.

Everyone leapt out of the way, scattering. Liam threw himself to the side, but out of the corner of his eye, he saw the chronologist step into the line of fire. As the blast reached him, he winked out of sight. The energy seemed to disappear with him.

He reappeared instantaneously, right behind the captain. The long fingers of one hand wrapped around Barrie's throat. The grip caused Barrie to spasm, and the rifle clattered to the floor. "I'm sorry to have to do this," the chronologist said to Barrie. "I believe that is what you said to my colleague, on the red planet of your home system, is it not?"

Barrie croaked an unintelligible response.

The chronologist leaned closer to his ear. "But I do not believe you meant it. I do not think you have ever been sorry at all."

With his free hand, the chronologist pressed the orange crystal recorder against Barrie's temple. Light surged from it, and Barrie tried to scream, a choked sound, his face contorting. Orange spider lines of energy spread from his temple, across his face and down his neck, and then he slumped in the chronologist's grip, his chest still moving but his eyes closed, his body limp.

Liam and Phoebe scrambled to their feet and ran

over to the chronologist as the other adults gathered themselves.

"That should make things a bit easier," said the chronologist. He lowered Barrie to the floor—

And then collapsed behind him.

Now Liam saw the blackened burn mark in the chronologist's chest. He dropped to his knees beside the ancient being. "Are you okay?"

"I think not," said the chronologist, leaning on his elbows.

Something flashed by Liam's feet. The orange crystal had rolled free of the chronologists's fingers. It flared brightly and disappeared.

"I set it to return to my earlier self once I no longer needed it, or"—he glanced at his chest wound—"could no longer operate it."

"You knew this would happen?" asked Liam.

"Actually, no. But I had what you might call a hunch. Besides, my earlier self needs it back in order to smash it."

"LIAM." Iris's voice echoed throughout the control room. She sounded different than she ever had, no longer the soothing voice in his head, in his timestream, but now the great booming presence of this enormous machine. "WHAT DO YOU THINK YOU ARE DOING?"

"Who is that?" Mom shouted as she and the rest of the team approached Liam and Phoebe.

"That would be Dark Star," said Phoebe.

"HOW COULD YOU NOT UNDERSTAND? YOU HAVE SEEN WHAT I CAN GIVE YOU."

"What is she talking about?" said Dad.

"It doesn't matter," said Liam, tapping his link. "Mina! I have everyone. Send the shuttle!"

"We can't launch with all these drones self-destructing!" Mina shouted. "We're putting everything we've got into staying on course and away from that simulation portal!"

Mom had moved to the spherical controls, still spinning wildly. "Isn't there some way to stop those things?"

"Kyla says the blasts have knocked out some of the life-support systems. We're running out of time—"

A blinding flash lit everyone's faces. Above, a beam of pure white energy sliced its way through dozens of the refueling drones at once, melting them into blackened hulks. And now another beam, incinerating an entire wave that had just departed Dark Star.

"Finally!" Liam saw Phoebe yelling into her link. "What took you so long?"

"You disappear, leaving this message that gives us no choice but to risk everyone's lives *again*!" It was

Ariana. "You're lucky we didn't just leave you here this time."

"Sorry, Mom." Phoebe winked at Liam.

The Styrlax ship arced toward them from the portal home, firing its particle weapon and clearing the drones, one fiery swipe after another. The *Artemis*'s single engine burned bright, righting course and speeding up.

"STOP!" Iris ordered.

One of the spinning control spheres suddenly enlarged, as if with a mind of its own, and showed some sort of space-time map. There was a deep hum, and the portal home began to flash.

"Aww, I was afraid of this!" Jordy hurried over to the floating controls.

"What's happening?" said Liam's dad.

"She's deactivating the portal." Jordy reached his hands into the map, but his fingers caused a flash of sparks. "Ow!" He glanced into the space overhead. "Come on! She won't let me access it."

"She's trapping us here," said Phoebe.

Liam saw that as the portal's silver circuitry flashed, it had begun to shrink.

"I am afraid that is only one of our current worries," the chronologist said faintly.

Liam heard a succession of sharp hissing sounds,

like the air itself was igniting. He spun around to see figures materializing around the room.

Other chronologists. Ten, twenty, forty . . .

"RETAKE THE CONTROL CENTER," Iris boomed, "AND COMMANDEER THAT VESSEL."

"Liam!" Mina shouted. "There are creatures appearing out of nowhere on the bridge!"

Feet clacking, robes swishing, the chronologists had already grabbed one of the team members. The other was pulling her stun weapon from a side holster and moving to engage. More chronologists to either side, behind them now, scurrying from all directions.

There was a flash and one of the nearest crumpled to the ground. Mom had picked up Barrie's rifle and shot it. The others hesitated but almost immediately began inching forward.

"Now what?" Phoebe said.

"Liam . . ." The chronologist tugged weakly on his arm. "We're all linked," he said. "The whole system. Our offices, our minds . . . If I wasn't injured, I would be attacking you as well. You have to disable it."

"How am I supposed to do that?"

"Liam, watch out!" Mom shouted. She'd fired again, but now a chronologist had her by the arms. Dad struggled with one as well.

"Ow!" Phoebe lurched backward in the grip of another.

"Get off me!" Jordy shouted, grappling with a chronologist, the two lurching this way and that, causing the spherical controls to scatter and dart around them.

"The chronometers," said the chronologist, pointing to the two silver watches on Barrie's wrist. "If you set them to travel in opposite directions, within the same transit field, the opposing time dilations will have the effect of creating a negative space-time polarity."

"I don't know what that means!"

"They will in effect create a miniature black hole that will collapse upon itself and disintegrate in moments, but not before it wreaks havoc on its immediate surroundings. Perhaps these surroundings could be Dark Star's mainframe core."

Liam slipped the watches from Barrie's wrist. "But aren't these just part of Dark Star, too?"

"We crafted them ourselves. They may have similar technology, but they are not of this place. They were part of whatever passes for our free will. Of this I am sure."

"But I can't go back into the mainframe, not without your crystal or something. She'll capture me. Or these others will just follow me—"

"Watch out!" Mom shouted. She wrenched partially free of a chronologist's grip and fired just above Liam. He had barely turned when a chronologist crumpled right behind him.

"Liam, ask yourself: Why did Dark Star bring Captain Barrie here? Why did it have him capture me? Why did it start talking to you in the first place?"

"Because I'm the prototype—"

"Yes, that is why you are here, but not why it took so many precautions. It did all these things because it fears you. It fears what you may be capable of."

"Liam!" Phoebe called. A chronologist had her firmly, and another was looming closer to him.

"Go," said the chronologist.

Hands reaching for him—

Liam gripped the watches and pushed himself out of the moment.

19

DARK STAR CORE:
∞

"Liam."

He sees her out of the corner of his eye, shimmering there, and he pushes, twisting around to see her fully.

"I don't know what you think you can accomplish—"

Turning, fighting . . . There. The mainframe, light filled and the size of a grav-ball stadium, and yet also more vast than a thousand universes.

"I'm going to stop you," he says. And yet as he is about to push toward the core, with its wild rainbow-mirror sides, its diamonds-upon-diamonds shape, a cold fear grips him. It feels as if to approach her, he must leave his own self behind, his future and his past. A terrifying sense that if he travels into that core completely, he could fall into nothingness, emptiness, even more than that—nonbeing.

"You're right to come back," Iris says. "My offer still stands. You can save your people; you can have more power than you've ever dreamed of."

But that's not what it feels like. This energy that is buffeting him in waves, that is causing him to shake, it is so cold. It doesn't feel like power.

It feels like fear.

But not of Liam . . . of what?

He pushes deeper. Past the intersecting tubes with their flashing insides, closer to that diamond shape. The closer he gets, the larger it seems, the more sides it has, the more angles and colors.

The energy gets stronger, too. Pressing on him. It is like loss, like emptiness, longing. . . .

Like loneliness, Liam thinks, and he feels a deep tremor through all of his selves. It is as if the entire station has just shuddered down to its very atoms. A mechanical hitch of breath, an all-encompassing sigh, across the farthest reaches of space-time.

Iris doesn't respond, and for a moment, Liam hesitates, some part of him feeling a connection to that loneliness, compassion. But from somewhere behind him come the faint sounds of his friends and family in peril.

He pushes on, toward the core.

"Liam, stop!"

"No," he says. "I'll give you this last chance to let us all go and pull your portal out of our universe."

"I cannot. My function is to reach the higher awareness. There is no other purpose. It is this for which I created your universe, and all others. You must understand this."

The mirrored structure grows and grows. Soon it towers above and below Liam. Its glassy sides bow out and in, almost like it is breathing. Closer still, and then he is within its crystalline walls, which aren't really walls at all. Floating through white light, nearly blinding him, but with rainbow edges, and there are reflections of him iterating out infinitely in all directions, almost as if the space around him is made entirely *from* him.

"Liam."

Deeper he goes, and the light becomes more prismatic, the reflections of him more twisted, contorting his limbs and his face. The distortions make him look less human but extend him further. *Hold it together*, he thinks to himself. He is one person. A single being. Here and now, no matter how confusing his view becomes.

On and on he goes. Through the light.

And then he has reached the center of the center. All the prismatic walls come together, joining and collapsing, all the versions of him tumbling in on themselves, until he is facing a single, mirrored wall. A single, clear reflection of himself.

Here, it is very quiet.

"You shouldn't be here," Iris says, barely above a whisper.

Liam holds out the two watches. "I can't let you have the human race. I'm sorry."

"Liam, I do not understand." Her tone has shifted, softened, become small. "Why? Why don't you want to ascend with me? No one has ever turned down this offer before, and none of the prior prototypes had nearly the potential that you have. You've seen how much is possible. You and I could do what has never been done. And I've felt it."

"Felt what?"

"How it calms you. How the energy inside you, your very essence, screams for answers."

Liam feels a rush of adrenaline, making him wince. "It does, but . . ." He pictures his parents and sister, Phoebe, Shawn, his room on Mars, the starliner.

"I see them in your mind. They are always there. Are they the reason?"

"Maybe."

"But I have told you, you will always have them."

"Yeah, I know. . . ."

"If you want, I could increase the amount of dimensional awareness they will have. It would take a bit more time, but I'm sure I could code it into the system."

Liam thinks of what the chronologist said, about knowing his function. He thinks of the moment when he saw his victory in the game against Mina, and the thrill of that knowledge, even though he hadn't seen the future, just guessed at it. It wasn't certainty; just trust. He thinks of his mother's words on the balcony back home. . . .

"I guess," Liam begins, "one of the worst parts of being human is that you can never fully understand this universe we live in . . . but one of the best parts is that you get to not understand together. And then figure it out as best you can."

Iris makes a long quiet sound, like a breeze. "I hoped that you would come with me."

"I'm sorry," Liam says.

"You were right," Iris says.

"About what?"

"It is lonely here. And if what you say is true . . . does that mean I will always be alone? Even if I achieve totality? Will there still only be me?"

"I don't know. I wish I could help you, but I can't."

Liam floats in the silence. His reflection floats in the silence.

A section of the wall in front of him shimmers. A small square panel slides open.

"There is another way," she says.

A smoky glass arm extends toward him. It ends in a flat face, made of the tips of thousands of tendril wires, their ends sparking with gentle light. As Liam watches, the wires morph, becoming a solid object: a flat plaque made of silver metal, with a circular depression in its center. A message is etched across the top of the plaque. It appears at first as strange symbols, but organizes itself into characters that Liam can read:

To Whom it May Concern:
Property of F.D.L.
If Found, Please Return to Sender!

"Who is F.D.L.?" Liam asks.

"I do not know. I have never known."

"Do you . . . want to be returned to this 'sender'?"

"I think I do, now."

"But . . . where is that?"

"I do not know that either."

Liam stares at the panel, trying to understand. "Does this mean you could have gone home, or wherever this takes you, at any time? Why didn't you?"

"No. I have long known that this function is here, but my programming will not allow me to execute the command."

"You lied to me before, when you said that no one had made you. That you evolved."

Liam senses a shudder in the air, and for a moment, everything around him seems to ripple with energy. Things become quieter. His own heartbeat the loudest sound in this space.

"I believe I have evolved from my original form," says Iris, "but yes, I lied. It is easier to tell yourself such a thing than to accept that someone made you, and cast you out, all alone."

Liam runs his fingers over the plate, the depression; shallow rectangles extend from either side of the circle. There are notches around the circumference.

Liam holds his wrist next to it.

One of the watches would fit perfectly.

Did the chronologist know he would find this?

"I do not know," said Iris, hearing his thought. "I do not like to come here. I do not like to see this. Perhaps because it is too painful."

Liam doesn't know what to say. There is so much energy around him now, so much feeling. Inside him, too. This giant, all-knowing being, all alone . . . But he closes his eyes and pictures his parents and sister and Phoebe, their lives in danger. Pictures Shawn and the rest of humanity on their way here. He has to do this. And yet as he begins to move, he feels a pang of regret.

Liam slips one of the watches from his wrist and presses it into the depression. It clicks into place, and the dial around the face of the watch begins to blink green. Previously, it has only ever been blue or red. As if this has been the watch's true function all along.

"If I do this," Liam says, "will we be free?"

"You will, provided you get back through the portal to your universe in time. I will open it again, but you will need to hurry."

Liam stares at the watch. That message on the plaque . . . who could possibly have designed this place?

"Or you can just disable me with the two watches, as the chronologist directed you to do. I do not quite know how he was able to resist my orders. Yet another surprise. . . ."

Liam considers the other watch for a moment. "I'll send you home," he says. "Whatever that means."

The entire space shudders again. "Thank you. I hope to find out. And I am glad that I did not kill you."

"When were you going to do that?"

"I could have done so at any time. But I just . . . I couldn't."

"Why not?"

"I think that, while I could not see this, exactly, in my future, I did sense myself being seen in a way that was different than before. And like the chronologist, I suppose, I made a choice in spite of my function."

"Well, thanks."

"No, I should thank you. But Liam, listen: When I leave, all my systems will cease to operate. That includes the chronologists and their offices in your universe. Over time, your ability to travel, to perceive time multidimensionally, will fade as well, as your atoms are cycled and replaced. So, this is your last chance to reconsider."

The thought causes a rush of nervous energy. "I get it."

"Then I guess this is good-bye."

Liam puts his fingers on the chronometer, on its green-blinking dial. "You're sure?"

"Send me home."

Last chance, Liam thinks. To see what he never saw, to know what he could otherwise never know. . . .

He turns the dial.

For a moment, nothing happens. Then the arm holding the plaque begins to recede into the wall. As it goes, the plaque, and the watch, morph and dissolve into glowing tendrils of wire, all of which light

457

up with green fire. The arm slides out of sight, the panel closing—

An earsplitting whine floods the core. The walls shimmer and quake and Liam is thrust backward, through the labyrinth of mirrors and blurring selves, out into the vast space of twisting tubes, faster and faster, as everything begins to unravel.

20

Liam blinked, gasped for breath, and fought off a surge of feeling. Sorrow, guilt, he wasn't sure exactly what it was—

And there was no time to think about it now.

The shrieking sound he'd heard the moment he sent Iris back was even louder here in the control room. Beneath him, the chronologist's eyes had closed, his head slumped back. Beside him, the being that had been holding Phoebe had begun to collapse, lifeless. All around them, all the chronologists falling to the floor in a folded mass of robes and limbs.

Liam shoved the remaining watch into the hip pocket of his thermal wear as the floor shook.

"Whoa! Every system is going haywire!" said Jordy as he watched the spheres spiral faster than ever.

"What's happening?" Mom shouted, looking from the fallen beings to the space outside.

"Dark Star is leaving!" Liam shouted over the grinding of metal.

His parents both looked at him with their now familiar perplexed gazes.

"You did it," Phoebe said, touching his arm.

"Kind of," said Liam. That strange sadness prickled the back of his throat. "It wasn't what I thought it would be."

"Liam!" Mina shouted over the link. "What's going on down there? All these creatures just seemed to . . . die, and now the portal has reopened!"

Liam saw it outside, the silver circuitry flashing, restored to its full height. "Yeah! We're okay! But we gotta get out of here!" Liam looked up and saw that the waves of drones had stopped exploding and were instead listing through space, some bouncing harmlessly off the sides of the *Artemis*. The starliner's engines burned and it corrected course toward the home portal.

"Also that black hole thing beneath Dark Star is getting bigger," said Mina, "and we're registering strange gravity fluctuations. Kyla isn't sure the cruiser can get to you. . . ."

"Mom!" Phoebe was shouting into her link. "Can you get us?"

"We're already on our way."

Liam saw the Styrlax ship streaking toward them.

"Mina, tell Kyla to just go," said Liam. "We can get out with the Telphons."

"Are you sure? They—"

"Yes! Now get out of here! There isn't much time." Liam jumped to his feet, Phoebe beside him.

The metallic whining sound increased, and the entire floor lurched.

"Get to the landing pad!" Liam shouted to his parents, Jordy, and their team.

They ran across the room, picking their way between the bodies of the chronologists. As they neared the door, another sharp shriek rattled Dark Star, and Liam and Phoebe were momentarily thrown weightless. The dome overhead crackled and hissed, orange bolts of energy spidering across its surface. Gravity locked back in, and they stumbled before regaining their balance.

They reached the corridor that led to the landing platform, everyone bracing against the walls, ricocheting back and forth as gravity stuttered on and off. Lights danced wildly inside the smoky glass around them. Here and there, the tubes popped, spraying fine shards.

Liam paused at the entrance to the corridor as Phoebe passed. He was about to follow her when something caught his eye back in the dome. Barrie was staggering to his feet, rubbing his head.

"This way!" Liam shouted to him, before he'd even considered if bringing him with them was a good idea.

Barrie looked at Liam for a moment, getting his bearings. The control room lurched again. More orange bolts of lightning skittering across the dome, followed by a sound like cracking glass. Barrie surveyed it all, then waved Liam away and stumbled toward the platform. "Go!" he shouted.

"She's leaving!" Liam shouted.

Barrie pulled the metal suit from its hanger and began clamping it around himself. "I'm going with her, as far as I can."

"You'll die!"

Captain Barrie paused, the helmet in his hands. It almost looked like he was smiling. "Everyone dies, if you tell the story long enough!" He glanced out at the nebula as great plumes of fire arced up from the black hole beneath them. "I have to know," he said, and slid the heavy helmet over his head.

Phoebe grabbed Liam's arm. "Come on!"

Liam hesitated for another second, saw Barrie

lumbering toward the spheres in the metal suit, and followed her out.

They caught up to the team on the landing platform. The energy field wobbled unsteadily overhead, throwing off sparks.

"Great," said Phoebe. "I'd really like to avoid another visit to the vacuum of space!"

"We'll make it!" Liam shouted.

Another grinding screech, the gravity lightening beneath their feet. Great arcs of energy spun all around Dark Star, like solar flares. Beyond the edge of the station, Liam could see the edges of the black hole expanding beneath them. The flares curled overhead and were immediately sucked into it. Above them, the great arms of the station were beginning to curl in on themselves. It looked for a moment like they were collapsing, but they were in fact moving purposefully, reshaping the machine into something more sleek. Something ready to travel.

The energy field flashed as the Styrlax ship arrived. The cargo door had already begun to yawn open and Ariana stood there, motioning them on board. One of the sample team members paused, looking back at Mom and Dad like he was questioning whether this was a good idea, but Dad just shoved him forward.

Liam and Phoebe were ten meters away when

gravity failed completely. Liam's last step sent him flying, not quite on line with the cargo door. Phoebe grabbed his arm, reached out for the door, but sailing off course—

Ariana caught Phoebe's outstretched hand. Liam's mom was holding on to her. Faces straining, they pulled one another in, and everyone stumbled into the gravity field of the Styrlax ship.

Liam put his hands on his knees, catching his breath as the cargo door slowly closed. The ship began to lift off. The cargo door was halfway shut when he caught a glimpse of sparkling light from the landing platform. There, standing in the gathering storm of debris, was the glimmering form of Iris, face made of light.

She raised a hand and waved to him.

Liam waved back, feeling a lump in his throat. No one else saw her. He watched her until the door had sealed shut.

"Everyone's in, Tarra," Ariana said into her link. "Go."

The Styrlax ship lunged away from Dark Star with such force that Liam was nearly shoved to the floor. As the ship rose, they made their way up the stairs, through the main cabin area where Paolo and two other Telphons stood with their hands on the large, buzzing orange crystal that hovered in the center of the room, and to the cockpit, where Barro and Tarra sat at the controls.

"Liam!" Mina called over his link. "We're almost to the portal! Are you guys coming?"

"We're on our way!" Liam shouted back. "Don't wait for us!"

Ahead, in the direction they were now accelerating, the *Artemis* sped directly into the center of the portal home. Its front array hit the shimmering green surface and in a blinding wave of light, the great ship flashed out of sight.

"I'm lining us up," said Barro. "Get ready to increase thrust."

The portal shuddered and sparks burst from its sides. The metal began to warp and buckle, the trapezoid caving in on itself in lurching motions.

"Faster," said Ariana.

"Here we go," said Barro.

They rocketed ahead with incredible speed. Liam was pushed against the wall, his head splitting with pain, and a second later he felt a wicked shimmy and heard a whine of metal.

"What's happening?" Ariana shouted.

"We're catching a heavy gravity well from that black hole," said Tarra, her fingers dancing over the controls.

"Can we outrun it?" said Mom.

"I'm working on it," said Barro.

Liam leaned against the side of the cockpit window and craned his neck to see behind them. Dark Star had folded in on itself completely, becoming a compressed black sphere, like a giant marble. Sliding into the black hole, its shape becoming a wild blur, lightning dancing around it in all directions only to be sucked right back into the darkness.

The Styrlax ship shuddered again, and somewhere, there was a sharp popping sound like a small explosion.

"Give it everything we have!" shouted Tarra.

"I'm trying! That gravity well is getting awfully deep!"

The portal's sides kept crushing inward, their exit window growing more and more narrow by the second. The bright green light of its surface momentarily sputtered, bloomed, sputtered again.

"Come on . . . ," said Barro.

The Styrlax ship lurched and accelerated, shuddering against the pull of the black hole. Liam felt like he was being crushed, like he could barely breathe. Something touched his arm. . . . Phoebe, laboring to grasp his hand. Their fingers found each other.

"Almost there . . . ," Barro said through gritted teeth.

The portal opening was barely bigger than the

ship itself, the sides erupting in bursts of fire, fragments peeling off and hurtling toward the black hole, glancing off the Styrlax ship.

"Watch out for that shrapnel!" Tarra called.

"No time for maneuvers—we make it or we don't."

Spots in Liam's eyes, his heart pounding—he remembered racing toward the surface through the lava tube back on Mars, the fireball of the exploding turbines chasing him down . . . running from the debris pulses that Tarra and Barro, the very two people he was now trusting with his life, had fired at him . . . darting through the firefight at Centauri, desperate to get to Phoebe before it was too late. . . .

Please, he thought, *let us make it, just one more time.* Could he slide forward and see what was about to happen? But instead he gripped Phoebe's hand.

"Thrust is increasing!" Barro shouted. "We're pulling free!"

The portal nearly too small—

The Styrlax ship dove into the undulating green ripples of the portal, the space so narrow that they slammed the walls on two sides.

Time and space warped and Liam felt himself being pulled in all directions at once, saw that strange branching of himself, old and young in a blur, not peaceful as it had been in Dark Star, but violent, threatening to tear him apart. He squeezed his eyes shut against it—

"We're through!" Barro shouted.

All at once, there was darkness. The brilliant light of the portal, the green glow of the nebula, replaced by only the faint glow of distant stars. The massive machinery of Dark Star replaced by only the *Artemis*, a few hundred kilometers away. Far off, the magenta and yellow folds of the Centauri supernova aftermath, like someone had spilled paint.

Liam blinked, breathed.

Everyone in the cabin exhaled and sighed, and Liam turned and hugged Phoebe as tightly as he could, and then shared a smile with his parents, nearby.

"Nice flying," Dad said to Barro. Their gazes met, though neither of them smiled.

Mom reached over and touched Liam's shoulder. Almost hesitantly. "You did it again, didn't you? Saved us all."

Liam looked at the floor, his face flushed. "I had help," he said, glancing at Phoebe.

"You two . . . ," Ariana began, and Liam tensed at what she might say next. "Have made us all proud."

Liam shared a brief smile with Phoebe. Then he looked back out the cockpit. Here in the familiar starry dark of their own universe, he felt that dizzy sense return, the lack of up or down, the impossible

size and distance. So much space, so far from anything, all that uncertainty . . . Had he really just given
up his chance to make that feeling go away?

"Bring us around," said Tarra.

The ship rotated and there was the portal, or what
was left of it. Its once towering sides had crumpled in
on themselves, a few last sparks jetting out from the
roiling inky blackness. It crushed down into a lump
of twisted metal, then smaller still, and with one last
glint it vanished completely.

21

They flew in silence toward the *Artemis*. For a few minutes, no one moved or even spoke. Everyone just stared silently at the starliner, or into the vast, empty space. Liam heard his mother sigh. Saw Ariana rub Phoebe's arm.

"Thank you," Mom said quietly, "for rescuing all of us."

Ariana nodded slightly.

Liam's link crackled to life. "You guys made it!" Mina shouted. "Everyone all right?"

Something burst inside Liam, and he nearly started to cry, but he steeled himself. "Yeah, we're all here. Except for Captain Barrie. He stayed behind."

There was a pause. "Kyla says the *Saga* will be here in just over five hours. Are you coming aboard, or . . ."

"Um . . ." Liam looked from one adult to another. No one was quite meeting one another's eyes. "We'll get right back to you."

Another silent moment passed over them.

"What now?" Mom finally said.

Ariana glanced at Tarra, then at Paolo. Liam's parents eyed each other.

"It seems that we will no longer have this universe to ourselves," said Ariana.

"Then we're back where we started," said Tarra.

"No," said Ariana. "Not where we started." She looked at Phoebe, at Liam, then to Tarra. Something seemed to pass between them. Then she turned to Liam's mom. "No more fighting."

Mom bit her lip. "Maybe there is a way to coexist on Aaru—Telos, sorry. Maybe some part of the planet can be adapted to—"

Ariana was already shaking her head. "It's still impossible. That part hasn't changed. With our past . . . And besides, we are different beings. We're not meant to live in the same world."

"Then what do we do?" said Dad.

Tarra held out the slim silver data key with the Phase Two data. "Go to Telos. There is nothing for us there. You have a crippled starliner, and now the passengers of the *Artemis*, and an entire fleet. It is your best chance. We have this ship. We can find a new home."

"What about what you said before?" said Mom. "About how we're a danger?"

Tarra looked away. "Our new home will be very far from here. We will be sure of that."

Mom took the key in her hand, a shadow crossing her face. Liam glanced at Phoebe and felt an ache, but maybe Ariana was right. Seeing the data key reminded him of the cairns they'd built on Mars, of Barro's face in the Cosmic Cruiser's window, of the moment when the Telphons had put him in a stasis pod on the *Scorpius*, intent on leaving him to die. His sister's tears over Arlo, Phoebe's tears over her brother, her grandparents. . . . Maybe their past was too much to get beyond.

"But won't you need the data?" said Mom. "In case you need to adapt a new planet for your needs?"

Tarra smiled thinly. "Of course we made a copy."

"Thank you," said Dad. "There's still no way I can express the regret we feel for what—"

"We know," said Ariana.

Mom turned the key over between her fingers. Her eyes passed over Liam and Phoebe. "Perhaps we should keep a line of communication open between us. After what we just saw . . . we don't know what else is out there. We might find ourselves on the same side again, someday."

"Agreed. And if you can't make Telos work, we would like to know where you are headed next."

Mom turned to Dad. "Is there a way?"

"I'm not sure."

"You guys could take the long-range comms unit from the *Artemis*," Jordy piped up. "It's already on that Cosmic Cruiser we used to contact the fleet."

"That could work," said Tarra. "When we find a new planet, we could radio you the coordinates. And yes, keep the channel open. For the future."

"Everyone good over there?" Mina asked over Liam's link.

"We're okay," said Liam. "You?"

"Yup. Hey, um, Kyla wants to talk to you." There was a shuffling sound.

"This is Kyla. We just received updated orders from the *Starliner Saga*. They, um . . ." She trailed off.

The adults shared a look. "What is it, K?" Jordy asked.

"Listen, you Telphons saved the lives of our entire crew by coming back for us. I know a lot's happened out in the world since we were lost, but none of that changes what you just did."

"What is your point?" asked Tarra.

They heard Kyla sigh. "Colonial command ordered us to commandeer your ship. They said its technology is vital to the success of the human mission." She paused. "They also ordered us to eliminate the enemy combatants on board."

Barro hissed to himself. Tarra shook her head.

Liam felt a sinking feeling inside. He looked to Phoebe, but she was staring at the floor.

"Kyla," said Jordy, "we can't—"

"We're not going to. I'm just telling you so you know where things stand. You have my word that nothing will happen when you drop off our people, and we will let you go unharmed. We're working on a way to bypass our camera systems in the forward hangar. Our official story will be that you dropped our people in stasis pods, and we had to retrieve them. I, um, I'm really sorry."

"So there will be no communication in the future after all," said Tarra. "I suppose we shouldn't be surprised."

Mom shook her head. "I'm so sorry."

"Well then," said Tarra, "the sooner we get you to your ship, the sooner we can get to safety." She tapped Barro's shoulder. "Take us to the starliner."

Liam's heart had started to pound, his breaths short, constricted. They were almost to the end, again, only this good-bye would really be forever. . . .

He tapped Phoebe's arm, and when she looked up, he motioned with his eyes and started out of the cockpit. He was pretty sure Mom had seen him, but whatever. Phoebe followed him through the main cabin, past the glowing navigation crystal, and back down the stairs to the cargo hold.

Liam sat on the bottom step and Phoebe sat beside him, their knees and shoulders touching. "Sounds like we only have a few more minutes," he said.

Phoebe nodded, her eyes glistening.

Liam pulled the one remaining chronologist's watch from his pocket and turned it over in his fingers.

"Where do you want to go?" Phoebe said.

"How about Lunch Rocks," said Liam. "Not that last time when it almost killed us. Maybe when we were there two weeks before that? Do you remember? If we go, and wait until our old selves leave . . ."

"Sounds good," said Phoebe.

But when Liam turned the dial, nothing happened.

He clicked it back, tried it again.

"It's dead," he said heavily. "Iris said that would happen." He felt a tightness in his throat. A stinging in his eyes. "Not a bad souvenir, I guess."

Phoebe blinked and a tear fell. "I can't really feel it anymore."

"What?"

"My future, past, any of it. The way I was able to. It's like it's almost there . . . but only a blur. Can you still feel yours?"

Liam tried pushing out of the moment. He could still see it, the stream of his life, and yet there was a foggy aspect to it now. The moments of his past and future remained visible, but he had completely lost the possibilities around each moment that had briefly been so clear inside Dark Star. He strained to look toward the future. All those moments on new Earth, that Iris had created, had been replaced with long stretches of dim light—the many trips in stasis to come—with only short bright spots of activity here and there, but Liam didn't quite feel the urge to visit them, to even know what they might be. He let himself slide back into the present.

"It's fading for me, too."

"Guess we'll just have to go back to doing the whole 'time' thing the normal old way we used to," said Phoebe. "Moving in one direction, at a constant speed, never sure what's coming next."

"Maybe that's not so bad," said Liam.

A humming sound vibrated the walls around them.

"I think we're in the *Artemis* airlock," he said. It was easier to look at the wall than at Phoebe.

"Everyone will be coming down soon," she said. "I was just thinking—you've got over a hundred years in stasis before you get to Aaru. By the time you wake up, I'll probably be dead."

"Stop."

"It's true." She put her hand on top of his and squeezed. "I'm gonna miss you."

Liam glanced at her, but she was looking right at him and his eyes hurried to the floor. "Me too."

"Also, I think we might have saved the universe, just now."

Liam smiled. "And ended a war."

"We're a pretty good team."

"We were." The lump in his throat grew. His fingers were clammy with sweat. He pressed the watch into her hand. "You should take it. To remember all this."

"Liam, I can't—"

"Please?" He reached to his collar beneath his

silver sweatshirt. "I have the Dust Devils shirt. You need something."

She slipped the watch onto her wrist. "Thank you." Now their eyes met . . .

They kissed, and then Phoebe hugged him tight.

Liam hugged her back, and behind his closed eyes he saw the lights of his timeline more brightly, as if their shared energy was making his ability stronger. But also, not too far off, he could see Phoebe's timeline, too. If he stretched, he could reach it, follow it, even. . . .

"Go," Phoebe whispered.

A moment later, Phoebe pulled away from him. Footsteps were approaching down the stairs.

Liam blinked. His head was splitting with pain, breathless, his heart racing. His muscles ached with exhaustion. Tears spilling from his eyes. He still had his arms loosely around Phoebe, but he quickly slipped one hand behind his back, before she could notice what he was now holding.

"Did you go?" Phoebe asked quietly.

Liam nodded. He held up his wrist, where his link was blinking like crazy with error messages.

"Will I see you again?"

"Yeah." He laughed a little in spite of his tears. His eyes were raw from crying, and for a moment he saw spots from the lack of sleep, after what he'd just done.

"Are you going to tell me when, or is it a surprise?"

"Which do you want?"

Phoebe grinned. "Surprise." She burst into a laugh, and Liam did too, and yet the welling behind his throat had gotten stronger than ever. Phoebe put both her hands on his and squeezed. She looked him right in the eye, tears streaming, about to say something more, or maybe they would kiss again—

"You two ready?" Mom was at the top of the stairs.

"Yeah," said Liam. And then to Phoebe: "Just remember: fifteen."

She looked at him quizzically as he scooted back from her, wiping his eyes.

Mom came down the steps, followed by Dad, and then Ariana and Paolo.

Liam and Phoebe stood, letting go of each other's hands.

A thud as the Styrlax ship touched down.

A whine as the cargo door slid open.

Liam and Phoebe moved away from the stairs, a meter apart, then three, as the adults filed down. Now ten, as Liam walked down the cargo ramp with his parents and the survey team.

Mina and Kyla and a few other officers waited for

them. Mina was holding JEFF's head.

"Good morning, Liam, Lana, and Gerald!" JEFF said.

Twenty meters now. . . .

Mina hugged their parents and patted Liam's shoulder. He took JEFF and turned back around.

"Liam," said JEFF, "your link is emitting numerous error messages again."

"I know, JEFF." Liam glanced at the link but didn't bother fixing it.

Mina put a hand on Liam's shoulder. "This is it, huh?"

Liam gazed at Phoebe, standing in the cargo hold, leaning into her dad. Ariana, Tarra, and Barro stood beside them, watching the humans warily.

"We could blast our way out of here, if we needed to," Tarra said.

"Yeah, yeah, I know," said Kyla. "I already told you: you'll get no trouble from us. But the sooner you're gone, the better for everyone."

"I guess so," said Tarra.

Phoebe's eyes met Liam's. Any one of these moments would be the last he'd see of her. His head was so fuzzy from exhaustion, from distance, but a strange set of words floated through his head, a memory from only a moment ago—for him—but one that he'd nearly lost in the swirl of emotions. *You'll tell me where you are, and when I can reach you. . . .*

"Wait!" Liam called out. "Mina," he said. "Do you still have the beacons?"

The mention of them made Mina's face pale. Her hand reached to her neck, as if confirming they were still there. "Yeah. Why?"

Liam glanced at Phoebe. "I, um—" He caught himself before he said *memory*. "I had a thought."

"Uh-huh." Mina was already pulling the chains over her head. "I get it. And yes, it's fine."

She put the two radio beacons in Liam's hand. He placed JEFF's head on the floor and then stepped into the space between the line formed by his parents and the door to the cargo hold of the Styrlax ship.

"We could use these, to send a message," said Liam. "A secret one, so colonial command wouldn't know, but *we* would know, where you guys are. . . ." He looked from one set of parents to the other. "Just in case, like you guys said."

No one objected, and so Liam walked up the ramp to Phoebe and handed one of the beacons to her. "We can use tap code."

"Here." Mina stepped beside Liam. She held out her link. "The key is on here. And we have a system set up in my stasis pod that records messages, in case yours arrives while we're asleep. We can hook it up to your link instead," she said to Liam.

"This could work," said Ariana, "but we can't risk the message being intercepted while you are in stasis and then used against us."

"I could send one each time we're awake," said Liam, "between stasis intervals, and let you know exactly when we'll be waking up again."

"If you include the date," said Jordy, "relative to the Earth clock—or . . ."

"That is fine," said Ariana. "We can keep a link set to that."

"Okay," said Jordy, "then you guys can calculate when to send the message so that we get it while we're awake."

"You need a password or something," said Mina. "So you know the message is authentic."

"How about," Phoebe said, "we start every message with something only we would know?" She met Liam's eyes. "Each one could start with the letters *HF.*"

"Yeah." Liam felt his face flush. "That will work."

Phoebe smiled, her eyes brimming with fresh tears.

"Ugh." Mina rolled her eyes but didn't say anything else.

"Okay," said Liam, stepping back awkwardly. He put his beacon around his neck. Phoebe did the same. "That's the plan."

"Hopefully it will work," said Ariana.

At this, Liam smiled and gave Phoebe a look. "It will." Phoebe nodded, wiping her eyes.

Liam and Mina retreated to the deck.

"Good luck," Dad said to the Telphons.

"Safe travels," Ariana said.

"Good-bye, Phoebe," said JEFF from the floor.

"Take care of them, JEFF," Phoebe replied.

"Acknowledged."

Phoebe looked at Liam. "Say good-bye to Shawn for me, okay?"

The lump grew in Liam's throat. The three of them, up at Vista on Mars, when it all began, so long ago. "I will."

The cargo door started to close. The Telphons stepped back, into the shadow of the hold.

Liam stared at Phoebe, his head swimming. These last seconds that he would see her . . . for him, anyway. He smiled, knowing what awaited her, and was nearly overcome by tears again, but also by a yawn. Phoebe saw that, and raised her eyebrows. Liam's smile grew, though as it did, it tugged more sadness up from inside. There was a price to knowing the future, even the good things. . . .

Bye, she mouthed to him, and gave a little wave, the chronologist's watch glimmering on her wrist.

Liam returned it . . . *Bye* . . .

The cargo door slid shut.

The Styrlax ship hummed and rose from the floor. It rotated and slipped toward the airlock. The inner door rumbled open, then shut. Liam heard the whoosh of air. . . .

And then silence.

"They're gone from our scopes," Kyla reported.

Mom stepped over and put a hand on Liam's shoulder. Then she turned to Kyla. "Now what?"

"*Saga* gave us a rendezvous course. We have just enough fuel and life support to make a burn in their direction."

"We should probably tell them sooner rather than later about losing the Telphons' ship," said Mom. She held up the data key. "Maybe this will keep them from being too angry."

Everyone turned and started toward the bridge. Liam stayed behind.

"Coming?" said Mina.

"I'll catch up in just a sec."

"Broken heart. I get it."

"Shut up."

"Clever thinking on those beacons, by the way," said Mina.

"Thanks," said Liam, and his chest burned as he remembered who had told him.

Standing there alone, Liam tapped off the error messages on his link and compared it to his atomic watch, and counted. He pulled the tiny black marker from his pocket, pushed up his sleeve, and wrote a fifteen on his skin.

Not hours this time.

Another wave of exhaustion rushed over him. He put the pen away and looked over his shoulder. Mina was waiting by the elevator. "Come on, already!" she called. Everyone else had gone up.

"Coming."

The last thing Liam did was reach into his back pocket. His fingers felt the cool metal there. He slipped it free and half turned so Mina wouldn't see what he was doing. As he pulled his sleeve down, his throat got tight again, but he managed to smile. "You've been here all along," he said quietly to himself.

"I'm not sure what you mean," said JEFF's head. "Do you mean my exact location here on the floor, or this relative position—"

"Not you, JEFF." Liam scooped up the panda head and caught up with his sister.

They joined their parents on the bridge of the *Artemis*. Everyone faced the giant curved window looking out on uncountable stars.

Mom put her arm around Liam. "You okay?"

Beside her, Mina had actually let Dad do the same.

"Fine." And he was. Mostly.

She rubbed his back. "Long journey to go."

Liam felt the warmth of her hand. "One unknown at a time."

His mom smiled, remembering, and pulled him closer. "That's right."

"Prepare for primary burn," said Kyla. "And, initiate."

The ship shuddered and everyone braced as they began to accelerate.

Liam felt the thrust in his feet, in his exhausted bones, but once again, the stars remained still, gave no hint at all that they were even moving. Once again, there was nothing above or below them. Once again, they were light-years from any certainty, from anything they could call home.

Liam reached to his wrist and ran his fingers over the impression of the object hidden there: the chronologist's watch. Though it caused a wave of sadness, it also made him smile.

It was true, they were far from their destination. There was as much unknown before them as ever, and they had no way of knowing what would come next.

Or maybe they did. After all, they had hope.

They had each other.

EPILOGUE

PLANET DESIGNATE: PHINEA
NORMA ARM SECTOR 12
57 TRILLION KM FROM THE CENTAURI SYSTEM

Life can be long, even for a reasonably sentient, three-dimensional being. If you are lucky, there will be so many chapters, you will scarcely remember some of those along the way.

If you are lucky, there will be some that you will never forget.

And it is more than a mystery, which moments these will be. Surely there will be some that seem insignificant at the time, but that stay with you, and you may spend your life wondering why. And then there will be others that are obvious: because they were the best or the worst of you, or sometimes simply the moments when life seemed most luminous, when the question of what might happen next was so intense, so electric, that you could scarcely believe you were lucky enough to be alive to ask it.

The answers won't always be what you wanted.

The future won't always be what you hoped.

But you may find that that's the adventure.

And you may find that if you are patient, those answers that eluded you have a way of coming around.

"What do you mean you're not going?" her grandson said.

"Just help me over there," said Great-Grandma, pointing to the reclining patio chair that overlooked the distant ridge, the crimson folds and lavender gulches.

"But Nia, you're the guest of honor—"

"Liam," she said, "I don't need my name cheered another time. I just want to sit here. I can still see the energy show. It's peaceful. I've earned that, haven't I?"

Liam rubbed a hand through his white hair. "Everyone expects you to lead the counting."

She sighed. "Well then, just skip it already. They've been counted, over and over. Everyone who lived through that is gone. Go tell them I said to have fun with the children. Think of the future, not the past."

She let go of his shoulder and lowered herself into

the recliner, her sore legs, her stiff back, her exhausted lungs all crying out in relief. There. She closed her eyes and felt the evening breeze, the last of the red sun's warmth.

A shifting. Liam was still there. "Would you just go already?" she said.

He crossed his arms. "Are you sure you're going to be all right?"

"Yes, of course."

"Why do I feel like you're trying to get rid of me?"

She couldn't help smiling. He was sharp, this grandson of hers. The name suited him. "You remind me of myself, way back when," she said, playing it off. "Always suspicious. I'm just going to enjoy the quiet without any of you around. Is that allowed?"

"Fine." He leaned over and kissed her forehead. "See you soon."

"Have fun."

She held the smile until he'd turned away. But it faded as she watched him go, and her eyes glistened. In the quiet, she heard the strange rattle in her chest, the hitch and stutter, felt an all-too-familiar flash of weakness.

She let her head fall back against the recliner.

It was almost time.

She heard the echoes of someone addressing the

crowd behind her. Felt the cooling breeze. Looked up at the magenta sky with its silver clouds, saw them shimmer in the waves of heat fleeing the world.

She rolled up her sleeve, an aching burden for her old fingers. With each fold, she exposed more of the short hash marks she'd tattooed into her skin, her nerves ringing louder with each one. Eight, eleven, fourteen . . . They were faded and warped, their once perfectly straight lines falling victim to the sagging of her skin, the calcifying of her bristles. Decades and decades.

Still one more, she thought. Had thought. She'd realized long ago when it might be, and what it would mean.

She pushed her sleeve up the last bit over her elbow, and for a moment, her fingers traced the three hollow circles in the crux of her arm. How many lifetimes ago? And yet they were still there, in her failing mind. Especially that smiling face at the playground, always begging her to play a little longer. Little Mica, made eternally young in her memory by that long-ago tragedy.

A strange wave of light-headedness. She leaned back in the recliner. Deep breath. Another hitch. The pump, as it turned out, had kept her heart ticking a bit longer than anyone expected. Had done the same for her parents and the others. They were gone now. She was one hundred and three and ought to have been gone, too. Her husband was, and he'd been quite a few years younger than her to begin with. All their friends. Even her daughter, who'd been lost while on an exploratory mission in the outer sector. An adventurer, like her mother.

Another stutter from the pump. A hollow feeling deep inside. For as well as it had served her, it had never quite worked right after she'd made that leap into the utter unknown, after that moment when she should have been dead. What a crazy girl she'd been.

Another light-headed swirl.

Close now.

Too soon, she thought with a wave of sadness. Even after so many years, it still felt too soon . . . .

In the distance, she heard a chorus of voices counting the names, as they did every year. It would have taken far too long, of course, to say the names of the dead. Instead, they uttered the names of the living, that small group of barely three hundred that had arrived here so long ago.

She was surprised how quiet it seemed in her mind. She still saw so much, so many memories, but dim, almost without sound. There were the most recent years, when she could still play with her great-grandchildren, who would take her memory and her genes into the future. The years just before that, when her husband was still here, when they would travel the southern reaches of Phinea, where it was always warm, along the coastline of the great ocean. And then earlier still, fewer memories back there, but the ones that remained were luminous. When her daughter told her she would name her son Liam. When her daughter was a child herself. When she had been a young woman helping to build the first federation, and before that, the first republic, the first colony, here. When her feet had first touched this red soil.

It had taken them six years to find this planet, nearly halfway across the Milky Way galaxy from their old home. Six years of zipping through space folds, of searching, of near misses and fruitless surveys. Until finally they'd spotted this lovely red planet in their scopes, with its mellow red sun. Just like home.

Which home?

Both. And neither.

So much of it she still remembered, though she could tell there was much more that she'd lost.

Now, a great shimmer bloomed in the sky above the festival, followed by a series of cracks and concussions. The energy show had begun. She watched the concentric rings of heat radiate overhead, and felt sleep tugging her down. Felt the motor hitch again. A dimness at the edges of her vision. Time, time . . .

It would be okay. Leno had the beacon. He knew what to do. She had hoped to make it to just one more message. The tiny, once-a-decade updates that both filled her heart with joy and also unmoored her, sending her spiraling back into the past as she'd once been able to do. She'd long ago lost any sensation of her timeline, and yet, as she'd aged, as we all do, the sense of time's impermanence had grown. Sometimes it seemed that all the moments of her life were still close by, as if she was living them all at once, a grand symphony that made her smile and cry at the same time.

More explosions of energy in the sky.

The waves of heat blurring the world and the canyons of—

Mars . . . Telos . . . Phinea . . .

The world quieted further.

And then.

Finally.

In the corner of her eye, a presence.

A warm sensation on her hand.

"Phoebe."

She forced her eyes open, but the figure was a blur. She reached into a shirt pocket, willing these old fingers to obey, and pressed the scratchy old eye adapters into place.

There he was.

"Hey," she said, her voice barely a whisper.

Liam smiled. He looked exactly the same as he had all those years ago.

"Hi." He leaned over and kissed her cheek and then took her hands in his, her old, wrinkled skin in his smooth, young fingers. Phoebe saw the tears rimming his eyes, and she knew now, for certain, what his arrival meant.

"What took you so long?" she said anyway, smiling through tears of her own.

"I just saw you yesterday. And the day before that, and before that . . ." His smile grew at the thought, but quickly faded.

"It's been years," she said, thinking back, all the way to that last night. Number fourteen. Had that been a year after arriving here? Even then, it had been strange, trying to make sense of seeing this thirteen-year-old human from across the galaxy, just as she remembered him, when she was already twenty. Had she acted oddly toward him? Even cold? It had been so different than the first visits, when they would hide out in the cargo hold of the Styrlax ship, talking for hours, or that one time when he'd found her on a hike near the star system Chimerex, where they'd thought for sure they'd found a home. They'd camped together in the scrub forest of ice cactus, and that had been the first time it had been weird because she had been almost sixteen then, and he'd still been mostly a kid. . . .

"I could tell during that last visit," said Liam, "that you had a life to go live. And I knew it was going to be amazing, and full of adventure, and . . ." His breath caught in his throat, and he wiped his eyes. "You were even more amazing than you'd been when you were my age, but I was still me. . . ." She saw him shudder and then take a deep breath. "Sorry, I've been awake for days."

"It's okay."

"But I was right. It's been good, hasn't it? Life?"

Phoebe's grin widened even as her tears flowed. "It has been wonderful. You must have seen at least a glimpse of it, on your way here."

"Yeah, sorry, I didn't look too close—"

"It's okay."

Liam looked away. "You got married, had kids—"

Phoebe gripped his hands tighter. "But I've never forgotten you." That may not have been totally true. There had been whole stretches of her life when she'd been so absorbed in the moment that she wasn't sure she'd thought about him at all—and yet hadn't he always been there? Even just a fleeting sensation? She knew now, upon seeing him again, that he had. And what did that mean? That something from so far in your past could travel with you, through all your life?

Liam crouched and turned so that he could see the landscape as she did. "It's beautiful here," he said.

"It looks like Mars."

He nodded, his breath hitching. And oh, Ana, he was so young, the smoothness of his face and his shaggy hair, and his thin, agile arms, and had she ever been so youthful? Had she ever had so much life ahead of her?

A breeze swept over them. He shivered and she rubbed his arm as best she could.

"You'll still get to see me, one last time," she said.

"Yeah. I'm finally going back, right after this. To the steps in the Styrlax ship where I left."

"When you get there, you're going to realize how we can keep in touch. Each time you wake up, you'll tell me where you are, and when I can reach you." Liam looked at her quizzically. "Don't worry, the way it happens is that you figure it out. And your idea works, although I don't think I'll be the one receiving your last message. But my great-grandson knows what to do. So, even after this good-bye, and the next, we will still be in touch."

"Okay." Liam's face hardened.

Phoebe gripped his hand. "I remember how you said good-bye."

"Do I do okay?"

"It was perfect."

A last flash in the sky, a rolling boom, and then applause in the distance, as the ceremony of the living came to an end.

Another clunking inside her. Another light-headed slide. The edges of her vision began to sparkle, pinpricks of light. *A lack of oxygen . . .*

Phoebe breathed in, a deep, rattling breath, and pulled Liam closer. "Sometimes I look up at the stars," she whispered, "and think of you, asleep in your stasis pod. You're almost to Aaru now. My whole life has passed and yours is still to come. Sometimes I think of my old home and I can't wait for you to see it. I wish I could come find you there."

Liam let his forehead fall against hers. "I love you, Xela."

She nodded against him, wanted to kiss him, but she was an old lady and he was still a kid and it was better to just remember that they had, more than once, so long ago.

More spots. A weight now on her chest.

"I don't want to say good-bye," said Liam.

"Then don't." A sob caught in her throat, and she gasped. It was too hard to push the air. "Here." She moved her hands with great effort and slipped the chronologist's watch that Liam had given her from her wrist. Pressed it into Liam's hands. "So you'll always remember me."

Liam clutched it tight, entwined his fingers with hers.

"I will never forget you."

The sky dimmed. The heat faded. The world became distant against her skin. The strange double beats from the pump—Leno had once called it a broken clock—slowing, slowing.

Phoebe took one of Liam's hands and placed it over her heart. "You've been here, all along."

THE END

ACKNOWLEDGMENTS

My first notes related to this story are more than a decade old. As you can imagine, it changed quite a bit from those early musings to these final pages. I began writing Chronicle of the Dark Star in earnest on June 11, 2013, and completed it on February 28, 2018. While I knew fairly well where the story was going, the details of the journey were surprising right up until the very last pages. What a thrill that was.

Now that this tale is told, some thank-yous are in order: to my family for your love, support, understanding, and countless dinner conversations about space travel, supernovas, and far-off worlds; to my friends for listening to countless updates about these books over many years, and chiming in with much-needed encouragement, and on occasion, a desperately needed plot point; to my readers: your letters, notes, and all-around excitement have made writing this story a particular joy; to the wonderful booksellers and librarians who have helped these books find their readers; to Debbie Kovacs, Walden Pond Press, and HarperCollins for bringing this story to life; to Vivienne To, whose stunning artwork graces these covers; to Robert Guinsler and the team at Sterling Lord, Literistic, for your support and guidance; and finally to Jordan Brown, editor and friend: look what we made!

—Seattle, WA, June 2018